S0-ASI-884

3 9077 00909565 7

SHORT STORIES

PRI   Prize stories 1962 :
       The O. Henry awards

1962   Short st
Prize Stories
O. Henry
memorial award
prize stories

ebster

Public Library

I Van Ingen Drive
Webster, NY 14580
716-872-7075

PRIZE STORIES 1962:
THE O. HENRY AWARDS

O. Henry memorial award

PRIZE STORIES 1962:

THE
O. HENRY AWARDS

Edited and With
an Introduction by

RICHARD POIRIER

DOUBLEDAY & COMPANY, INC.
GARDEN CITY, NEW YORK
1962

Library of Congress Catalog Card Number 21–9372
Copyright © 1962 by Doubleday & Company, Inc.
All Rights Reserved
Printed in the United States of America
First Edition

1962

CONTENTS

INTRODUCTION by Richard Poirier   7

KATHERINE ANNE PORTER, "Holiday," *The Atlantic Monthly,* December 1960   19

THOMAS PYNCHON, "Under the Rose," *The Noble Savage,* Number 3   49

TOM COLE, "Familiar Usage in Leningrad," *The Atlantic Monthly,* July 1961   79

SHIRLEY W. SCHOONOVER, "The Star Blanket," *The Transatlantic Review,* Spring 1961   99

DAVID SHABER, "Professorio Collegio," *Venture,* Winter 1960–61   121

MARY DEASY, "The People with the Charm," *The Yale Review,* Autumn 1960   137

SHIRLEY ANN GRAU, "Eight O'Clock One Morning," *The Reporter,* June 22, 1961   153

DAVID JACKSON, "The English Gardens," *Partisan Review,* March–April 1961   161

JOHN GRAVES, "The Aztec Dog," *The Colorado Quarterly,* Summer 1961   201

THOMAS E. ADAMS, "Sled," *The Sewanee Review,* Winter 1961   217

6 CONTENTS

MIRIAM MCKENZIE, "Déjà Vu," *New World Writing,*
Number 18   227

MAUREEN HOWARD, "Bridgeport Bus," *The Hudson Review,*
Winter 1960–61   239

REYNOLDS PRICE, "The Warrior Princess Ozimba," *The
Virginia Quarterly Review,* Summer 1961   251

THOMAS WHITBREAD, "The Rememberer," *The Paris Review,*
Summer–Fall 1960   259

JOHN UPDIKE, "The Doctor's Wife," *The New Yorker,*
February 11, 1961   275

MAGAZINES CONSULTED   285

INTRODUCTION

FIRST PRIZE: Katherine Anne Porter, for "Holiday"
SECOND PRIZE: Thomas Pynchon, for "Under the Rose"
THIRD PRIZE: Tom Cole, for "Familiar Usage in Leningrad"

There have been so few American novels, and even fewer stories, concerned with politics that the reader may be surprised to discover, as indeed I was, that the three stories leading this volume define important elements of their meaning in political terms. Even in those instances in American literature where politics is somewhere near the center of attention, Henry Adams' *Democracy*, for example, or Robert Penn Warren's *All the King's Men*, there is no acknowledgment that it can be inherently interesting as ideology or that political ideas can, as in George Orwell and Arthur Koestler, provide in themselves the substance of drama. There is scant admission even among contemporary American writers that "in our time," as Thomas Mann puts it, "the destiny of man presents its meaning in political terms." For anyone interested in a much fuller treatment of the subject than this introduction will allow, there is the rewarding study by Irving Howe: *Politics and the Novel*. What Mr. Howe observes of earlier American novelists—that they sometimes treated political ideology as if it were merely a form of private experience—is true in the present instances. And yet this phenomenon is cause, to my mind, more for satisfaction than regret. It is another indication of how suspicious the best of our writers have always been of any kind of system, any publicly accredited ideas, any conventional modes of expression provided by political allegiances, no less than by social and religious ones. These three stories thus afford a representative, if small, example of the degree to which our writers still insist upon shaping even political ideas to the dimensions of personal, sometimes eccentric vision, of the extent to which their uses of language can give us a sense of relationships among people more subtle than those defined strictly in political terms.

Many will remember some earlier stories by Katherine Anne Porter that are more conspicuously "political" than the one for which this year's first prize is awarded. "Flowering Judas," "Pale Horse, Pale Rider," and "The Leaning Tower" are among the most distinguished examples. "Pale Horse, Pale Rider," being closer to circumstances of which we can take a personal measure, creates the atmosphere of political crisis; in this case, of World War I. It shows how through subscription to the conformist public idioms of a "united people" there can be a corresponding loss of the ability to fashion speech that brings individuals into more satisfying intimacies. The epidemic of flu which separates the lovers through death is a version, we are made to feel, of an epidemic of platitude and cliché—again no respecter of persons—which threatens their lives with another sort of remoteness and isolation. "Holiday" is by no means as obviously political as these earlier stories, but it is equally concerned, within the dimensions of a large family and a farming community, with forms of social cohesion. At the point where the story does receive a specifically political accent, it is with a significantly witty kind of allusiveness to Marxist theory. Miss Porter is still, that is, making political rigidities surrender to what is essentially a literary adaptation, as if they were only the source for metaphors and as if the metaphors need in no way be responsible to the official form of the political ideas to which they allude.

This sort of adventurousness is not what the story at first leads us to expect. The situation is not at all astonishing, and the reader may experience at the beginning, with its faintly platitudinous phrasing, some tired confidence in a predictable development. What we actually find, as we continue, is an extremely tough-minded recognition of the limits of sympathy and human contact and a corresponding restraint upon the eloquence of the concluding scene. The story is full of rural conservatism, of the suspicion that programmatic efforts in response to suffering betray an ignorance of the peculiar needs of individuals and of the ability, through ingenuity as much as endurance, to satisfy them. The story is about people whose communal labor has created relationships among them, and between them and their natural environment, so close that literally nothing except death can disrupt them.

While we may for a time not choose to see the implications of this family life extended into such political terms as "rural conservatism," we must at one point recognize that they are given an unmistakable and comic political coloration. I refer to the scene in which the old patriarch of the Müller family, the biggest landowner and the richest farmer in the county, is shown with *Das Kapital*, of which he is a convinced reader. Though the scene is only a vignette, it is substantial and odd enough to call attention to itself. In fact, it summons round it the meanings more deeply embedded elsewhere in the story and then calls them comically into play. Marx is attractive to the old man not for any shared sentiments about the exploitation of labor. We can guess that he would respect the call that the "workers of the world unite" because it is work itself, not class consciousness, that unites the family, including, most significantly, the deformed daughter, Ottilie, who is in fact immoderately exploited for her labor in the family kitchen. The feeling of unity among members of the family is so unselfconscious that they never express it sentimentally, and it allows them only one, very practical question about the crippled daughter: How is she to be made useful? The answer is that only through work can she remain united to the workers of her mutely beloved world.

The brilliance of the story, however, is not in its attitudes—in their strictly political allusiveness, so witty and exploratory. Miss Porter's achievement is in expressing these attitudes most fully by the implications of her style, making it appear that she has not conceived of them in any terminology as overt as mine. She is a most self-possessed writer, never given here, and seldom elsewhere, to techniques and symbolisms that would summarize her meanings. The scene with father Müller looks at first like a merely anecdotal detail, a bit of picturesque gossip for the narrator's friends back home. In the description of the harness on the carriage, of the natural scenery, of the family at dinner, there is a spontaneity of detail and emphasis, giving way now and then to a controlled lyricism, which never beckons us toward the metaphoric meanings implicitly there. The suggestions, often having to do with those working relationships between seemingly disparate elements on the Müller farm, need to be called to the surface of what some readers may take only as an attractively full pictorialism. Like all forms of reticence and tact, Miss Porter's takes great self-assurance, the reserve of someone with ultimate confidence in what, if called upon, she can provide. In this she shares the virtues of the family as well as their unobtrusive generosity. Their lives, like the story itself, are full of extravagance of detail, of pain and natural disturbance which threaten to fracture established relationships. All of these are admitted and responded to by the family and in the style of the narration, and yet the melodramatic possibilities are always held in check by unhurried, firmly cadenced rhythms. The control, actually revealed by the acknowledgments of all that endanger it, is heard, too, in the voice of the narrator, essentially Miss Porter herself. The voice is never detached from its coherence with the inner workings of the family in order to sound the more spectacular notes of a distant observer, and it establishes a relationship between the reader and this family that allows a practical, rather than pastoral, reverence for the simple and obvious necessities of life.

Since Thomas Pynchon, in "Under the Rose," is writing about spies, neither he nor they can afford much reverence for the obvious. The originality of his story, however, is a matter of its shape even more than its subject, and by virtue of its author's relative newness (he has so far published only a few stories), it offers the occasion for saying once again that this volume ideally should announce the yearly emergence of new writers whose personal grasp of their material necessarily reveals itself in departures from routine, in their impatience with values that belong not to their personal discoveries but to conventions, either social or literary, of earlier fiction. It is gratifying to include now, as in last year's collection, not only a number of writers who will be new to most readers, but several whose stories are the first they have ever published.

The feat of Mr. Pynchon's storytelling is that it succeeds in being extraordinarily serious about our historical moment even while being inalterably remote in its people or situations from anything that we can imagine nowadays as contemporary. We are meant to feel the gap as part of the significance of the story, since in a most general way it is concerned with the time, at the turn of the century, when the gap occurred. It is about the process in which politics ceases to express the complexities and eccentricities of the persons involved and instead becomes their fate. With all the trappings of a romantic novel and many that belong to romantic opera, to which it insistently directs us by allusions to *Manon*, it is nonetheless a philosophical romance about spying. Those who read by skipping might just as well skip this story entirely, since they will miss not only the comedy, and the meaning of often difficult speculative passages, but even much of what is happening. To read the story is to find that it is continually inquisitive about the significance to modern life of what we take to be merely the machinery of historical adventure stories about international spying. The trick is admirably carried off, not by any species of literary parody, though this is abundant. Rather than being allowed to rest at a point of ironic detachment, we are drawn into the very process of "spying." It becomes for us more than a mere adventure; it becomes an activity of perception. The story is close to interior monologue, and what could be more curious than the interior monologue of a spy in 1898? He is continually the *voyeur*, on the watch for tiny signs that to us are relatively unimportant, since we are never involved in the issues that make him a *voyeur*—not love, or sex, or even crime, but that remote crisis at Fashoda that never became a war, and those fading historical figures, Kitchener and Marchand, our spotty knowledge of whom is, oddly, what makes us indifferent to them as characters. They belong to history, not to fiction, and cannot, existing only as public figures, do anything to surprise us. We are thus left with the conduct of the action as the thing of interest, rather than the actions themselves. Those actions take place "under the rose" indeed, *sub rosa*, as for spies—especially in Egypt, one of whose gods, Horus, the god of silence, has a rose as his symbol. But more significantly, they occur "under" the rose of love, that not infrequent romantic image, where we observe all the tricks of female talent, as the hero calls them, of observation, of the decoding of signs and gestures—all of these for no personal end at all, no romantic expansion, such as the hero of opera can attain by the same wiles, no flowering of knowledge into love.

It is not possible here to trace the remarkable deftness by which this story is made to be, subtly and painfully, about the fatal alternatives of modern international politics. The achievement is not the result of the more editorial passages, full as these are of a wisdom gained from working in a style that forces the author into close involvement with complications of meaning. The accomplishment is instead in the way the style draws us remarkably into the hero, so that we are ultimately willing to find ourselves in him, to see as our own what he calls his "personal apocalypse," and the threat he feels of a general one, as of our time. The apocalypse does come for him, as it can for us, when he learns that politics has become a depersonalized force, that it has stripped him totally of power by taking away all significance from his tricks, his decoys, his games—the imagination by which he thought to manipulate alternatives rather than succumb to them. Life may well be a game we play for mortal stakes, but when the element of "game" becomes meaningless we must either turn away from confrontations in the presence, as here, of the Sphinx, and live in contented impotence like Goodfellow, or, like Porpentine, die beneath it, acting out the most literal implications of our gamesmanship by surrendering to moral abstraction and thence to violence. The story owes much to the political novels of Joseph Conrad in that the predicaments that it evokes become general not by the author's insistence but by the intensity with which he makes them particular.

Politics in fiction, even in the few examples we are considering, can take many different forms, but one to which each of these stories implicitly objects is summed up in the phrase "artificial system." The term is Nathaniel Hawthorne's, and there are no more brilliantly skeptical renderings of "system" in our literature than the best of his political stories, "My Kinsman, Major Molineux" and "The Maypole of Merrymount." Criticized in the phrase is any effort to claim that some particular arrangement of words or ideas is equivalent to reality itself, whether the arrangement call itself society, political ideology, or even art. So strong is the power of these on our minds, so persuasive are they, that we cease to recognize their artificiality and accept them as images of the very nature of things. We lose the freedom to see, even to imagine other possible arrangements, much less create them. Politics can in this way take a form which to some writers is similar to the conventions of their art, and they can choose to deal with it out of a similar impulse—to liberate their own and the readers' imagination from its confinements.

Tom Cole's "Familiar Usage in Leningrad," his first published story, recognizes this impulse as a part of his theme, though it might be said that his style does not stimulate us, to the degree of Miss Porter's or Mr. Pynchon's, to some new and fresh awareness of possible meanings, of multiple shapes which the story might take in our experience. Mr. Cole's story of American-Russian confrontations is more overtly political, more topical than any in the volume, not excepting Shirley Ann Grau's "Eight O'Clock One Morning." Through the brief love affair of his young American hero with a Russian girl, he shows the degree to which, even when taken close to that hidden but not essentially mysterious life, an intelligent and sensitive young man may still be ruled by various stereotypes differing very little from the accepted ones of American and Soviet mythologies. Throughout the story there is a play of "we" and "they" indulged in both by the Russians and the group of American guides, of whom the hero is not too comfortable a member. The topicality of the situation is of a degree almost journalistic, and Mr. Cole's alertness to the stylistic equivalents of conventionalized attitudes is apparent in his own stylistic exploitation of journalism. He thus brilliantly recognizes the latent threat of superficiality in the *donnée* of the story by making his hero succumb at various times to it. The opening pages are intended to sound like journalistic reporting, very sensitive to detail, very accurately written, very poised—and of a certain triviality. This is not a "story" at all in the opening pages, but a reported event. This is true, this is how it *is:* sticky soda water and flies buzzing in the cabin of a Soviet plane that is stunningly handsome, as things can be in Russia, on the outside.

When Jeremy leaves the group in Leningrad, he seems for a moment to have escaped from the simple-minded comparative thinking of his compatriots and his hosts, to be ready for some more personal, less intimidated and intimidating view of things. And yet, by then allowing his hero to locate himself in the city mostly by his recollections of literature, Mr. Cole intends to show us that when his traveler's perceptions are not guided by politics they are as fully determined by art, by Russian literature written for the most part before the Revolution. Only when the narrator finally meets Elizaveta do we begin to notice a distinct shift from the style of travelogue to what we recognize as a story of intimate experience and emotion. But Mr. Cole is never unaware of the horns of his dilemma, that art conventionalizes our responses as much as politics can, that one is not necessarily an escape from the limitations of the other. The scenes with Elizaveta are often blatantly antipolitical, only to become, as the hero registers them, just as blatantly literary. The hero's picture of the old ladies who live with Elizaveta is in the direct line of Gorki, and his whole judgment of the girl's character is a literary judgment, a "they" view drawn from the *past*, which is necessarily embodied in the novels he has read, and only in that degree different from the similarly prefabricated views of his political contemporaries, both American and Russian. The effectiveness of the last scene, when Elizaveta flashes into life at the moment of separation, is that the American is thereby drawn back into politics as a reality of personal experience—essentially it is government intrusion that prevents their being together—and not merely, as he has wanted to think, a reality only in the impersonal area of international competition. Elizaveta's outburst is distinctly political: "What do you *want* of this world? . . . Sometimes I think you Americans *are* corrupt. You always must *own* things. That's the only relationship you can understand." Yet the story traces out a more complicated series of possible relationships in the mind of the hero than Elizaveta herself could be aware of. The complication attests to the degree to which Jeremy's mind must work through preordained alternatives of relationship before it reaches the point where it can even recognize what is for him the most personal, the least artificial, and the most tender one.

The possible relationships created by each of these stories—between the characters, between them and the author, between the reader and all of these—are revealed necessarily in the sounds and significances of phrasing. It is primarily through phraseology that we are brought into any sort of relationship to a narrative, and it is by attending to it that we discover whether or not a particular story can, as D. H. Lawrence expresses it in *Lady Chatterley's Lover*, "inform and lead into new places the flow of our sympathetic consciousness and lead our sympathy away in recoil from things gone dead." Lawrence is less concerned with the attitudes of a writer here than with his way of rendering them, with what he calls "the novel, properly handled," with the qualities of expression that direct our attention as we read into some essentially exploratory ways of witnessing reality. While it can be argued that there is no such thing as an original subject in literature, we aren't necessarily impoverished thereby so long as we show that there are always new possible arrangements of words and images, sounds of the human voice addressing itself to admittedly familiar subjects in a way we haven't heard before. There has been space here to consider only the variety with which the three prize stories give personal definitions to that most publicly defined of subjects which is politics. There are, needless to say, many other things to write about and, as the juxtaposition of some of the stories might indicate, many ways of looking at roughly the same thing. These stories are meant to be alike only in this—that each should offer the reader the most essential pleasure of fiction or poetry: the excitement of watching, of listening to what Robert Frost calls "the feat of words."

PRIZE STORIES 1962:
THE O. HENRY AWARDS

KATHERINE ANNE PORTER was born at Indian Creek, Texas, in 1890. She was educated in the South and has been awarded numerous honors for her writing. Miss Porter, who now lives in Washington, D.C., has traveled extensively in the United States, Europe, and Mexico and has taught in several universities. Her published works include two collections of short stories, *Flowering Judas* and *The Leaning Tower*, and a book of three short novels, *Pale Horse, Pale Rider*. A fourth novel, *Ship of Fools*, will be published in 1962.

HOLIDAY

from *The Atlantic Monthly*

At that time I was too young for some of the troubles I was having, and I had not yet learned what to do with them. It no longer can matter what kind of troubles they were, or what finally became of them. It seemed to me then there was nothing to do but run away from them, though all my tradition, background, and training had taught me unanswerably that no one except a coward ever runs away from anything. What nonsense! They should have taught me the difference between courage and foolhardiness, instead of leaving me to find it out for myself. I learned finally that if I still had the sense I was born with, I would take off like a deer at the first warning of certain dangers. But this story I am about to tell you happened before this great truth impressed itself upon me—that we do not run from the troubles and dangers that are truly ours, and it is better to learn what they are earlier than later. And if we don't run from the others, we are fools.

I confided to my friend Louise, a former schoolmate about my own age, not my troubles but my little problem: I wanted to go

Copyright 1960 by The Atlantic Monthly Company, Boston 16, Massachusetts.

somewhere for a spring holiday, by myself, to the country, and it
should be very simple and nice and, of course, not expensive, and
she was not to tell anyone where I had gone; but if she liked,
I would send her word now and then, if anything interesting was
happening. She said she loved getting letters but hated answering
them; and she knew the very place for me, and she would not tell
anybody anything. Louise had then—she has it still—something
near to genius for making improbable persons, places, and situations sound attractive. She told amusing stories that did not turn
grim on you until a little while later, when by chance you saw and
heard for yourself. So with this story. Everything was just as Louise
had said, if you like, and everything was, at the same time, quite
different.

"I know the very place," said Louise. "A family of real old-
fashioned German peasants, in the deep blackland Texas farm
country, a household in real patriarchal style—the kind of thing
you'd hate to live with but is very nice to visit. Old father, God
Almighty himself, with whiskers and all; old mother, matriarch in
men's shoes; endless daughters and sons and sons-in-law, and fat
babies falling about the place; and fat puppies—my favorite was
a darling little black thing named Kuno—cows, calves, and sheep
and lambs and goats and turkeys and guineas roaming up and
down the shallow green hills, ducks and geese on the ponds. I
was there in the summer when the peaches and watermelons were
in—"

"This is the end of March," I said, doubtfully.

"Spring comes early there," said Louise. "I'll write to the Müllers about you, you just get ready to go."

"Just where is this paradise?"

"Not far from the Louisiana line," said Louise. "I'll ask them
to give you my attic—oh, that was a sweet place! It's a big room,
with the roof sloping to the floor on each side, and the roof leaks a
little when it rains, so the shingles are all stained in beautiful
streaks, all black and gray and mossy green, and in one corner there
used to be a stack of dime novels, The Duchess, Ouida, Mrs.
E.D.E.N. Southworth, Ella Wheeler Wilcox's poems—one summer
they had a lady boarder who was a great reader, and she went
off and left her library. I loved it! And everybody was so healthy

and goodhearted, and the weather was perfect. . . . How long do you want to stay?"

I hadn't thought of this, so I said at random, "About a month."

A few days later I found myself tossed off like an express package from a dirty little crawling train onto the sodden platform of a country station, where the stationmaster emerged and locked up the waiting room before the train had got round the bend. As he clumped by me he shifted his wad of tobacco to his cheek and asked, "Where you goin'?"

"To the Müller farm," I said, standing beside my small trunk and suitcase with the bitter wind cutting my shoulders through my thin coat.

"Anybody meet you?" he asked, not pausing.

"They *said* so."

"All right," he said, and got into his little ragged buckboard with a sway-backed horse and drove away.

I turned my trunk on its side and sat on it facing the wind and the desolate mud-colored shapeless scene and began making up my first letter to Louise. First I was going to tell her that unless she meant to be a novelist, there was no excuse for her having so much imagination. In daily life, I was going to tell her, there are also such useful things as the plain facts that should be stuck to, through thick and thin. Anything else led to confusion like this. I was beginning to enjoy my letter to Louise when a sturdy boy about twelve years old crossed the platform. As he neared me, he took off his rough cap and bunched it in his thick hand, dirt-stained at the knuckles. His round cheeks, his round nose, his round chin were a cool, healthy red. In the globe of his face, as neatly circular as if drawn in bright crayon, his narrow, long, tip-tilted eyes, clear as pale-blue water, seemed out of place, as if two incompatible strains had collided in making him. They were beautiful eyes, and the rest of the face was not to be taken seriously. A blue woolen blouse buttoned up to his chin ended abruptly at his waist as if he would outgrow it in another half hour, and his blue drill breeches flapped about his ankles. His old clodhopper shoes were several sizes too big for him. Altogether, it was plain he was not the first one to wear his clothes. He was a cheerful, detached, self-possessed apparition against the tumbled brown earth and ragged dark sky, and I smiled at him as well as I could with a face that felt like wet clay.

He smiled back slightly without meeting my eye, motioning for me to take up my suitcase. He swung my trunk to his head and tottered across the uneven platform, down the steps slippery with mud, where I expected to see him crushed beneath his burden like an ant under a stone. He heaved the trunk into the back of his wagon with a fine smash, took my suitcase and tossed it after, then climbed up over one front wheel while I scrambled my way up over the other.

The pony, shaggy as a wintering bear, eased himself into a grudging trot, while the boy, bowed over with his cap pulled down over his ears and eyebrows, held the reins slack and fell into a brown study. I examined the harness, a real mystery. It met and clung in all sorts of unexpected places; it parted company in what appeared to be strategic seats of jointure. It was mended sketchily in risky places with bits of hairy rope. Other seemingly unimportant parts were bound together irrevocably with wire. The bridle was too long for the pony's stocky head, so he had shaken the bit out of his mouth at the start, apparently, and went his own way at his own pace.

Our vehicle was an exhausted specimen of something called a spring wagon, who knows why? There were no springs, and the shallow enclosed platform at the back, suitable for carrying various plunder, was worn away until it barely reached midway of the back wheels, one side of it steadily scraping the iron tire. The wheels themselves spun not dully around and around in the way of common wheels, but elliptically, being loosened at the hubs, so that we proceeded with a drunken, hilarious swagger, like the rolling motion of a small boat on a choppy sea.

The soaked brown fields fell away on either side of the lane, all rough with winter-worn stubble ready to sink and become earth again. The scanty leafless woods ran along an edge of the field nearby. There was nothing beautiful in those woods now except the promise of spring, for I detested bleakness, but it gave me pleasure to think that beyond this there might be something else beautiful in its own being, a river shaped and contained by its banks, or a field stripped down to its true meaning, plowed and ready for the seed. The road turned abruptly and was almost hidden for a moment, and we were going through the woods. Closer sight of the crooked branches assured me that spring was beginning, if sparely, reluctantly; the leaves were budding in tiny cones of watery green besprinkling all the new shoots; a thin sedate rain began again to fall, not so opaque as a fog, but a mist that merely deepened overhead, and lowered, until the clouds became rain in one swathing, delicate gray.

As we emerged from the woods, the boy roused himself and pointed forward, in silence. We were approaching the farm along the skirts of a fine peach orchard, now faintly colored with young buds, but there was nothing to disguise the gaunt and aching ugliness of the farmhouse itself. In this Texas valley, so gently modulated with small crests and shallows, "rolling country" as the farmers say, the house was set on the peak of the barest rise of ground, as if the most infertile spot had been thriftily chosen for building a shelter. It stood there staring and naked, an intruding stranger, strange even beside the barns ranged generously along the back, low-eaved and weathered to the color of stone.

The narrow windows and the steeply sloping roof oppressed me; I wished to turn away and go back. I had come a long way to be so disappointed, I thought, and yet I must go on, for there could be nothing here for me more painful than what I had left. But as we drew near the house, now hardly visible except for the yellow lamplight in the back, perhaps in the kitchen, my feelings changed again toward warmth and tenderness, or perhaps just an apprehension that I could feel so, maybe, again.

The wagon drew up before the porch, and I started climbing down. No sooner had my foot touched ground than an enormous black dog of the detestable German shepherd breed leaped silently at me, and as silently I covered my face with my arms and leaped back. "Kuno, down!" shouted the boy, lunging at him. The front door flew open and a young girl with yellow hair ran down the steps and seized the ugly beast by the scruff. "He does not mean anything," she said seriously in English. "He is only a dog."

Just Louise's darling little puppy Kuno, I thought, a year or so older. Kuno whined, apologized by bowing and scraping one front paw on the ground, and the girl holding his scruff said, shyly and proudly, "I teach him that. He has always such bad manners, but I teach him!"

I had arrived, it seemed, at the moment when the evening chores were about to begin. The entire Müller household streamed out of the door, each man and woman going about the affairs of the moment. The young girl walked with me up the porch steps and said, "This is my brother Hans," and a young man paused to shake hands and passed by. "This is my brother Fritz," she said, and Fritz took my hand and dropped it as he went. "My sister Annetje," said the young girl, and a quiet young woman with a baby draped loosely like a scarf over her shoulder smiled and held out her hand. Hand after hand went by, their palms variously younger or older, broad or small, male or female, but all thick hard decent peasant hands, warm and strong. And in every face I saw again the pale, tilted eyes, on every head that taffy-colored hair, as though they might all be brothers and sisters, though Annetje's husband and still another daughter's husband had gone by after greeting me. In the wide hall with a door at front and back, full of cloudy light and the smell of soap, the old mother, also on her way out, stopped to offer her hand. She was a tall strong-looking woman wearing a three-cornered black wool shawl on her head, her skirts looped up over a brown flannel petticoat. Not from her did the young ones get those water-clear eyes. Hers were black and shrewd and searching, a band of hair showed black streaked with gray, her seamed dry face was brown as seasoned bark, and she walked in her rubber boots with the stride of a man. She shook my hand briefly and said in German English that I was welcome, smiling and showing her blackened teeth.

"This is my girl Hatsy," she told me, "and she will show you to your room." Hatsy took my hand as if I were a child needing a guide. I followed her up a flight of steps steep as a ladder, and there we were, in Louise's attic room, with the sloping roof. Yes, the shingles were stained all the colors she had said. There were the dime novels heaped in the corner. For once, Louise had got it straight, and it was homely and familiar, as if I had seen it before. "My mother says we could give you a better place on the downstairs," said Hatsy, in her soft blurred English, "but *she* said in her letter you would like it so." I told her indeed I did like it so. She went down the steep stairs then, and her brother came up as if he were climbing a tree, with the trunk on his head and the suitcase in his right hand, and I could not see what kept the trunk from crashing back to the bottom, as he used the left hand to climb with. He put his burden down and straightened up, wriggling his shoulders and panting only a little. I thanked him and he pushed his cap back and pulled it forward again, which I took for some sort of polite response, and clattered out hugely. Looking out of my window a few minutes later, I saw him setting off across the fields carrying a lighted lantern and a large steel trap.

I began changing my first letter to Louise. "I'm going to like it here. I don't quite know why, but it's going to be all right. Maybe I can tell you later—"

The sound of the German speech in the household below was part of the pleasantness, for they were not talking to me and did not expect me to answer. All the German I understood then was contained in five small deadly sentimental songs of Heine's, learned by heart; and this was a very different tongue, Low German corrupted by three generations in a foreign country. A dozen miles away, where Texas and Louisiana melted together in a rotting swamp whose sluggish undertow of decay nourished the roots of pine and cedar, a colony of French immigrants had lived out two hundred years of exile, not wholly incorruptible, but mystically faithful to the marrow of their bones, obstinately speaking their old French, by then as strange to the French as it was to the English. I had known many of these families during a certain long summer happily remembered, and here, listening to another language nobody could understand except those of this small farming community, I knew that I was again in a house of perpetual exile. These were solid, practical, hard-bitten, landholding German peasants who stuck their mattocks into the earth deep and held fast wherever they were, because to them life and the land were one indivisible thing; but never in any wise did they confuse nationality with habitation.

I liked the thick warm voices, and it was good not to have to understand what they were saying. I loved that silence which means freedom from the constant pressure of other minds and other opinions and other feelings, that freedom to fold up in quiet and go back to my own center, to find out again, for it is always a rediscovery, what kind of creature it is that rules me finally, makes all the decisions no matter who thinks they make them, even I; who little by little takes everything away except the one thing I cannot live without, and who will one day say, "Now I am all you have left—take me." I paused there a good while listening to this muted unknown language which was silence with music in it; I could be moved and touched but not troubled by it, as by the crying of frogs or the wind in the trees.

The catalpa tree at my window would, I noticed, when it came into leaf, shut off my view of the barns and the fields beyond. When in bloom the branches would almost reach through the window. But now they were a thin screen through which the calves, splotchy red and white, moved prettily against the weathered darkness of the sheds. The brown fields would soon be green again; the sheep would not look then as they did now, merely lumps of moving earth, but would be washed by the rains and become clean gray. All the beauty of the landscape now was in the harmony of the valley rolling fluently away to the wood's edge. It was an inland country, with the forlorn look of all unloved things; winter in this part of the South is a moribund coma, not the Northern death sleep with the sure promise of resurrection. But in my South, my loved and never-forgotten country, after her long sickness, with only a slight stirring, an opening of the eyes between one breath and the next, between night and day, the earth revives and bursts into the plenty of spring with fruit and flowers together, spring and summer at once under the hot shimmering blue sky.

The freshening wind promised another light sedate rain to come at evening. The voices below-stairs dispersed, rose again, separately calling from the yards and barns. The old woman strode down the path toward the cow sheds, Hatsy running behind her. The woman wore her wooden yoke, with the milking pails covered and closed with iron hasps, slung easily across her shoulders, but her daughter carried two tin milking pails on her arm. When they pushed back the bars of cedar which opened onto the fields, the cows came through lowing and crowding, and the calves scampered each to his own dam with reaching, opened mouths. Then there was the battle of separating the hungry children from their mothers when they had taken their scanty share. The old woman slapped their little haunches with her open palm, Hatsy dragged at their halters, her feet slipping wide in the mud, the cows bellowed and brandished their horns, the calves bawled like rebellious babies. Hatsy's long yellow braids whisked round her shoulders, her laughter was a shrill streak of gaiety above the angry cow voices and the raucous shouting of the old woman.

From the kitchen porch below came the sound of splashing water, the creaking of the pump handle, and the stamping boots of men. I sat in the window watching the darkness come on slowly. All the sounds of the place gathered under the roof while the lamps were being lighted. My own small lamp had a handle on the oil bowl, like a cup's. There was also a lantern with a frosted chimney hanging by a nail on the wall. A voice called to me from the foot of my stairs and I looked down into the face of a dark-skinned, flaxen-haired young woman, far advanced in pregnancy, and carrying a prosperous year-old boy on her hip, one arm clutching him to her, the other raised above her head so that her lantern shone upon their heads. "The supper is now ready," she said, and waited for me to come down before turning away.

In the large square room the whole family was gathering at a long table covered with a red checkered cotton cloth, heaped-up platters of steaming food at either end. A crippled and badly deformed servant girl was setting down pitchers of milk. Her head was so bowed over, her face was almost hidden, and her whole body was maimed in some painful, mysterious way, probably congenital, I supposed, though she seemed wiry and tough. Her knotted hands shook continually, her wagging head kept pace with her restless elbows. She ran unsteadily around the table scattering plates, dodging whoever stood in her way; no one moved aside for her, or spoke to her, or even glanced after her when she vanished into the kitchen.

The men moved forward to their chairs. Father Müller took his patriarch's place at the head of the table, Mother Müller looming behind him like a dark boulder. The young men ranged themselves about one side, the married ones with their wives standing back of their chairs to serve them, for three generations in this country had not made them self-conscious or disturbed their ancient customs. The two sons-in-law and three sons rolled down their shirt sleeves before beginning to eat. Their faces were polished with recent scrubbing and their open collars were damp.

Mother Müller pointed to me, then waved her hand at her household, telling off their names rapidly once more. I was a stranger and a guest, so was seated on the men's side of the table, and Hatsy, whose real name turned out to be Huldah, the maiden of the family, was seated on the children's side of the board, attending to them and keeping them in order. These infants ranged from two years to ten, five in number—not counting the one still straddling his mother's hip behind his father's chair—divided between the two married daughters. The children ravened and gorged and reached their hands into the sugar bowl to sprinkle sugar on everything they ate, solemnly elated over their food and paying no attention to Hatsy, who struggled with them only a little less energetically than she did with the calves, and ate almost nothing. She was about seventeen years old, pale-lipped and too thin, and her sleek fine butter-yellow hair, streaked light and dark, real German peasant hair, gave her an air of fragility. But she shared the big-boned structure, the enormous energy and animal force that was like a bodily presence itself in the room; and seeing Father Müller's pale-gray deep-set choleric eyes and high cheekbones, it was easy to trace the family resemblance around the table: it was plain that poor Mother Müller had never had a child of her own—black-eyed, black-haired South Germany people. True, she had borne them, but that was all; they belonged to their father. Even the tawny Gretchen, expecting another baby, obviously the pet of the family, with the sly smiling manner of a spoiled child, who wore the contented air of a lazy, healthy young animal, seeming always about to yawn, had hair like pulled taffy and those slanted clear eyes. She stood now easing the weight of her little boy on her husband's chair back, reaching with her left arm over his shoulder to refill his plate from time to time.

Annetje's baby drooled comfortably down her back, while she spooned things from platters and bowls for her husband. Whenever their eyes met, they smiled with a gentle, reserved warmth in their eyes, the smile of long and sure friendship.

Father Müller did not in the least believe in his children's marrying and leaving home. Marry, yes, of course; but must that take a son or daughter from him? He always could provide work and a place in the household for his daughters' husbands, and in time he would do the same for his sons' wives. A new room had lately been built on, to the northeast, Annetje explained to me, leaning above her husband's head and talking across the table, for Hatsy to live in when she should be married. Hatsy turned very beautifully pink and ducked her head almost into her plate, then looked up boldly and said, "*Jah, jah,* I am marrit now soon!" Everybody laughed except Mother Müller, who said in German that girls at home never knew when they were well off—no, they must go bringing in husbands. This remark did not seem to hurt anybody's feelings, and Gretchen said it was nice that I was going to be here for the wedding. This reminded Annetje of something, and she spoke in English to the table at large, saying that the Lutheran pastor had advised her to attend church oftener and put her young ones in Sunday School, so that God would give her a blessing with her next child. I counted around again, and sure enough, with Gretchen's unborn, there were eight children at that table under the age of ten; somebody was going to need a blessing in all that crowd, no doubt. Father Müller delivered a short speech to his daughter in German, then turned to me and said, "What I say iss, it iss all craziness to go to church and pay a preacher goot money to talk his nonsense. Say rather that he pay me to come and lissen, then I vill go!" His eyes glared with sudden fierceness above his square speckled gray and yellow beard that sprouted directly out from the high cheekbones. "He thinks, so, that my time maybe costs nothing? That iss goot! Let him pay me!"

Mother Müller snorted and shuffled her feet. "Ach, you talk, you talk! Now you vill make the pastor goot and mad if he hears. Vot ve do, if he vill not chrissen the babies?"

"You give him goot money, he vill chrissen," shouted Father Müller. "You vait und see!"

"Ah sure, dot iss so," agreed Mother Müller. "Only do not let him hear!"

There was a gust of excited talk in German, with much rapping of knife handles on the table. I gave up trying to understand, but watched their faces. It sounded like a pitched battle, but they were agreeing about something. They were united in their tribal skepticisms, as in everything else. I got a powerful impression that they were all, even the sons-in-law, one human being divided into several separate appearances. The crippled servant girl brought in more food and gathered up plates and went away in her limping run, and she seemed to me the only individual in the house. Even I felt divided into many fragments, having left or lost a part of myself in every place I had traveled, in every life mine had touched, above all, in every death of someone near to me that had carried into the grave some part of my living cells. But the servant, she was whole, and belonged nowhere.

I settled easily enough into the marginal life of the household ways and habits. Day began early at the Müllers', and we ate breakfast by yellow lamplight, with the gray damp winds blowing with spring softness through the open windows. The men swallowed their last cups of steaming coffee standing, with their hats on, and went out to harness the horses to the plows at sunrise. Annetje, with her fat baby slung over her shoulder, could sweep a room or make a bed with one hand, all finished before the day was well begun; and she spent the rest of the day outdoors, caring for the chickens and the pigs. Now and then she came in with a shallow box full of newly hatched chickens, abject dabs of wet fluff, and put them on a table in her bedroom where she might tend them carefully on their first day. Mother Müller strode about hugely, giving orders right and left, while Father Müller, smoothing his whiskers and lighting his pipe, drove away to town with Mother Müller calling out after him final directions and instructions about household needs. He never spoke a word to her or looked at her and appeared not to be listening, but he always returned in a few hours with every commission performed exactly. After I had made my own bed and set my attic in order, there was nothing at all for me to do, and I walked out of this enthusiastic bustle into the lane, feeling extremely useless. But the repose, the almost hysterical inertia of their minds in the midst of this muscular life, communicated itself to me little by little, and I absorbed it gratefully in silence and felt all the hidden knotted painful places in my own mind beginning to loosen. It was easier to breathe, and I might weep, if I pleased. In a very few days I no longer felt like weeping.

One morning I saw Hatsy spading up the kitchen garden plot, and my offer to help, to spread the seeds and cover them, was accepted. We worked at this for several hours each morning, until the warmth of the sun and the stooping posture induced in me a comfortable vertigo. I forgot to count the days, they were one like the other except as the colors of the air changed, deepening and warming to keep step with the advancing season, and the earth grew firmer underfoot with the swelling tangle of crowding roots.

The children, so hungry and noisy at the table, were peaceable little folk who played silent engrossed games in the front yard. They were always kneading mud into loaves and pies and carrying their battered dolls and cotton rag animals through the operations of domestic life. They fed them, put them to bed; they got them up and fed them again, set them to their chores making more mud loaves; or they would harness themselves to their carts and gallop away to a great shady chestnut tree on the opposite side of the house. Here the tree became the *Turnverein*, and they themselves were again human beings, solemnly ambling about in a dance and going through the motions of drinking beer. Miraculously changed once more into horses, they harnessed themselves and galloped home. They came at call to be fed and put to sleep with the docility of their own toys or animal playmates. Their mothers handled them with instinctive, constant gentleness; they never seemed to be troubled by them. They were as devoted and care-taking as a cat with her kittens.

Sometimes I took Annetje's next to youngest child, a baby of two years, in her little wagon, and we would go down through the orchard and into the lane for a short distance. I would turn again into a smaller lane, smoother because less traveled, and we would go slowly between the aisles of mulberry trees where the fruit was beginning to hang and curl like green furry worms. The baby would sit in a compact mound of flannel and calico, her pale-blue eyes tilted and shining under her cap, her little lower teeth showing in a rapt smile. Sometimes several of the other children would follow along quietly. When I turned, they all turned without question, and we would proceed back to the house as sedately as we had set out.

The narrow lane, I discovered, led to the river, and it became my favorite walk. Almost every day I went along the edge of the naked wood, passionately occupied with looking for signs of spring. The changes there were so subtle and gradual, I found one day that branches of willows and sprays of blackberry vine alike were covered with fine points of green; the color had changed overnight, or so it seemed, and I knew that tomorrow the whole valley and wood and edge of the river would be quick and feathery with golden green blowing in the winds.

And it was so. On that day I did not leave the river until after dark and came home through the marsh with the owls and night-jars crying over my head, calling in a strange broken chorus in the woods until the farthest answering cry was a ghostly echo. When I went through the orchard the trees were freshly budded out with pale bloom, the branches were immobile in the thin darkness, but the flower clusters shivered in a soundless dance of delicately woven light, whirling as airily as leaves in a breeze, as rhythmically as water in a fountain. Every tree was budded out with this living, pulsing fire as fragile and cool as bubbles. When I opened the gate their light shone on my hands like fox fire. When I looked back, the shimmer of golden light was there, it was no dream.

Hatsy was on her knees in the dining room, washing the floor with heavy dark rags. She always did this work at night, so the men with their heavy boots would not be tracking it up again and it would be immaculate in the morning. She turned her young face to me in a stupor of fatigue. "Ottilie! Ottilie!" she called loudly, and before I could speak, she said, "Ottilie will give you supper. It is waiting, all ready." I tried to tell her that I was not hungry, but she wished to reassure me. "Look, we all must eat. Now, or then, it's no trouble." She sat back on her heels, and raising her head, looked over the window sill at the orchard. She smiled and paused for a moment and said happily, "Now it is come spring. Every spring we have that." She bent again over the great pail of water with her mops.

The crippled servant came in, stumbling perilously on the slippery floor, and set a dish before me, lentils with sausage and red chopped cabbage. It was hot and savory and I was truly grateful, for I found I was hungry, after all. I looked at her—so her name was Ottilie?—and said, "Thank you." "She can't talk," said Hatsy, simply, stating a fact that need not be emphasized. The blurred, dark face was neither young nor old, but crumpled into crisscross wrinkles, irrelevant either to age or suffering; simply wrinkles, patternless blackened seams as if the perishable flesh had been wrung in a hard cruel fist. Yet in that mutilated face I saw high cheekbones, slanted water-blue eyes, the pupils very large and strained with the anxiety of one peering into a darkness full of danger. She jarred heavily against the table as she turned, her bowed back trembling with the perpetual working of her withered arms, and ran away in aimless, driven haste.

Hatsy sat on her heels again for a moment, tossed her braids back over her shoulder, and said, "That is Ottilie. She is not sick now. She is only like that since she was sick when she was baby. But she can work so well as I can. She cooks. But she cannot talk so you can understand." She went up on her knees, bowed over, and began to scrub again, with new energy. She was really a network of thin taut ligaments and long muscles elastic as woven steel. She would always work too hard, and be tired all her life, and never know that this was anything but perfectly natural; everybody worked all the time, because there was always more work waiting when they had finished what they were doing then. I ate my supper and took my plate to the kitchen and set it on the table. Ottilie was sitting in a kitchen chair with her feet in the open oven, her arms folded, and her head waggling a little. She did not see or hear me.

At home, Hatsy wore an old brown corduroy dress and galoshes without stockings. Her skirts were short enough to show her thin legs, slightly crooked below the knees, as if she had walked too early. "Hatsy, she's a good, quick girl," said Mother Müller, to whom praising anybody or anything did not come easily. On Saturdays, Hatsy took a voluminous bath in a big tub in the closet back of the kitchen, where also were stored the extra chamber pots, slop jars, and water jugs. She then unplaited her yellow hair and bound up the crinkled floss with a wreath of pink cotton rosebuds, put on her pale-blue China silk dress, and went to the *Turnverein* to dance and drink a seidel of dark-brown beer with her devoted suitor, who resembled her brothers enough to be her brother. On Sundays, the entire family went to the *Turnverein* after copious washings, getting into starched dresses and shirts, and getting the baskets of food stored in the wagons. The servant, Ottilie, would rush out to see them off, standing with both shaking arms folded over her forehead, shading her troubled eyes to watch them to the turn of the lane. Her muteness seemed nearly absolute; she had no coherent language of signs. Yet three times a day she spread that enormous table with solid food, freshly baked bread, huge platters of vegetables, immoderate roasts of meat, extravagant tarts, strudels, pies—enough for twenty people. If neighbors came in for an afternoon on some holiday, Ottilie would stumble into the big north room, the parlor, with its golden-oak melodeon, a harsh-green Brussels carpet, Nottingham lace curtains, crocheted lace antimacassars on the chair backs, to serve them coffee with cream and sugar and thick slices of yellow cake.

Mother Müller sat but seldom in her parlor, and always with an air of formal unease, her knotted big fingers cramped in a cluster. But Father Müller often sat there in the evenings, where no one ventured to follow him unless commanded; he sometimes played chess with his elder son-in-law, who had learned a good while ago that Father Müller was a good player who abhorred an easy victory, and he dared not do less than put up the best fight he was able, but even so, if Father Müller felt himself winning too often, he would roar, "No, you are not trying! You are not doing your best. Now we stop this nonsense!", and the son-in-law would find himself dismissed in temporary disgrace.

Most evenings, however, Father Müller sat by himself and read *Das Kapital*. He would settle deeply into the red plush base rocker and spread the volume upon a low table before him. It was an early edition in blotty black German type, stained and ragged in its leather cover, the pages falling apart, a very bible. He knew whole chapters almost by heart, and added nothing to, took nothing from, the canonical, once-delivered text. I cannot say at that time of my life I had never heard of *Das Kapital*, but I had certainly never known anyone who had read it, though if anyone mentioned it, it was always with profound disapproval. It was not a book one had to read in order to reject it. And here was this respectable old farmer who accepted its dogma as a religion—that is to say, its legendary inapplicable precepts were just, right, proper, one must believe in them, of course; but life, everyday living, was another and unrelated thing. Father Müller was the wealthiest man in his community; almost every neighboring farmer rented land from him, and some of them worked it on the share system. He explained this to me one evening after he had given up trying to teach me chess. He was not surprised that I could not learn, at least not in one lesson, and he was not surprised either that I knew nothing about *Das Kapital*. He explained his own arrangements to me thus: "These men, they cannot buy their land. The land must be bought, for *Kapital* owns it, and *Kapital* will not give back to the worker the land that is his. Well, somehow, I can always buy land. Why? I do not know. I only know that with my first land here I made good crops to buy more land, and so I rent it cheap, more than anybody else I rent it cheap, I lend money so my neighbors do not fall into the hands of the bank, and so I am not *Kapital*. Someday these workers, they can buy land from me, for less than they can get it anywhere else. Well, that is what I can do, that is all." He turned over a page, and his angry gray eyes looked out at me under his shaggy brows. "I buy my land with my hard work, all my life, and I rent it cheap to my neighbors, and then they say they will not elect my son-in-law, my Annetje's husband, to be sheriff because I am atheist. So then I say, all right, but next year you pay more for your land or more shares of your crops. If I am atheist, I will act like one. So, my Annetje's husband is sheriff, that is all."

He had put a stubby forefinger on a line to mark his place, and now he sank himself into his book, and I left quietly without saying good night.

The *Turnverein* was an octagonal pavilion set in a cleared space in a patch of woods belonging to Father Müller. The German colony came here to sit about in the cool shade, while a small brass band played cloppity country dances. The girls danced with energy and direction, their starched petticoats rustling like dry leaves. The boys were more awkward, but willing; they clutched their partners' waists and left crumpled sweaty spots where they clutched. Here Mother Müller took her ease after a hard week. Her gaunt limbs would relax, her knees spread squarely apart, and she would gossip over her beer with the women of her own generation.

On the other side of the pavilion, Father Müller would sit with the sober grandfathers, their long curved pipes wagging on their chests as they discussed local politics with profound gravity, their hard peasant fatalism tempered only a little by a shrewd worldly distrust of all officeholders not personally known to them, all political plans except their own immediate ones. When Father Müller talked, they listened respectfully, with faith in him as a strong man, head of his own house and his community. They nodded slowly whenever he took his pipe from his mouth and gestured, holding it by the bowl as if it were a stone he was getting ready to throw.

On our way back from the *Turnverein* one evening, Mother Müller said to me, "Well, now, by the grace of Gott it is all settled between Hatsy and her man. It is next Sunday by this time they will be marrit."

All the folk who usually went to the *Turnverein* on Sundays came instead to the Müller house for the wedding. They brought useful presents, mostly bed linen, pillow covers, a white counterpane, with a few ornaments for the bridal chamber; and the bridegroom's gift to the bride was a necklace, a double string of red coral twigs. Just before the short ceremony began, he slipped the necklace over her head with trembling hands. She smiled up at him shakily and helped him disentangle her short veil from the coral, then they joined hands and turned their faces to the pastor, not letting go until time for the exchange of rings—the widest, thickest, reddest gold bands to be found, no doubt—and at that moment they both stopped smiling and turned a little pale. The groom recovered first, and bent over—he was considerably taller than she—and kissed her on the forehead. His eyes were a deep blue, and his hair not really Müller taffy color, but a light chestnut; a good-looking, gentle-tempered boy, I decided, and he looked at Hatsy as if he liked what he saw. They knelt and clasped hands again for the final prayer, then stood together and exchanged the bridal kiss, a very chaste reserved one, still not on the lips. Then everybody came to shake hands and the men all kissed the bride and the women all kissed the groom. Some of the women whispered in Hatsy's ear, and all burst out laughing except Hatsy, who turned red from her forehead to her throat. She whispered in turn to her husband, who nodded in agreement. She then tried to slip away quietly, but the watchful young girls were after her, and shortly we saw her running through the blossoming orchard, holding up her white ruffled skirts, with all the girls in pursuit, shrieking and calling like excited hunters, for the first to overtake and touch her would be the next bride. They returned, breathless, dragging the lucky one with them, and held her, against her ecstatic resistance, while all the young boys kissed her.

The guests stayed on for a huge supper, and Ottilie came in, wearing a fresh blue apron, sweat beaded in the wrinkles of her forehead and around her formless mouth, and passed the food around the table. The men ate first, and then Hatsy came in with the women for the first time, still wearing her square little veil of white cotton net bound on her hair with peach blossoms shattered in the bride's race. After supper, one of the girls played waltzes and polkas on the melodeon, and everyone danced. The bridegroom drew gallons of beer from a keg set up in the hall, and at midnight everybody went away, warmly emotional and happy. I went down to the kitchen for a pitcher of hot water. The servant was still setting things to rights, hobbling between table and cupboard. Her face was a brown smudge of anxiety, her eyes were wide and dazed. Her uncertain hands rattled among the pans, but nothing could make her seem real, or in any way connected with the life around her. Yet when I set my pitcher on the stove, she lifted the heavy kettle and poured the scalding water into it without spilling a drop.

The clear honey green of the early morning sky was a mirror of the bright earth. At the edge of the woods there had sprung a reticent blooming of small white and pale-colored flowers. The peach trees were now each a separate nosegay of shell rose and white. I left the house, meaning to take the short path across to the lane of mulberries. The women were deep in the house, the men were away to the fields, the animals were turned into the pastures, and only Ottilie was visible, sitting on the steps of the back porch peeling potatoes. She gazed in my direction with eyes that fell short of me, and seemed to focus on a point midway between us, and gave no sign. Then she dropped her knife and rose, her mouth opened and closed several times, she strained toward me, motioning with her right hand. I went to her, her hands came out and clutched my sleeve, and for a moment I feared to hear her voice. There was no sound from her, but she drew me along after her, full of some mysterious purpose of her own. She opened the door of a dingy, bitter-smelling room, windowless, which opened off the kitchen, beside the closet where Hatsy took her baths. A lumpy narrow cot and a chest of drawers supporting a blistered looking-glass almost filled the space. Ottilie's lips moved, struggling for speech, as she pulled and tumbled over a heap of rubbish in the top drawer. She took out a photograph and put it in my hands. It was in the old style, faded to a dirty yellow, mounted on cardboard elaborately clipped and gilded at the edges.

I saw a girl child about five years old, a pretty smiling German baby, looking curiously like a slightly elder sister of Annetje's two-year-old, wearing a frilled frock and a prodigious curl of blonde hair on the crown of her head. The strong legs, round as sausages, were encased in long white ribbed stockings, and the square firm feet were laced into old-fashioned soft-soled black boots. Ottilie peered over the picture, twisted her neck, and looked up into my face. I saw the slanted water-blue eyes and the high cheekbones of the Müllers again, mutilated, almost destroyed, but unmistakable. This child was what she had been, and she was without doubt the elder sister of Annetje and Gretchen and Hatsy; in urgent pantomime she insisted that this was so—she patted the picture and her own face, and strove terribly to speak. She pointed to the name written carefully on the back, Ottilie, and touched her mouth with her bent knuckles. Her head wagged in her perpetual nod; her shaking hand seemed to flap the photograph at me in a roguish humor. The bit of cardboard connected her at once somehow to the world of human beings I knew; for an instant some filament lighter than cobweb spun itself out between that living center in her and in me, a filament from some center that held us all bound to our inescapable common source, so that her life and mine were kin, even a part of each other, and the painfulness and strangeness of her vanished. She knew well that she had been Ottilie, with those steady legs and watching eyes, and she was Ottilie still within herself. For a moment, being alive, she knew she suffered, for she stood and shook with silent crying, smearing away her tears with the open palm of her hand. Even while her cheeks were wet, her face changed. Her eyes cleared and fixed themselves upon that point in space which seemed for her to contain her unaccountable and terrible troubles. She turned her head as if she had heard a voice and disappeared in her staggering run into the kitchen, leaving the drawer open and the photograph face downward on the chest.

At midday meal she came hurrying and splashing coffee on the white floor, restored to her own secret existence of perpetual amazement, and again I had become a stranger to her like all the rest, but she was no stranger to me, and could not be again.

The youngest brother came in, holding up an opossum he had caught in his trap. He swung the furry body from side to side, his eyes fairly narrowed with pride as he showed us the mangled creature. "No, it is cruel, even for the wild animals," said gentle Annetje to me, "but boys love to kill, they love to hurt things. I am always afraid he will trap poor Kuno." I thought privately that Kuno, a wolfish, ungracious beast, might well prove a match for any trap. Annetje was full of silent, tender solicitudes. The kittens, the puppies, the chicks, the lambs and calves were her special care. She was the only one of the women who caressed the weanling calves when she set the pans of milk before them. Her child seemed as much a part of her as if it were not yet born. Still, she seemed to have forgotten that Ottilie was her sister. So had all the others. I remembered how Hatsy had spoken her name but had not said she was her sister. Their silence about her was, I realized, exactly that—simple forgetfulness. She moved among them as invisible to their imaginations as a ghost. Ottilie their sister was something painful that had happened long ago and now was past and done for; they could not live with that memory or its visible reminder— they forgot her in pure self-defense. But I could not forget her. She drifted into my mind like a bit of weed carried in a current and caught there, floating but fixed, refusing to be carried away. I

reasoned it out. The Müllers, what else could they have done with
Ottilie? By a physical accident in her childhood, she had been
stripped of everything but her mere existence. It was not a society
or a class that pampered its invalids and the unfit. So long as one
lived, one did one's share. This was her place, in this family she
had been born and must die; did she suffer? No one asked, no
one looked to see. Suffering went with life, suffering and labor.
While one lived one worked, that was all, and without complaints,
for no one had time to listen, and everybody had his own troubles.
So, what else could they have done with Ottilie? As for me, I
could do nothing but promise myself that I would forget her, too;
and to remember her for the rest of my life.

Sitting at the long table, I would watch Ottilie clattering about
in her tormented haste, bringing in that endless food that represented all her life's labors. My mind would follow her into the
kitchen, where I could see her peering into the great simmering
kettles, the crowded oven, her ruined hands always lifting and
stirring, and paring and chopping, her whole body a mere machine
of torture. Straight up to the surface of my mind the thought would
come urgently, clearly, as if driving time toward the desired
event: Let it be now, let it be *now*. Not even tomorrow, no,
today. Let her sit down quietly in her rickety chair by the stove
and fold those arms, and let us find her there like that, with her
head fallen forward on her knees. I would wait, hoping she might
not come again, ever again, through that door I gazed at with
wincing eyes, as if I might see something unendurable enter. Then
she would come, and it was only Ottilie, after all, in the bosom of
her family, and one of its most useful and competent members;
and they with a deep right instinct had learned to live with her
disaster on its own terms, and hers; they had accepted and then
made use of what was for them only one more painful event in a
world full of troubles, many of them much worse than this. So, a
step at a time, I followed the Müllers as nearly as I could in their
acceptance of Ottilie and the use they made of her life, for in some
way that I could not quite explain to myself, I found great virtue
and courage in their steadiness and refusal to feel sorry for anybody,
least of all for themselves.

Gretchen bore her child, a son, conveniently between the hours of supper and bedtime, one evening of friendly domestic-sounding rain. The next day brought neighboring women from miles around, and the child was bandied about among them as if he were a new kind of medicine ball. Sedate and shy at dances, emotional at weddings, they were ribald and jocose at births. Over coffee and beer the talk grew broad, the hearty gutturals were swallowed in the belly of laughter; those honest hard-working wives and mothers saw life for a few hours as a hearty low joke, and it did them good. The baby bawled and suckled like a young calf, and the men of the family came in for a look and added their joyful improprieties.

Cloudy weather drove them home earlier than they had meant to go. The whole sky was lined with smoky black and gray vapor hanging in ragged wisps like soot in a chimney. The edges of the woods turned dull purple as the horizon reddened slowly, then faded, and all across the sky ran a deep shuddering mumble of thunder. All the Müllers hurried about getting into rubber boots and oilcloth overalls, shouting to each other, making their plan of action. The youngest boy came over the ridge of the hill with Kuno helping him to drive the sheep into the fold. Kuno was barking, the sheep were baaing and bleating, the horses freed from the plows were excited; they whinnied and trotted at the lengths of their halters, their ears laid back. The cows were bawling in distress and the calves cried back to them. All the men went out among the animals to round them up and quiet them and get them enclosed safely. Even as Mother Müller, her half-dozen petticoats looped about her thighs and tucked into her hip boots, was striding to join them in the barns, the cloud rack was split end to end by a shattering blow of lightning, and the cloudburst struck the house with the impact of a wave against a ship. The wind broke the window-panes and the floods poured through. The roof beams strained and the walls bent inward, but the house stood to its foundations. The children were huddled into the inner bedroom with Gretchen. "Come and sit on the bed with me now," she told them calmly, "and be still." She sat up with a shawl around her, suckling the baby. Annetje came then and left her baby with Gretchen, too; and standing at the doorstep with one arm caught over the porch rail, reached down into the furious waters which were rising to the very threshold and dragged in a half-drowned lamb. I followed her. We could not make ourselves heard above the cannonade of thunder, but together we carried the creature into the hall under the stairs, where we rubbed the drowned fleece with rags and pressed his stomach to free him from the water and finally got him sitting up with his feet tucked under him. Annetje was merry with triumph and kept saying in delight, "Alive, alive! Look!"

We left him there when we heard the men shouting and beating at the kitchen door and ran to open it for them. They came in, Mother Müller among them, wearing her yoke and milk pails. She stood there with the water pouring from her skirts, the three-cornered piece of black oilcloth on her head dripping, her rubber boots wrinkled down with the weight of her petticoats. She and Father Müller stood near each other, looking like two gnarled lightning-struck old trees, his beard and oilcloth garments streaming, both their faces suddenly dark and old and tired, tired once for all; they would never be rested again in their lives. Father Müller suddenly roared at her, "Go get yourself dry clothes. Do you want to make yourself sick?"

"Ho," she said, taking off her milk yoke and setting the pails on the floor. "Go change yourself. I bring you dry socks." One of the boys told me she had carried a day-old calf on her back up a ladder against the inside wall of the barn and had put it safely in the hayloft behind a barricade of bales. Then she had lined up the cows in the stable, and sitting on her milking stool in the rising water, she had milked them all. She seemed to think nothing of it.

"Hatsy," she called, "come help with this milk!" Little pale Hatsy came flying, barefoot because she had been called in the midst of taking off her wet shoes. Her new husband followed her, rather shy of his mother-in-law.

"Let me," he said, wishing to spare his dear bride such heavy work, and started to lift the great pails. "No!" shouted Mother Müller, so the poor young man nearly jumped out of his shirt. "Not you. The milk is not business for a man." He fell back and stood there with dark rivulets of mud seeping from his boots, watching Hatsy pour the milk into pans. Mother Müller started to follow her husband to attend him, but said at the door, "Where is Ottilie?", and no one knew, no one had seen her. "Find her," said Mother Müller. "Tell her we want supper, now."

Hatsy motioned to her husband, and together they tiptoed to the door of Ottilie's room and opened it silently. The light from the kitchen showed them Ottilie, sitting by herself, folded up on the edge of the bed. Hatsy threw the door wide open for more light and called in a high penetrating voice as if to a deaf person or one at a great distance, "Ottilie! Suppertime. We are hungry!", and the young pair left the kitchen to look under the stairway to see how Annetje's lamb was getting on. Then Annetje, Hatsy, and I began sweeping the dirty water and broken glass from the floors of the hall and dining room.

The storm lightened gradually, but the flooding rain continued. At supper there was talk about the loss of animals and their replacement. All the crops must be replanted, the season's labor was for nothing. They were all tired and wet, but they ate heartily and calmly, to strengthen themselves against all the labor of repairing and restoring which must begin early tomorrow morning.

By morning the drumming on the roof had almost ceased; from my window I looked upon a sepia-colored plain of water moving slowly to the valley. The roofs of the barns sagged like the ridge-poles of a tent, and a number of drowned animals floated or were caught against the fences. At breakfast, Mother Müller sat groaning over her coffee cup. "Ach," she said, "what it is to have such a pain in the head. Here too." She thumped her chest. "All over. Ach, Gott, I'm sick." She got up sighing hoarsely, her cheeks flushed, calling Hatsy and Annetje to help her in the barn.

They all came back very soon, their skirts draggled to the knees, and the two sisters were supporting their mother, who was speechless and could hardly stand. They put her to bed, where she lay without moving, her face scarlet. Everybody was confused; no one knew what to do. They tucked the quilts about her, and she threw them off. They offered her coffee, cold water, beer, but she turned her head away. The sons came in and stood beside her and joined the cry: "*Mutterchen, Mutti, Mutti,* what can we do? Tell us, what do you need?" But she could not tell them. It was impossible to ride the twelve miles to town for a doctor; fences and bridges were down, the roads were washed out. The family crowded into the room, unnerved, in panic, lost unless the sick woman should come to herself and tell them what to do for her. Father Müller came in, and kneeling beside her, he took hold of her hands and spoke to her most lovingly, and when she did not answer him, he broke out crying openly, in a loud voice, the great tears rolling, "Ach, Gott, Gott. A hundert tousand tollars in the bank" —he glared around at his family and spoke broken English to them, as if he were a stranger to himself and had forgotten his own language—"and tell me, tell, what goot does it?"

This frightened them, and all at once, together, they screamed and called and implored her in a tumult utterly beyond control. The noise of their grief and terror filled the place. In the midst of this, Mother Müller died.

In the midafternoon the rain passed, and the sun was a disk of brass in a cruelly bright sky. The waters flowed thickly down to the river, leaving the hill bald and brown, with the fences lying in a flattened tangle, the young peach trees stripped of bloom and sagging at the roots. In the woods had occurred a violent eruption of ripe foliage of a jungle thickness, glossy and burning, a massing of hot peacock green with cobalt shadows.

The household was in such silence, I had to listen carefully to know that anyone lived there. Everyone, even the younger children, moved on tiptoe and spoke in whispers. All afternoon the thud of hammers and the whine of a saw went on monotonously in the barn loft. At dark, the men brought in a shiny coffin of new yellow pine with rope handles and set it in the hall. It lay there on the floor for an hour or so, where anyone passing had to step over it. Then Annetje and Hatsy, who had been washing and dressing the body, appeared in the doorway and motioned. "You bring it in now."

Mother Müller lay in state in the parlor throughout the night, in her black silk dress with a scrap of white lace at the collar and a small lace cap on her hair. Her husband sat in the plush chair near her, looking at her face, which was very contemplative, gentle, and remote. He wept at intervals, silently, wiping his face with a big handkerchief. His daughters brought him coffee from time to time. He fell asleep there toward morning.

The light burned in the kitchen nearly all night, too, and the sound of Ottilie's heavy boots thumping about unsteadily was accompanied by the locust whirring of the coffee mill and the smell of baking bread. Hatsy came to my room. "There's coffee and cake," she said, "you'd better have some," and turned away crying, crumbling her slice in her hand. We stood about and ate in silence. Ottilie brought in a fresh pot of coffee, her eyes bleared and fixed, her gait as aimless-looking and hurried as ever, and when she spilled some on her own hand, she did not seem to feel it.

For a day longer they waited; then the youngest boy went to fetch the Lutheran pastor, and a few neighbors came back with them. By noon many more had arrived, spattered with mud, the horses heaving and sweating. At every greeting the family gave way and wept afresh, as naturally and openly as children. Their faces were drenched and soft with their tears; there was a comfortable relaxed look in the muscles of their faces. It was good to let go, to have something to weep for that nobody need excuse or explain. Their tears were at once a luxury and a cure of souls. They wept away the hard core of secret trouble that is in the heart of each separate man, secure in a communal grief; in sharing it, they consoled each other. For a while, they would visit the grave and remember, and then life would arrange itself again in another order, yet it would be the same. Already the thoughts of the living were turning to tomorrow, when they would be at the work of rebuilding and replanting and repairing—even now, today, they would hurry back from the burial to milk the cows and feed the chickens, and they might weep again and again for several days, until their tears should heal them at last.

On that day I realized, for the first time, not death, but the terror of dying. When they took the coffin out to the little country hearse and I saw that the procession was about to form, I went to my room and lay down. Staring at the ceiling, I heard and felt the ominous order and purpose in the movements and sounds below—the creaking harness and hoofbeats and grating wheels, the muted grave voices—and it was as if my blood fainted and receded with fright, while my mind stayed wide-awake to receive the awful impress. Yet when I knew they were leaving the yard, the terror began to leave me. As the sounds receded, I lay there not thinking, not feeling, in a mere drowse of relief and weariness.

Through my half-sleep I heard the howling of a dog. It seemed to be in a dream, and I was troubled to awaken. I dreamed that Kuno was caught in the trap; then I thought he was really caught, it was no dream and I must wake, because there was no one but me to let him out. I came broad awake, the cry rushed upon me like a wind, and it was not the howl of a dog. I ran downstairs and looked into Gretchen's room. She was curled up around her baby, and they were both asleep. I ran to the kitchen.

Ottilie was sitting in her broken chair with her feet in the edge of the open oven, where the heat had died away. Her hands hung at her sides, the fingers crooked into the palm; her head lay back on her shoulders, and she howled with a great wrench of her body, an upward reach of the neck, without tears. At sight of me she got up and came over to me and laid her head on my breast, and her hands dangled forward a moment. Shuddering, she babbled and howled and waved her arms in a frenzy through the open window over the stripped branches of the orchard toward the lane where the procession had straightened out into formal order. I took hold of her arms where the unnaturally corded muscles clenched and strained under her coarse sleeves; I led her out to the steps and left her sitting there, her head wagging.

In the barnyard there remained only the broken-down spring wagon and the shaggy pony that had brought me to the farm on the first day. The harness was still a mystery, but somehow I managed to join pony, harness, and wagon not too insecurely, or so I could only hope; and I pushed and hauled and tugged at Ottilie and lifted her until she was in the seat and I had the reins in hand. We careened down the road at a grudging trot, the pony jolting like a churn, the wheels spinning elliptically in a truly broad comedy swagger. I watched the jovial antics of those wheels with attention, hoping for the best. We slithered into round pits of green mud and jogged perilously into culverts where small bridges had been. Once, in what was left of the main road, I stood up to see if I might overtake the funeral train; yes, there it was, going inchmeal up the road over the little hill, a bumbling train of black beetles crawling helter-skelter over clods.

Ottilie, now silent, was doubled upon herself, slipping loosely on the edge of the seat. I caught hold of her stout belt with my free hand, and my fingers slipped between her clothes and bare flesh, ribbed and gaunt and dry against my knuckles. My sense of her realness, her humanity, this shattered being that was a woman, was so shocking to me that a howl as doglike and despairing as her own rose in me unuttered and died again, to be a perpetual ghost. Ottilie slanted her eyes and peered at me, and I gazed back. The knotted wrinkles of her face were grotesquely changed, she gave a choked little whimper, and suddenly she laughed out, a kind of yelp but unmistakably laughter, and clapped her hands for joy, the grinning mouth and suffering eyes turned to the sky. Her head nodded and wagged with the clownish humor of our trundling lurching progress. The feel of the hot sun on her back, the bright air, the jolly senseless staggering of the wheels, the peacock green of the heavens: something of these had reached her. She was happy and gay, and she gurgled and rocked in her seat, leaning upon me and waving loosely around her as if to show me what wonders she saw.

Drawing the pony to a standstill, I studied her face for a while and pondered my ironical mistake. There was nothing I could do for Ottilie, selfishly as I wished to ease my heart of her; she was beyond my reach as well as any other human reach, and yet, had I not come nearer to her than I had to anyone else in my attempt to deny and bridge the distance between us, or rather, her distance from me? Well, we were both equally the fools of life, equally fellow fugitives from death. We had escaped for one day more at least. We would celebrate our good luck, we would have a little stolen holiday, a breath of spring air and freedom on this lovely, festive afternoon.

Ottilie fidgeted, uneasy at our stopping. I flapped the reins, the pony moved on, we turned across the shallow ditch where the small road divided from the main traveled one. I measured the sun westering gently; there would be time enough to drive to the river down the lane of mulberries and to get back to the house before the mourners returned. There would be plenty of time for Ottilie to have supper ready. They need not even know she had been gone.

THOMAS PYNCHON has had short stories published in *Epoch*, *New World Writing*, *The Kenyon Review*, and *The Noble Savage*. A novel will be published by J. B. Lippincott Company, sometime in 1962.

UNDER THE ROSE

from *The Noble Savage*

As the afternoon progressed, yellow clouds began to gather over Place Mohammed Ali, casting a tendril or two back toward the Libyan desert. A wind from the southwest swept quietly up rue Ibrahim and across the square, bringing the chill of the desert into the city.

Then let it rain, Porpentine thought: rain soon. He sat at a small wrought-iron table in front of a café, smoking Turkish cigarettes with a third cup of coffee, ulster thrown over the back of an adjoining chair. Today he wore light tweeds and a felt hat with muslin tied round it to protect his neck from the sun; he was leery of the sun. Clouds moved in now to dim it out. Porpentine shifted in his seat, took a watch from his waistcoat pocket, consulted it, replaced it. Turned once more to look out at the Europeans milling about the square: some hurrying into the Banque Impériale Ottomane, others lingering by shopwindows, seating themselves at cafés. His face was carefully arranged: nerveless, rakish-expectant; he might have been there to meet a lady.

All for the benefit of anyone who cared. God knew how many there were. In practice it narrowed down to those in the employ of Moldweorp, the veteran spy. One somehow always tacked on "the veteran spy." It might have been a throwback to an earlier time, when such epithets were one reward for any proof of heroism or

Copyright © 1961 by The World Publishing Company.

manhood. Or possibly because now, with a century rushing head-long to its end and with it a tradition in espionage where everything was tacitly on a gentlemanly basis, where the playing-fields of Eton had conditioned (one might say) premilitary conduct as well, the label was a way of fixing identity in this special *haut monde* before death—individual or collective—stung it to stillness forever. Por-pentine himself was called *"il semplice inglese"* by those who cared.

Last week in Brindisi their compassion had been relentless as always; it gave them a certain moral advantage, realizing as they did that Porpentine was somehow incapable of returning it. Tender and sheepish, therefore, they wove their paths to cross his own at random. Mirrored, too, his private tactics: living in the most fre-quented hotels, sitting at the tourist cafés, traveling always by the respectable, public routes. Which surely upset him most; as if, Porpentine once having fashioned such proper innocence, any use of it by others—especially Moldweorp's agents—involved some violation of patent right. They would pirate if they could his child's gaze, his plump angel's smile. For nearly fifteen years he'd fled their sympathy; since the lobby of the Hotel Bristol, Naples, on a winter evening in '83, when everyone you knew in spying's free-masonry seemed to be waiting. For Khartum to fall, for the crisis in Afghanistan to keep growing until it could be given the name of sure apocalypse. There he had come, as he'd known he must at some stage of the game, to face the already aged face of Mold-weorp himself, the prizeman or maestro, feel the old man's hand solicitous on his arm and hear the earnest whisper: "Things are reaching a head; we may be for it, all of us. Do be careful." What response? What possible? Only a scrutiny, almost desperate, for any fine trace of insincerity. Of course he'd found none there; and so turned, quickly, flaming, unable to cover a certain helplessness. Hoist thus by his own petard at every subsequent encounter as well, Porpentine by the dog-days of '98 seemed, in contrast, to have grown cold, unkind. They would continue to use so fortunate an engine: would never seek his life, violate The Rules, forbear what had become for them pleasure.

He sat now wondering if either of the two at Brindisi had fol-lowed him to Alexandria. Certain he had seen no one on the Venice boat, he reviewed possibilities. An Austrian Lloyd steamer from Trieste also touched at Brindisi; was the only other they would have taken. Today was Monday. Porpentine had left on a Friday. The Trieste boat left on Thursday and arrived late Sunday. So that (a) at second-worst he had six days, or (b) at worst, they knew. In which case they had left the day before Porpentine and were already here.

He watched the sun darken and the wind flutter the leaves of acacias around Place Mohammed Ali. In the distance his name was being called. He turned to watch Goodfellow, blond and jovial, striding toward him down rue Cherif Pacha, wearing a dress suit and a pith helmet two sizes too large. "I say," Goodfellow cried. "Porpentine, I've met a remarkable young lady." Porpentine lit another cigarette and closed his eyes. All of Goodfellow's young ladies were remarkable. After two and a half years as partners one got used to an incidental progress of feminine attachments to Goodfellow's right arm: as if every capital of Europe were Margate and the promenade a continent long. If Goodfellow knew half his salary was sent out every month to a wife in Liverpool he showed none of it, rollicking along unperturbed, cock-a-hoop. Porpentine had seen his running mate's dossier but decided some time ago that the wife at least was none of his affair. He listened now as Goodfellow drew up a chair and summoned a waiter in wretched Arabic: "Hat fingan kahwa bisukkar, ya weled."

"Goodfellow," Porpentine said, "you don't have to—"

"Ya weled, ya weled," Goodfellow roared. The waiter was French and did not understand Arabic. "Ah," Goodfellow said, "coffee then. Café, you know."

"How are the digs?" asked Porpentine.

"First-rate." Goodfellow was staying at the Hotel Khedival, seven blocks away. There being a temporary hitch in finances, only one could afford the usual accommodations. Porpentine was staying with a friend in the Turkish quarter. "About this girl," Goodfellow said. "Party tonight at the Austrian Consulate. Her escort, Goodfellow: linguist, adventurer, diplomat . . ."

"Name," said Porpentine.

"Victoria Wren. Traveling with family, videlicet: Sir Alastair Wren, F.R.C.O., sister Mildred. Mother deceased. Departing for Cairo tomorrow. Cook's tour down the Nile." Porpentine waited.

"Lunatic archaeologist," Goodfellow seemed reluctant. "One Bongo-Shaftsbury. Young, addlepated. Harmless."

"Aha."

"Tch-tch. Too highly strung. Should drink less café-fort."

"Possibly," Porpentine said. Goodfellow's coffee arrived. Porpentine continued: "You know we'll end up chancing it anyway. We always do." Goodfellow grinned absently and stirred his coffee.

"I have already taken steps. Bitter rivalry for the young lady's attentions between myself and Bongo-Shaftsbury. Fellow is a perfect ass. Is mad to see the Theban ruins at Luxor."

"Of course," Porpentine said. He arose and tossed the ulster around his shoulders. It had begun to rain. Goodfellow handed him a small white envelope with the Austrian crest on the back.

"Eight, I suppose," said Porpentine.

"Right you are. You must see this girl."

It was then that one of Porpentine's seizures came upon him. The profession was lonely and in constant though not always deadly earnest. At regular intervals he found need to play the buffoon. "A bit of skylarking," he called it. It made him, he believed, more human. "I will be there with false mustaches," he now informed Goodfellow, "impersonating an Italian count." He stood gaily at attention, pressed an imaginary hand: "*Carissima signorina.*" He bowed, kissed the air.

"You're insane," from Goodfellow, amiable.

"*Pazzo son!*" Porpentine began to sing in a wavering tenor. "*Guardate, come io piango ed imploro . . .*" His Italian was not perfect. Cockney inflections danced through. A group of English tourists, hurrying in out of the rain, glanced back at him, curious.

"Enough," Goodfellow winced. "'Twas Turin, I remember. Torino. Was it not? '93. I escorted a marchesina with a mole on her back and Cremonini sang Des Grieux. You, Porpentine, desecrate the memory."

But the antic Porpentine leaped in the air, clicked his heels; stood posturing, fist on chest, the other arm outstretched. "*Come io chiedo pietà!*" The waiter looked on with a pained smile; it began to rain harder. Goodfellow sat in the rain sipping his coffee. Drops of rain rattled on the pith helmet. "The sister isn't bad," he observed as Porpentine frolicked out in the square. "Mildred, you know. Though only eleven." At length it occurred to him that his dress suit was becoming soaked. He arose, left a piastre and a millième on the table and nodded to Porpentine, who now stood watching him. The square was empty except for the equestrian statue of Mohammed Ali. How many times had they faced each other this way, dwarfed horizontal and vertical by any plaza's late-afternoon landscape? Could an argument from design be predicated on that moment only, then the two must have been displaceable, like minor chess-pieces, anywhere across the board of Europe. Both of a color (though one hanging back diagonal in deference to his chief), both scanning any embassy's parquetry for signs of the Opposition, any statue's face for a reassurance of self-agency (perhaps, unhappily, self-humanity), they would try not to remember that every city's square, however you cut it, remains inanimate after all. Soon the two men turned almost formally, to part in opposite directions: Goodfellow back toward the hotel, Porpentine into rue Ras-et-Tin and the Turkish quarter. Until eight he would ponder the Situation.

At the moment it was a bad job all round. Sirdar Kitchener, England's newest colonial hero, recently victorious at Khartum, was just now some four hundred miles farther down the White Nile, foraging about in the jungle. A General Marchand was also rumored to be in the vicinity. Britain wanted no part of France in the Nile Valley. M. Delcassé, Foreign Minister of a newly formed French cabinet, would as soon go to war as not if there were any trouble when the two detachments met. As meet, everyone realized by now, they would. Kitchener had been instructed not to take any offensive and to avoid all provocation. Russia would support France in case of war, while England had a temporary rapprochement with Germany, which of course meant Italy and Austria as well.

Moldweorp's chief amusement, Porpentine reflected, had always been to harass. All he asked was that eventually there be a war. Not just a small incidental skirmish in the race to carve up Africa, but one pip-pip, jolly-ho, up-goes-the-balloon Armageddon for Europe. Once Porpentine might have been puzzled that his opposite number should desire war so passionately. Now he took it for granted that at some point in these fifteen years of hare-and-hounds he himself had conceived the private mission of keeping off Armageddon. An alignment like this, he felt, could only have taken place in a Western World where spying was becoming less an individual than a group enterprise, where the events of 1848 and the activities of anarchists and radicals all over the Continent seemed to proclaim that history was being made no longer through the *virtù* of single princes but rather by man in the mass; by trends and tendencies and impersonal curves on a lattice of pale blue lines. So it was inevitably single combat between the veteran spy and *il semplice inglese*. They stood alone—God knew where— on deserted lists. Goodfellow knew of the private battle, as doubt- less did Moldweorp's subordinates. They all took on the roles of solicitous seconds, attending to the strictly national interests while their chiefs circled and parried above them on some unreachable level. It happened that Porpentine worked nominally for England and Moldweorp for Germany, but this was accident: they would probably have chosen the same sides had their employments been reversed. For he and Moldweorp, Porpentine knew, were cut from the same pattern: comrade Machiavellians, still playing the games of Renaissance Italian politics in a world that had outgrown them. The self-assumed roles became only, then, assertions of a kind of pride, first of all in a profession which still remembered the free- booting agility of Lord Palmerston. Fortunately for Porpentine the Foreign Office had enough of the old spirit left to give him nearly a free hand. Although if they did suspect he'd have no way of knowing. Where his personal mission coincided with diplomatic policy, Porpentine would send back a report to London, and no one ever seemed to complain.

The key man now for Porpentine seemed to be Lord Cromer, the British Consul-General at Cairo, an extremely able diplomat and cautious enough to avoid any rash impulses: war, for example. Could Moldweorp have an assassination in the works? A trip to Cairo seemed in order. As innocent as possible; that went without saying.

The Austrian Consulate was across the street from the Hotel Khedival, the festivities there unexceptional. Goodfellow sat at the bottom of a wide flight of marble steps with a girl who could not have been more than eighteen and who, like the gown she wore, seemed awkwardly bouffant and provincial. The rain had shrunken Goodfellow's formal attire; his coat looked tight under the armpits and across the stomach; the blond hair had been disarranged by the desert wind, the face was flushed, uncomfortable. Watching him, Porpentine came aware of his own appearance: quaint, anomalous, his evening clothes purchased the same year General Gordon was done in by the Mahdi. Hopelessly passé at gatherings like this, he often played a game in which he was, say, Gordon returned from the dead and headless; that odd, at least, among a resplendent muster of stars, ribbons, and exotic Orders. That out of date, certainly: the Sirdar had retaken Khartum, the outrage was avenged, but people had forgotten. He'd seen the fabled hero of the China wars once, standing on the ramparts at Gravesend. At the time Porpentine had been ten or so and likely to be dazzled; he was. But something had happened between there and the Hotel Bristol. He had thought about Moldweorp that night and about the likelihood of some apocalypse; perhaps a little too on his own sense of estrangement. But not at all about Chinese Gordon, lonely and enigmatic at the mouth of that boyhood Thames; whose hair it was said had turned white in the space of a day as he waited for death in the besieged city of Khartum.

Porpentine looked about the Consulate, checking off diplomatic personnel: Sir Charles Cookson, Mr. Hewat, M. Girard, Hr. von Hartmann, Cav. Romano, Comte de Zogheb, &c., &c. Right ho. All present and accounted for. Except for the Russian Vice-Consul, M. de Villiers. And oddly enough one's host, Count Khevenhüller-Metsch. Could they be together?

He moved over to the steps where Goodfellow sat desperate, yarning about nonexistent adventures in South Africa. The girl regarded him breathless and smiling. Porpentine wondered if he should sing: It isn't the girl I saw you with in Brighton; who, who, who's your lady friend? He said:

"I say." Goodfellow, relieved and more enthusiastic than necessary, introduced them.

"Miss Victoria Wren."

Porpentine smiled, nodded, searched all over for a cigarette. "How do you do, Miss."

"She's been hearing about our show with Dr. Jameson and the Boers," said Goodfellow.

"You were in the Transvaal together," the girl marveled. Porpentine thought: he can do whatever he wants with this one. Whatever he asks her.

"We've been together for some time, Miss." She bloomed, she billowed; Porpentine, shy, withdrew behind pale cheeks, pursed lips. As if her glow were a reminder of any Yorkshire sunset, or at least some vestige of a vision of Home which neither he nor Goodfellow could afford—or when you came down to it, cared—to remember, they did share in her presence this common evasiveness.

A low growl sounded behind Porpentine. Goodfellow cringed, smiled weakly, introduced Sir Alastair Wren Victoria's father. It became clear almost immediately that he was not fond of Goodfellow. With him was a robust, myopic girl of eleven; the sister. Mildred was in Egypt, she soon informed Porpentine, to gather rock specimens, being daft for rocks in the same way Sir Alastair was for large and ancient pipe-organs. He had toured Germany the previous year, alienating the populations of various cathedral towns by recruiting small boys to toil away half-days at a clip keeping the bellows going: and then underpaying. Frightfully, added Victoria. There was, he continued, no decent pipe-organ anywhere on the African continent (which Porpentine could hardly doubt). Goodfellow mentioned an enthusiasm for the barrel-organ, and had Sir Alastair ever tried his hand at one. The peer growled ominously. Out of the corner of his eye Porpentine saw Count Khevenhüller-Metsch come out of an adjoining room, steering the Russian vice-consul by the arm and talking wistfully; M. de Villiers punctuated the conversation with mirthful little barks. Aha, Porpentine thought. Mildred had produced from her reticule a large rock, which she now held up to Porpentine for inspection. She had found it out near the site of the ancient Pharos, it contained trilobite fossils. Porpentine could not respond; it was his old weakness. A bar was set up on the mezzanine; he loped up the marble stairs after promising to bring punch (lemonade, of course, for Mildred).

Someone touched his arm as he waited at the bar. He turned and saw one of the two from Brindisi, who said: "Lovely girl." It was the first word he could remember any of them speaking to him directly in fifteen years. He only wondered, uneasy, if they reserved such artifice for times of singular crisis. He picked up the drinks, smiled all angelic; turned, started down the stairs. On the second step he tripped and fell: proceeded whirling and bouncing, followed by sounds of glass breaking and a spray of Chablis punch and lemonade, to the bottom. He'd learned in the army how to take falls. He looked up bashful at Sir Alastair Wren, who nodded in approval.

"Saw a fellow do that in a music-hall once," he said. "You're much better, Porpentine. Really."

"Do it again," Mildred said. Porpentine extracted a cigarette, lay there for a bit smoking. "How about late supper at the Fink," Goodfellow suggested. Porpentine got to his feet. "You remember the chaps we met in Brindisi." Goodfellow nodded, impassive, betraying no tics or tightenings; one of the things Porpentine admired him for. But: "Going home," Sir Alastair muttered, yanking fiercely at Mildred's hand. "Behave yourselves." So Porpentine found himself playing chaperon. He proposed another try for punch. When they got to the mezzanine Moldweorp's man had disappeared. Porpentine wedged one foot between the balusters and looked down, surveying rapidly the faces below. "No," he said. Goodfellow handed him a cup of punch.

"I can't wait to see the Nile," Victoria had been saying, "the pyramids, the Sphinx."

"Cairo," Goodfellow added.

"Yes," Porpentine agreed, "Cairo."

Directly across rue de Rosette was the Fink restaurant. They dashed across the street through the rain, Victoria's cloak ballooning about her; she laughed, delighted with the rain. The crowd inside was entirely European. Porpentine recognized a few faces from the Venice boat. After her first glass of white Vöslauer the girl began to talk. Blithe and so green, she pronounced her o's with a sigh, as if fainting from love. She was Catholic; had been to a convent school near her home, a place called Lardwick-in-the-Fen. This was her first trip abroad. She talked a great deal about her religion: had, for a time, considered the son of God as a young lady will consider any eligible bachelor. But had realized eventually that of course he was not but maintained instead an immense

harem clad in black, decked with rosaries. She would never stand
for such competition, had therefore left the novitiate after a matter
of weeks but not the Church: that, with its sad-faced statuary, its
odor of candles and incense, formed along with an uncle Evelyn
the twin foci of her serene orbit. The uncle, a wild or renegade sun-
downer, would arrive from Australia once a year bringing no gifts
but prepared to weave as many yarns as the sisters could cope with.
As far as Victoria remembered, he had never repeated himself. So
she was given enough material to evolve between visits a private
and imaginary sphere of influence, which she played with and
within constantly: developing, exploring, manipulating. Especially
during Mass: for here was the stage, the dramatic field already
prepared, serviceable to a seedtime fancy. And so it came about
that God wore a wide-awake hat and fought skirmishes with an
aboriginal Satan out at the antipodes of the firmament, in the
name and for the safekeeping of any Victoria.

Now the desire to feel pity can be seductive; it was always so
for Porpentine. At this point he could only flick a rapid glance at
Goodfellow's face and think with the sort of admiration pity once
foundered in makes detestable: a stroke of genius, the Jameson
raid. He chose that, he knew. He always knows. So do I.

One had to. He'd realized long before that women had no mo-
nopoly on what is called intuition; that in most men the faculty
was latent, only becoming developed or painfully heightened at all
in professions like this. But men being positivists and women more
dreamy, having hunches still remained at base a feminine talent;
so that like it or not they all—Moldweorp, Goodfellow, the pair
from Brindisi—had to be part woman. Perhaps even in this main-
tenance of a threshold for compassion one dared not go beneath
was some sort of recognition.

But like a Yorkshire sunset, certain things could not be afforded.
Porpentine had realized this as a fledgling. You do not feel pity
for the men you have to kill or the people you have to hurt. You
do not feel any more than a vague *esprit de corps* toward the
agents you are working with. Above all, you do not fall in love.
Not if you want to succeed in espionage. God knew what preado-
lescent agonies were responsible; but somehow Porpentine had
remained true to that code. He had grown up possessing a sly mind

and was too honest not to use it. He stole from street-hawkers, could stack a deck at fifteen, would run away whenever fighting was useless. So that at some point, prowling any mews or alley in midcentury London, the supreme rightness of "the game for its own sake" must have occurred to him, and acted as an irresistible vector aimed toward 1900. Now he would say that any itinerary, with all its doublings-back, emergency stops, and hundred-kilometer feints remained transitory or accidental. Certainly it was convenient, necessary; but never gave an indication of the deeper truth that all of them operated in no conceivable Europe but rather in a zone forsaken by God, between the tropics of diplomacy, lines they were forbidden forever to cross. One had consequently to play that idealized colonial Englishman who, alone in the jungle, shaves every day, dresses for dinner every night, and is committed to St. George and no quarter as an article of love. Curious irony in that, of course. Porpentine grimaced to himself. Because both sides, his and Moldweorp's, had each in a different way done the unforgivable: had gone native. Somehow it had come about that one day neither man cared any longer which government he was working for. As if that prospect of a Final Clash were unable by men like them, through whatever frenzied twists and turns, to be evaded. Something had come to pass: who could guess what, or even when? In the Crimea, at Spicheren, at Khartum; it could make no difference. But so suddenly that there was a finite leap or omission in the maturing process—one fell asleep exhausted among immediacies: F.O. dispatches, Parliamentary resolutions; and awakened to find a tall specter grinning and gibbering over the foot of the bed, know that he was there to stay—hadn't they seen the apocalypse as an excuse for a glorious beano, a grand way to see the old century and their respective careers go out?

"You are so like him," the girl was saying, "my uncle Evelyn: tall, and fair, and oh! not really Lardwick-in-the-Fenish at all."

"Haw, haw," Goodfellow replied.

Hearing the languishment in that voice, Porpentine wondered idly if she were bud or bloom; or perhaps a petal blown off and having nothing to belong to any more. It was difficult to tell—getting more so every year—and he did not know if this were old age beginning to creep up on him at last or some flaw in the generation itself. His own had budded, bloomed, and, sensing some blight in the air, folded its petals up again like certain flowers at sunset. Would it be any use asking her?

"My God," Goodfellow said. They looked up to see an emaciated figure in evening clothes whose head seemed that of a nettled sparrow-hawk. The head guffawed, retaining its fierce expression. Victoria bubbled over in a laugh. "It's Hugh!" she cried, delighted.

"Indeed," echoed a voice inside. "Help me get it off, someone." Porpentine, obliging, stood on a chair to tug off the head.

"Hugh Bongo-Shaftsbury," said Goodfellow, ungracious.

"Harmakhis." Bongo-Shaftsbury indicated the hollow ceramic hawk-head. "God of Heliopolis and chief deity of Lower Egypt. Utterly genuine, this: a mask used in the ancient rituals." He seated himself next to Victoria. Goodfellow scowled. "Literally Horus on the horizon, also represented as a lion with the head of a man. Like the Sphinx."

"Oh," Victoria sighed, "the Sphinx." Enchanted, which did puzzle Porpentine: for this was a violation, was it not, so much rapture over the mongrel gods of Egypt? Her ideal should rightfully have been pure manhood or pure hawkhood; hardly the mixture.

They decided not to have liqueurs but to stay with the Vöslauer, which was off-vintage but only went for ten piastres.

"How far down the Nile do you intend to go?" asked Porpentine. "Mr. Goodfellow has mentioned your interest in Luxor."

"I feel it is fresh territory, sir," replied Bongo-Shaftsbury. "No first-rate work around the area since Grébaut discovered the tomb of the Theban priests back in 'ninety-one. Of course one should have a look round the pyramids at Gizeh, but that is pretty much old hat since Mr. Flinders Petrie's painstaking inspection of sixteen or seventeen years ago."

"I imagine," murmured Porpentine. He could have got the data, of course, from any Baedeker. At least there was a certain intensity or single-minded concern with matters archaeological which Porpentine was sure would drive Sir Alastair to frenzy before the Cook's tour was completed. Unless, like Porpentine and Goodfellow, Bongo-Shaftsbury intended to go no further than Cairo.

Porpentine hummed the aria from *Manon Lescaut* as Victoria

poised prettily between the other two, attempting to keep equilibrium. The crowd in the restaurant had thinned out and across the street the Consulate was dark, save two or three lights in the upstairs rooms. Perhaps in a month all the windows would be blazing; perhaps the world would be blazing. Projected, the courses of Marchand and Kitchener would cross near Fashoda, in the district of Behr el-Abyad, some forty miles above the source of the White Nile. Lord Lansdowne, Secretary of State for War, had predicted 25 September as meeting-date in a secret dispatch to Cairo: a message both Porpentine and Moldweorp had seen. All at once a tic came dancing across Bongo-Shaftsbury's face; there was a time-lag of about five seconds before Porpentine—either intuitively or because of his suspicions about the archaeologist—reckoned who it was that stood behind his chair. Goodfellow nodded, sick and timid; said, civilly enough: "Lepsius, I say. Tired of the climate in Brindisi?" Lepsius. Porpentine hadn't even known the name. Goodfellow would have, of course. "Sudden business called me to Egypt," the agent hissed. Goodfellow sniffed at his wine. Soon: "Your traveling companion? I had rather hoped to see him again."

"Gone to Switzerland," Lepsius said. "The mountains, the clean winds. One can have enough, one day, of the sordidness of that South." They never lied. Who was his new partner?

"Unless you go far enough south," Goodfellow said. "I imagine far enough down the Nile one gets back to a kind of primitive cleanness."

Porpentine had been watching Bongo-Shaftsbury closely, since the tic. The face, lean and ravaged like the body, remained expressionless now; but that initial lapse had set Porpentine on his guard.

"Doesn't the law of the wild beast prevail down there?" Lepsius said. "There are no property rights, only fighting; and the victor wins all. Glory, life, power and property, all."

"Perhaps," Goodfellow said. "But in Europe, you know, we are civilized. Fortunately. Jungle-law is inadmissible."

Soon Lepsius took his leave, expressing the hope they would meet again at Cairo. Goodfellow was certain they would. Bongo-Shaftsbury had continued to sit unmoving and unreadable.

"What a queer gentleman," Victoria said.

"Is it queer," Bongo-Shaftsbury said, deliberately reckless, "to favor the clean over the impure?"

So. Porpentine had wearied of self-congratulation ten years ago. Goodfellow looked embarrassed. So: cleanness. After the deluge, the long famine, the earthquake. A desert-region's cleanness: bleached bones, tombs of dead cultures. Armageddon would sweep the house of Europe so. Did that make Porpentine champion only of cobwebs, rubbish, offscourings? He remembered a night-visit in Rome, years ago, to a contact who lived over a bordello near the Pantheon. Moldweorp himself had followed, taking station near a street-lamp to wait. In the middle of the interview Porpentine chanced to look out the window. A streetwalker was propositioning Moldweorp. They could not hear the conversation, only see a slow and unkind fury recast his features to a wrath-mask; only watch him raise his cane and begin to slash methodically at the girl until she lay ragged at his feet. Porpentine was first to break out of that paralysis, open the door, and race down to the street. When he reached her Moldweorp was gone. His comfort was automatic, perhaps out of some abstract sense of duty, while she screamed into the tweed of his coat. *"Mi chiamava sozzura,"* she could say: he called me filth. Porpentine had tried to forget the incident. Not because it was ugly but because it showed his terrible flaw so clear: reminding him it was not Moldweorp he hated so much as a perverse idea of what is clean; not the girl he sympathized with so much as her humanity. Fate, it occurred to him then, chooses weird agents. Moldweorp somehow could love and hate individually. The roles being, it seemed, reversed, Porpentine found it necessary to believe if one appointed oneself savior of humanity that perhaps one must love that humanity only in the abstract. For any descent to the personal level can make a purpose less pure. Whereas a disgust at individual human perversity might as easily avalanche into a rage for apocalypse. He could never bring himself to hate the Moldweorp crew, any more than they could avoid genuine anxiety over his welfare. Worse, Porpentine could never make a try for any of them; would remain instead an inept Cremonini singing Des Grieux, expressing certain passions by calculated musical covenant, would never leave a stage where vehe-

mences and tendresses are merely forte and piano, where the Paris
gate at Amiens foreshortens mathematically and is illuminated by
the precise glow of calcium light. He remembered his performance
in the rain that afternoon: he like Victoria needed the proper setting. Anything intensely European, it seemed, inspired him to
heights of inanity.

It got late; only two or three tourists left scattered about the
room. Victoria showed no signs of fatigue, Goodfellow and Bongo-
Shaftsbury argued politics. A waiter lounged two tables away, im-
patient. He had the delicate build and high narrow skull of the
Copt, and Porpentine realized this had been the only non-Euro-
pean in the place, all along. Any such discord should have been
spotted immediately: Porpentine's slip. He had no use for Egypt,
had sensitive skin and avoided its sun as if any tinge of it might
make part of him the East's own. He cared about regions not on
the Continent only so far as they might affect its fortunes and no
further; the Fink restaurant could as well have been an inferior
Voisin's.

At length the party arose, paid, left. Victoria skipped ahead
across rue Cherif Pacha to the hotel. Behind them a closed carriage came rattling out of the drive beside the Austrian Consulate
and dashed away hell-for-leather down rue de Rosette, into the wet
night.

"Someone is in a hurry," Bongo-Shaftsbury noted.

"Indeed," said Goodfellow. To Porpentine: "At the Gare du
Caire. The train leaves at eight." Porpentine gave them all good
night and returned to his *pied-à-terre* in the Turkish quarter. Such
choice of lodgings violated nothing; for he considered the Porte
part of the Western World. He fell asleep reading an old and mutilated edition of *Antony and Cleopatra* and wondering if it were
still possible to fall under the spell of Egypt: its tropic unreality, its
curious gods.

At 7:40 he stood on the platform of the Gare, watching the
porters from Cook's and Gaze's pile boxes and trunks. Across the
double line of tracks was a small park, green with palms and acacias. Porpentine kept to the shadow of the station-house. Soon the
others arrived. He noticed the tiniest flicker of communication pass
between Bongo-Shaftsbury and Lepsius. The morning express

pulled in, amid sudden commotion on the platform. Porpentine turned to see Lepsius in pursuit of an Arab, who had apparently stolen his valise. Goodfellow had already gone into action. Sprinting across the platform, blond mane flapping wild, he cornered the Arab in a doorway, took back the valise and surrendered his quarry to a fat policeman in a pith helmet. Lepsius watched him snake-eyed and silent as he handed back the valise.

Aboard the train they split up into two adjoining compartments, Victoria, her father, and Goodfellow sharing the one next the rear platform. Porpentine felt that Sir Alastair would have been less miserable in his company, but wanted to be sure of Bongo-Shaftsbury. The train pulled out at five past eight, heading into the sun. Porpentine leaned back and let Mildred ramble on about mineralogy. Bongo-Shaftsbury kept silent until the train had passed Sidi Gaber and swung toward the southeast.

He said: "Do you play with dolls, Mildred?" Porpentine gazed out the window. He felt something unpleasant was about to happen. He could see a procession of dark-colored camels with their drivers, moving slowly along the embankments of a canal. Far down the canal were the small white sails of barges.

"When I'm not out after rocks," said Mildred.

Bongo-Shaftsbury said: "I'll wager you do not have any dolls that walk, or speak, or are able to jump rope. Now do you."

Porpentine tried to concentrate on a group of Arabs who lazed about far down the embankment, evaporating part of the water in Lake Mareotis for salt. The train was going at top speed. He soon lost them in the distance.

"No," said Mildred, doubtful.

Bongo-Shaftsbury said: "But have you never seen dolls like that? Such lovely dolls, and clockwork inside. Dolls that do everything perfectly, because of the machinery. Not like real little boys and girls at all. Real children cry, and act sullen, and won't behave. These dolls are much nicer."

On the right now were fallow cotton-fields and mud huts. Occasionally one of the fellahin would be seen going down to the canal for water. Almost out of his field of vision Porpentine saw Bongo-Shaftsbury's hands, long and starved-nervous, lying still, one on each knee.

"They sound quite nice," said Mildred. Though she knew she was being talked down to her voice was unsteady. Possibly something in the archaeologist's face frightened her.

Bongo-Shaftsbury said: "Would you like to see one, Mildred?" It was going too far. For the man had been talking to Porpentine, the girl was being used. For what? Something was wrong.

"Have you one with you?" she wondered, timid. Despite himself Porpentine moved his head away from the window to watch Bongo-Shaftsbury.

Who smiled: "Oh yes." And pushed back the sleeve of his coat to remove a cuff-link. He began to roll back the cuff of his shirt. Then thrust the naked underside of his forearm at the girl. Porpentine recoiled, thinking: Lord love a duck. Bongo-Shaftsbury is insane. Shiny and black against the unsunned flesh was a miniature electric switch, single-pole, double-throw, sewn into the skin. Thin silver wires ran from its terminals up the arm, disappearing under the sleeve.

The young often show a facile acceptance of the horrible. Mildred began to shake. "No," she said, "no: you are not one."

"But I am," protested Bongo-Shaftsbury, smiling, "Mildred. The wires run up into my brain. When the switch is closed like this I act the way I do now. When it is thrown the other—"

The girl shrank away. "Papa," she cried.

"Everything works by electricity," Bongo-Shaftsbury explained, soothing. "And it is simple, and clean."

"Stop it," Porpentine said.

Bongo-Shaftsbury whirled to him. "Why?" he whispered. "Why? For her? Touched by her fright, are you? Or is it for yourself?"

Porpentine retreated, bashful. "One doesn't frighten a child, sir."

"General principles. Damn you." He looked petulant, ready to cry.

There was noise out in the passageway. Goodfellow had been shouting in pain. Porpentine leaped up, shoving Bongo-Shaftsbury aside, and rushed out into the passageway. The door to the rear platform was open: in front of it Goodfellow and an Arab fought, tangled and clawing. Porpentine saw the flash of a pistol-barrel. He moved in cautiously, circling, choosing his point. When the

Arab's throat was exposed sufficiently Porpentine kicked, catching him across the windpipe. He collapsed rattling. Goodfellow took the pistol. Pushed back his forelock, sides heaving. "Ta."

"Same one?" Porpentine said.

"No. The railroad police are conscientious. And it is possible, you know, to tell them apart. This is different."

"Cover him, then." To the Arab: "*Auz e. Ma tkhafsh minni.*" The Arab's head rolled toward Porpentine, he tried to grin but his eyes were sick. A blue mark was appearing on his throat. He could not talk. Sir Alastair and Victoria had appeared, anxious.

"May have been a friend of the fellow I caught back at the Gare," Goodfellow explained easily. Porpentine helped the Arab to his feet. "*Ruh.* Go back. Don't let us see you again." The Arab moved off.

"You're not going to let him go?" Sir Alastair rumbled. Goodfellow was magnanimous. He gave a short speech about charity and turning the other cheek which was well received by Victoria but which seemed to nauseate her father. The party resumed their places in the compartments, though Mildred had decided to stay with Sir Alastair.

Half an hour later the train pulled into Damanhur. Porpentine saw Lepsius get off two cars ahead and go inside the station-house. Around them stretched the green country of the Delta. Two minutes later the Arab got off and cut across on a diagonal to the buffet entrance; met Lepsius coming out with a bottle of red wine. He was rubbing the mark on his throat and apparently wanted to speak to Lepsius. The agent glared and cuffed him across the head. "No bakshish," he announced. Porpentine settled back, closed his eyes without looking at Bongo-Shaftsbury. Without even saying aha. The train began to move. So. What did they call clean, then? Not observing The Rules, surely. If so they had reversed course. They'd never played so foul before. Could it mean that this meeting at Fashoda would be important: might even be The One? He opened his eyes to watch Bongo-Shaftsbury, engrossed in a book: Sidney J. Webb's *Industrial Democracy.* Porpentine shrugged. Time was his fellow professionals became adept through practice. Learned ciphers by breaking them, customs officials by evading them, some opponents by killing them. Now the new ones read

books: young lads, full of theory and (he'd decided) a faith in
nothing but the perfection of their own internal machinery. He
flinched, remembering the knife-switch, fastened to Bongo-Shaftsbury's arm like a malignant insect. Moldweorp must have been
the oldest spy active but in professional ethics he and Porpentine
did belong to the same generation. Porpentine doubted if Moldweorp approved of the young man opposite.

Their silence continued for twenty-five miles. The express
passed by farms which began to look more and more prosperous,
fellahin who worked in the fields at a faster pace, small factories
and heaps of ancient ruin and tall flowering tamarisks. The Nile
was in flood: stretching away from them, a glittering network of
irrigation canals and small basins caught the water, conducted it
through wheat and barley fields which extended to the horizon.
The train reached the Rosetta arm of the Nile; crossed high over
it by a long, narrow iron bridge, entered the station at Kafr ez-
Zaiyat, where it stopped. Bongo-Shaftsbury closed the book, arose
and left the compartment. A few moments later Goodfellow entered, holding Mildred by the hand.

"He felt you might want to get some sleep," Goodfellow said.
"I should have thought. I was preoccupied with Mildred's sister."
Porpentine snorted, shut his eyes and fell asleep before the train
started to move. He awoke half an hour out of Cairo. "All secure,"
Goodfellow said. The outlines of the pyramids were visible off to
the west. Closer to the city gardens and villas began to appear. The
train reached Cairo's Principal Station about noon.

Somehow, Goodfellow and Victoria managed to be in a phaeton
and away before the rest of the party got on the platform.
"Damme," Sir Alastair puzzled, "what are they doing, eloping?"
Bongo-Shaftsbury looked properly outwitted. Porpentine, having
slept, felt rather in a holiday mood. "*Arabiyeh*," he roared, gleeful.
A dilapidated pinto-colored barouche came clattering up and Porpentine pointed after the phaeton: "A double piastre if you catch
them." The driver grinned; Porpentine hustled everyone into the
carriage. Sir Alastair protested, muttering about Mr. Conan Doyle.
Bongo-Shaftsbury guffawed and away they galloped, around a
sharp curve to the left, over the el-Lemun bridge and pell-mell
down Sharia Bab el-Hadid. Mildred made faces at other tourists

on foot or riding donkeys, Sir Alastair smiled tentatively. Ahead
Porpentine could see Victoria in the phaeton tiny and graceful,
holding Goodfellow's arm and leaning back to let the wind blow
her hair.

The two carriages arrived at Shepheard's Hotel in a dead heat.
All but Porpentine alighted and moved toward the hotel. "Check
me in," he called to Goodfellow, "I must see a friend." The friend
was a porter at the Hotel Victoria, four blocks south and west.
While Porpentine sat in the kitchen discussing game birds with a
mad chef he had known at Cannes, the porter crossed the street to
the British Consulate, going in by the servants' entrance. He
emerged after fifteen minutes and returned to the hotel. Soon an
order for lunch was brought in to the kitchen. "*Crème*" had been
misspelled to read "*chem.*"; "*Lyonnaise*" was spelled without an *e*.
Both were underlined. Porpentine nodded, thanked everyone, and
left. He caught a cab and rode up Sharia el-Maghrabi, through the
luxurious park at the end; soon arrived at the Crédit Lyonnais.
Nearby was a small pharmacy. He entered and asked about the
prescription for laudanum he had brought in to be filled the day
before. He was handed an envelope whose contents, once more in
the cab, he checked. A raise of £50 for him and Goodfellow: good
news. They would both be able to stay at Shepheard's.

Back at the hotel they set about decoding their instructions.
F.O. knew nothing about an assassination plot. Of course not.
No reason for one, if you were thinking only about the immediate
question of who would control the Nile Valley. Porpentine wondered what had happened to diplomacy. He knew people who
had worked under Palmerston, a shy, humorous old man for whom
the business was a jolly game of blindman's-buff, where every day
one reached out and touched, and was touched by, the Specter's
cold hand.

"We're on our own, then," Goodfellow pointed out.

"Ah," Porpentine agreed. "Suppose we work it this way: set a
thief to catch one. Make plans to do Cromer in ourselves. Go
through the motions only, of course. That way whenever they get
an opportunity, we can be right on the spot to prevent them."

"Stalk the Consul-General," Goodfellow grew enthusiastic, "like
a bloody grouse. Why we haven't done that since—"

"Never mind," Porpentine said.

That night Porpentine commissioned a cab and roved about the city until early morning. The coded instructions had told them nothing more than to bide time: Goodfellow was taking care of that, having escorted Victoria to an Italian summer-theater performance at the Ezbekiyeh Garden. In the course of the night Porpentine visited a girl who lived in the Quartier Rosetti and was the mistress of a junior clerk in the British Consulate; a jewel merchant in the Muski who had lent financial support to the Mahdists and did not wish now that the movement was crushed to have his sympathies known; a minor Esthetic who had fled England on a narcotics charge to the land of no extradition and who was a distant cousin of the valet to Mr. Raphael Borg, the British Consul; and a pimp named Varkumian who claimed to know every assassin in Cairo. From this fine crew Porpentine returned to his room at three in the morning. But hesitated at the door, having heard movement behind it. Only one thing for it: at the end of the corridor was this window with a ledge outside. He grimaced. But then everyone knew that spies were continually crawling about window-ledges, high above the streets of exotic cities. Feeling an utter fool, Porpentine climbed out and got on the ledge. He looked down: there was a drop of about fifteen feet into some bushes. Yawning he made his way quickly but clumsily toward the corner of the building. The ledge became narrower at the corner. As he stood with each foot on a different side and the edge of the building bisecting him from eyebrows to abdomen he lost his balance and fell. On the way down it occurred to him to use an obscene word; he hit the shrubbery with a crash, rolled, and lay there tapping his fingers. After he had smoked half a cigarette he got to his feet and noticed a tree next his own window, easily climbable. He ascended puffing and cursing; crawled out on a limb, straddled it, and peered inside.

Goodfellow and the girl lay on Porpentine's bed, white and exhausted-looking by street-light: her eyes, mouth, and nipples were little dark bruises against the flesh. She cradled Goodfellow's white head in a net or weaving of fingers while he cried, streaking her breasts with tears. "I'm sorry," he was saying, "the Transvaal, a wound. They told me it was not serious." Porpentine, having no

idea how this sort of thing worked, fell back on alternatives: (a)
Goodfellow was being honorable, (b) was truly impotent and had
therefore lied to Porpentine about a long list of conquests, (c)
simply had no intention of getting involved with Victoria. Which-
ever it was, Porpentine felt as always an alien. He swung down by
one arm from the limb, nonplused, until the stub of the cigarette
burned down to his fingers and made him swear softly; and because he knew it was not really the burn he cursed he began to
worry. It was not only seeing Goodfellow weak. He dropped into
the bushes and lay there thinking about his own threshold, sus-
tained proudly for twenty years of service. Though it had been
hammered at before, he suspected this was the first time it had
shown itself truly vulnerable. A pang of superstitious terror caught
him flat on his back in the bushes. It seemed he knew, for a space
of seconds, that this indeed was The One. Apocalypse would
surely begin at Fashoda if for no other reason than that he felt
his own so at hand. But soon: gradually, with each lungful of a
fresh cigarette's smoke, the old control seeped back to him; and
he got at last to his feet, still shaky, walked around to the hotel
entrance and up to his room. This time he pretended to've lost his
key, making bewildered noises to cover the girl as she gathered her
clothing and fled through connecting doors to her own room. All
he felt by the time Goodfellow opened was embarrassment, and
that he had lived with for a long time.

The theater had presented *Manon Lescaut*. In the shower next
morning Goodfellow attempted to sing "*Donna non vidi mai.*"
"Stop," said Porpentine. "Would you like to hear how it should be
done?" Goodfellow howled. "I doubt you could sing Ta-ra-ra-
boom-di-ay without mucking it up."

But Porpentine could not resist. He thought it a harmless com-
promise. "*A dirle io t'amo,*" he caroled, "*a nuova vita l'alma mia si
desta.*" It was appalling; one got the impression he had once
worked in a music-hall. He was no Des Grieux. Des Grieux knows,
soon as he sees that young lady just off the diligence from Arras,
what will happen. He does not make false starts or feints, this
chevalier, has nothing to decode, no double game to play. Porpentine envied him. As he dressed he whistled the aria. Last night's
moment of weakness bloomed again behind his eyes. He thought:

if I step below the threshold, you know, I shall never get back again.

At two that afternoon the Consul-General emerged from the front door of the Consulate and entered a carriage. Porpentine watched from a deserted room on the third floor of the Hotel Victoria. Lord Cromer was a perfect target but this vantage at least was unavailable to any hired assassin-in-opposition as long as Porpentine's friends kept on the alert. The archaeologist had taken Victoria and Mildred to tour the bazaars and the Tombs of the Khalifs. Goodfellow was sitting in a closed landau directly under the window. Unobtrusive (as Porpentine watched) he started off behind the carriage, keeping at a safe distance. Porpentine left the hotel, strolled up Sharia el-Maghrabi. At the next corner he noticed a church off to his right; heard loud organ music. On a sudden whim he entered the church. Sure enough, it was Sir Alastair, booming away. It took the unmusical Porpentine some five minutes to come aware of the devastation Sir Alastair was wreaking on the keys and pedals. Music laced the interior of the tiny, Gothic house with certain intricate veinings, weird petal-shapes. But it was violent and somehow Southern foliage. Head and fingers uncontrollable for a neglect of his daughter's or any purity, for the music's own shape, for Bach—was it Bach?—himself? Foreign and a touch shabby, uncomprehending, how could Porpentine say. But was yet unable to pull away until the music stopped abruptly, leaving the church's cavity to reverberate. Only then did he withdraw unseen out into the sun, adjusting his neck-cloth as if it were all the difference between wholeness and disintegration.

Lord Cromer was doing nothing to protect himself, Goodfellow reported that night. Porpentine, having rechecked with the valet's cousin, knew the word had gone through. He shrugged, calling the Consul-General a nitwit: tomorrow was 25 September. He left the hotel at eleven and went by carriage to a *Brauhaus* a few blocks north of the Ezbekiyeh Garden. He sat alone at a small table against the wall, listening to maudlin accordion music which must surely have been old as Bach; closed his eyes, letting a cigarette droop from his lips. A waitress brought Munich beer.

"Mr. Porpentine." He looked up. "I followed you." He nodded, smiled; Victoria sat down. "Papa would die if he ever found out," gazing at him defiant. The accordion stopped. The waitress left two Krugers.

He pursed his lips, ruthful in that quiet. So she'd sought out and found the woman in him; the very first civilian to do so. He did not go through any routine of asking how she knew. She could not have seen him through the window. He said:

"He was sitting in the German church this afternoon, playing Bach as if it were all he had left. So that he may have guessed."

She hung her head, a mustache of foam on her upper lip. From across the canal came the faint whistle of the express for Alexandria. "You love Goodfellow," he hazarded. Never had he been down so far: he was a tourist here. Could have used, at the moment, any Baedeker of the heart. Almost drowned in a fresh wailing of the accordion her whisper came: yes. Then had Goodfellow told her. . . . He raised his eyebrows, she shook her head no. Amazing, the knowing of one another, these wordless flickerings. "Whatever I may think I have guessed," she said. "Of course you can't trust me, but I have to say it. It's true." How far down could one go, before . . . Desperate, Porpentine: "What do you want me to do, then?" She, twisting ringlets round her fingers, would not look at him. Soon: "Nothing. Only understand." If Porpentine had believed in the devil he would have said: you have been sent. Go back and tell him, them, it is no use. The accordionist spotted Porpentine and the girl, recognized them as English. "Had the devil any son," he sang mischievous in German, "it was surely Palmerston." A few Germans laughed, Porpentine winced: the song was fifty years old at least. But a few still remembered.

Varkumian came weaving his way among tables, late. Victoria saw him and excused herself. Varkumian's report was brief: no action. Porpentine sighed. It left only one thing to do. Throw a scare into the Consulate, put them on their guard.

So next day they began "stalking" Cromer in earnest. Porpentine woke up in a foul mood. He donned a red beard and a pearl-gray morning hat and visited the Consulate, posing as an Irish tourist. The staff weren't having any: he got ejected forcibly. Goodfellow had a better idea: "Lob a bomb," he cried. Happily his knowledge of munitions was faulty as his aim. The bomb, instead of falling safely on the lawn, soared in through a window of the Consulate, sending one of the proverbial charwomen into hysterics (though it proved of course to be a dud) and nearly getting Goodfellow arrested.

At noon Porpentine visited the kitchen of the Hotel Victoria to find the place in a turmoil. The meeting at Fashoda had taken place. The Situation had turned to a Crisis. Upset, he dashed out into the street, commandeered a carriage, and tore off in search of Goodfellow. He found him two hours later sleeping in his hotel room where Porpentine had left him. In a rage he emptied a pitcher of ice-water over Goodfellow's head. Bongo-Shaftsbury appeared in the doorway grinning. Porpentine hurled the empty pitcher at him as he vanished down the corridor. "Where's the Consul-General?" Goodfellow inquired, amiable and sleepy. "Get dressed," bellowed Porpentine.

They found the clerk's mistress lying lazy in a patch of sunlight, peeling a mandarin orange. She told them Cromer was planning to attend the opera at eight. Up to then, she could not say. They went to the shop of the chemist, who had nothing for them. Barreling through the Garden Porpentine asked about the Wrens. They were at Heliopolis, as far as Goodfellow knew. "What the bloody hell is wrong with everyone?" Porpentine wanted to know. "Nobody knows anything." They could do nothing till eight; so sat in front of a café in the Garden and drank wine. Egypt's sun beat down, somehow threatening. There was no shade. The fear that had found him night before last now crawled along the flanks of Porpentine's jaw and up his temples. Even Goodfellow seemed nervous.

At a quarter to eight they strolled along the path to the theater, purchased tickets in the orchestra, and settled down to wait. Soon the Consul-General's party arrived and sat near them. Lepsius and Bongo-Shaftsbury drifted in from either side and stationed themselves in boxes; forming, with Lord Cromer as vertex, an angle of 120 degrees. "Bother," said Goodfellow. "We should have got some elevation." Four policemen came marching down the center aisle, glanced up at Bongo-Shaftsbury. He pointed to Porpentine. "My Gawd," Goodfellow moaned. Porpentine closed his eyes. He'd blown it, all right. This was what happened when one blundered right in. The policemen surrounded them, stood at attention.

"All right," Porpentine said. He and Goodfellow arose and were escorted out of the theater. "We shall desire your passports," one of them said. Behind them on the breeze came the first sprightly chords of the opening scene. They marched down a narrow path, two police behind, two in front. Signals had, of course, been arranged years before. "I shall want to see the British Consul," Porpentine said and spun, drawing an old single-shot pistol. Goodfellow had the other two covered. The policeman who had asked for their passports glowered. "No one said they would be armed," another protested. Methodically, with four raps to the skull, the policemen were neutralized and rolled into the underbrush. "A fool trick," Goodfellow muttered: "we were lucky." Porpentine was already running back toward the theater. They took the stairs two at a time and searched for an empty box. "Here," Goodfellow said. They edged into the box. It was almost directly across from Bongo-Shaftsbury's. That would put them next to Lepsius. "Keep down," Porpentine said. They crouched, peering between small golden balusters. On stage Edmondo and the students chaffed the Romantic, horny Des Grieux. Bongo-Shaftsbury was checking the action of a small pistol. "Stand by," Goodfellow whispered. The postilion horn of the diligence was heard. The coach came rattling and creaking into the inn courtyard. Bongo-Shaftsbury raised his pistol. Porpentine said: "Lepsius. Next door." Goodfellow withdrew. The diligence bounced to a halt. Porpentine centered his sights on Bongo-Shaftsbury, then let the muzzle drift down and to the right until it pointed at Lord Cromer. It occurred to him that he could end everything for himself right now, never have to worry about Europe again. He had a sick moment of uncertainty. Now how serious had anyone ever been? Was aping Bongo-Shaftsbury's tactics any less real than opposing them? Like a bloody grouse, Goodfellow had said. Manon was helped down from the coach. Des Grieux gaped, was transfixed, read his destiny on her eyes. Someone was standing behind Porpentine. He glanced back, quickly in that moment of hopeless love, and saw Moldweorp there looking decayed, incredibly old, face set in a hideous though compassionate smile. Panicking, Porpentine turned and fired blindly, perhaps at Bongo-Shaftsbury, perhaps at Lord Cromer. He could not see and would never be sure which one he had intended as target. Bongo-Shaftsbury shoved the pistol inside his coat and disappeared. A fight was on out in the corridor. Porpentine pushed the old man aside and ran out in time to see Lepsius tear away from Goodfellow and flee toward the stairs. "Please, dear fellow," Moldweorp gasped. "Don't go after them. You are outnumbered." Porpentine had reached the top step. "Three to two," he muttered.

"More than three. My chief and his, and staff personnel . . ." Which stopped Porpentine dead. "Your—"

"I have been under orders, you know." The old man sounded apologetic. Then, all in a nostalgic rush: "The Situation, don't you know, it is serious this time, we are all for it—"

Porpentine looked back, exasperated. "Go away," he yelled, "go away and die." And was certain only in a dim way that the interchange of words had now, at last, been decisive.

"The big chief himself," Goodfellow remarked as they ran down the stairs. "Things must be bad." A hundred yards ahead Bongo-Shaftsbury and Lepsius leaped into a carriage. Surprisingly nimble, Moldweorp had taken a short cut. He emerged from an exit to the left of Porpentine and Goodfellow and joined the others. "Let them go," Goodfellow said.

"Are you still taking orders from me?" Without waiting for an answer Porpentine found a phaeton, got in and swung around to pursue. Goodfellow grabbed on and hauled himself up. They galloped down Sharia Kamel Pasha, scattering donkeys, tourists, and dragomans. In front of Shepheard's they nearly ran down Victoria, who had come out into the street. They lost ten seconds while Goodfellow helped her aboard. Porpentine could not protest. Again she had known. Something had passed out of his hands. He was only beginning to recognize, somewhere, a quite enormous betrayal.

It was no longer single combat. Had it ever been? Lepsius, Bongo-Shaftsbury, all the others, had been more than merely tools or physical extensions of Moldweorp. They were all in it; all had a stake, acted as a unit. Under orders. Whose orders? Anything human? He doubted: like a bright hallucination against Cairo's night-sky he saw (it may have been only a line of cloud) a bell-shaped curve, remembered perhaps from some younger F.O. operative's mathematics text. Unlike Constantine on the verge of battle, he could not afford, this late, to be converted at any sign. Only curse himself, silent, for wanting so to believe in a fight according to the duello, even in this period of history. But they—no, it—had not been playing those rules. Only statistical odds. When had he stopped facing an adversary and taken on a Force, a Quantity?

The bell curve is the curve for a normal or Gaussian distribution. An invisible clapper hangs beneath it. Porpentine (though only half-suspecting) was being tolled down.

The carriage ahead took a sharp left, moving toward the canal. There it turned left again, and raced alongside the thin ribbon of water. The moon had risen, half of it, fat and white. "They're going for the Nile Bridge," Goodfellow said. They passed the Khedive's palace and clattered over the bridge. The river flowed dark and viscous under them. On the other side they turned south and sped through moonlight between the Nile and the grounds of the viceregal palace. Ahead the quarry swung right. "Damned if it isn't the road to the pyramids," Goodfellow said. Porpentine nodded: "About five and a half miles." They made the turn and passed the prison and the village of Gizeh, hit a curve, crossed the railroad tracks and headed due west. "Oh," Victoria said quietly, "we're going to see the Sphinx."

"In the moonlight," Goodfellow added, wry. "Leave her alone," Porpentine said. They were silent for the rest of the way, making little gain. Around them irrigation ditches interlaced and sparkled. The two carriages passed fellahin villages and water-wheels. No sound at all in the night save wheels and hoofbeats. And the wind of their passage. As they neared the edge of the desert Goodfellow said, "We're catching up." The road began to slope upward. Protected from the desert by a wall five feet high, it wound around to the left, ascending. Ahead of them suddenly the other carriage lurched and crashed into the wall. The occupants scrambled out and climbed the rest of the way on foot. Porpentine continued on around the curve, stopping about 100 yards from the great pyramid of Kheops. Moldweorp, Lepsius, and Bongo-Shaftsbury were nowhere in sight.

"Let's have a look about," Porpentine said. They rounded the corner of the pyramid. The Sphinx crouched 600 yards to the south. "Damn," Goodfellow said. Victoria pointed. "There," she cried:

"going toward the Sphinx." They moved over the rough ground at a dead run. Moldweorp had apparently twisted his ankle. The other two were helping him. Porpentine drew his pistol. "You are for it, old man," he shouted. Bongo-Shaftsbury turned and fired. Goodfellow said: "What are we going to do with them anyway? Let them go." Porpentine did not answer. A moment or so later they brought the Moldweorp agents to bay against the right flank of the great Sphinx.

"Put it down," Bongo-Shaftsbury wheezed. "That is a single-shot, I have a revolver." Porpentine had not reloaded. He shrugged, grinned, tossed the pistol into the sand. Beside him Victoria looked up rapt at the lion, man, or god towering over them. Bongo-Shaftsbury pushed up his shirt-cuff, opened the switch and closed it the other way. A boyish gesture. Lepsius stood in the shadows, Moldweorp smiled. "Now," Bongo-Shaftsbury said. "Let them go," Porpentine said. Bongo-Shaftsbury nodded. "It is no concern of theirs," he agreed. "This is between you and the Chief, is it not?" Ho, ho, thought Porpentine: couldn't it have been? Like Des Grieux he must have his delusion even now; could never admit himself entirely a gull. Goodfellow took Victoria's hand and they moved away, back toward the carriage, the girl gazing back restless, eyes glowing at the Sphinx.

"You screamed at the Chief," Bongo-Shaftsbury announced. "You said: go away and die."

Porpentine put his hands behind his back. Of course. Had they been waiting for this, then? For fifteen years? He'd crossed some threshold without knowing. Mongrel now, no longer pure. He turned to watch Victoria move away, all tender and winsome for her Sphinx. Mongrel, he supposed, is only another way of saying human. After the final step you could not, nothing could, be clean. It was almost as if they'd tried for Goodfellow because he had stepped below the threshold that morning at the Gare du Caire. Now Porpentine had performed his own fatal act of love or charity by screaming at the Chief. And found out, shortly after, what he'd really screamed at. The two—act and betrayal—canceled out. Canceled to zero. Did they always? Oh God. He turned again to Moldweorp.

His Manon?

"You have been good enemies," he said at last. It sounded wrong to him. Perhaps if there had been more time, time to learn the new role . . .

It was all they needed. Goodfellow heard the shot, turned in time to see Porpentine fall to the sand. He cried out; watched the three turn and move away. Perhaps they would walk straight out into the Libyan desert and keep walking till they reached the shore of some sea. Soon he turned to the girl, shaking his head. He took her hand and they went to find the phaeton. Sixteen years later, of course, he was in Sarajevo, loitering among crowds assembled to greet the Archduke Francis Ferdinand. Rumors of an assassination, a possible spark to apocalypse. He must be there to prevent it if he could. His body had become stooped and much of his hair had fallen out. From time to time he squeezed the hand of his latest conquest, a blond barmaid with a mustache who described him to her friends as a simple-minded Englishman, not much good in bed but liberal with his money.

TOM COLE was born in Paterson, New Jersey, in 1933. He received his B.A. degree from Harvard in 1954, served in the army, and in 1958 received an M.A. degree in Slavic (also from Harvard). He has traveled extensively in Italy, Sicily, and Greece and worked in the Soviet Union. Mr. Cole is married and lives in Boston where he teaches Russian at M.I.T. This is his first story to be published.

FAMILIAR USAGE IN LENINGRAD

from *The Atlantic Monthly*

Not until he saw the silver swept-back jet with "Aeroflot" printed along its length in clean Cyrillic letters did Jeremy Pearl believe that he was really going to be free of Moscow. Two days of blessed relief. He mingled with the crowd at the boarding gate, under the morning sun, as cheerful and inconspicuous and perspiring as anyone there. The loudspeaker resounded pleasantly in his ears—the first pleasant loudspeaker he had heard in a month—calling flights to Kiev, Tpilisi, Tashkent, and finally his own, to Leningrad. Holiday mood swelled within him now, and gratitude toward the winged cylinder that was to lift him away. Really, these jets were splendid achievements.

Achievements: he winced at the word. After a month in Moscow, Jeremy had had more than enough of achievements, whether Ours or Theirs. A guide in the architecture section of the American Exhibition, he was weary of hearing his own voice praising the new glass skyscrapers along Park Avenue and weary of hearing the loudspeakers in Moscow grunting the latest news of pig-iron tonnage from the Donbas. Driving out to the airport that morning, he had even been afraid to comment on the towering sunrise for fear

Copyright 1961 by The Atlantic Monthly Company, Boston 16, Massachusetts.

that the taxi driver would start praising it as an achievement; socialist, capitalist, empyrean—what difference did it make? So he had not begun a conversation, which was a pity, because he hadn't yet met a Moscow cabby who lacked his malicious bit of gossip about Khrushchev, the upper set, or the black market. Without a word, the two of them had rattled past the miles of yellowish block housing and the summer fields, in a brown car curiously like a Chevrolet of the late 1940s. But now, wedged into the lively crowd boarding the plane, he insisted, most firmly, to himself: No, a jet is *not* an achievement, nor a symbol, nor a statistic. It is a thing, handsome and ingenious, designed for human needs. People— Russians—grew cheerful at the prospect of flying in one. He, too, would be cheerful.

As he strapped on his safety belt, he listened with pleasure to the two young officers across the aisle arguing about the exact number of minutes the flight would take until the first touch on Leningrad runway. They settled on a bet payable in vodka, and the nearer leaned over toward Jeremy to request his services as official timer. They seemed to have no immediate sense of his being a foreigner; this pleased him, and the long college weekends spent memorizing Russian verbs passed through his mind in grim but satisfying review. He looked at his watch, saying, "Do you think I'll have time to look at this again before we land?"

The nearer officer grinned in a self-congratulatory way all too familiar to Jeremy and said, "TU-104." He had a metal tooth.

"TU-104," Jeremy agreed.

TU-104. He thought of all those Russians at the Exhibition asking him with a child's good-natured intensity how long Nixon's flight to Moscow had taken and announcing that "our Kozlov" had flown from New York in "our TU-104" in eleven and a half hours. Then those metal-toothed grins, mixed with mock compassion, as if Nixon had obviously crawled all the way on his hands and knees, when Jeremy admitted to not knowing how many hours the American jet had taken. TU-104. Did the hundredth and thousandth person to ask an identical question really have a sense that the question still existed? Faces seemed to say so, crowding in upon him, eager or doubtful or hostile, workers' or students' or agitators' faces, faces from Sverdlovsk and Kharkov and Tomsk, lined or blunt or not recently shaved, too many faces, for thirty-two days. It was not only his having worked too long in Moscow's suspicious air, pressed into its bulbous chaos, that had tired Jeremy. It was being plunged into Mass Questions for the first time. He had been a bookish young man, and now he was battered every day by eight or ten hours of bragging and apologizing and arguing. On the second day he had remembered that these pouring crowds were composed of Russian people; by the fourth he could perceive only Soviet population units, endlessly repeating themselves, except for a very few, and all wanting to talk with heat about We and They.

Who cared, finally? At this heretical thought he glanced around guiltily—a new habit. The officers had stopped consulting the altimeter set like a clock into the cabin's wall up front, because they were fascinated by Jeremy's loafers. Soon they would want to talk, to be hospitable and jolly, to compare the number of cubic meters in their respective university dormitories—Moscow versus Harvard—to chat about all the things Jeremy once had thought he had come to the Soviet Union to hear. It would be decent, honest, We and They talk, urgent with peace and friendship until certain taboo words came up: governments, missiles, Hungary, Guatemala. So he turned, guiltily, to the window and watched the last traces of the city below. Even the white mass of the university disappeared, the world's largest inhabited stone cake; and the Moscow River gave a last glint. The fields over which they were flying now were not checkered like those of Europe or Pennsylvania. They were broad and Russian and dull, fading away into vague forests.

He was glad to be leaving Moscow for a while, since he certainly wasn't the type to be exhibited to mobs. Look: a genuine, pudgy piece of Americana with thick glasses! He was tired of Russians barging up to him at the Exhibition, asking, "Who are you?" Or, rather, "What is your father?" What snobs these workers and peasants were! My father is an accountant, a man who keeps columns of figures for capitalists. Then the agitators' superior smiles, full of implication: You see, Comrades, you needn't discuss with this round young person; his family exploits the masses. Once, when an agitator had started the father routine with him, Jeremy had leaned over to a charming Russian girl in the crowd and whispered, "I'll tell you a secret. My father is a nervous Jewish Marxist."

"So is mine," the girl answered, and winked. Then she vanished across the hot black pavement, beyond the crowds, her blue print summer dress flying after her. It had been a relationship of typical length for Jeremy Pearl, considering that he had liked the girl and she was attractive. For an hour afterward, he had been too rattled to make his brilliant explanation of America's entry into Korea. Well, in thirty-two days and nights he had only succeeded in grazing a few lives, at best. And he was tired, furthermore, of the other American guides in their identical blue sweaters, all busy and young and admiring themselves in their roles of guides and taking notes. Shiny guide fish out of school water, flopping and gulping because there turned out to be so much conflict in the world. He congratulated himself on having severed connections from the jovial shoal that was also spending these two days of leave in Leningrad; he grinned to remember their faces when he had told them he was only going to the Hermitage anyway, to see some Lorenzo Lottos and Giorgione's bright-red *Judith*. Let them have something to talk about on the train.

The stewardess was at his arm, watching him mumble to himself. She asked again, "*Ne khotite fruktovoi vody?*" The ubiquitous gas water, in heavy glasses. Do you know, he asked the girl silently, that the Soviets have achieved the world's worst cherry soda? She jiggled the tray a little impatiently, but smiled at him. She had no make-up; she wore a simple white blouse; some wisps of her hair were rebellious. Who ever heard of a stewardess shaped like a dumpling? "*Spasibo,*" he said aloud, and took a glass.

As soon as the sweet gas water came out, so did the flies. They flew busy circles around the sun motes, buzzing and colliding as if the TU-104 were any Moscow restaurant. They dipped their hairy bodies into the gas water and tried to escape with their sugar bubbles before being swatted with rolled-up *Pravdas*. A passenger called on God to curse the Aeroflot. Wonderful, thought Jeremy, socialist self-criticism in action. Then the cabin door opened and an oldish man stepped out, wearing work trousers and an undershirt. "Citizens," he said, "I want to explain about the flies." An angry murmur went up. "We apologize," the man said, brushing at his ear. "It is only during the hot months that we have this—inconvenience, but we fly such a full schedule with so many Comrades on vacation that there is no time to fumigate between flights. Of course, we do have fly swatter brigades—strong ladies," and the man's eye yielded a twinkle. "But they only get the flies unfit to survive. The clever ones all hide under the arms of the seats. Comrades, what can we do? It's nature. Thank you." He bowed and withdrew as the passengers clapped and hooted. The officers caught Jeremy's eye and did begin a conversation on We and They, insects and airlines, which Jeremy enjoyed. The jet landed before they knew it, lowering past bogs and stunted fir trees, and he shook hands, exchanging wishes of peace and friendship for the ten thousandth time that summer. All three had forgotten the bet when they separated, relaxed and benign, into the midmorning. Jeremy was in an excellent mood for his visit to the Hermitage.

But he did not see the Hermitage that day. Soviet red tape wound around and around his singleness, forcing him to debate at every turn the Intourist assumption that because he was not a delegation, he did not exist. While groups from Iowa, Indonesia, and East Germany bustled by, he had ample time to study wall portraits of Lenin and Chinese dignitaries. Two hours to get a place in a limousine for the city; an hour and a half to find an overstuffed room at the Hotel Astoria; two hours to win a place at table in the hotel dining room and have cold salmon, tomato salad, and blinchiki brought to him.

It was after four o'clock when he finally stood out in the cooling air. Too late for the museums, he wandered through the great northern spaciousness of Leningrad's center, the planned streets and squares, the imitative but gracious palaces, neoclassical, rococo, peeling now but still defying the marshy Finnish winds with strange pastel greens and yellows, with porticoes and rows of columns; surely never so many columns erected anywhere else so far from the Mediterranean. The city still rose out of the brimming Neva waters like a mirage—"Peter's creation." Jeremy felt strangely at home. Beneath the cupola of the Isaac Cathedral and the admiralty building's golden needle glinting toward the oblique sun, he walked through a shadow into the European past, when the city's delegations had been Quarenghis and Rastrellis invited to design an architecture complete for their hosts. He let himself into the city of Peter and Catherine, of summer's white nights in Pushkin and Dostoevsky, of winter's three o'clock sunsets in Gogol. He refused to draw gray conclusions from the squalor pressing on all sides; if there was squalor side by side with dignity, let it be called picturesque, for he did not want to make decisions. It was New York and Peiping that required decisions: what have men wrought there? And, of course, Moscow, with its awful momentousness in the air, the ringing of the bell at the Kremlin gate to announce the silent blind limousines swooshing forth into the emptiness of Red Square. But in Leningrad, Peter's town, the momentousness had passed by. At least for a traveler.

He whistled softly as he strolled under a huge coffered archway into the square fronting the Winter Palace. The square was immense beyond belief, as if miles of marshland—half the frontier of Finland—had been drained and paved and bordered with a neat gardenlike set of palaces. The shaft of the Alexander monument stood stunted amid the whelming space. Toy Russian figures walked singly or in twos at drab intervals. Jeremy's imagination raced; he was standing in the unfillable Palace Square he had read about: "The first time there is a crowd in Petersburg, the city will be crushed . . . a crowd would mean a revolution." He stood alone, he and the Alexander column and the few toy figures, but in his mind the carriages rolled up to the green Winter Palace behind horses supple and glossy under the lanterns; the bejeweled and haughty—Speranskis and Karenins and Volkonskis—poured out, dwarfed by the immensities. And tiny Trotsky mastering the raging square with words.

A sudden wind swept across from the Neva. He put his hands deep into his pockets and slouched off across the square, now bleak as a tundra. He had almost reached the archway again and was beginning to wonder what to do next when he found a crisply folded paper in his right pocket. It was obviously not a ruble note, because all his rubles came in wads or sheaves. He put on his horn-rimmed glasses and held the paper close to his eyes in the dimming light. "To Elizaveta" was written in a cursory American hand. Elizaveta? Yes, the note from that tall boy, Bob What's-his-name, who had come to the exhibition from the Vienna Youth Conference via the north. "Met this great girl in Leningrad, you see? Speaks English like a dream. Want her to drop down here before I go to Tashkent. Listen, get this note to her when you're up there, will you, Jerry? Be a friend. She may introduce you to some interesting people; you could use some—" Thinking of Bob What's-his-name, Jeremy started to crumple the note and look for a sewer. But he reconsidered. The girl's address was on the Nevsky Prospect, quite far from the river. He could take a slow twilight stroll along the Nevsky and talk to Gogol. With luck, the address would be hard to find, so that his evening would be almost accounted for. Then, back to the hotel: caviar, hot tea with extra sugar, and to bed. Tomorrow, the Hermitage all day.

"Just step out onto the Nevsky, and it already smells of strolling," said Gogol to Jeremy. "True, true," he answered. The Prospect was still wide, lively, and clean, at least as far as he could tell in the dusk. Strollers there were: the men in sandals and bell-bottomed trousers, women in neat jackets over print dresses, children in sailors' outfits. Behind him, the admiralty spire had just lost its high tip of sunlight, while in the government cheese and wine shops the lights were coming on, splashing the patient queues. People were arm in arm, and Jeremy was with Gogol.

By the time he found the address, the Prospect had peacefully deteriorated. Elizaveta's building had five stories, poor and damp-looking, in a neighborhood that seemed still to be quivering from the Nazi siege. Jeremy turned into an open entranceway leading to a series of murky inner courtyards. He decided not to ask anyone for directions to the right staircase, because he had no idea of the mood of the Leningrad authorities toward Americans paying calls. Bob What's-his-name, who didn't speak a word of Russian, must have visited the house. But, still—Jeremy stumbled awhile in suffocating darkness. The shutters on the inner courtyard were all pulled, although it was still August. Pallid electric bulbs burned in the entryways; someone was practicing a Rachmaninoff prelude on an inadequate piano. Finally he climbed a dark staircase, toward the fourth floor. The wrought-iron railing wobbled in his hand. Doors along the way, two to a landing, were incredibly decrepit, with some unheard-of kind of stuffing falling out of them as if they were old quilts. The place was impregnated with a sour smell, a mingling of cabbage, sweat, bad plaster, and nineteenth-century rainfalls. Past and present blurred in Jeremy's mind again. Gogol, quite uninvited, warned him that if they were frying fish in the kitchen, there would probably be so much smoke that he wouldn't even be able to see the cockroaches. "Take your big nose and go away," Jeremy said. He knocked on the door, much too loudly.

After a moment, the door opened one third, and a crumpled old face looked up at him. Another old lady, less crumpled than the first, stood in the background. "*Dobryi vecher,*" he said, trying to greet both of them. "I'd like to speak to Elizaveta if I may." They shuffled away, leaving the door as it was, and he heard one of them saying "a cultured young man. . . ." Jeremy could see an icon of the Virgin and an upholstered couch shaped like a donkey's back. Then a slender girl stood in his line of sight—rather tall, with an unfinished thought on her face and a curl to the corners of her eyes and mouth that gave her a smile even if she wasn't smiling. As she was not now. She wore the usual Russian print dress; her summer-brown hair was braided. In one hand she had a folder of papers and a pencil imprisoned by her thumb. She waited, neutrally. "Yes," she said, "what is it, Comrade?"

"I'm sorry to trouble you when you are working," Jeremy said, "but there is a note for you, from an American named Bob—" She grabbed not the note but Jeremy's wrist, and pulled him inside, slamming the door.

"Are you an American?" she whispered, in English, looking at his face and then at his loafers.

"Yes, I am. I work at the Exhibition in Moscow."

"Then don't you know you should not have come here? It is very dangerous. Has anyone seen you? Oh God, that stupid—" Elizaveta still seemed to be smiling because of the strange curve to her face.

"No one saw me," he said. "I'm sorry, I didn't think—"

"Speak Russian," Elizaveta snapped. "Those old witches will have a fit." The two ladies were sewing in a corner by the same lamp, with the inevitable fringed orange shade. One room for all: there was a bed in another corner, probably Elizaveta's, because a lamp-lit writing desk was next to it, and a small glass-enclosed bookcase with standard Russian authors. A cot was made up near the couch, and a wooden table with a bowl of cucumbers stood in the middle of the room. A second golden icon, of Saint George, and a print of old Petersburg hung on the walls. Jeremy started to explain, in Russian, that Bob had given him no information at all about the Leningrad situation, but the more crumpled lady crept up, pulling her black shawl close, and said, "It is time for *him* to go." Jeremy edged toward the door.

"But maybe *he* is not ready to go," Elizaveta said angrily, taking hold of his sleeve.

"Liza," the old lady croaked, "your foreign friends are going to ruin us. Especially if they are so idiotic—"

"He's not my friend, and it's not his fault. He just arrived from Moscow and knows nothing about—"

"It's time for him to go!" said the other lady. She was frantic. "To *go!*"

Jeremy stood, miserably. Elizaveta was still holding his sleeve. She looked at him with quick sympathy. "This is terrible for you. You were only trying to do a favor."

"To *go!* To *go!*" wailed the second lady from her corner, as the first crossed herself, mumbling.

"Oh, shut up!" Elizaveta said. She threw on a brown cloth coat, took Jeremy's arm, and steered him onto the stairs. "Let's go for a walk, Kolya," she said loudly, as if to an audience on the stairs. "Toward your brother's."

The door slammed behind them. She propelled him out through the courtyards and onto the night-filled Nevsky without letting him say a word. He was still burning with embarrassment when they had joined the strollers going back toward the river.

"Please forgive me," he stammered. "I certainly didn't mean— It was the last thing—"

"Don't mind the old ladies. The less they have to live for, the more they worry about it."

She was not looking at him. He considered saying, "I apologize. Deeply. Good-by," but she still had an automatic hold on his arm. "Who are they?" he asked instead.

"Who are who? Oh, them. My grandmother and her friend. I think the friend is *her* grandmother, but they're ashamed of it. We all love each other madly."

"I don't see very well in the dark," Jeremy said. "Do you mind telling me whether you are smiling or not?"

"Perhaps. I remain, however, inscrutable."

True. He had no idea whether or not her anger was still near the surface.

"My name is Jeremy," he said. "You know, something like the prophet." He had pronounced it in English.

"Of course, *Ieremia*. My grandmother knows all the prophets by heart, which accounts for the wisdom of her approach to life. I am so furious at her, and you, and Bob."

A block of silence. Jeremy said, "What do you do?"

"I am a translator. Which reminds me. You know, *Ieremia*, that you speak a very clean, exact Russian. If I were not so mortified over this evening, we could perfect it. Why did you learn Russian so well?"

"I like it."

"Are you a spy?"

"Yes." This time Jeremy knew that she was smiling, because they passed under a street lamp—three high bright globes in the pawnbroker's pattern—and her teeth flashed a little. Suddenly she pushed him into a doorway and said, "Well, let me show you how to be a good spy. First, take off that stupid tie. Come on." It was his regular striped traveling tie. But he took it off. "Now open your top button and put out your shirt collar—wide, like this—over your jacket. Good. Now off with those glasses. Too American. Lean toward me when I take your arm, put a smug expression on your face—excellent—and we have an ambitious young Soviet engineer out with his solemn translator friend. Perfect couple."

They walked a while more, into the old Petersburg section, across the Griboyedov Canal and past the former Kazan Cathedral, now an antireligious museum. He was afraid to ask questions that would show how little he knew of the city. He cleared his throat as if in preparation for an important remark. "The streets of Leningrad," he said, "are very clean."

"Of course they are," she said. "We have a program of compulsory-voluntary immaculateness."

"You mean one can't even have dirt if one wants to? One's own small pile of dirt?"

"Really, you bourgeoisie have such decadent ideas."

"But I represent the Western democracies," said Jeremy. "I am shocked that you Russians cannot have freedom of dirt."

"Citizen Little Man, we have greater goals in mind. Your obsolete private dirt will have to go. You may share all the rich collective dirt you want at the kolkhoz."

"You know," Jeremy said, "this being a Little Man is not comfortable. They chased me down these very streets with bronze hoofs. They stole my greatcoat after I went without tea to save for it. Now they take away my pile of dirt. What a life."

"Ah, Little Man, I sympathize. They took away your Czar."

"They took away my nobility," he said.

"They took away your room."

"They took away my family."

"And now they want your dirt," said Elizaveta.

"And now they want my dirt. After midnight I come out alone on the Nevsky and drop cigarette butts in my favorite gutters. But in the morning—"

"Nothing?"

"Nothing."

"A socialist triumph."

"Communist repression. One night I left old copies of *Izvestia* everywhere."

"Vicious capitalist espionage!"

"Courageous democratic action. But what's the use?"

"None," said Elizaveta. "Any other questions? Feel free to ask questions. The people must be educated."

"That's true. You must catch up to and overtake America."

"But *you* must meet the Soviet challenge, economically, militarily—"

"Who knows?" Jeremy said.

"Who knows?" agreed Elizaveta.

They had reached the river. In the glisten of the fast water, lights from eighteenth-century windows threatened to move downstream but held their own, at the last minute, against the current. Jeremy put on his glasses. He and Elizaveta laughed, in great relief, delighted with each other.

There were few cars along the embankment. Elizaveta's face was in the darkness, but her eyes, like the river, caught little points of reflected light. Jeremy imagined that he could still see the unfinished thought on her face and could feel in her slenderness the pathos of all the slim girls and admirable ladies who filled his memory from the pages of Turgenev and Tolstoy. A wave of feeling surprised him, a *frisson* down through his ankles; he felt that he was shaken in a confusion as to who or where he was, where the pages of his imagination ended and where he had actually begun to stand in the night above the River Neva with this girl close to him.

Elizaveta extended a slim finger and touched Jeremy's right cheek. "Little Person," she said. She began to trace patterns along his cheekbone and the soft center below it.

"I see that you understand very well who I am," he said. He took off his glasses again and shoved them into his jacket pocket. Elizaveta's finger continued to drift across his face. The night became a blur. He reached his hand through the night toward the place where he remembered her face to be, saying, "But you are an Aleksandra or a Natasha."

"No," she said, "no!", and she pressed his palm full against her face. "I'm a Little Person too, the least in the world." He could feel her face moving against his palm as she spoke. "Only the Little Persons are still alive." He moved closer to her and heard her words as whispers of breath against his ear. "Ieremi,"—she had softened the name—"the others are all dead. They want us to be dead with them. They don't want us to feel what it is to be alive."

Suddenly he felt her lips on his, with a terrible hunger. They kissed again and again and held to each other, afraid to let go; he felt her hands pressing at his temples. Before they parted, the glistening Neva waters that had passed them at the beginning had long since flowed into the Gulf of Finland. Passers-by, ever fewer, smiled at them. The two leaned against the stone parapet, watching the swift wide waters that came newly on, and they hardly knew where to begin finding words again. Time was short between them. They had no place to go, Jeremy thought; it was already late. To-morrow was the important word in their lives. "Tomorrow," he said, just as Elizaveta hesitantly asked, "What are you going to do tomorrow?"

She had instructed him in the art of meeting invisibly during daylight. He was to find her in the morning crowd near the anti-religious museum—there was always a crowd near the antireligious museum, which had a jolly waxworks exhibition of bad priests and obscurantists—and then he was to pass through her field of vision, walking slowly. She would follow him down the Nevsky at a gradually decreasing distance until they were side by side. "Fad-ing together," she called it; a way of meeting "questionable human beings" without there having been a place where so-and-so was seen greeting so-and-so. That night, as he fell asleep, Jeremy wondered, a little petulantly, why he hadn't learned this before, until he realized that she would be the first Russian he was going to meet privately in daytime.

In his room at the Astoria, he awoke to sunlight on the ornate mirror with another start of confusion as to where and who. He put on his glasses. The room was Russified Victorian. Gilt, fringed cushions, angels carved from heavy wood, furniture resting on thumping big lions' feet. He hadn't even learned her last name. In fact, he couldn't remember what she looked like. There was a sense of her cleanliness and slenderness in the dusk, her words and touch; delicious, but he would never recognize her in a crowd. It was over. Typical, typical, Jeremy muttered as he pulled on his clothes.

He ran in terror from the beaming fat waitress who wanted him to sit down for three hours over tea in a glass and fried eggs. In the square he bought two sweet rolls from a girl in a white smock at a pushcart, and he half trotted, munching, toward the meeting place. The Nevsky Prospect was streaming with people on their way to office work, looking almost as wilted as their old brief cases. The sun was hot. Jeremy arrived at the semicircular colonnade of the former Kazan Cathedral a half hour early, and he was just about to find twenty reasons why it was so unfortunate an imitation

of St. Peter's when he saw her. She was unmistakable, as slim and
fresh as he remembered, with her light-brown hair brushed back, a
touch of lipstick. She was wearing a neat sweater buttoned up the
front and even a string of glass beads. She looked through him as
if he were one of the wax statues inside. Oh, yes, of course:
Jeremy remembered and walked obediently away toward the looming yellow admiralty building.

In a moment he felt an arm slip into his and he smelled lavender
soap. She laughed into his ear. "Good morning, *gospodin* spy.
What's the password?"

Jeremy said, "No answer, Elizabeth," which makes a foolish
rhyme in Russian, no better than See you later, alligator. But she
seemed satisfied. Now that it was true that he was going to spend
the day with a marvelous Russian girl, he decided not to waste it.
Daytime: sociological information; evening: love. Accordingly, he
began his interrogation. "I don't even know your last name," he
said.

"I don't have one," she answered. "Or, rather, I did have one
until the Revolution, but they took it away. They renamed me
Steelworks. Steelworks in the name of Kirov. But you can call me
just Liza." She used *ty*—"thee"—with him, which threw Jeremy
even more off balance, since he had learned all his conversational
Russian in the polite form. He stumbled twice, trying to begin a
sentence. Elizaveta laughed again. "You're pretending to have trouble so that we'll have to speak English. Well, we won't. It's too
inconvenient, and too—cold."

They never got to the Hermitage. Lorenzo Lotto, Elizaveta said
laughing, Jeremy would always have with him; for her, he had only
one day. She wanted to go where they could "talk all the time and
chase each other and run in the sun."

They were in a taxi, driving through scanty landscape toward
Peterhof. The Gulf of Finland, seeming frigid and forlorn even in
August, lay to their right, with Kronstadt's bristle of cranes in the
distance. To the left, the birch-scattered flatness never blessed by
nature and too recently blasted by the siege. Charred hulks of the
old estate houses stood on slight rises of the ground. Jeremy would
have asked the cab driver for his memories of the war if Elizaveta
had not assumed a Ukrainian accent, pronouncing all her g's like

h's, and told the driver they were both summer vacationers in town for two days. She also introduced Jeremy as a young Party official from Albania who really knew Russian quite well. The driver pretended great interest in Albania, so Jeremy gave a report on conditions there, stressing agricultural problems and Muslim reaction, while Elizaveta ran her finger up and down his back. After the driver had thanked Jeremy for the tip, he pointed good-naturedly. "You're not from Albania, Comrade, and she is not Ukrainian."

"Quite right," Jeremy said. "I'm American." This sent the driver into gales of laughter.

He said, "And she, I suppose, is also American, from Hollywood [*Golivud*]. And I'm from Hawaii [*Gavai*]. Very warm in *Gavai*." He was still muttering happily to himself about Hawaii as he drove off.

The two spent their bright hours in the park at Peterhof under the high gross majesty of the palace on its hill—the only hill within miles—with the splash of all its fountains and the blue marine canal gathering their waters to flow into the sea, that northern finger of sea for which eighteenth-century czars were so grateful. Elizaveta described the rubble left by the siege, and pointed with pride to the restorations, complete even to Tritons and Venuses descending in a brilliant gilded cascade. Suddenly she said to Jeremy, "You don't like them, do you?"

"Well—" he said. The restorations were too garish; the glittering yellow sculpture reminded him of golf trophies.

"You realize, my dear boy, what the people went through here and what it means to have this place as theirs again?"

Jeremy looked worried. He was afraid he would start spouting about art and society. "Poor Ieremi," Elizaveta said, touching his chin. Her mood had changed again. "I'm not going to make you argue. This is a day for Little Persons."

And it was. They ran through the parks. They splashed in every fountain capable of being splashed in, bought ice cream from saintly ladies in white, and then they were shivering together at the prow of the excursion boat back to Leningrad across the cold gray wash of the gulf. The city was a long blur ahead of them, except where the golden needle of the Petropavlovsk fortress caught a late gleam of sun and cauterized the dimness.

It was the edge of night when they were in front of the stolid Astoria Hotel, certainly not to say good-by, but not knowing where to go. Jeremy was saying, "Elizaveta, come up to my room. It's quiet and private. You'll love it; it has a lamp with an orange fringed shade and a picture of a nice peasant girl gathering something—radishes, I think—that makes her very happy."

"Oh, Ieremi, I want to very much. More than you want me to, I think. But it's impossible."

"Don't radishes make you happy?"

Elizaveta smiled, perhaps. "Very. And so do you. But if they find me in a foreigner's room at the Astoria, I'm through. I have a bad name already." He raised his eyebrows, but she said, "No, we have no time to go into that. Anyway, our public crimes are personal matters. Don't meddle. I haven't asked you how you treat Negroes."

"I promise to salute every Negro I meet if you will come to my room."

"Ieremi, it would be horrible for you, too. Tass would give it bigger propaganda right now than a new Sputnik. How they would love to find an American lecher spreading his poisons around the Soviet masses. I would have to testify that you lured me with visions of Wall Street. What would your mother think?"

"You're playing with me, aren't you?"

"Playing with you? Do you have any idea what this game may cost? Do you really think—? Oh, never mind. Next thing, you will accuse me of self-pity, then flightiness. Go ahead. I'll give you ten minutes for the whole list."

"I'm sorry," he said. "I always seem to be sorry. I suppose I wanted to be serious for a moment."

"For seriousness we definitely have no time, sweet friend." Elizaveta took his hand in both of hers and pulled him toward the hotel entrance. "Come on," she said, "we can have some wine and we can dance upstairs in the ballroom. Excellent cure for seriousness."

"But won't that be just as—inconvenient? For you?"

"No, no. It's so crowded and obvious that they will never notice us. Just don't forget to be one half the perfect Soviet couple. Smug expression. And let me speak most of the time—which I would probably do anyway."

While they were riding up in the elevator, Elizaveta whispered, "What Russian word can you pronounce most easily?"

"Radishes," Jeremy whispered.

"Good. If anyone official wants to talk to you, just say 'radishes.'"

The Astoria ballroom. High ceiling, shiny waxed floor, small round tables packed in as tightly as salmon eggs, palm fronds hanging helplessly, corks popping from mediocre Georgian wine, an eight-piece band, Guy Lombardo style, pot-shaped middle-class couples pushing each other anxiously back and forth to a series of variations on *Moscow Evenings*.

"Lord," Jeremy whispered. "They're all from the Bronx."

The headwaiter seated them at a table with an imperturbably well-nourished, fortyish couple. He wore a dark suit and a wide tie with a pattern that looked like watermelons; she had a frilly white blouse and too much perfume. She was slicing a Kiev cutlet that oozed with butter, and he was toying with the fatty embroidery of his poached sturgeon. "They really don't know how to play dance music here," she was saying. "In Paris it's different. We've been to Paris," she said, turning to Elizaveta. And then to Jeremy, "Don't you think so?"

"Radishes," Jeremy said.

"Pardon?" said she.

But Elizaveta was already on her feet, saying, "You know, Kolya, I don't think we have time for dinner after all. Your brother will be waiting."

They were out in the street, looking up at the tall baroque dome of the Isaac Cathedral. "God save us from the Astoria ballroom," said Jeremy. Elizaveta seemed thoughtful. "Do you know anything about the Bronx?" he asked.

"No, unless you mean those wild horses in your *kovboi* stories."

Jeremy locked Elizaveta in a tremendous bear hug. "Oh, absurd, absurd," he said, in English.

"I don't know exactly what you mean," said Elizaveta in Russian, "but it's true." She struggled to free her arms, and then put them around his neck.

They clung together. This time Jeremy felt desire run through

him like summer lightning. He tried to kiss the corners of her lips,
where the smiles were. Elizaveta whispered and began to touch his
face with soft kisses. "Oh, I don't care," she said. "Come on. Pay
another visit to my apartment. This time I invite you."

"But—"

She put her finger over his lips. "No one will notice. You look
completely Russian now. I've ruined you."

The last hint of summer dusk hung on and on, as it does in the
north. They leaned close, strolling down the wide Nevsky again.
Finally he asked, "Will the grandmothers be out?"

"Of course not. They are much too old."

"But, couldn't they drop into the communal kitchen or something?" He heard his voice growing plaintive.

"No, no, no, they always eat early." Elizaveta laughed softly.
"They won't mind us. They'll sit in the far corner and turn their
backs and bend over their sewing. They have an incredible amount
of sewing to do."

"But, still—"

"Oh, Ieremi, dear boy, it won't be embarrassing. We just have to
be a little quieter than you are used to being in the Western
democracies. Unless you can solve our housing within ten minutes." They walked on in silence, past the dark colonnade of the
antireligious museum where they had "faded together" in the
morning. Elizaveta clung still more closely to his arm. "You'll see,
Ieremi. It won't be so bad. We're all used to it."

"Well, I'm not." He tried to sound good-natured.

"But that's just the way it is."

"The way it *is*?" he asked, in desolation. "Is that the way it was
with Bob What's-his-name and every other What's-his-name?"

She stopped dead. "What do you *want* of this world?" she asked,
coldly. "I suppose you think you've said something cruel. It's worse
than that; it's stupid. Sometimes I think you Americans *are* corrupt.
You always must *own* things. That's the only relationship you can
understand." She turned away from him.

Oh, God, thought Jeremy, here it is, the inevitable.

But Elizaveta led him instead to a street lamp, and she took his
worried face in her hands. "Ieremi," she said, "timid boy, accept
what I am offering. Love is the one thing here that is not com-

plicated. Perhaps with you it is just the opposite, but now you are *chez nous* and you must do as we do. Agreed?" His throat would not let him say the word. "Agreed?" asked Elizaveta.

"Yes, agreed," he said.

They walked along through the murk-filled inner courtyards, up the cabbaged stairway with its doors waning in decrepitude, Jeremy playing silent word games to ease his embarrassment: I'm always inhibited when the room is inhabited. He admired the slope of Elizaveta's slim back as she put the key into the lock, without making a sound, and then they were in the modest room with its golden Saint George and the Virgin, and sway-backed couches, sets of Tolstoy and Chekhov, orange-fringed lamps, and the one solid table with its bowl of cucumbers. Both the old ladies shook hands with Jeremy, addressing him as "young man." The more crumpled asked him whether he would like a cucumber, and the other began to suggest, somewhat indirectly, that since he was a foreigner it was getting to be time for him to go. But when they saw that Elizaveta was stretching a brown blanket like a curtain in front of her bed, suspending it from the book cabinet and a clothing rack, reaching up on tiptoe with her arms upraised, the two ladies smiled and nodded and patted Jeremy's arm. Then they bundled off toward their sewing corner. Russian women. Elizaveta accepted him quietly into the deep shadows she had created, where love is the one thing not complicated.

They were walking, hand in hand, down the gloom of the Nevsky's tag end, toward the Moscow Station. It was late in the evening. The Red Arrow was leaving Leningrad in half an hour, and Jeremy had to be on it in order to stand at his post when the Exhibition floodgates opened at eleven the next morning. Empty buses ground by. "I haven't even asked you about your family," he said.

"Don't. We are Russians. When we aren't busy killing each other, someone rolls in the artillery from Europe. Only my brother and I were left after the siege. He went out to grow corn in Siberia. And I stayed on."

"Why?"

"Oh, I still love poor Leningrad. I hold the grandmothers' hands,

and go to concerts, and wait for people like you." Elizaveta leaned
fondly against his arm for a moment. Then she said, "Ieremi, the
station is no place for a Russian to be with a foreigner either. We
shall have to fade apart."

"*Nu ladno*. Well"—he hesitated—"all right. But when can we
meet again?"

She shook her head. "Ieremi, I'm in trouble as it is."

He tried to slow the pace of their walk. He closed his eyes and
leaned more heavily toward Elizaveta. He began to hum. Then he
said, "I suppose you admire all your Russian *Romeo and Juliet*
music—Prokofiev, Tchaikovsky."

She laughed, too quietly. "You're not very subtle, you know. I
suppose I like the Prokofiev, somewhat. But I love Mozart, like you.
Did you forget already, stupid boy?" He opened his eyes. They
were in a blurred square with a monument, and the Moscow Station bulked ahead.

"Liza," he said, "where will we be after we fade apart? Tell me."

"I don't know. I don't know, my friend. Where we were before,
it seems. Nowhere."

"You just don't understand!" he burst out. "Maybe you can be
brave like a Turgenev woman, and maybe you think life is fine with
me because our police don't follow me at night. Maybe you think a
moment's love is the solution for everything."

"Please, Ieremi! Please, please! We've had something. Isn't that
more than nothing? Who are we to—?" She could not go on. She
burst into wild tears, amazing him, and kissed his face. Then she
was gone, running, while he still leaned toward the place where she
had been, as a stalk leans after the wind.

Steam rose in clouds past the windows; a samovar in the train
buffet was softly brewing. Through the station a loudspeaker
echoed, announcing the departure of the Red Arrow for Moscow.
Its voice bulged with the tedious Soviet assumption that the departure of every train will be welcomed by history.

SHIRLEY W. SCHOONOVER was born in Biwabik, Minnesota. She attended the University of Minnesota and the University of Nebraska, where she became interested in writing. Miss Schoonover lives in Lincoln, Nebraska, and is currently working on a novel and a collection of short stories. Her first story appeared in *New Campus Writing III* in 1959.

THE STAR BLANKET

from *The Transatlantic Review*

They had walked miles that day. They walked miles every day that they changed grazing land. The man and woman followed the sheep silently, the only conversation was that of the sheep as they flowed down the hills. The dogs were merely extensions of the man's will, moving to his short whistles, guiding the wooly mass down from the summer grazing lands to the winter flatlands. The man raised his right hand and the dogs fell to the ground, allowing the sheep to stop and graze.

The man threw his pack to the ground and sat next to it.

"Ought to be good grazing farther on down." He pulled tobacco from his shirt pocket and bit off a corner.

The woman remained standing, looking up the side of the mountain they had descended and down the foothills.

"All the steps it took for us to get down here. All the steps it'll take for us to reach winter pasture. Who'd think there were that many steps to a mountain?" She shook her head and eased one booted foot against the other.

"You sure waste your time thinking about steps in mountains. If you want to get from one place to another it always takes steps."

Copyright 1961 by Joseph McCrindle. By permission of The Transatlantic Review 1961.

He rolled the tobacco around his tongue, savoring the fresh flavor, the bite on his tongue.

"And when we go back up the mountain again, what a waste of steps. We don't even leave marks to remember from one spring to another. Or even spring to fall."

"Don't worry about it, we don't need marks, we find the best grass, that's enough." He stood up and whistled the dogs into action.

The rest of the day they spent following the sheep down the shallow hills, down to a valley that would hold them all the California winter.

As they went the man kept his eyes to the ground remarking the grass and the dryness. "It's going to be a hard winter in the mountains." From time to time he would spit brown juice onto the gray grass.

The woman walked behind him, carrying her pack, looking at the sky and the progress of the sun and clouds. She watched the man ahead of her, thinking, "He never looks at the sky unless it's going to rain or snow. He doesn't notice the sheep-clouds or the feather-clouds, just the rain clouds." She stumbled over a hummock of grass and the man turned and laughed at her.

"Get your nose out of the clouds, they won't save you any steps."

"I was just watching the sky, and the clouds running down it."

"No use watching the sky, it'll be there tonight and tomorrow. It's not good for anything except weather."

"Sometimes I think a thing doesn't always have to be used to be good. The sky is good to look at." She spoke softly to herself, not seeing the land around her; rather seeing into the land and the sky in dimensions she could not explain, but merely sense.

"What?" The man called back, then, watching her unseeing progress down the hillside, he turned, grinned, and walked on, head down.

That night they bedded the sheep down in an outcropping of gray boulders and sandy ledges. The dogs gathered the sheep like needles gathering beads, and scolded them into a bumping, blatting, wooly scuffle of bodies.

The man and woman sat beside their fire, drinking black sour coffee from tin cups. The man threw small shards of wood into the fire, and thought about the sheep and the dogs, and his need for another dog.

The woman lay on her back, half dozing, lying against the earth, feeling its outward thrust against her back.

"Do you suppose the mountains are growing?" She asked her husband.

"I don't suppose anything so crazy. These mountains have been here all my life, never grew an inch that I saw." He squinted at her through the fire. His pale eyes took on a white cast from the flames; and as he looked, his face changed, becoming cunning and sensual. He arose and went to her. He lay beside her, taking her body with his hard hands, gripping her rather than caressing her. She lay passive, looking at him with mildly wondering eyes. When he was through he left her and rolled up in his blanket to sleep. She continued to stare up into the sky, past the stars.

She had come to him from her father in exchange for three pregnant ewes. She had been thirteen then, and a plain, quiet girl. Her father had been a sheep rancher who had fallen into difficulty, and with a large family of girls, it was expedient to bestow his middle daughter upon a wandering sheep herder who promised to keep her. She had been a good wife to the shepherd, having a quiet gentleness with the lambing ewes, and a quickness of foot when needed to herd the sheep. She had lived these two years with him in the mountains and the flat lands; wearing levis and flannel shirts, cropping her hair once a year like the sheep, and had pleased him in the secret moments of their life together. He had taken her with him into the small town that was their outside world every spring during the shearing time, until a vagrant cowboy had noticed her feminine form under the heavy shirt.

"I'd sure like to take your daughter into the dance tonight." His eyes had spoken more than the words, and understanding flashed between the men.

"My wife ain't free to go dancing. We're going back to the sheep tonight."

"Sheep herder!" The cowboy narrowed his eyes at them. He mounted his horse and, looking tall and arrogant, he said, "Maybe we could wash the smell off your woman, but right now it would be like bedding a lousy sheep."

The man never took her into town again, instead he left her to tend the sheep when he made his trading trips. She was no more lonely during these trips than when he was with her.

The next day they reached their small cabin which was their winter shelter. It was adequate for shelter and no more. The man had built it ten years before, and owned the acres that surrounded it. They established themselves in it, the sheep in a large pen, the woman cooked supper in the iron stove. The man dozed while the woman folded blankets into the bed and pushed the table and chairs into a new design against the wall. She heated water and bathed herself, washing her hair and body over and over with yellow soap until she felt clean of the sheep dust and grit of the trail.

"You going into town tomorrow?" she asked.

"Yeah. I'm taking some of the lambs for selling. We need stock for the winter, so clear out the shelves for whatever I can pick up." He turned noisily onto his side.

"Bring me something from town," she spoke softly to his back; hands brushing through her hair, drying it, twisting it into a knot at the back of her neck.

"What like? I can't spend money on foolishness."

"Just something little for me to look at. I saw a picture card when we were at the cowboys' camp. That was pretty. I could look at that and think of what other places there are."

"You want that card? I'll bring you a new shirt and pants, they're pretty when they're new."

"No, something for me to look at and hold. I don't want to use everything. Remember that fair we saw that first trip? They had cards and pretty boxes with shells. Bring me a pretty box with shells. I could look at it and touch the shells . . ."

"I'll see what there is to bring that doesn't cost too dear. Come to bed now so we can sleep."

When he had gone into town with the lambs she shook out the blankets and swept the floor.

All the day long and night that he was gone she thought about the town and the rushing cattle in the stockyard, the lighted cafes, and the pretty goods in the store and the town women who wore colorful dresses.

"If he brings me the box I'll keep it on the table all winter. I can see the watermarks on the shells and think of all the miles they've come to be here." She hummed to herself and tended the sheep.

When he came home she waited, breathless, while he unpacked the borrowed mule. He unloaded a package of wadded shirts and denim pants, wool socks, and a pair of boots for her. She watched him, and put away the sacked flour, coffee, sugar, tobacco, and tins of food. She dug through the sacks looking for the thing she had asked for.

"Did you bring me something pretty?" She hugged her arms to her chest.

"I spent all I could on things we need. I can't see what you needed that box for." He unwrapped a dozen tins of snuff and stacked them on the table. "Here's something you like, lump sugar for your coffee." He handed her a box of sugar.

She took the sugar from him and put it on the shelf.

"No thanks, hey? Well, I can get my thanks in bed." He touched her shirt front with a hard, accustomed hand.

"Look outside in the sheep pen. There's something else I got in town."

She went slowly outside. In the gray mass of sheep stood a large, dark shape. It was a horse, standing solemnly in the half dark, looking toward her with mysterious black eyes. A fringe of forelock covered its eyes so that it seemed to look at her from a shadow. She entered the pen and pushed the sheep aside to walk to the horse. It stood unmoving when she touched its nose. She ran her hand up between its ears and stroked its neck. Its head drooped and it sighed. It neither welcomed her nor rejected her, but stood accepting her attention without resistance.

The man buffeted his way through the sheep and stood before her. "I got him free from that cowboy we saw last spring. He was going to shoot the horse because it's windbroke and can't keep up with the cattle."

The woman looked at them both. He put his arm possessively around the horse's neck. "I can use him for packing our stuff up

mountain next spring. One thing's sure, he won't be running away
from us, he's too windbroke."

"He's a pretty thing," she said.

"Well, see, I brought you something to look at. He isn't much
good for anything but looking at right now, but come spring he
can be used." He slapped the horse's shoulder and turned away.
The horse looked at the woman and closed its eyes.

During the winter the dogs herded the sheep into nearby valleys for pasture. The horse grazed with the sheep, following them
listlessly from spot to spot. The dogs nipped its heels and made it
trot, causing it to breathe heavily in a wheezing, whuffling short-
ness of breath. The woman, seeing this, would call the dogs to
stop; but they, listening to the man, would loll their tongues at
her and dart at the horse until the man whistled them down.

At night, when the sheep were penned, the horse would stand
at the fence looking off into the mountains. The man would sit
beside the stove oiling his rifle, splicing tanned hides into a rope.
The woman would sit on the floor staring into the grated opening
of the stove, listening to the night sounds. It was during one of
these nights that she said: "I think I'm starting a baby."

"Well, that's good." He stopped his work to touch her hair.
"When did this happen?"

"I think three months ago. I haven't had any woman signs for
that long, and my belt's too tight."

She stood while he felt her belly and sides.

"A baby, hey?" He thrust his hand within her shirt to her breasts.
"You are fattening up and filling out. Next time I go into town,
I'll bring you some more sugar and some canned fruit. You feel all
right?"

"Oh, yes. I think it'll be born in the summer. Could you bring
me some cloth to make it some clothes?"

"Yeah, I guess I could. Flannel, I expect, and some pins and
thread. You'll have to pack it with you when we go up mountain."
He held her to him and kissed her head. "Give me a boy. He'd be
a big help and we could keep more sheep."

That night when they were in bed and he lay against her he
repeated, "Give me a boy. Give me a boy."

When he slept she rose to one elbow and watched him. In

sleep his face was the tender version of the day face, the pale eyes were hidden beneath a short run of lashes, the animal cunning mouth was relaxed into softer lines, tinted by tobacco juice and perpetual windburn. In sleep his face allowed no more knowledge of him than did his day face, it was so utterly expressionless. Whatever imagination or feeling he might have had was covered by the continuous need for material satisfaction. He had been orphaned at six years and had herded sheep for other men until he had begun his own flock. Since he had lost his parents, he had lost all identity except as a shepherd in the mountains. His dreams were of wool and sheep and the steadily increasing roll of money in a tin container under the floor. Some nights he panted like a dog in his sleep, dreaming of the heights and the slow unwinding of the pasture lands up into the emptiness of the sky.

He had first seen his wife while she was tending her father's sheep on a winter pasture; sitting in the scrubby grass bent over some knitting. She was thirteen, just budding from a youth into womanliness. Her small, round head bent so seriously over woman's work touched some memory of his dead mother; her brown boyish hands knitting steadily and her yet unformed, unmarred face struck him in the groin with a kind of sad desire both to possess her and father her. In his late thirties, he had had few dealings with women, and so instead of courting her, he spoke with her father.

"She's a little bit strange," said the father. "She reads books and wanders off alone into the hills and we never know when she'll come back. But if you want her and figure you can put up with her ways, take her."

The girl had stood silently watching from the doorway of her father's house. For the exchange of three sheep she was given to the man. Her mother had spoken to her, bidding: "I never had time to tell you what to expect from a man. I can't tell you now except to be good to him. When he comes to you at night, take him." The girl had looked at her mother with mute eyes. "There's no way to find out about men and their ways except by doing. In ten years you'll not remember what it was like not to know a man. It seems to have been going on forever, and it will go on that way until he's too old." The mother held her daughter for the last time.

"If you can take joy from his man's ways, that's good. If you can't, try to give him what you can, there's some joy in that too." She kissed her daughter's round forehead. "Now go to him, he seems to be kind, and you'd have to marry some one someday."

The man had taken her away with him into the cabin he had built. He watched her arrange her small store of clothing on the high shelf. She walked about the room, touching the table and the chairs. She looked into the cupboard at the supplies, patted the dogs and touched the window ledge. Her presence in the room made it a less lonely place for the man and he smiled at her hands when they touched the dogs.

The room was a new and lonely place for the girl. The smells of the man and dogs, wet fur and wool, the low flickering fire in the stove, the absence of her mother made her aware of being pitched out into an alien world. The presence of the man, his physical urge toward her, made her feel shut in and apprehensive. She had some knowledge of what her mother had meant, but only enough to keep her nerves tense. She remembered the rams in mating season, their arrogant, almost cruel way of commanding the ewes; the ewes falling to their knees under the onslaught of the rams, the heavy odors of life regenerating itself. She tried to think if her father had ever looked at her mother that way, and the patience of her mother's eyes when night came.

"Come now, you've seen all the things I have." The man took her arm and held her close against his chest, stroking her hair and back gently. He took her to the bed and watched her undress to the pale baby skin. She lay beneath the wool blanket, eyes closed.

"If I must learn man's ways, let it be now. Don't let it hurt. Don't let him hurt me."

When the man touched her shoulder she flinched and opened her eyes. She stared at him and clasped her hands over her breasts, hiding them and herself from his maleness.

"Ah, now, I won't hurt you." He said, "Let me hold your hand and we'll talk a bit."

She gave her hand to him and pulled the cover up to her chin.

"You're still afraid, hey? I won't hurt you." He leaned over her and touched her face with his. "You're so small, more like my child than my wife." He touched her body under the blanket, gently, as if plucking a fragile plant. She turned her face to his shoulder and closed her eyes. He stroked her body carefully; she sensing the rushing of his passion; he building his desire slowly so as not to frighten her.

"Will you let me?" he asked her. She had fallen into a musing state. She nodded.

When he was through he turned her head and looked at her.

"Well, now, it didn't hurt, did it?" She looked at him with patient eyes and shook her head. He took her hand and rested with her until they both fell asleep.

During the years before she became pregnant her figure filled out into feminine contours. Her waist lengthened and diminished to a fitting slimness, her breasts lost the baby roundness and drooped slightly, her hips and buttocks rounded to firm, earth-round lines. Her walk changed from a girl's gait to a purposeful stride, although she still walked as if paying no attention to the earth, but walked slightly above it.

She and the man spoke little, they shared all their activities, but his mind rested on the sheep while hers mused over the eternally silent mountains and the dimension of sound and color.

In the spring of her pregnancy and after the lambing, they made their way back over the foothills and into the mountain pasture-lands.

The woman had become fond of the horse; feeling that it and she shared the same state of uselessness. The horse had recovered some of its broken wind and moved more alertly. Daily it was packed with their supplies and carried them silently after the sheep. The man walked ahead, whistling the dogs into the familiar patterns of action, watching the new grasses come up before them. The woman stepped behind him watching the rain mists climb higher up the mountain each day, seeing the horse move ahead of her, flicking its tail against the constant flies, reaching for the short grasses along the way. She drew pleasure from the horse's grace and its increasing strength and wildness. At night when the horse was unpacked, it would roll on the earth, rubbing its skin against the sharp strength of the mountain side, rising and kicking itself into the air. At these times she would clasp her hands and laugh while the horse nickered to her and coaxed her for the secret lumps of sugar she kept for it. The time came when she would ride the horse around the camp, calling the dogs to romp with her and the horse. She and the horse would pick their way from the camp to sudden ledges of the mountain and look down through the ground fog to the foothills, catching glimpses of occasional rivers and lights from other campfires. She would always return with the horse running and snorting, both looking wild and fresh from mysterious journeys in the night. The man would wait for her return and she would prepare the supper.

"What do you find in the night to look so happy about?"

"Oh, we look for the different stars. We saw camplights down east of us. We smelled the pines up mountain. It's all so different from the day. The stars are different up here from down land."

"The stars are always the same. No matter where you are." He drank his coffee and sat back. "You're getting as strange now as you were when I first brought you home."

"Strange? No, I'm not." She looked at him anxiously.

"It's that horse. You ride him too much, and you're away from me too much. You need to settle down to thinking about regular things like the sheep and the camp. You're going to have a baby soon, you should think about that."

"I do. Everytime he moves, I think about him. I made up a song to him." She began humming to herself.

"Songs." The man grunted. "I mean the sewing of clothes, that thread and cloth cost too dear to be wasted."

She looked at him and smiled. "I have been sewing. But my mind keeps straying to the other things he'll need."

"What else will he need? Plenty of flannel there."

"Oh, I meant the sun to shine on him; the stars to sparkle at him at night. I hear little voices in the wind singing for him. I want him to have flowers to look at and pull apart."

The man looked at her and shook his head. He settled into his blankets for the night.

The woman continued sewing straight white seams up and down squares of flannel. She threaded and re-threaded the needle, dreaming of her child.

That night while she was sewing she saw stars falling, running down the hill of the skies and disappearing behind the mountain. She wondered to herself, "If the stars never change, why do some fall out of the sky?" She watched hard for some minutes to see if certain stars would lose their place and fall. But they didn't. Rather, as if from some place beyond the familiar stars, the falling stars appeared and then began their descent. The idea of familiar and new stars held her breathless, and she spoke to the child within her.

"Did you know that there are old stars and new ones? Or maybe the old ones are those that fall out of the sky, and we just see their ending." She fell asleep and dreamed of the falling stars.

The next morning she was struck with the idea of making a blanket for the baby with stars on it. "I remember when I was little, ma had a blanket with patches and designs on it. I want to make the same kind of blanket, but with stars on it."

The man looked at her and jostled her arm. "Stars on a blanket, hey? Well, if you've got any of that cloth left you could make it, I suppose. But what's the use of it?"

She smiled, "There doesn't have to be a use for it except for me to look at. I look at the stars at night, and this way, I can carry the baby in them when he's born. And he can look at them when it's cloudy."

They walked many strenuous miles that day and came to a camp of cowboys and cattle. They settled near it and walked to the campfire. The cowboys greeted them with jokes and glances at her burdened figure. They sat around the campfire and shared supper and coffee.

"Yeah, this is as high as we'll take the cattle. You're welcome to the rest of this mountain," the foreman said.

"We'll go up to the broken pass and summer graze there," the man said, offering the cowboys his tobacco, and accepting a hand-rolled cigarette.

"Your wife going to have that baby soon?" the foreman asked.

"In about two months, she figures."

"You'd better send her down the mountain then. She'll need help with it." The foreman was father to seven children, and knew of the difficulties of childbirth.

"Oh, could I go down to a ranch?" she asked.

"You figure she'll need help? I'll be with her when the baby comes." Her husband exhaled cigarette smoke and glanced at his wife.

"Bringing babies is woman's work. You never know what might happen. Bring her down to our ranch, we have an old woman there who brings lots of babies."

"Well, I guess I can spare her for a couple of weeks." He took his wife's hand and held it on his knee.

"Why don't you let her stay at the ranch until you come back down mountain? She can pay her way by helping the cook. And she'll need the rest. You don't want her bringing the baby back up mountain."

"Oh, I'd like that." The woman sat back thinking about the society of other women, the talk she missed, and the help she'd have when the baby came. "I could make the star blanket then, if somebody would help me."

"Star blanket?" The foreman looked at her and then at her husband.

"Yeah. She got a notion the other night she wants to make a blanket for the baby with stars on it. No use in it, though."

"What kind of blanket is that, Missus?" The foreman spoke kindly.

"I thought I'd make a white blanket with blue stars on it. The baby could look at them when it's cloudy, and it could know what stars are right off."

"I have an old blanket like that." He stood up and went to his pack, pulling out a small saddle blanket of some Indian design. He held it out to her. "You can have it if you want."

She took it in her hands and smiled at him. The blanket was white bordered with bands of black and blue and with blue stars and lightning shapes. It was heavy, coarsely woven wool. "That's pretty. I take it with many thanks." She smiled again at him and stroked the stars.

"You don't have to give my wife anything like that." Her husband frowned in gratitude.

"No, no, take it. You can keep it for the baby, and it will be warm for him in the winter."

The foreman turned to the husband, "I mean what I say about

sending her down mountain when her time comes. You've got that horse, it'll carry her down in a couple of days."

"I'll have to think about it."

"Mister, don't take this unkindly. I've watched the two of you go up and down the mountain these years, and I know you're tight with a dollar. But don't be tight with your wife or your baby. You can't ever get them back when they're dead. So just risk the sheep for that last month and send her down to the ranch." He turned to the woman. "When you feel your time coming, ma'am, you just start down the mountain. If you need help down, I'll be glad to ride down with you."

"Thank you. I'll try to come down without help." She touched her stomach and sighed. "But how will I know when it's time?"

"My wife says when the baby moves down so you can breathe again, that's the time to get ready. So you just get on that horse and start down."

That night the cowboys talked and told stories about their lives with the cattle. The man and woman watched and listened. As it is with all lonely men they sang the melancholy songs and played handmade guitars. The woman saw them as beautiful and kindly strangers who shared her loneliness on the mountain. She saw the glint of their saddle decorations in the night light and watched their dark figures slump in the darkening, starfilled night. They spoke of towns she had never seen, one spoke of the ocean and its strangeness. He showed her some shells he had brought from the ocean shore. She held them and touched the water-etched designs. The cowboy had linked the shells together on a hand-braided cord. The shells tinkled together and shone blue and white under the stars.

"See, ma'am, the inside is shiny and smooth. The outside is rougher and dull." He turned the shells over and over. "Folks say that they've found shells like this up here in the mountains."

"What? Shells in the mountains?" She looked at him for the joke.

"Ma'am, I'm not fooling you. When I was down on the coast last year, I ran into a fellow who told me so. He said if we keep our eyes open in the raw parts of the mountain, sometime we might spot marks of shells and plants that live under the water.

I've been looking ever since then. But I haven't seen any." He poured the last of the coffee into her cup. "If you get up higher you might just keep your eyes open. You might find some. This fellow told me these mountains are still young. And that they've hardly finished growing."

"I never heard of such a thing." She looked at him sharply to see if he was making fun of her.

"The way he tells it, the mountains grew up out of ocean water, pushing and shoving each other, and carrying the shells and plants with them." He looked at her earnestly.

"I've heard some tall stories in my day, but this takes them all." Her husband rolled into his blankets and eyed the cowboy. "Don't fill her head up with any stranger ideas than she already has."

"Tell me the rest. How young are these mountains?" She leaned forward to hear every word.

"Ma'am, they're way older than we are. They've been here before white men or Indians ever came, but this fellow said that they are babies compared to mountains in other parts of the world."

She looked away from him to the mountain looming over them. "Could we tell if they were still growing?"

"I figure if this mountain ever starts to grow again, we can forget about getting off. I don't think a mountain's growing pains would be easy to take. This man said that when mountains grow they grow from the inside out, and parts break off." He smiled at her and said, "He didn't think they'd be growing any more for years, so don't you worry about it, ma'am."

"Thank you for telling me about it. My husband thinks I'm strange for thinking such things." She looked apprehensively at her sleeping husband.

"No, ma'am, you're not strange. There's a lot to be known about this world, and the only way I figure you can find out anything is to wonder about it and ask somebody. I've got some books back at the ranch, you're welcome to read them and look at the pictures."

"Thank you, I look forward to reading them. How did you get them?"

"Every winter when we're in slow times I go out to the towns and look around. There's ways to find books and ways to learn things. All you have to do is go out and hunt for them."

"Why do you look for books?"

"Ma'am, I guess I'm just part cat. When I see something I've got to know all I can about it. That star blanket you wanted. I think you're smart to give it to your baby. He'll grow up looking at the stars and maybe be a better or smarter man than his dad. I don't mean disrespect toward your husband, but every little shove we can give to another person, means they'll go a lot farther than we did."

He stood up and moved away from her. "I'd better let you get some sleep now. You listen to Jake and go down mountain when your time comes. And you read all the books you want. When winter comes, if you want, I'll bring you some more."

She lay rolled up in her blankets looking into the darkness where the cowboy had disappeared. Her mind hummed and murmured with the things he had told her. And he hadn't thought her strange for her thought and questions. She hugged the star blanket to her and fell into a deep sleep.

The sounds of men moving and the barking of dogs woke her. She lay for minutes watching the men in the dawnlight squatting over their coffee cups and tin plates. When her husband leaned over her, she smiled and struggled to her feet. They shared breakfast with the cowboys and left the camp. They had walked a mile when they heard a horse coming behind. They stopped and saw the cowboy riding up the slope. When he reached them, he stopped his horse and handed the woman the string of shells.

"I thought you might like these for that baby, ma'am. I'll be going down to the ocean again in a couple of years, and I'll get more." He saluted her with his hat and turned his horse.

"Thank you! Thank you!" she called after him.

"Well, he's a strange one. You forget all that fooling with shells and books." Her husband turned up the mountain and whistled at the dogs. She followed him, holding the string of shells and wondering at the cowboy's goodness.

That summer as they followed the sheep higher into the mountain she looked for marks in the raw sections of the ledges. She wandered from the sheep trail onto ledges and shelves, scratching into the sliding shale for the shell marks. But she found none.

She gazed into the side of the mountain as if willing it to disclose its hidden shells. As her size and awkwardness increased she was forced to ride the horse for the major part of the day, or stay in camp while her husband took the sheep to new grazing. When she was left alone she sewed more garments for the child or took slow walks with the horse, talking to it about the cowboy and what he had said to her. The horse had become doglike in its devotion to her and followed her, nuzzling her pockets for the sugar. She sat long hours on the mountain side, making bouquets of the spring flowers, garlanding the horse's mane with them, and laughing when he ate them indiscriminately.

The man changed with the summer, growing more irritable. He would watch her while she turned the shells over in her hands, or take out the star blanket and count the stars on it. He watched her find things on the mountain and rejoice over them, things that he had seen, unseeing, for years. What new dimensions she found and lived in were not of his liking, and he grew to dislike and then hate the mountain and her preoccupation with it.

"Next spring," he said, "we're going up another mountain. This one's been over grazed, and it's too crowded."

She glanced at him and then up at the ledged peak.

"We'll find new places on the next mountain. Maybe it will have shells like the cowboy said."

"You're wasting time looking for shells on a mountain. That kind of talk is for kids and old folks, we're looking for grazing land." He frowned at her and held her arm tightly. "You forget that kind of talk. And forget that cowboy."

"I won't. You always think I'm strange. But I'm not. I can wonder about anything I want to." She pulled away from him.

"You're thinking about that cowboy. I heard you talking to him, and looking at him." He raged at her, suddenly jealous, suddenly aware that she was more than a convenience.

He took her by the shoulders and shook her. She glared at him and ground her teeth. He released her and went to the fire. They had supper and lay down to sleep. After a few minutes he went to her and took her body fiercely to his. She lay passive, looking at him with a fresh awareness of his body. She felt the coarse hairs of his body and the perspiration running down his face. At once she remembered his kindness to her on that first night. What had made him change over the years? She felt the thrusting of his body and a quick discomfort about the child. She tried to push him away, saying, "Stop. The baby. You're hurting me."

He continued to thrust against her, determined to reclaim her from the mountain, to bring her back to the docile wife she had been. Through the haze of desire and his own loneliness he finally heard her words and their meaning. He stopped, resting heavily against her, looking into her eyes. She resisted him now not only with her body, but with her will. He turned away from her body and lay beside her. They lay side by side on the mountain slope. He gazing at her with a lonely despair; she lying silent, no longer resisting him, but mute and aloof, part of the mountain, removed utterly from his grasp, eyes turned inward to the remote workings of her own mind and body.

She lay resting softly against the mountain, listening somehow to the silent workings of the child within her, feeling the kicking and stretching of the unborn, sensing a rebellious anger in its movements. She touched her stomach, marveling at the fruitful fullness that jutted imperiously against the black night sky.

"Mountains grow from the inside out." It was that way with her. The vigorous, active wonder within her was pushing her body out of shape to accommodate its own demands, lying heavily against her spine. She stretched a hand out against the peaceful tilting mountain slope, feeling the roundness of it, imagining the massed bones and structure beneath. She nestled against the curve of the mountain and slept.

The next day they reached the summer grazing land. The mountain here was open for miles to flats of grassland and small ponds filled with ice water from underground springs. The sheep would graze for weeks before exhausting the ground cover. The man and woman set up a tent against a windfall of trees, gathered the broken, sun-dried wood into stacks for their small summer fire, and prepared for the weeks of wandering after the sheep during the day and returning at night to the same spot.

The woman continued her search for shells, although aware that none would be found in the grass-grown flats. She walked with the sheep and the horse, disappearing into the alleys that led up and into the mountain. From time to time she saw deer and rabbits staring out from the mountain's secret avenues, heard birds calling above her and felt the silence of the mountain. She walked daily higher through the trees and ledges, following dead stream beds into echoing chambers of the mountain's interior. As she picked her way deeper into the mountain she lost track of what she was looking for; listening to the stillness of the mountain and the creak of trees. She followed the mysterious silent voice of the mountain as it led her farther from her husband and his sheep to some invisible, lost, unspeaking essence that beckoned her and charmed her senses with a provocative, almost sensual desire. When night fell on the mountain she would drift down through the ground mists to the camp, lost in the wanderings of her mind, to prepare supper.

Her nights were filled with the campfire, her husband and his talk of the sheep, the alien duties of cooking and eating. She cooked and ate in silence, looking at the pots and plates, trying to recognize some familiar quality about them. Her husband's face, once so involved with herself as to be her own identity, now was foreign and harsh.

He would look at her over his plate, wondering at her silence. He spoke to her and received no answer.

"I shot a deer today," he'd say. "We'll have meat every day now and dry the rest." He'd pause and wait for her reply. None came.

"How's your sewing? You finish all that flannel?" He stoked his mouth with tobacco and closed the tin.

"Hey! Answer me!" He threw a stick at her.

She turned her head in his direction, inquiringly.

"Talk to me!" He threw another stick at her.

"Yes." She smiled in his direction, her eyes looking through him into the dark beyond.

"You are queerer now than you used to be." He rolled the to-bacco in his mouth. "Is it the baby?"

"The baby is fine. We walked into the mountain today. There's something up there." She took out the star blanket and unrolled it over her knees.

"What's up there? I suppose there's deer and a few bear. You be careful when you go alone." He peered at her, watching her hands stroking the stars on the blanket.

"No, there's something up there that I can't find. I can almost hear it. Sometimes when I come around the corner of a ravine I think it will be standing there. But it never is."

"You take a dog with you tomorrow. And take the rifle."

"No. The dogs might frighten it away. And I don't want to shoot it. I want to find it and see what it is."

Her husband stood up, throwing the remaining coffee into the fire. "Well, you better stay close to camp. Your time is almost here and you don't figure that thing in the mountain is going to help you any, do you?"

"No, I just want to find it." She opened her blankets for the night. "I feel like the baby is moving down. When can I start for the ranch?"

"I don't figure on letting you go. You talk so strange they might not let you come back." He lay next to her, holding her head in his hands. "You going crazy on me?"

She shook her head. "No, can't you tell there's something waiting in the mountain?"

"There isn't anything in that mountain but deer and bear." He pulled her down to his chest. "Now you just forget that crazy talk and think about how you're going to have that baby here in camp."

"You promised I could go to the ranch and have a woman help me."

She huddled beside him, her distended abdomen pushing him away from her as his arms tightened about her.

"No, I've been thinking. You go down mountain to that ranch and read those books about shells and growing mountains and you'll get so crazy you won't come back."

"I will come back. Oh, let me go down. I'm afraid of being alone when the baby comes."

"What help you need, I'll give you. If I can bring sheep, I can bring a baby." He looked at her cunningly, "If you stay here you can hunt for that thing."

She looked levely at him. "You are breaking your promise."

"Promises are for people who can use them. This promise is

better used broken. I'll take care of you and the boy when he comes."

Her eyes flickered and she looked away toward the horse.

"I'll be taking the horse with me everyday from now on, so you won't be trying to sneak out on him." He spoke with his eyes closed.

"I don't like you for this," she said. "If the baby is hurt by your keeping me here, it's all your blame."

"No blame will be coming. I'll take care of that." He slept leaning against her, holding her body as if to keep her with him even in sleep.

During the rest of her time, the woman walked restlessly through the mountain's interiors. She spoke to the mountain and the thing that haunted her. "Let me have the baby easily and quickly, don't let the baby be hurt." The listening air around her echoed upon the mountain walls, "Hurt."

Early in the morning her labor began. She went into the tent and lay on the blankets. Her husband watched her face and said, "I'll just take the sheep out to the grazing and come right back." She nodded and he left.

When he didn't return when she expected him, she crept out of the tent to watch for him. She lay on her side against the yielding slope, resting between pains, holding the star blanket to her, twisting it between her hands when the pains reached their peak, relaxing when the pains subsided.

She watched the sun climb the hill of the sky and descend. At times it seemed as if she must fall off the shoulder of the earth and down into the sky. Moments went by that she clung to the side of the mountain, feeling a pulsebeat under her, hearing a beating in the air as if the mountain were heaving with her and falling out from under her. She was sweating heavily, her body sliding within her clothes, her hands were slippery in the grass and on the blanket. The pains increased in rapidity and strength until she was constantly knotted with them, breathing harshly through her mouth. She was swept from the side of the mountain at one second, and pushed back into it at the next. Then, suddenly, the child was forced from her body into the air, and the mountain stopped twisting beneath her. She lay spent, watching the moun-

tain fall back into place above her. Then she sat up and reached
for the child. Its face turned up to hers, utterly lifeless. The cord
between the child and the afterbirth had strangled it, choking off
its first cry. She looked down at it dumbly, hearing a forlorn wail
from beyond her ken. She held the dead child to her, rocking it.
She twisted the cord from its neck, and covered the child and all
in the star blanket.

When the man returned he found her sitting on the slope, holding the dead child wrapped in its bloodied star blanket.

"I lost my way in those ravines. How's the boy?"

"He's dead. He choked on the cord." She smoothed the blanket
over the child.

"Let me see. Huh. He never got his breath." The man turned
the child about in the blanket, touching the round, puckered face,
the blunt features, the scruff of hair.

"Well, you rest. I'll bury him in the trees." He walked away with
the child.

"No, don't bury him up here. Let me take him down so he can
have a mark on his grave." She went after the man, reaching for
the child.

"No need in that. He died here and he can stay here." He laid
the baby under a tree and dug a shallow grave. She stood, leaning
against the tree, eyes averted. He buried the child and covered the
small enclosure with branches and stones. "This tree can be his
mark. He never needed more than that."

The woman sat beside the grave and dropped leaves gently on
it, seeming to hear a heartbeat from the buried child. She laid her
head down on the branches and closed her eyes. "I'll stay here
with him until morning. He might be lonely and afraid all alone."

The man nodded and walked to the camp.

That night, lying next to her child's grave she listened to the
sounds of the mountain and dreamed about the child.

In the morning the man prepared to take the sheep away to the
grazing. The woman went to the fire and cleaned herself. When
the man spoke to her she said: "You take the sheep today. I want
the horse."

The man looked at her. She found her string of shells and put
them into a pocket. "I'm going down mountain."

"What for, you don't need help any more."

"I'm going down mountain," she said stubbornly, "I let you strangle my baby with your ideas of keeping and using."

"I didn't strangle the baby." He stepped toward her, hands out.

"No, not likely, but it's the same." She called the horse and turned down the mountain.

"You figure you're going to find some shells?" He called at her, running after the horse. "You won't find any. Ever. There's no use looking!"

"I want to look. I want to see what it's like to look."

"You'll be back. You'll see. There's no use in it at all!"

"No, no use at all." She looked at him for the last time and rode down the mountain.

DAVID SHABER, born in 1929 in Cleveland, attended Western Reserve University, then Yale. He has taught at Allegheny College and Smith College. In addition to his writing, Mr. Shaber is involved in theatrical production. His work has appeared in *The Best Short Plays of 1952–53, Folio, The Grecourt Review, The Transatlantic Review, Venture,* and *Prize Stories 1961.*

PROFESSORIO COLLEGIO

from *Venture*

They turned into the street called Park Avenue, red-brick-hobbled and tar-streaked in the late summer sun. Except for being a little wider and straighter it was to Ira much like the rest of the streets he had ridden with Milt that hot, apartment-hunting afternoon; not one of them what could be called a professional piece of pavement set solid in its own contours but each merely unrolled across the top of the ground, improvised in face of the encroaching countryside that Ira could see through every backyard threatening to make the town no town at all.

"Man, I love it down here!" he heard Milt say, giving the steering wheel an exultant by-Jove smack with the flat of his hand. "Of course, I know I shouldn't talk," Milt went on, suddenly grave, to Ira. "You're the boy that has to be satisfied, not me. After all, it's going to be your apartment—if it should turn out to be okay, that is—and you're the boy. But I swear I can't help myself, you know? I mean, did you ever see such houses?"

Ira looked across the absolutely flat lawns at the houses. Weathered a uniform gray, all were vaguely out of plumb, a porch sagging here, an eccentric door-jamb there, as though something had

Copyright 1961 by Venture Publications, Inc. By permission of Venture.

let go inside, leaving them more leaned together than built. He
wiped his forehead with the handkerchief he had carried in his
hand for the last hour and thought of how he had looked forward
to establishing himself in his own apartment.

"This street does it to me every time," Milt was saying. "I have
to admit I honest to God am nuts about this street." Ira smiled
uncertainly. He had met Milt for the first time when he, Ira, had
come up to be interviewed for the instructorship at the college two
months previous. When he had discovered that Milt, like himself,
had literary ambitions, the bond was sealed. Now, contemplating
the round, crew-cut face of his new friend and the T-shirt sleeves
stretched like comfortable elastic bands around his biceps, he
thought Milt looked like no college professor he had ever seen.
What does he look like instead, Ira wondered. God, what do I
look like instead?

"I wish I was a little more familiar with the town, that's all,"
Ira said, and arched his back away from the seat, trying to lure
any stray late-afternoon breath down the inside of his own T shirt.
But the air in the car was utterly still and he slumped back again.
"Actually, I'm not sure I get the feel of it all yet."

"Of *course* you don't." Milt deliberated briefly, gathering his
sentences before going on. "Of course you don't. And what's more,
I don't think you should expect to. Ira, you're going to be a *fine*
teacher. That's all you have to worry about." After such delibera-
tive pauses, Milt's opinions had the considered ring of academic
research and in this way he made a great many surprising things
seem for Ira patently and reassuringly a part of the educational
process. The other two processes were, as far as Ira could tell, Art
and Life, and each had a vocabulary of its own.

"But, Jesus," Milt said, returning now to Art, "Jesus, just take
a look at those houses, that's all. Some place to live, huh? I mean,
when you think what this must've been. Man," he shook his head,
"I love it." He was halfway up the walk to the house displaying
the red-crayoned card *Apartment To Rent; Ask At Rear* before he
realized Ira was not with him. When he saw Milt waiting, Ira
opened the car door and put one foot out on the curb, on his lap
the folded newspaper he had bought that morning before he
started out.

"I was just checking the address," he said.

At the rear there were hollyhocks brittle in the August sun and the improbable odor of Parmesan cheese. With Ira hanging back, Milt rattled the screen door, then lifted his head in a long, happy smell. Ira wiped under his chin with the handkerchief. For a moment, even though he could hear muffled sounds from within, he thought no one might come and looked studiously at the newspaper. Then the woman's voice called, nervously and hoarsely Italian, "Yes, yes, please, you go up-a-stairs. It's a private entrance, you go right up-a-stairs and look all-a you want. You look all-a you want, please."

Milt winked at him and went promptly up the wooden steps that hung alongside the house, taking them two at a time. Ira heard the woman's voice go on rapidly in Italian and through the darkness beyond the screen door now he could make out a small man sitting in his undershirt at a porcelain table. The man was holding a coffee cup in both hands, elbows on the table and while the woman spoke made no response other than to grunt or nod indifferently. When he put the cup down and turned to look at the door, Ira went quickly up the stairs, holding carefully to the wooden rail.

Upstairs, the decor was maintained largely by the liberal use of blue-tinted mirrors. They hung in assorted blue circles on the kitchen wall, over the dark brown dresser in what was meant to be the bedroom, and when Milt, pacing delightedly from one room to another chanting, "*How* about this, *how* about this," passed the coffee table in the living room his smile had a bluish cast in the reflected light from the table-top, which was a mirror of blue glass.

"You see. You see, it's a nice-a place."

Ira turned and saw the woman of the voice below, immense and darkly moustached, enter the room. Still wheezing from the stairs, she gathered her arms about her bosom and gasped hoarsely at Milt, "You look. Around. Like I tell-a you?"

From then on events were only intermittently clear to Ira. There seemed to be some questions from Milt of hot water and telephones and from the woman answers of ovens and guaranteed steam heat plus the frequent assurance that the Last-a Boy stay here two years.

"And you could-a move in as soon as-a you want," she offered to Milt at one point.

"No, no," said Milt, "I'm not the one." Smiling at the woman, he pointed to Ira. "He's the one. I'm just a friend showing him around because he's new in town. He's the one."

"Ohhh," said the woman.

Ira nodded and smiled.

Milt hooked a thumb toward him and said impressively, "Professorio Collegio."

"Ohh," said the woman.

Ira nodded and smiled again. He was still nodding and smiling when they left her a few minutes later at the top of the stairs, her arms folded, contemplating the downward trip and calling after them, "Last-a boy stay here two years." Below, as he ducked past the overgrown hollyhocks, Ira saw from the corner of his eye the man in his undershirt staring through the darkness at the screen door.

In the car again Milt said, "Did I tell you? Did I tell you?" He leaned forward to put the key in the ignition, then glanced through the windshield and hesitated dramatically, shaking his head. "Man, this street."

"Yeah," said Ira. He was looking at the houses. "My God, do you suppose they're all crawling with blue glass like that?"

"Like what?"

"Like what," Ira echoed derisively.

"I didn't know it bothered you that much." Still bent to the steering wheel, Milt raised his head.

"I didn't say it bothered me, exactly. It just felt like an old Ginger Rogers movie, that's all. I just kept waiting for Ginger to waltz in, that's all."

"You know, that's interesting." Milt spoke carefully, turning to see Ira take off his watch and wipe his wrist with the handkerchief. "Of course, to me that blue stuff and everything, to me it's actually part of the basic charm of the place. I'm telling you, this was really the street."

"Yeah, I guess it was." Ira strapped on his watch again. "Well, we going to sit here the rest of the afternoon, or what?"

"Not to mention," Milt went on, "not to mention the material you could pick up from that momma. I know I'd take it just to live over her. Man, I think she's a gold mine."

"I know you do, *paisan*," Ira laughed. He shook his head. "*Professorio Collegio*. Oh, brother."

"What was wrong with that?" asked Milt, flushing.

"Oh, nothing. *Professorio Collegio*—that's all!"

Milt tossed the newspaper to Ira's lap. "Go ahead, cross it off if you don't like it." He punched the key into the ignition, and they jerked away from the curb.

Ira looked at his finger tips. They were soiled and greasy with ink from continually re-pressing the creases in the paper. "I don't know. Maybe I should look for something unfurnished."

"You got money for a stove and refrigerator?"

"Milt, I just don't understand that. I mean, God, in Cleveland every unfurnished apartment has at least *some* sort of stove and refrigerator."

"This isn't Cleveland."

"But, Jesus, you wouldn't think there'd be that much difference in eighty miles, would you?"

"Don't worry about the difference."

"Who's worried? It just happened to strike me, that's all. Jesus, who's worried?" Ira said. He took a deep breath and picked up the paper again.

When they turned the next corner Milt said, "Well, I don't know where to go. We've been through everything in town." They drove in silence for another block. "And *excuse* me, but for sixty-five bucks a month you're not going to get a better deal in this town, I can tell you that. In fact, I'm still trying to understand what more you want."

"I didn't say I wanted more," Ira said. "I never said I wanted more."

"My God, she even threw in the phone for free."

"Yes, she did, she did." Ira wiped under his chin with the handkerchief. "Of course, all kinds of other factors enter into it," he said, glancing back to the paper. "You know."

"For instance."

"Oh, I don't know. Well, for instance," he said casually, still looking at the paper, "and this is only a minor consideration, but just for instance, there's my folks to think of. You know. I mean, graduate school was one thing. Sure, I lived in all kinds of holes, what the hell did I care. You know graduate school—"

"Look, I don't know what you expect," Milt interrupted, "but if you think this place is a hole—"

"Who said anything about this place? Jesus, wait a minute, will you?" said Ira in a grieved tone. "I was just mentioning graduate school, because to my folks I'm a big professor now. You know. And actually Cleveland is only eighty miles away."

"So?"

"So it's only eighty miles, and if I know the folks they'll be here every other weekend at least, dragging my grandmother and God knows who else. Naturally, the place I have will be important to them, especially since this will be the first apartment of my own for them to show off. I'm out of graduate school now, and they think it's time I re-entered the world of the living, I suppose. I don't know. Anyhow, I ought to *try* and find something semi-respectable, so they don't have to worry about bringing people," said Ira.

Milt settled back carefully before he spoke. "Ira, I can understand perfectly how your mother and father feel but I'm afraid they'll have to learn they can't run up here every three days. You won't have time for them, Buster. You're a teacher."

"Oh, they don't have to be hit by a train," Ira said. "They'll come once or twice and they'll see how busy I am, and that'll be the end of it. But even if they're only eventually here four or five times, why embarrass them? As long as it doesn't cost me anything, y'understand," he added hastily. "And for instance, I've never had all my books at graduate school, and my Dad and I built these bookcases so I could finally have them with me. I could never jam *them* in that little blue heaven. I mean, there are a great many other factors, as well. Basically, I'm just not sure the place is quite what I saw for myself, that's all."

Again they were silent for a block, when through the window something caught Ira's eye.

"Hey, wait a minute," he said, twisting now to look through the back of the car. "Wasn't that a For Rent sign?"

"Was it?" Milt asked.

"Yes, in the window of that brick job, right on the corner. Let's take a look."

"Oh, that one. Ira, you don't want to go back there," Milt said.

"Sure I do," Ira said. "Why don't I?"

"Because it'll ruin you, that's why. I know the apartment, and it'll ruin you for anything else. It's a gorgeous joint, but in the first place the rent is ridiculous, and in the second place it's unfurnished."

"What do you mean, gorgeous?"

"I mean gorgeous," Milt said. "A regular luxury building. Helen and I looked at a suite there when we first came to town. Believe me, you'll be ruined."

"Okay, but *how* gorgeous?"

"Ira, listen, it's unfurnished."

"I still don't know what you mean by gorgeous," Ira said.

Milt looked at him. Then he pulled the car over.

"All right," he said, watching the traffic, waiting for a chance to turn around. "It's your funeral."

They parked behind the cream and salmon-colored Cadillac in the drive. Ira led the way to the door and pushed the button beneath the polished brass nameplate. Somewhere inside there was a faint sound of chimes. "You know it's unfurnished," the woman said when she came to the door and looked at them. She was deeply tanned and when she raised her hand to brush back a careless wave, Ira caught a glimpse of silver fingernails against the even brown of her forehead.

"Yes, I understand it is," Ira answered quickly. He reached to tuck in his T shirt where it had come out in back. "You see, we're from the college. I mean, we're instructors on the staff."

"Well, it's this way," the woman said, and Ira, followed by Milt, walked quickly after her into the soft shadows of the hall. As they went up the broad double stairway the polished mahogany balustrade slid smoothly under his hand.

It was over thirty minutes before they came down again, thirty minutes of double sinks, disposals and blond woodwork, of three and a half rooms with high ceilings, walls in pastel Sanitas and walk-in closets. There was a bath in leaf-green tile, a window seat under dormer windows, and a short pipe, now capped, sticking up through the kitchen floor where the stove had been. On the last step coming down, Ira ran his finger slowly, reluctantly off the groove in the mahogany banister.

"I'll definitely be checking back with you on this," he said to the woman at the door. "Definitely." He looked up once more through the stairwell to the third floor. "The whole thing is that stove and refrigerator."

"All right. If you're interested you can get in touch with me," the woman said and closed the door.

Going back to the car they said nothing. Ira climbed in and sat limply. "Well, take me home," he said at length. "I'm ruined."

"Sure you are," said Milt. "I told you."

Ira leaned forward so he could look through the windshield at the third floor and wiped his forehead with his handkerchief. "Boy," he said fervently, "what would you give? Just what would you *give*, that's all." He could not stop smiling. "Couldn't you just see my folks finding me there? I mean, just for instance." And now he laughed out loud. "Man, am I ruined."

"All right, take it then."

"What?"

"Sure. Go ahead, what the hell," Milt said.

"Oh, Milt, come on. How could I take it, will you tell me? Where does a measly instructor come off laying out one-ten a month for an apartment? I mean, *how* could I take it?"

"Yeah. I guess it isn't really feasible," said Milt, as they backed out of the drive away from the Cadillac.

"Of course, it isn't," Ira said.

"Too bad," said Milt.

They waited in silence for the light at the corner. When it changed they made the turn toward town.

"Actually, though," Ira said slowly, "*actually*, though, if I could somehow maneuver a stove and refrigerator it might not be *completely* out of the question." He continued casually after a moment. "Naturally, that still does leave the rest of the stuff."

They did not look at each other.

"Well, of course, *I* think you'd kill that place with too much furniture," Milt said thoughtfully.

"I'm glad you said that," Ira nodded vigorously, "I'm awfully glad you said that, because that's what I thought, too."

"Oh, you'd absolutely kill it," said Milt.

"Only a few simple pieces," Ira said, "that's all."

"That's right, keep it simple. Keep the lines clean. A few chairs, maybe, and a foam rubber couch—"

"And I can knock that together myself—"

"Why not? Why not?"

"And the bookcases will do a lot for the living room, anyhow, when I get them there. I mean, I keep the dust jackets on my books, and they're pretty colorful," Ira said earnestly. "Now I don't know for sure about the stove and refrigerator, y'understand, but I may have an idea. I don't want to say anything more about it until I know definitely, but I just *may* have an idea." His voice dropped a notch. "Of course, it's still a helluvan extravagance, Milt."

"As a matter of fact," Milt said deliberately, "it's exactly twice what the woman was asking for the other place, if you want to be specific. But you know what I think? I think you should take it. Listen, each person has to have one luxury. It's essential. Believe me, Buster, when school starts a decent place to come home to will be mighty important."

"Well, that's the way I figure," Ira said. "And I do want to work at home, too. You know. I mean, I didn't want to say before, but I do know I couldn't actually get any *writing* done in that blue heaven we looked at."

"Ira, you want to be careful," Milt said and frowned. "You can't always expect—"

"Oh, don't misunderstand me, I can write anywhere," Ira interrupted blandly. "That isn't what I meant. In fact, you remember last night when you got into the relationship between the educational experience and the Messianic Impulse, and I happened to bring up this stupid little campus musical I wrote? The first thing that got me really interested in writing? Well, I neglected to mention *where* I wrote it. Brother, *there's* a story I ought to write some day." They had reached the main shopping block in town. Milt pulled over to the curb at the drug store across from the supermarket. "Where you going?" asked Ira.

"I told Helen I'd pick up a few things for dinner."

"Sit a minute," Ira said. "This is worth hearing, I want you to hear this. See, I had the whole second act to do over Christmas, and I didn't know where to go. To work, I mean. The fraternity house was out—there's always a bunch of make-out artists who use it as headquarters over the holidays. Boy, that's one thing I found out about myself. When I work, really work, I can't have anyone near me. In the next room, even. Which means home was out, too. *Obviously*."

"That's something we all go through," Milt said.

"Yes, but wait a minute, I just want to tell you," Ira said, raising his hand for silence. "I finally arranged for this apartment right in town, from two graduate students who were going to be gone over Christmas. My God, I even remember I gave them ten bucks for the place, too. All I had to do was feed the cats. They had two kittens they'd picked up somewhere—Noodnick and Where's Charley, I never knew which was which. Otherwise, that was it. I didn't even give my mother the phone number, because I knew she'd be down or calling every twenty minutes if I did. Just packed a bag and went."

"Sounds like an ideal set-up to me," said Milt. "I could use something like that myself for a couple weeks."

"You could, huh," said Ira. "With the bed unmade except for an old gray sheet—I swear, it was actually gray—and greasy pans all over the sink—the whole place smelled of lamb chops, anyhow—and crumbs and dust over everything sixteen inches thick? Sure, it *sounds* ideal, but Jesus. Squalor Incorporated, I swear. Thank God my folks *didn't* see it." Ira laughed. "Boy, I set up camp in the living room and didn't budge—only from the couch where I slept to the little table where I wrote. It was the weirdest five days I ever spent in my young life, I'll tell you that."

He raised the hand with the handkerchief to his forehead, then hesitated midway and laughed. "I remember, after a while down there I got to feeling I didn't exist, actually. I mean, I didn't go out except for sandwiches and catfood, and nobody knowing where I was and sleeping in my clothes, just working until I'd get tired and then sacking out and never knowing what time it was when I got up—well, it was like nothing was real, like I wasn't really there, or anywhere. I don't know how to explain it, it was so crazy. For instance, I'm sitting at the table once, and I hear the kitchen window open. Then I see this hand come in from the porch and dump a bowlful of fishheads on the floor for the cats." Milt winced. "Sure, that's bad enough, but the point is, *I* was supposed to feed the cats. I mean, I said I would. But she didn't even come around to the front door. Just this hand coming in the window and dumping it and walking away, like I wasn't there, like nobody was there. It was just like I didn't exist, that's all. Oh, it really got to be something cute. Like, you ever been afraid to blink?"

"To blink?"

"See, I'd wake up and lie there on that couch not knowing what time it was, and ask myself, who am I? I'd just lie there asking myself who am I, who am I, who am I, over and over. I mean, right out loud. And the more I asked it, the more it seemed like I wasn't in my body at all, like I didn't have anything to do with me. All of a sudden I'd get scared that if I so much as moved a muscle, if I didn't stay absolutely rigid, the real part of me would float out of me up to the ceiling. Sometimes my hands would ache for an hour afterwards, I'd have them clenched so tight. I'd just lie there rigid, trying not to blink, not even to move an eyelash, asking myself who am I. Oh, it was cute."

Milt's eyes wandered out the window.

"Anyhow," Ira said, "when I woke up one morning around the fifth day, I found Noodnick and Where's Charley playing on my chest with one of the fishheads."

"Jesus," Milt said.

"Yeah," said Ira. "That was all, Brother. I was out of there with the second act finished that night. But the point of the whole thing is, I wrote, didn't I? And if I could write there, I guess I can write anywhere. That's what I meant about the blue place being bad for writing. By comparison, I meant. Now, of course, you take this *last* place," Ira said. "That would be a positive pleasure. God, who couldn't work there?"

"Not to mention how nice it would be for your folks when they come up," said Milt. "Man, they'll love it."

"Oh, no question about it. Milt, this is an *apartment*, you know what I mean? Of course, I don't know for sure about the stove and refrigerator. I'll have to check and I don't want to say any more about it. But I may have an angle, who knows?" Ira sat up abruptly and pounded his fist into the palm of his hand. "You know, I just may take the place, how do you like that?"

"Oh man, what a year this could be," Milt said happily. "And, Jesus, I really think you're going to be a fine teacher, too. I knew it when I first laid eyes on you at the interview." Milt opened the car door. "Ira, you're going to be *fine*," he said. "Really fine."

Milt crossed the street to the supermarket. As soon as he saw him disappear inside, Ira got out of the car and hurried to the drug store. Inside, he asked for a dollar's worth of change, then stepped into the phone booth. While waiting for his number he tried to turn on the little fan overhead but it would not start and he reached for his handkerchief. Then his father answered and the operator said sixty-five cents please. As the first coin hit, his father said, "What is it, Ira?" His father felt about pay phones much as he did about slot machines and while Ira dropped in the coins he kept saying, "Ira? What is it, Ira?"

"Dad, it's me," Ira said finally. He heard his father say, "Ira," away from the phone and knew his mother must be there in the kitchen, too. "Dad?" he said.

"Yes, what is it?"

"Something just came up and I wanted to talk to you."

"You had to call?" his father asked. "I thought you were coming home."

"I am, but this thing came up, and actually it's fairly urgent, it really is." He paused for a moment. "Dad, I finally found an apartment."

"So?"

"Well, I wanted to tell you, and to ask—"

"Is this why you called—to tell me you had an apartment?" his father interrupted at the other end.

"All right, wait a minute, will you? There are some simple problems about it that I wanted to discuss with you. I just wanted to *ask* you, that's all."

"Go ahead. Ask," his father said. "I don't know why you had to call, but go ahead."

Ira looked for a dry spot on the handkerchief. "Well, you see, the place is unfurnished, and I wondered if—"

"What do you mean, unfurnished? You have no furniture."

"Oh, I'm not worried. I'll scrape something simple together. I mean, that's not—"

"How?" his father interrupted. "What are you talking about?"

"Oh, it's all right, I'll manage. That's no problem, actually. The real problem is a stove and a refrigerator and what I *wondered* was—"

"Ira wants to take an unfurnished apartment," his father said off the phone. "Oh, my God," Ira heard his mother say.

"Dad—" Ira called into the phone.

"Without a stove and refrigerator," his father went on.

"Is he crazy?" his mother said.

"Dad, listen—" Ira said.

"Ira, how can you take an unfurnished apartment?" his father said, into the phone again.

"Well, I'm trying to tell you, aren't I? Jesus, I—"

"How much is the rent?"

"—What?"

"The rent. How much is it?"

"Oh. Sixty-five a month. I guess."

"You *guess?*"

"*I* don't know."

Off the phone his father said, "Sixty-five a month for an unfurnished apartment." "Oh, my God," Ira heard the answer. "When is he coming home?"

"Ira, you'd better come home," his father said.

"Tell him I'll put supper on for him," his mother said.

"Your mother's going to put supper on for you," into the phone.

Ira said, "Well, it looks as though I'll *have* to wait until I'm home before we can discuss this with any *semblance* of sanity."

"All right. Your mother's got supper on." As he hung up, his father said, "Please, Ira. *Think* a little."

Coming out of the store, he saw Milt looking at him quizzically from the car. "Cigarettes," Ira said brightly, holding up the package he had bought after leaving the phone booth. "Listen, Milt," he went on, "would you mind terribly if I took a raincheck on supper tonight? It's this angle on the stove and refrigerator. I mean, it's just an angle, that's all."

He kissed his mother as he always did when he got home and immediately went upstairs. Entering his room he hesitated, looking at the two bookcases neatly filled with books. They were large and leaned a little away from the wall. Ira had tried wedging them backwards to fit flush, but then there was a gap at the bottom, so he had taken the wedges out and left them that way. Ira put his hand on the top shelf of the nearest case and rubbed slowly back and forth. The shelves were rough and not sanded or varnished; Ira was going to do that after he settled them in his apartment. He continued to stroke the wood absently until his mother called him to come down and eat, it was on the table.

After they had finished, his father pushed back from the table, glanced at his mother and said to him, "Now, Ira, what's about this apartment?"

"Nothing," Ira said quietly. "It's an apartment, that's all."

"Did you take it yet?" his mother asked.

"Of course not. How could I take it without some sort of stove and refrigerator?"

"Well, *that's* something, anyhow," she said to his father. There was a pause while Ira lighted a cigarette. His father looked at his mother.

"You mean *I'm* supposed to find you a stove and refrigerator," he said.

"I just thought you might have some idea where I could pick them up. Second-hand, I mean. They don't have to be much."

"I'm sure they don't. Ira, you must be out of your mind. Where would I get such ideas?"

"I just thought you might know somebody. Listen, it happens to be important to have a decent place when you teach," Ira said.

"You mean all new instructors have apartments like that?" his father asked.

"It's all right, never mind," Ira said. "I was thinking on my way home, anyhow. I mean, I'll find the things for myself." His father and mother exchanged smiles. "It just happens to be a gorgeous apartment, that's all."

"I should hope so for sixty-five a month in a little town, unfurnished," his father said. "Didn't you look at any other places, furnished?"

After a moment Ira answered, "Sure, we looked at other places."

"Weren't any of them cheaper?"

"A little bit. Some of them. I don't know."

His father leaned forward and tapped his finger on the table. "And this stove and refrigerator you're going to find—how're you going to get them down there?"

"What's the difference?"

"No, just tell me."

"Dad, in a trailer. I mean, you can rent trailers for practically nothing. I thought maybe you and mother could bring it with you one of the times you come down," Ira said.

"Ira, it's eighty miles. You talk like it was around the corner." He looked at Ira's mother.

"Yes, your father can't run out there every minute," his mother said.

"I just thought maybe some Sunday with the Kohrmans—"

"Ira, the Kohrmans aren't interested in running out to your apartment," she said.

"My God, it's only eighty miles," Ira said faintly.

"Only eighty miles," said his father, smiling and shaking his head at his wife.

"Of course," she said to Ira, "we'll try and come out once to help settle you, if we can."

"Ira, I'm sorry, but I just don't have the time to run out there every minute," said his father.

"Oh, sure, sure, I understand. I mean, I understand that," Ira said. He got up suddenly. "If anybody phones for me, I'll be upstairs."

"Who would phone? Nobody knows you're in town," his mother said. "And, Ira," she called after him, "I don't care how warm it is, please don't come to the table in your undershirt."

In his room, Ira went directly to one of the bookcases and took out the first book. He opened it, then closed it again, feeling it closed with both hands, and put it back. Then he took the next book. He went down one shelf this way, taking the books out one by one, not reading them, just taking the books out and putting them back. Halfway through the second shelf Ira sat in the small bedroom chair near the bookcase. He put the book he was holding down on his lap and bridged his forehead with his hand. He sat like that for some time before closing his eyes.

The sound of a voice awoke him. For a moment he did not remember where he was. Then he recognized his bookcases and realized it was his mother speaking on the phone in her bedroom. He could hear her distinctly. "Yes, that's right," she said and paused.

"That's right, an *un*furnished apartment. Can you imagine him?"

When his legs went rigid the book on his lap fell loudly to the floor, and from the next room his mother called, "Ira, are you all right? Are you all right, Ira?" Ira stared at the ceiling, very careful not to move, the knuckles of his clenched hands bloodless. It was several moments before he allowed himself to blink.

Meanwhile, he told her he was fine.

MARY DEASY was born in Cincinnati, Ohio, and attended the University of Cincinnati and the Cincinnati Conservatory of Music, where she received a Bachelor of Music degree. She has published seven novels, which have been widely translated, and her short stories have appeared in *Mademoiselle, Harper's, The Atlantic Monthly,* and *The Yale Review.* This is her third story to be included in O. Henry Award volumes, and several others have appeared in collections of *The Best American Short Stories.*

THE PEOPLE WITH THE CHARM

from *The Yale Review*

"And what about that Mrs. Duggan, if she calls again?" Mrs. Feeney said. "Shall I tell her to leave this house in peace for a change tonight?"

"That won't be necessary," Monsignor Boyle said. He cracked another walnut carefully between the silver nutcrackers, glancing across the table at Father Mazzoni with his narrow smile. "Father Mazzoni will take care of that."

"Three nights running," Mrs. Feeney said. "She ought to know by this time that the man has no intention of dying. He'll live to see all of us under the sod."

She had gathered up the last of the dishes from the table, but she lingered there in the doorway of the big dark dining room as she always did when dinner was over, holding on to the opportunity to talk to Monsignor when he wasn't off in his study or in the parlor with visitors, or out helping some family in the parish celebrate a wedding or a christening or an anniversary. She could have talked to Father Mazzoni at any time, of course, except when he was busy with his religious duties, but she seldom bothered to look

The Yale Review, copyright 1960 by Yale University Press.

into the parlor when he was there alone. Usually, when she did, it was only to remark that it would be a good deal better for him to go out and take a long walk for himself than to sit cooped up there in the house like a moulting bird with the fidgets, or to complain because he had disarranged Monsignor's magazines on the table beside the armchair.

"Monsignor hasn't time for magazines," she said to him firmly, "but he takes these to give callers something proper to read if it happens they've to wait to see him. *That's* what he takes them for, not to have them mucked about till they look like a dozen of those kids down at the drugstore have been at them, *with* their cokes and their ice-cream sodas."

Father Mazzoni was a very young priest, and it was not so many years since he had been warned away from the magazine rack in a drugstore himself, though in a neighborhood a good deal less prosperous than the one St. Anne's parish included. He knew he ought to have been firmer about the matter—after all, the magazines didn't belong to Mrs. Feeney any more than they belonged to him, and Monsignor had told him to "help himself to the whole place" when he had first been sent to St. Anne's a year before—but after a while he had stopped picking up the magazines at all. Instead, when the weather was even passable, he had taken to wandering out to the back yard, where there was a hedge for privacy and neither parishioners nor Mrs. Feeney for whom to have to keep up an appearance. The people next door were not Catholics, and the only ones in the family he ever saw in their yard were an eleven-year-old named Francine Stoke and her six-year-old half-brother, Henry Carlson. He hadn't even become acquainted with them till he had started a garden in the spring and they had come over to the hedge to watch.

"Father Mazzoni has his packing to do," Mrs. Feeney was suggesting, to Monsignor. "The last assistant you had here, that Father Heston, I was a month clearing out the things he'd left. *And* his tennis rackets, if you please, he was forever writing me from that new place of his, would I find them and send them on to him, *and* this pair of old shoes he said he had, *and* a tobacco pouch that had *Made in India* stamped inside. This time anything that's left behind goes straight to St. Vincent de Paul's, and that's the end of it."

"I'm sure you'll have no trouble with Father Mazzoni," Monsignor Boyle said. "Father Mazzoni's a very reliable young man." He nodded across the table to Father Mazzoni, the smile lingering on his narrow, clever, agreeable face. "The Boss was saying that very thing to me only the other day," he said. "'What poor old Mick Flynn needs up there at St. John Evangelist's is a dependable young fellow who can hold the parish together for him without running it any farther into the ground than Mick and the good Lord have already done between them'—I believe that was the way he put it. He told me he thought very highly of the work you've done here at St. Anne's."

It was no good reminding Monsignor that if the Archbishop really thought so highly of his, Father Mazzoni's, work, he wouldn't be burying him in a little town and a little church as assistant to a fumbling old priest who wouldn't have needed an assistant at all if he had had the health and energy to look after his few parishioners. Monsignor knew as well as he did how the situation really stood—even better, in fact, since he was undoubtedly the one who had engineered the whole thing. He and the Archbishop were old friends and classmates, and it would have needed no more than a discreet word from him to do it. "That young Father Mazzoni you've sent me, John—well, he's a nice lad, and I've no doubt he'll polish up into a fine parish priest one of these days, but isn't he a bit of a rough diamond for St. Anne's just now?" Father Mazzoni could almost hear him saying it. He knew well enough that he was a solemn, awkward young man, and that he was so silent with some of Monsignor Boyle's grand rich parishioners that they must have wondered sometimes whether he had a tongue in his head at all except for the Latin in the Mass, but all the same it was painful to him to think of Monsignor and the Archbishop discussing him and finding him wanting. And what made it worse was that Monsignor was so polite and considerate about it that he couldn't even be angry with him; he could only envy, in silent despair, the inimitable *savoir-faire* with which he was carrying off a disagreeable situation.

This evening Monsignor had been invited to drop in at an anni-

versary reception for one of the city councilmen and his wife, so
he left the dining room early, and Father Mazzoni, faced with the
alternatives of barricading himself in his own room against Mrs.
Feeney's overeager offers to speed his packing and of a cheerless
February evening outside, chose the latter and went out to the
back garden. The early winter dusk was already so thick there that
he could scarcely make out the bare, hummocky ground just beyond the spirea and weigela where he had planted his little garden
the spring before, and he walked on back, poking rather forlornly
with the toe of his shoe at a last stump of cornstalk still decaying
on the ground. The garden had been one of Mrs. Feeney's abomi-
nations—the parish house and its surroundings were, for her, of
too august a gentility to be desecrated by lettuce and beans—but
he had planted it in his first naïve confidence in Monsignor's
lavish "help yourself to the whole place," and by the time he had
found out his error it was too late.

Still, some of his happiest moments at St. Anne's had been
spent out here, weeding the lettuce patch, staking up the tomato
plants on broiling summer afternoons, with Francine Stoke and
Henry Carlson watching him across the hedge. Francine was a
rather weedy-looking little girl herself, thin even for the scrawny
age of eleven, and with indeterminate colored hair, but they had
understood each other almost from the first moment they had confronted each other across the hedge, she with her little brother,
Henry Carlson, attached to her like an appendage.

"My name is Francine Stoke," she had said to him on that
first day, and he had said, "I'm Father Mazzoni," and she had
said, "Yes, I know all about you. You're the new priest who's come
to live with Monsignor Boyle and Mrs. Feeney, and my mother
says you're Italian."

She had a great interest in nationalities, he discovered that first
day, and had catalogued everyone she knew along that line. Her
mother, she told him, was half French and half English, and her
own father was all English, but Henry Carlson's father was Swedish, so that Henry was half Swedish too.

"Isn't that peculiar?" she asked him earnestly. "To have your
own brother half Swedish, when you're not Swedish at all?"

He said no, he didn't think so; things like that often happened when somebody's father died and their mother married again.

"Oh, but my father isn't dead," Francine said promptly. "He's divorced; I see him every summer." She added: "My mother says his relationship with her was a failure; that's why we don't live with him any more."

Father Mazzoni could think of nothing in particular to say to that, so he had returned to his spading and had made the dirt fly for a few minutes. He had seen his neighbor, Mrs. Carlson, a lovely and expensive-looking lady who affected very high heels, very dark sunglasses, and very vivid colors in make-up and clothing, as she made the hurried passage from her front door to her car, and they had exchanged *Good mornings*, but no more than that, because he had the feeling that she disapproved of him. Or perhaps that was too strong a word; like most charming, successful, happy people she simply did not bother to see a young man who was neither charming, successful, nor happy himself.

"We had a beautiful house then," Francine said reflectively to him, across the hedge. "I mean, when we lived with *my* father instead of Henry's. It was every bit as nice as this one. But my mother says what difference does a house make if you don't like the people who live in it."

"That seems sensible," Father Mazzoni cautiously agreed.

He rested on his spade for a moment and measured with his eyes the plot of ground before him, planning where he would put the tomatoes and where he would put the beans. He was a little nervous about the line the conversation was taking; that was before he had learned to know Francine well, and to realize that in talking to her he had no need to be encumbered by the dignities or penalties of his position. She lived, indeed, in the strange world of precocious childhood, with her childish values carefully hidden away because they had already met prematurely with ridicule or disillusionment, and her grown-up values merely parroted by rote, because she had not yet learned by experience what they meant. She and Henry dropped into a companionable silence with him now, and then attacked him minutely on the subject of exactly what he intended to plant; after that she went back to her former subject and informed him that her mother had a great deal of charm.

"She says that's all a person needs in life," she said. "Charm—that's it. Do you think that's right?"

"Well," Father Mazzoni said, grasping at his theology in spite of politeness, "there are a few other things—"

"My mother doesn't think so," Francine said. "She says charm has got her everything in this world she ever wanted." She paused a moment. "I'm going to have charm when I grow up," she asserted then.

Father Mazzoni looked at her weedy figure and indeterminate hair and wondered, but he kept his disbelief to himself.

"My mother says it's an absolute necessity," Francine went on. "She says there isn't a thing in the world more important for a woman—or for a man, either." She looked down judiciously at her small, stolid brother beside her. "Now Henry," she said, "hasn't any charm at all. He never will have. My mother says so."

Father Mazzoni had the feeling that she was trying to estimate what amount of that commodity he had himself, but, if she decided he was lacking in it, it didn't seem to affect their relationship. As the summer went on, they became very good friends; hardly a day went by that she and Henry Carlson didn't come down to the hedge to inspect the progress of the tomatoes and the beans, and when she returned at the beginning of September from a month in camp one of the first things she did was to go to see the changes in the garden. He gave her and Henry each a ripe tomato, warm from the vine, and she told him how she had won first prize for swimming at camp. She fished the medal out of her blouse pocket for him to admire.

"That's a tarpon on it," she said. "They're very good swimmers too. My father caught one once, in Florida."

Father Mazzoni said that it was a beautiful medal.

"I think so," she said. "But my mother says swimming isn't important as long as you've got slick-looking legs in a bathing suit."

She dropped the medal back into her pocket and began questioning him on what he had done while they were gone. She had a great curiosity about what went on inside the four walls of the parish house: she had asked him once, for example, whether he and Monsignor Boyle really sat down after dinner with their cigars or their pipes and their evening papers, just like the other men on the block who went downtown to their offices every day. And what did they talk about to each other at mealtimes, and were they like a family, that had disagreements and shouted at one another sometimes, or was being a priest like being in the army, where you always had to be respectful to everybody who was higher up than you were? Father Mazzoni always tried to answer her questions clearly, but he had an idea that she still did not understand the situation. Once she asked him if Mrs. Feeney had a husband, and when he said she had had one, but he was dead, she had asked him was Monsignor Boyle's wife dead too, and was that why he and Mrs. Feeney lived together?

This evening, standing over the ruins of his last summer's garden in the cold February dusk, he found himself looking across at the lighted windows of the house next door, wondering if he dared go over and say good-by to Francine Stoke and Henry Carlson. He had never been inside the Carlson house, and he felt that there was a sort of embarrassment in the way of a clergyman of a strange faith calling uninvited at anyone's house—as if he were a policeman, whose very uniform gave scandal by proclaiming that he was on official business. He was standing there, eying the house irresolutely, when he caught a glimpse of something moving in the yard next door. It was Francine Stoke running across the winter lawn toward him, looking oddly incomplete without Henry Carlson beside her. She came up to the hedge, and he saw that she had on only a light sweater over her dress.

"I saw you from my window," she said, breathing a little quickly from her run in the sharp night air. "I often sit up there, you know, without a light—thinking." She paused to note the effect of that, and then went on at once: "You're going away—aren't you? Mrs. Feeney told me."

"Did she?" Father Mazzoni said.

"Yes. She told me this afternoon when I came home from school; she said, 'Well, your friend's going away, so you can stop hanging over our hedge from this time out.' And I said, 'Who's going away?' And she said, 'Father Mazzoni.' She doesn't like me, does she?"

"Well—" Father Mazzoni temporized. After a moment he smiled a little, ruefully, and said, "Well, I guess she doesn't like me, either."

Francine Stoke looked at him seriously; he saw her small, weedy figure—she had grown during the past year, but she hadn't filled out—in the darkness.

"Is that why you're going away?" she asked him suddenly. "Because your relationship with Mrs. Feeney and Monsignor Boyle is a failure? Is that the reason?"

He said it wasn't, and he tried to explain it to her about the Archbishop's having to transfer young priests from one place to the other as they were needed, but he thought privately that her explanation was probably nearer the truth than his. His relationship with the other two people in the house *had* been a dismal failure—but then, he thought, in a sudden moment of anger, the fault had not been entirely his. He had come into their pleasant, happy, agreeable life with his diffidences and his awkwardness, and they had made him feel that he was an encumbrance of which they would rid themselves as soon as they decently could—exactly, he thought, as Francine Stoke was an encumbrance to her charming mother, as all the homely, left-handed people of this world were encumbrances in the lives of the more vivid, more sought-after ones who happened to be saddled with them. Mrs. Carlson was right, he said to himself grimly; in this life, at any rate, it was the people with the charm who succeeded.

He and Francine stood there in the cold damp night air and said good-by.

"You'd better go inside now," he said, looking at the thin sweater thrown around her shoulders. "You'll catch cold, and your mother will worry."

Francine shrugged. "No, she won't."

"Well, you'd better go on in anyway. And say good-by to Henry for me."

She nodded, but she was obviously thinking about something else. After a moment she asked him abruptly: "Do you know what I was doing upstairs in my room tonight? I was concentrating."

"Concentrating?"

"Yes." She looked at him tensely; he saw her young-old face, pinched with cold, through the darkness. "If you concentrate on something hard enough," she said, "it's bound to happen. I concentrate on being like my mother every day." She hesitated, frowning slightly, in the darkness. "Maybe if you'd concentrate on being like Monsignor Boyle—" she said. "Did you ever think of that?"

Father Mazzoni said that he had not.

"It's not that I'd *like* you to be like Monsignor Boyle," Francine said. "I like you just the way you are. But my mother says a person has to concentrate on improving themselves." She was silent for a moment, brooding. "I'm concentrating right now on getting valentines tomorrow," she confided. "Last year I only got six, and there was a girl in my class who got forty-two. My mother said she guessed every boy in that whole school who could write sent her one."

Father Mazzoni thought that he ought to be able to find something in his store of theological knowledge that would prove to Francine Stoke—and to him—that there were more important matters in an eleven-year-old girl's life than receiving forty-two valentines on Valentine's Day, but at the moment he could not discover it. He only said encouragingly that he was sure she would do better this year—and added, rather unconvincingly, that popularity was not everything.

"No, it's not," Francine agreed conscientiously. "But it's nice."

He watched her weedy little figure racing back over the frozen lawn toward the house next door; maybe, he thought, she was right about herself, and the good Lord would see to it that she grew up into a beautiful woman, who would satisfy even her mother's fierce criteria of success. But as he walked back slowly to the house, the mood of depression in which he had come out deepened. It occurred to him that he might very probably never see either her or Henry Carlson again. Possibly Father Flynn would not object if he started a garden at St. John Evangelist's in the spring, but his pleasure in it, he knew now, would not be the same if the two children were not there to look over the fence and share his pride and interest in what he grew.

He went into the house by the kitchen door. Mrs. Feeney was

washing dishes at the sink, but she looked up from her work as he came in.

"Monsignor said to remind you to call Father Flynn about your arrangements," she said to him. "*Our* young man will be here on Tuesday, you know."

"Yes, I know, Mrs. Feeney," he said.

And don't slam the door behind you when you leave, he thought bitterly; she might as well have said that too. If she were in any greater hurry to get him out of the house, she'd have to pack his things and call a taxi for him herself. He was going on toward the dining room, but she stopped him to inquire: "Who was that you were talking to out there? I thought I heard voices—didn't I?"

"It was Francine Stoke," he said. "The little girl next door. She wanted to say good-by."

Mrs. Feeney shrugged her shoulders over her soapy dish pan.

"Ah well, *she*'ll miss you, I suppose," she said. "I said to her myself this afternoon, 'There'll be no use your hanging over our hedge from this time out, because your friend is going away.' It's not natural for a child her age not to want to spend her time with other children her age," she added disapprovingly.

"She's had an unfortunate upbringing," Father Mazzoni said. He felt a slow anger beginning to glow in him again at her easy assumption of superiority, and a desire to defend the Francine Stokes of the world against her smoldered quietly under his rather abrupt, stammering statements. "She's hardly a child, in many ways," he said. "She'll have a hard time in life, because of it."

"Well, you're right enough about that," Mrs. Feeney agreed. She emptied the dish water into the sink and wrung out her dish cloth with victorious finality. "She's a plain little thing," she said. "There's one sure thing: she'll never get a husband in this world."

Father Mazzoni walked out into the empty parlor and stood there with his head down, positively rigid with resentment. It had been on the tip of his tongue to say to Mrs. Feeney that any man in his right mind, given the choice of her or Francine Stoke at a nubile age, wouldn't have hesitated a moment before choosing Francine, but he knew that Mrs. Feeney, whose respect for Roman collars had been tempered by twenty-five years of keeping house for them, would probably have countered by implying derisively that, even if he had been in a position to make the choice, he was still hardly the type to set himself up as a judge of what was an attractive woman. As he stood there in the quiet, alien elegance of the parlor, with its implications of a life half genial, half monkish, in its authentic souvenirs of the Holy Land and its aroma of fine Havana cigars, his own impotence before her triumphantly advanced superiorities, before the remembered faint charitable indulgence of Monsignor Boyle's presence, rose up in him and almost choked him. He and Francine Stoke, it seemed, stood outside the warm walls of human certainty and joy, doomed in their own timidities and failure before the tolerant *superbia*—he liked the Latin word—of the Mrs. Feeneys and the Monsignor Boyles and the Mrs. Carlsons.

Then the thought of the valentines occurred to him. It was such a ridiculous idea that he put it aside—but it returned at once, and suddenly he said to himself, "Why not?" and before he knew it he was walking out to the hall to get his hat and coat.

"Where are you going?" Mrs. Feeney called to him, her sharp ears hearing the front door open from the kitchen. "There's Monsignor out for the evening, and if that Mrs. Duggan calls again—"

"I won't be ten minutes," Father Mazzoni said, and left before she could say any more.

He walked up the street in the freezing darkness. The gift shops and the stationery stores would be closed, he knew, but fortunately the drugstores were still open. He passed by Parkhurst's to go on to Dogan's, where the parish house always dealt, and Mr. Dogan himself, a tall knifelike black-haired gloomy man, came up to wait on him. There was no soda fountain in Dogan's, and the store was deserted.

"I'd like to buy some valentines," Father Mazzoni said firmly. "Several—valentines."

Mr. Dogan looked a little surprised, but he led the way over to the greeting-card rack, where he offered a small supply for inspection.

"You may not find anything to suit you, Father," he said doubtfully, looking at Father Mazzoni as if he wondered what kind of valentine *would* suit a man in his position. "It's rather late, you know, and I don't have the selection I had a little earlier." He

watched Father Mazzoni rapidly scanning the rack. "Something
for your mother—?" he suggested delicately, indicating a lacy one
off down in the corner.

"I'll take them all," Father Mazzoni said.

He had made a rough count, and he calculated that there could
not possibly be more than two dozen; it was not nearly enough
for his purpose. Mr. Dogan, on the other hand, seemed to be
thinking privately that it was entirely too many—but Father Mazzoni reflected, with a sense of slight, reckless exhilaration, that, as
his acquaintance with Mr. Dogan was likely to be as sharply termi-
nated in the very near future as his friendship with Francine
Stoke, it really did not matter. He paid Mr. Dogan four dollars
and fifty-five cents for the twenty-three valentines—he had counted
them as Mr. Dogan had added them up—and then left with a
cheerful good night. The only thing he could do, he thought,
would be to go back to Parkhurst's; perhaps between the two of
them he could fill up his quota.

At Parkhurst's there was a vociferous clientele at the soda fountain, just out of the early movie, and he had to inspect the valentines on the greeting-card rack without the assistance of a clerk.
Few of them were of the sort he would have selected if he had had
a choice, but Parkhurst's was running as short of stock as Dogan's,
so he had to make do with what he found. He brought the whole
lot of them up to the blond young lady behind the counter, who
was almost too busy being admired by the customers to pay any
attention to him. When she finally found time to add up the prices,
she stared at him a little doubtfully, but the arithmetic involved
in the sale of twenty-six valentines, all at different amounts, was
too much of a problem for her to have much leisure left for wondering what he was going to do with them. Father Mazzoni was
reasonably certain that she overcharged him in the end, but he
was in a hurry, so he let it go. Then he walked back to the parish
house with his prizes.

When he let himself in, Mrs. Feeney was on the telephone in
the hall. He paused there for a moment, thinking in dismay that
it might be Mrs. Duggan again, and that in that case he would
certainly miss the late mail, but he soon caught the drift of the
conversation, which was on the subject of blue flowered silk, and

gathered that it was not a matter of life and death. He went on upstairs to his room. There, as soon as he had closed the door, he emptied the forty-nine valentines he had bought out on his desk, and sat down to address them to Miss Francine Stoke. He varied his handwriting so that they would not seem to come from the same person, and, remembering the habits of small boys, printed some of them largely in pencil.

When it came to signatures, he had a knottier problem to solve. He did not know the names of any of Francine's schoolmates, and, even if he had, it would hardly have been feasible for him to sign them to the valentines. But he recalled how he, as a boy of ten or twelve, had hidden his own romantic pangs behind an ambiguous *Guess who?*—and he inscribed these words boldly beneath the first tender verse. The valentines from Dogan's, he saw now, on inspecting them, were almost all in the sentimental style—there was one, all lace and red-satin hearts, that had cost a dollar, and came in an envelope of impressive size—while the ones from Parkhurst's were comic and occasionally rather unflattering. He felt, though, that he could not afford to discard any of them. For some time, in the quiet, priestly silence of the house, with only Mrs. Feeney's voice murmuring discreetly of feminine vanities below, he sat signing the bright-colored cards, inventing new disguises, or recalling them from his childhood as he went along. A *Friend, Your Sincere Friend, Your Secret Pal, You Know Who*—he went through the whole repertory of anonymity. Then he put all the valentines into their envelopes and sealed them shut.

The stamp compartment of his desk portfolio confronted him unexpectedly with another problem: he had only twenty-eight stamps, he found, to send forty-nine envelopes through the mail. He sat there for a moment, considering; then he walked out into the hall. Mrs. Feeney was just concluding her conversation below, and he called out to her boldly over the stair rail: "Mrs. Feeney! Have you any stamps?"

"Stamps?" She came to the foot of the stairs and looked up at him mistrustfully. "How many do you need?" she asked him, after a moment.

"Twenty-one. Would you have that many?"

"Twenty-one!" Her upturned face expressed astonishment.

"You're turning into a great letter-writer all of a sudden, aren't you?" she asked. "Are you going to write that many all in one night?"

"Never mind," Father Mazzoni said. "Have you got them?"

She came up the stairs, grumbling under her breath. He felt an odd sense of exhilaration, watching her; it was as if he were involving her as his accomplice in a secret plot of which she would have been certain to disapprove if he had told her of it. She went into her room, and came out a few minutes later with a long crumpled paper of stamps.

"Nineteen—twenty—twenty-one," she said. "That'll be eighty-four cents, *if* you please, Father; there's nothing like moving for making people forget their little debts, you know."

Father Mazzoni reached into his pocket and counted the change out into her hand. But she still did not give him the stamps; she stood looking at him, withholding them, with her long-sharpened instinct to ferret out the least source of news from behind priestly discretion.

"And what might you be wanting with all of these, if I may ask?" she said shrewdly. "It's the first I knew of it that you had so many people to write to."

The answer sprang to his tongue out of the irreverences of his buried childhood.

"You'd be surprised," he said, and reached politely for the stamps. He was not at all sure that she did not stand listening outside his door as he went inside to place the stamps on the twenty-one envelopes, for when he came out again, with the whole forty-nine of them, all shapes and sizes, in his hand, she was just retreating into her room.

"Back in ten minutes," he called to her cheerfully. "I want to catch the late collection at the corner."

If she guessed, he thought, as he went out again into the cold February darkness, so much the better; he would not tell her himself, but he would like her to know that she had aided him in preparing a minor triumph for Francine Stoke. He would like all of them to know—Mrs. Feeney, Mrs. Carlson, Monsignor Boyle, and even the Archbishop—that there were times when, with all their charm, they could not have everything their own way, that there were times when the homely, left-handed ones could have some of the triumphs of life for their own, if only they would look around and find the way.

His mood of heady exhilaration carried him to the corner mail-box, and he deposited the forty-nine valentines inside with the satisfaction of a man who has made a victorious gesture in the face of fate. But walking home through a beginning sleety drizzle, past the Carlson house with its lighted windows below, where Mrs. Carlson, no doubt, was basking in the pleasant warmth of Mr. Carlson's admiration, and of the admiration of any other people who happened to be present, while Francine Stoke concentrated solitarily on valentines in the darkness above, he felt suddenly that he had been a fool—one ridiculous, unwanted person making a clownish gesture to deceive for a moment another ridiculous, un-wanted person into believing she was really glamorous and loved. How could he possibly change things with forty-nine pieces of printed pasteboard? A sense of the futility of his own actions mocked him, and he saw the long black car in which Monsignor Boyle was being driven up to his front door by an attentive pa-rishioner, a fellow-guest, no doubt, at the reception, as a symbol of the difference between their lives.

He and Monsignor went up the steps together.

"A bad night," Monsignor said, politely making conversation. "I suppose—Mrs. Duggan called again?"

"No," Father Mazzoni said. "I only went out to mail some letters."

He saw the front door open before them; Mrs. Feeney, it seemed, had been keeping watch.

"Oh—Monsignor," she said at once, deferentially. "I didn't ex-pect you'd be home so early. That Mrs. Duggan just called again, if you'll believe it—" Her eyes fell on Father Mazzoni. "But here's Father Mazzoni back too, at last," she said pointedly. "I suppose you can spare the time to run over there for a few minutes, Fa-ther, now that you've got all that correspondence off your hands?"

Father Mazzoni said that he would have the time. He started off down the walk into the damp, blowing darkness; glancing back once, he saw the two of them silhouetted, against the quiet monk-ish elegance of the house, in the lighted doorway, and he felt, though he knew that Monsignor would never be so indiscreet, that they were smiling together over his awkward youth. A dull pain of humiliation passed over his heart; still, as he neared the mail-box in which the forty-nine valentines lay waiting, he felt once more the secret exhilaration of revolt beating like a small drum of defiance within his head.

SHIRLEY ANN GRAU was born in 1929 in New Orleans, Louisiana, and studied at Tulane University, where she received a B.A. in 1950. She is the author of *The Black Prince*, a collection of short stories, two novels, *The Hard Blue Sky* and *The House on Coliseum Street*, and short stories and articles which have appeared in *Mademoiselle*, *Holiday*, and *The New Yorker*.

EIGHT O'CLOCK ONE MORNING

from *The Reporter*

My mother is standing on the front porch when we come down at eight o'clock one morning. Soon as she hears us, she spins around and pops back inside the house.

"What you see?" I ask her.

"Go brush your teeth," she says.

"But we haven't had breakfast," Rosalie cries. "Not even one bite."

"Go get it then," my mother says.

My old man is waiting in the kitchen, the way he is every morning. He always gets up early and has breakfast first, so the three of us can have the table to ourselves.

"Hi kids," he tells us. "You all dressed up for school?"

"Good morning, sir," we say politely.

"That's fine," my mother says.

"Where's Taylor?" my father says.

"Where is he?" my mother asks.

"He's coming."

Taylor is the youngest. He's five and starting kindergarten today.

"Go tell Taylor to come down," my father says. "You Carrie, go call Taylor."

Copyright 1961 by The Reporter Magazine Company.

As I leave I hear them talk about Taylor. It's a way they have of saying his name over and over again. They're crazy about his name, which is a pretty fancy name for a snuffly kid. They heard it on television one night when my mother's stomach was bulging full with him. So that's why he's Taylor.

I don't go up, just stand at the foot of the stairs and yell after him. I keep yelling until he answers, which takes a while.

Then I go back in the kitchen. My mother is finishing lunch for the old man; she's wrapping up the sandwiches. She's trying to get him to do something too—you can tell by the tone in her voice.

"Just a little way," she is saying. "Go see can you find out anything."

"Okay," my father says.

But she can't stop. She rattles right on, as if he'd said no.

"I'd gone myself, only this man comes up to me—what's his name? Lives in the house with the pink shutters down the next block. He comes up to me while I'm standing on the front walk, trying to see what I can see, and he says: 'You go back inside, lady, there's going to be trouble.' And I see him tell the same thing to Marie Armand standing out in her front yard."

"Okay," my father says again.

My mother doesn't seem to hear him. "You wouldn't think school'd make all this trouble. There wasn't no trouble when Carrie started five years ago."

"Six," I say but they don't hear.

"And there wasn't trouble when Rosalie came around to going."

"Yeah," my father says.

"Why it's got to be Taylor gets all the trouble?"

My father says okay again. I watch him go out the door and put the lunch box on the seat of the truck that is standing in the driveway, the truck that says Harris Plumbing Company. That's my father and his brother.

"Where'd he go?" Rosalie asks. These days she talks in a high-pitched whiny voice she thinks she got from Marilyn Monroe.

"He's gone to look at the school," my mother says. "Now shut up and eat."

Just then Taylor comes down. "Shut up and eat too," my mother says to him before he can open his mouth.

In less than five minutes my father is back. "Keep the kids home," he says.

"My God!" my mother says. "Them under foot all day!"

"You ask me to go look, I go look."

My mother gets herself a cup of coffee, and I know she is upset because she doesn't even like the stuff.

"There's plenty of police around the school," my father says, "and there's some other characters around too. So keep the kids out of it."

"Home all day." My mother rubs her hands together sadly.

"Now listen, you kids," he says, "if I hear you been bad today, if your mama tells me one thing when I get back, you won't think you been so smart."

Rosalie asks me: "You think you can do my hair today?"

"Okay."

"No peroxide streaks," my mother says.

My father has fixed himself another cup of coffee too, and he sits down with it. He must feel something is wrong, or he wouldn't be hanging around like this. Other mornings he stays just long enough to see that we got our arms and legs.

All of a sudden, there's some yelling in the street. "Hu . . . hu." No words. Not that we can make out anyhow.

My father heaves himself up. And the telephone rings. His head snaps around like a mechanical doll's and he says, "Rosalie, go get it." Which isn't necessary because Rosalie always answers the phone in this house.

He turns back to the window. Now, the way the house is set, he can't see anything unless it's right in front—and by the sound of it, the racket is a little way down the street. So he's looking at nothing. But he keeps on looking anyhow.

Rosalie calls: "It's for Carrie."

My mother says: "Who is it?" And to me: "Sit down."

"Michael," Rosalie says. I go back to eating my corn flakes because I know I haven't got a chance in the world of getting that call.

We can hear my mother answer. "No," she is saying, "she can't come to the phone."

"What does that character want?" my father asks me.

"Ask mama," I tell him. "I'm not talking to him."

He glares at me for a minute and then he breaks into a grin. He always did like his girls to talk back to him.

"A fine boy friend you got," he says.

"He's all right."

When my mother comes back, my father asks: "He's cutting school?"

"Wouldn't tell me nothing, but I can guess."

"To run loose on the streets. . . . Keep these kids out of it."

"They're not going one step out the front door," my mother says.

There's more noise in the street—a kind of chant now. "Hu, hu . . ."—and this time I climb on a chair and look out with my father. You can't see too much, like I said—just every once in a while three or four kids passing: they look like they'd be in high school. They are wearing black leather jackets, most of them, though it is a bright hot day, and they are walking right down the middle of the street.

"You know them?" my father asks me.

I shake my head.

"Not any of them?"

So I tell him that I haven't ever seen a single one of them.

"I figured they wasn't from around here," my father says.

"What?" my mother asks. "What?"

"White niggers," my father says to the window glass. "God-damn white niggers, spoiling for trouble."

In a couple of minutes a yellow Public Service bus passes. And somebody starts throwing at it. A shower of things bang into it, ricochet off the steel sides, clatter down to the pavement. The passengers all duck down. You can see their hunched-over backs and the tops of their brown paper parcels. A window breaks and the bus drives on and all there is left is a pile of glass in the middle of the empty street.

Taylor begins to drink my father's coffee, which is right on the counter by him. He isn't allowed to have any for fear it will turn his skin yellow, but my old man is so busy at the window that he doesn't even notice what Taylor's doing. When he looks down and sees that the cup is empty, he just hands it back to my mother and says, "More."

My mother is putting things in the dishwasher, with short jumpy motions. She knocks a chunk off a good plate when she bangs it against the sink.

My father says: "That was ice they threw."

"What?" My mother juggles another plate, but catches it in time.

"What they threw at the bus—it was ice."

"Where'd they get that?" my mother asks.

"Lots of places," my father tells her. "Everybody's got ice."

"I wouldn't like to get hit by a piece of ice," Rosalie says.

"Stupid kids," my father says, and I can't make out whether he is talking about us or the people in the street.

There are more of them now, laughing and yelling like Mardi Gras Day. One boy, with a blond crewcut, sticks his toe in the pile of broken glass and sends it flying all over the street. Some of the kids are carrying Confederate flags and some of them are carrying mops. They're holding them straight up in the air, and they kind of look like heads on sticks, old women's heads with the hair hanging down.

I start to say something like that but I don't, because I see that nobody is going to hear me, nobody is going to listen.

"Oh my God!" my mother says all of a sudden and she rushes off, yelling back over her shoulder, "I got to tell Mama she better not come for lunch."

"She must heard about this."

There was the sound of the phone dialing little trickling sounds like water. "How would she know over there, way over there? I bet there's lots of people don't know."

My father grunts and doesn't say anything.

My mother comes back from the phone and says triumphantly: "She didn't know anything about it."

Rosalie asks: "Can we make some fudge?"

"Anything to keep you quiet," my mother tells her.

They both get down on their hands and knees and start looking around in one of the low cupboards for the proper size pan. Taylor has found his kitten and he's feeding it cat food out of the can with a spoon. You can hear him singing to it.

Then it happens. I hadn't been looking out, so the first I know of it is when my father says, "Son of a bitch!"

But he says it softly so that my mother and Rosalie, who have their heads inside the cupboard rattling pans, can't hear him. And if Taylor does he pays no attention.

I look out. A diaper-service truck (painted all blue and white) has pulled up in front of the Fortiers' across the street. The Negro driver must be awful brave or awful foolish or maybe he just doesn't know.

He has taken the clean diapers into the house and put the dirty ones in the back of the truck and closed the door.

When the kids first notice him he is back in the cab. He has just started the motor and he is barely moving when they catch up with him. There are a dozen or so of them, and they dash alongside. Some run directly in front and the truck stops. Two of them jump in the open door and grab for the driver, only they keep missing because another kid is beating away with an old mop. He is swinging it with all his strength at the driver but all he hits is the head of one of the boys who have hopped the cab. And all the time bits of things, rocks or maybe more ice, are rattling down on the truck.

My old man bangs through the kitchen door. I go after him, fast as I can. First thing I notice is how much noisier it is outside than it seemed from the other side of the glass. There's a lot of confused yelling, and the kid who got smacked by the mop handle is standing a little bit back, holding his head with both hands and roaring, louder than the rest.

My old man stops at his truck and takes out a short piece of pipe. Then he walks down to the edge of our lawn, right to where it meets the sidewalk.

The Negro driver has got the kids out of the cab now and has shut the door. Now they are standing in a circle outside pounding on the truck. I see the back window crack into a crazy star pattern when a rock hits it, but it doesn't shatter.

"Run over them!" my old man yells to the driver. "Run over the bastards."

He can't hear him, not inside the cab. Some of the kids do and turn around, but they don't make a move toward him.

The driver is racing his motor, but he isn't moving. You can see his dark face peering through the windshield.

Somebody yells: "You gotta have a rope!" I don't know who it is. Everybody is yelling something. We hear it again: "Go get a rope!" And that does it. My old man says something very quietly under his breath and starts over to the truck. He moves to the front of it, and he takes hold of the first collar he can. He yanks on it; the kid goes sailing over backwards and he grabs for another. And I remember the picture on his dresser, the picture of him in trunks when he used to box at St. Michael's Arena. And all this time, over everybody else, I can hear him yelling: "Put it in gear. Run over them. Use the God-damn truck."

Maybe the driver hears him, because after a while he does shift (he doesn't have the clutch all the way in and the gears grind and scrape) and he begins to inch forward. Between the two of them, the slow-moving truck and the guy who is throwing people around, they get a little clear space. And then a little more.

Finally the truck slips through.

Everybody stands in the street and looks after it. Everybody except my father, who comes stalking stiff-legged back to his own yard. The kids mill around muttering; some begin to drift toward us. My father straightens up, the length of pipe in his right hand.

They look at each other. Just stand and look. My father lets them do that for a minute.

Then he yells: "Get out of here!" And he starts swinging the pipe around his head.

They disappear all right. Run off like water on oil.

My old man comes up the walk, rubbing his shoulder and swearing.

By this time my mother is standing in the door and has both her hands slapped up against her mouth and Rosalie is behind her, trying to push her way into the door so she can see too. Back in the house you can hear Taylor singing to the cat and he doesn't know that anything has happened at all.

My old man puts the pipe on the lowest step and clears his throat and spits into the flower bed. He spits again, as if there's something in his mouth he can't get out. Then he turns and looks back down the street. And when he talks it is to the street.

"Niggers and white niggers," my father says. As if that explained everything.

DAVID JACKSON, born in Lead, South Dakota, in 1922, left the
University of California in 1947 to study languages at the Institut auf
dem Rosenberg, in St. Gallen, Switzerland, and writing at the University of Denver. He is married to the painter, Doris Jackson. He
lives in Stonington, Connecticut.

THE ENGLISH GARDENS

from *Partisan Review*

Despite the shabby black tight suit, octagonal rimmed spectacles,
and bent stovepipe hat, the fact remained that Meredith Wilder
was a handsome young man.

As usual, his tallness, his fine light eyes under dark brows, a
strength about him had made him welcome in every group of the
crowded Munich *Fasching* party. He seldom had much to say.
His voice being deep and pleasant made up for that. Everyone
knew Meredith as an American poet, and his appearance, in the
costume of Spitzweg's painting, "The Poor Poet," was sufficient
indication to all the Germans there that he had wit—if of a concealed, American, Abraham Lincoln variety.

Suddenly, his quota of drinks reached, Meredith surprised them
all—their standards perhaps lowered by alcohol—by throwing off
his reserve, pulling a red drapery around him, and launching into
Escamillo's *"Si tu m'aimes, Carmen, tu pourras tout à l'heure
être fière de moi!"* Whereupon Munich's great mezzo, flinging herself into his arms, sang back, *"Ah je t'aime, et que je meure si
j'ai jamais aimé quelqu'un autant que toi!"* And they were immediately surrounded by an admiring circle. Meredith flushed attractively with pleasure. Several hours later, the Princess von P.,
an editor and translator, rewarded him for his gallantries. She

Copyright 1961 by Partisan Review.

drew her lips from his, as they were saying goodnight, and echoed Carmen's words.

He started home, rosily, in the grey dawn of Ash Wednesday along Munich's Ludwigstrasse toward the arch of Siegestor. He hunched his shoulders under a black wool cape, for the March air was wet and went straight to the bones. He twirled a bent umbrella. The glow of the party was still upon him. He made his way past the buildings of the University, the arch, and into Leopoldstrasse, that grand avenue of Munich's bohemia, Schwabing. He was heading for his pension on the edge of the famous English Gardens.

But block by block the bloom faded. Soberness came to sit on his black cape and bent hat. The moment was coming when he would have to face his conscience. It had done a lot for him. Without it, life might have been easier, but not so successful. Looks, health, and a natural laziness were always at work persuading him to treat his poetic talent even more lightly than he did. But no, his conscience had provoked him, far more than any ambition, to work and polish and finally be recognized—by authorities as vague as the *Times Literary Supplement* and as partisan as the publisher of his volumes of verse (three were serious, one was a children's book)—as one of the leading young American poets.

About himself, Meredith was modest. For every critic who called his poetry too often shallow and mocking, there were three who protested that he had managed the hardest of all things: to speak lightly of tragic affairs. Through all of this he pursued his own way. Unlike Paul Klee's defiant, "To hell with uncle, let's get on with our building," Meredith's pun, "I can only fly where I fly —and so the Shallows always come back to Capistrano," hid his fear that, perhaps, those severer critics were right.

He had money, a small income left by his grandmother, and he had been through good eastern schools; teaching in one of them, now, but for this year when he was enjoying a leave of absence and a Guggenheim Fellowship. Ostensibly he was here in Munich in order to be near the source of nineteenth-century German poets—post-Schiller to pre-Rilke—about whom he was writing, a vague enterprise. To a few friends and himself he confessed that his greatest enthusiasm for these poets flowered when he was composing his request for the grant. Actually, he wanted to live a little, particularly in Munich, a city he had first seen and grown to love at the end of the war when he had been a Private First Class and an interpreter at nearby Dachau. Neither the horrors of the concentration camp nor the apparent unconsciousness of these horrors in neighboring Munich had damaged his affection for the city. His mind did not work that way. The Baroque, the Rococo, the high-flown nineteenth-century romance of painters and poets, the buildings of the Assam brothers, the palaces of Nymphenburg, the riches of Lenbach and Caspar David Friedrich —these held his attention. He liked the size of the city, knew its opera stars and ballet dancers and celebrities like Erich Kästner. He had late morning coffees with them and got into theaters on their passes. And, what's more, he felt confident he was a favorite of theirs.

Now again, he started humming. A way of pacifying his conscience—without actually writing a poem—had come to him: he would send off that letter about Munich he had promised to his last serious love affair. She was back in New York busy, no doubt, with her own literary life; yet she was arranging a series of readings for him, next year. She kept urging him to write such a letter, for she claimed she could sell it, somewhere.

Thinking, humming, warming to the idea, he turned into the small streets and squares pressed up against the English Gardens. As he approached the pension walls he was as usual softly singing a song of Müller's—not quite as Schubert had set it.

His landlady, the Gräfin von Erlach, had rented him the library of the house. It was a big square tall room, four walls of books broken only by two windows onto the garden. The only door was backed by shelves and, when closed, disappeared into a section devoted to the journals of English tourists. He had the habit of picking up one of these on his way to his bath or the w.c. There was a fireplace which said, in deeply engraved gold-filled letters, *"Nihil Volo Nisi Ut Ardeat"*—I wish only to burn, a motto he now took to heart. He stripped off his poor poet's clothes, stood there slapping the back of his neck, did some knee bends and stretched his shoulders and arms, and then pulled on a wartime flight mechanic's suit in which he liked to work. Rubbing his hands, he paced around the room as was his habit, circling his writing table at the windows like a tiger cornering its prey. The pension was quiet, they all still slept.

At last, he began: "Dear girl, the pension is quiet, they are all asleep, and I'm filled with the honor of working in the small hours and, finally, writing to you. Here will be the letter about Munich, do you think it is worthy of printers' ink? This removable preface contains my love; but it can be considered as stationary, if you would like to announce it to the world. And now to the subject:

"Munich is a vast imitation, and as such is fortifying. I find it, also, an important city. Walking up the Florentine Ludwigstrasse to the classical Roman Siegestor, into the Left Bank Leopold-strasse, I am conscious of hoping some original of mine, one day, will be taken into the sleeping mind of Munich. In order that, ever after, dreamlike copies would emerge.

"A Munich rusticated palace is the dream of a Southern Renaissance; a pony-tail hairdo of a Munich Teen-ager is a dream of American Daring.

"The English Gardens, where we would walk in late Spring, is, of course, the dream of a dream. It is a landscaped Arcadia. Four miles long, one wide, the Gardens hold acres of trees, canals, lakes. At some exact moment of a sultry late Spring day, the Gardens proclaim their origins in that great painter of the nineteenth century, Böcklin. The city has vanished. There are bird cries straight from his brush. The sun slants across lawns, figures in date-less clothes trail along some way off, a column from the Golden Age (perhaps a smokestack) meets your gaze. The murmur of waves (traffic), a cry, and there sport Undine and dryads and jolly naked fat mermen looking like Wallace Beery.

"Of course, the illusion is forever being broken, but pleasantly so. For this is an arena of tourists and bohemian Schwabing. And there is the old Schwabinger, the pre-Hitler, Expressionist veteran sitting around on nearly private benches. He, like his contempo-raries, wears a collection of sweaters and scarves and carries what must be music or manuscripts or drawings. The rich Schwabingers take up tables on the two levels of terraces at the *Seehaus*, a vast restaurant on the edge of an artificial lake. They have dogs and cats, sometimes canes. But even on sunny days, late afternoon, a

kind of mid-European fatalism prompts them to carry umbrellas.
And, often enough, the sunset disappears into a rising of clouds
and the rain falls. These old Schwabingers laugh and wave to
friends off at other tables. 'That is Greta von Spielerin,' you will be
told, 'a great actress in her time,' or 'He is Rudolph Kunstler—you
must know his political cartoons of the 'twenties.' Everyone is
familiar. Munich is a *Millionendorf*—a village of a million people."

Meredith had an illusion of the ease and pleasure of writing,
this morning. Why hadn't he got up early, before? The pension
usually took him over, took him into its intimacies. The maids
lingered and giggled in his room after they cleaned. The Gräfin
and he held long conversations of a literary turn, she in English,
he in German. She told him stories of her father's friends, the
poets Mörike and Keller. And Meredith was lazy and gregarious
and liked having his work interrupted. Now, the words were rolling
out:

"The Gardens are fine for you and me and the old Schwabinger.
But Munich's Teen-agers, the *Halbstarkern* (half-strongs), its de-
linquents, its young art and literary worlds have no time for the
Gardens (although they are said to be handy for quick sex).
Sitting around in espresso cafés along Leopold, or in the two to
three basement bars near the University, they slouch, drink a lot
of coffee, wear blue jeans which, after all these postwar years,
finally have a true, worn, James Dean style. The girls wear tight
sweaters and pale lips and messy Brigitte Bardot hair. They ignore
each other and draw on menus. They come and go indifferently,
dropping into chairs, dragging each other across rooms and streets
to drop down somewhere else. They smoke one cigarette after
another and stump them out, moodily. With the intensity of their
German natures they are imitating the current style. And this, I
gather, is Beat. I am tempted to warn them of the outcome in a
quatrain called, *The Digger*:

> '*I dig Jazz and James Joyce, man!*
> *I dig Zen and Horse!' you rave.*
> *That's nice. Dig everything you can.*
> *You'll get around to your own grave.*

But I would be wasting my time. They . . ." Abruptly, he stopped. The truth was he knew little about Beatniks. "Damn little," he told himself, drumming his fingers. But he was diverted by the pension garden coming up more clearly into light. He peered out, noting how wet and brown it was, seeing a snowbird tramp around under some leafless berry bushes. And the prospect of weeks more of greyness overwhelmed him. He began imagining The South. Italy. The Mediterranean. Next, he remembered his old friend and fellow-poet, Walter Norman, a resident of Venice. He pushed the typewriter aside and reached over for a post card from a handy pile he kept on his desk. They were all reproductions from the Schack Gallery (with the exception of a dozen pornographic Rubens he had found at the Pinakothek). He wrote:

"Dear Walter, it's the old season of discontent, up here in Krautland. And we are all partied out. I imagine you in hip boots strolling around San Marco. Would you like a caller, namely me, Meredith?"

With a sense of accomplishment, he rose, took off his mechanic's suit, climbed under the quilts of his bed, and, in the middle of a new thought, went to sleep.

Approaching Venice by sea, at this time, was yet another poet, Nicolas Manas.

Unlike Meredith Wilder, Nicolas knew all about the Beat Generation. It was a question, in fact, which was the creation of which.

Ten years ago, fresh from reform schools and jail (an experience that had rather strengthened his belief in the goodness of man), after an apprenticeship as a black-haired youth in the harsh trade of Getting Along With Fellow Cons, Nicolas emerged with an eye out for the easy thing and chanced upon the makings of a literary movement. This was happening in a bar and restaurant on MacDougal Street, down in Greenwich Village—where so many movements have seen the light of day. Cloaked in his fortune's smile, creased khaki pants, and a torn black shirt, Nicolas encountered some young men from New York and Columbia universities. A few beers later these young men perceived in Nicolas's tough, optimistic, code-like utterances a New Talent. As the days passed Nicolas's new friends (mostly graduate students whose long, rather

Spenserian verses had appeared in university magazines) were quoting to each other notes Nicolas was apt to leave in their various rooms. For example this one, in an upper West side rooming house:

Man, do you snore! A trumpet of angels! I'm going over to walk on the river. I'll be around.

Or this one left in a Village apartment:

You got sex on the brain. Let's f . . k the stars, that's for poets.

His literary pronouncements were quoted, too:

"I walked in there, yesterday, and Manas's reading a book. He's all excited and yells at me, 'Hey, this Shelley's great!' "

"Shelley! . . ?" fondly but cautiously.

"Yeh, Shelley. Nicolas says Shelley's the Man of the Times." A legend was beginning.

As Beatnik letters grew and Nicolas began to become a "poet," both found simple candor a chief piece of equipment. In Nicolas it was more *over*-candor. Reaching for the heart of the matter, expressing the truth of his reactions to, say, jazz, cars, sex, or in describing his disgust with his listener, or his listener's with *him*, he often seemed so close as to be behind the subject. "I heard ya laugh. I get it! Listen, I frighten you, you can't take this love I'm offerin'." It dazzled, it intimidated. Above all—it provoked. Candor having produced this atmosphere, a quick switch to boyishness, to "yeah?" and "gee!" was usually enough to get what he wanted: a beer, a convert, a fix (marijuana, heroin, or opium), or at least a "connection," or money, or a place to stay—a "pad" in the new jazz language. From New York to San Francisco, Boston, Mexico, and points North and South, these pads became the footfalls of his nights.

Nicolas's other talent was toughness, a verbal persuasion when all else failed. "What d'ya mean you can't put me up for the night?" his loud voice was heard in many crowded rooms. "You too good for us around here?" Or from the platform he would interrupt his reading of a poem to ask the audience, "You people ever hear of this Alfred S . . . ? Well, the other night . . ." (and here *he* would be interrupted by a perfectly timed cry from a fellow Beatnik, "Read the poetry, get on with the poetry for Chrissake!") and whatever had been denied Nicolas was usually forthcoming.

It was a kind of Action Blackmail, and as Nicolas and his movement rose to fame with the help of their favorite muse, Publicity
—tracking them with her feet of column print—threats, personal
charms and abuse, etc., were needed less and less. At last they
could abandon former methods, former haunts, even former fads
like Zen Buddhism, Chinese poets and things Eastern, or West
American, and face that traditional theater where so many Americans in the arts find themselves, Europe.

But in these more celebrated times, Nicolas's profitable jailbird
past made getting an extended travel passport difficult; not as difficult as he imagined, for he had never entertained the idea of going
to a lawyer or the State Department, yet it would have taken some
doing to get his own passport. The Law, the State, Authority, its
Consequences, were among Nicolas's deepest seated fears. Such
fear accounted for some of his oddest lines:

Long hair, is that *against the law?*
and:
America, brush your teeth!
At the same time, such fear produced a petulance praised as anger
in his poems. During the crisis of the passport he began confusing
his fear with his creative activity and crying, "If they'd just let me
write poems!" The outer fringes of his audiences imagined he
meant The Muses or The Cruelties of Poverty. The inner circle
understood well enough, but they were amazed when he explained
to them the elaborate means he'd devised for securing a passport:
"I got this cousin, looks like me, who'll apply. . . . Say, any you
guys know if that ink really runs? Well, my cousin'll apply, oh,
maybe over in Jersey—that'd throw 'em off the track—and . . ."
To protests of why all that trouble and why didn't Nicolas just go
down and inquire, he turned such a startled agonized face, cover-
ing it with his hands and shouting through them, "You don't *get*
it!" that looks were exchanged and days of long discussion followed. There were telephone calls to law students, dimly known;
runners returned carrying "the word," speeches were made, and it
was even day-dreamed that Nicolas stood every chance of being
the new Paul Robeson. This suggestion was reluctantly dropped
when Nicolas, defiant and snarling, warned them, "One word

about this to the papers" (a new phrase in Beatnik circles) "and you guys'll see the *end* of Manas, get it?"

At last, on the day a prewar Venezuelan freighter was to sail, Nicolas, muffled to his ears in a great scarf, more than usually unshaven, crowded into a taxi with several glum friends and drove off to Brooklyn. One or two of them still had hopes a reporter might have got wind of it, but other things held the attention of the Press—Russia's ultimatum on Berlin, for example. So Nicolas's boarding and departure were like those of millions before him— long, cold, with feeble waves and spastic smiles from the rail. He headed down the harbor and off to sea.

Several days had passed since Nicolas's arrival in Venice. His host, Walter Norman, was standing on the fringes of a crowd surrounding Nicolas's table at Ciro's bar. Though he couldn't see Nicolas, he knew his guest's expression, the tears on his face, by the loud declaiming he could hear:

"What do you bullshit prosers *feel?*"

Answer coming from a famous tough novelist who, ten years ago, had written an army life novel raising a row of sorts and then becoming a movie:

"What d'ya mean feel?"

"Hah! you don't even know. (Buy me a beer, big shot.) Look, it's like I either feel love or I jump in a canal! See?"

"Listen, poet, suicide's *the* homosexual act!"

At this Walter decided to leave. It was past four a.m. and he was out of lire, this week's and next's. Hearing Nicolas's shout, "You too cheap to buy me a beer even?" Walter threw open the swinging door and lunged into the Campo Larga 22 Marzo. Arms flailing, head down, Walter ambled along startling those late passersby who did not know him. He was a man full of unexpected fears and major courage. He was a familiar sight in Venice and given to loud, shouted retorts when taunted. "You may kiss the ass of——" (the name of the place where Mussolini was buried), a Norman cry in a vast baritone, had brought cheers and applause one evening from the cafés around the Morosini. Italians understood bravado. His fire-engine red suit, double-breasted with red buttons, or his white suit, white buttons, brought Venetians to a standstill of respect as he passed along talking to himself or to a

group of friends moving from a cocktail party someplace to a dinner someplace else.

Poetry and poets were the two chief concerns of Walter's life.
Tonight, talking aloud, now and then raising his head to address
the stars, he had temporarily put his problem with Nicolas out of
his mind and was brooding about something that had occurred to
him some hours before. "Everyone's a four-letter poet, nowadays!"
he was telling himself, crossing a small high-arched bridge, "Moss,
Hall, Pack, Reid, Bagg, Gunn . . . my God!" Amazed, he
stopped still. "What does it mean?" he demanded, throwing out
an arm, oblivious of the two staring gondoliers beneath him. He
walked on. "Let's see . . . hmmm. The old five-letter ones, Eliot,
Frost, Pound, Moore, Auden, we can safely put them in a group
—poor Manas, out of his time. But what of the *six*? Old Wilder,
me! Damn!" Striking his fist he stamped down the narrows into
Morosini. As he crossed that large campo, the problem of Meredith Wilder came back to mind; he debated what to say on a card.
It would not do for Manas and Wilder to meet. "*Impensabile!*"
Walter announced. (Unseen, a couple in shadows nearby guiltily
drew apart.) He knew that Nicolas went through all the mail
coming into or going out of the apartment. "Impudence!" Walter
cried, "but what can you do? Manas is one of the angels, we *all*
are. Why shouldn't Wilder lend a hand?" Walter snickered. He
remembered that Nicolas planned to stay several weeks, possibly
months, in Venice. His snickers faded away. When depressed,
Walter liked to sing a German song. Imitating Lotte Lenya singing *Moritaten*, furtively looking around and putting his key in the
lock of his door, he was actually thinking that, perhaps, Nicolas
ought to be persuaded to see more of Europe. Maybe he should
suggest Germany. Yet he felt vaguely ignoble planning to send
Manas off, so soon, and knowing he was sending him to plague
Wilder.

His post card, which he took right out again and mailed, was
a reproduction of Caravaggio's Chastisement of Love and it read:
"Dear Meredith, I am at present up to my, uh, hips in fellow poets.
Manas is here. And there are many Early Morning Scenes being
played out. Do you know him? Otherwise I would say 'do come.'
Lamely me, Walter."

Eight weeks later, Walter's mind was completely changed. His reluctance to impose Nicolas on Meredith was worn down by the unrelenting exploits and exploitation of his guest. Door after door in the city was being closed to the pair of them. The third week of May a new danger evolved in the young American girl, Mary Jane Lerner, who took to following them around. At first, Walter was little more than bored with her and her rapt concentration on Nicolas. When he discovered that her husband was the tall, husky, frequently drunk man he had stayed clear of in several bars, the matter took on another light. This was all brought to a head one long night Mary Jane and Nicolas spent in Walter's *salone* drinking Walter's last bottle of gin and smoking two marijuana cigarettes. Walter heard it all from his bedroom where Nicolas had locked him, and they heard Walter crying to himself, "A scandal! Throw them out! Her husband is *over six feet tall!*"

"Listen, Norman," Nicolas called back, "you're not beautiful enough for us out here!" And then he went on to tell Mary Jane she must stop nursing her husband in his drinking and go forth with the saints and angels. Mary Jane, who had somehow supplied the cigarettes as the price of admission to an evening with her hero sighed, agreed, and listened. Walter sighed and listened, too, and as far as he could tell Nicolas's attentions were limited to advice and the improvisations of several long poems, but would Mary Jane's husband believe it? "*Poco probabile*," he muttered before, near dawn, he fell into a troubled sleep. When he awoke he found his door unlocked and without hesitating rushed out, bought a train ticket to Munich and returned. After much shouting and threatening, Nicolas was put on the late-afternoon train North. Walter also provided three ten-dollar traveler's checks, an amount which happened to be all his ready cash as well as three dollars short of return fare.

You arrive in Munich on that train in the early morning. You have passed the mountains and towns of Austria in the night— although later Nicolas liked to say, "Man, there they were, those Alps, lookin' like *Jedermann* in *Lederhosen* and I yelled '*Guten Tag!*' out the window and they all looked at me on that train."

Actually, he spent the time dozing and flipping idly through the pages of a book on Greek myths, the margins of which he had used

for memorandums of addresses and other useful information. Also
he read an article on Munich which had been written by Meredith
Wilder, and he narrowed his eyes when he came to a poem which
was part of the article. "What a drag, man," he said to himself.
And this he stored away, too.

He stepped from the train in the warm morning spring sunlight
and glumly started for the exits. Soon old habits prevailed and
within twenty paces his walk became a saunter and he looked
around with his habitual speculative eye. He saw that *Männer
Toilette* was off to the right and decided to check that, later.
Ahead he saw signs for exchange above brass-framed windows set
in a brown marble wall. He stood in front of the exchange rates
sign as he searched in his pocket for a traveler's check. He seemed
to remember that in dealing in tens you moved a decimal point
and added a zero. Having done this in his mind, he moved over,
straddling his canvas sack, and leaned on the counter. All during
the transactions he kept one finger on the top edge of his passport,
as the clerk copied from it, and craned to watch the computer machine—his sullen dark unshaved suspicion forced the clerk to use
this machine. Nicolas had figured the amount to be forty marks
and twenty-five pfgs (whatever they were); he was pleased, but
straight-faced, to receive forty-*two* marks and thirty, "Forty-two
marks and thirty pfennigs," the clerk explained, "twenty pfennigs
for exchange charge."

"*Ja*," Nicolas answered in German, giving the clerk one last
grave glance, and telling himself he would come back here unless
this joker got fired in the meantime. He stuffed papers, money,
and passport away and, picking up his sack, headed off for the first-
class restaurant. Imagining himself two marks plus to the good, he
intended having a beer.

He chose a table next to three fellow Americans and listened
while he drank his beer. He had just decided that they were only
college students and that there was nothing to be had there when
he heard:

Hank: How'd you make out, then?
Doug: Christ! I was down to my last five marks. So I took my
        sack out in the English gardens.
Bill: The what?

Doug: This big park the other side of Munich. Dark as hell, take anything you want out there. Not a cop in a kilometer.

Hank: Now where?

Doug (on a note of formality): My mother and father are at the Königshof. They came in yesterday. How about you guys coming to lunch?

Bill: Free? Yes.

Looking over at them, appreciatively, Nicolas gave a loud laugh. But as he was not noticed he subsided and, finally, having finished his beer to the last drop, paid, left. That square article on the city had been confirmed in one point, The English Gardens. Meanwhile he made off toward the toilets. Any criminologist will tell you that public lavatories and parks provide fertile grounds for his species of study. They had often provided Nicolas with his "connections." Many an hour he had haunted one or the other in major cities in the United States, in Mexico City, Venice. A line from a long Manas poem proclaimed:

I'll tell you this, Unclesam, R.R. station johns have been better pals to me than the Travelers Aid.

It was not yet ten o'clock and the toilets were empty. Philosophically, Nicolas turned away. No sense loitering when he knew what to check next. Nevertheless, Munich's worth had been damaged by a small part. It was becoming Square, in his mind, and it would soon stand for all of Germany.

Outside the tall exit was a man in a green uniform with white belt, cap, and gloves. Nicolas went up to him:

"The English Gardens?"

"*Bitte?*" The policeman studied him.

"The English Gardens," Nicolas repeated, slowly, louder.

"*Ah! Englischer Garten!*" Understanding was followed by another long look and the question: "*Griechisch?*"

"*Danke,*" Nicolas replied, using one of his five German words. And then in a tougher voice he repeated, "The English Gardens!"

A young German walked by wheeling a bicycle. He stopped, he smiled, "Are you an American?"

"*Ja,*" Nicolas replied, looking him over.

"May I help you with your problem?"

"No problem, just wanna look at these English Gardens."

The student, for that's what he was, as Nicolas had expertly guessed before dismissing him as a possible connection, briefly explained to the policeman and then turned to Nicolas: "You get on that tram (do you say tram? oh) it is number fifteen, and you change to number seven, north. Tell the conductor *Sieben* . . . I had better write it."

Nicolas produced his copy of the Greek Myths. As the student searched for, found, and wrote in a blank margin he asked pleasantly, "You are a student?"

"You might say," Nicolas answered, but without the usual provocative undertone.

"Ah, splendid. You have a writer named Emerson who said . . ."

"*Ja, ja,* I know what he said," Nicolas cut in, taking the myth book back, "I'll see you around." With that, he walked over to the platform in the middle of the downtown street.

"Good-bye!" cried the student. But, ignored, he started off with his bicycle and a bewildered look. The policeman had watched the whole of it and now called, "*I* think he's a Greek!"

The sun came out as Nicolas was squinting down the track. He fished out a pair of dark glasses. In a few minutes, pushing past the others, he stood blocking the aisle by the conductor's stand of number fifteen. He showed the directions and a two-mark coin, took ticket and change and then deliberately surveyed the car. No one interesting, all seats taken. He moved himself perhaps a foot out of the way and stooped to see Munich's large uninteresting center move by. *Squaresville, man,* Nicolas composed in his mind. He had better write a post card to Walter. He opened the myth book again and there (along the margin next to Robert Graves's imaginative interpretation of the creation of the Dactyls from Rhea's finger tips) were the names of four Munich bars and Meredith Wilder's address. The bars were marked as Walter had marked them in a small black book kept in a nearly secret drawer. The code, which had probably something to do with sex or other interest, Nicolas was determined to find out and put to use. A card to Walter would get him an introduction to this Meredith, and that might be good for something. Nicolas called on his muse, a line came back:

Squaresville, man, and all the palazzos are crummy Palasts.

That ought to draw a laugh, Nicolas reasoned, as he stored the line away on the wax tape that was his mind.

And, indeed, his post card did draw from Walter a letter recommending his friend, the poet Nicolas Manas, to his friend Meredith Wilder. Five days later, on receiving it, Meredith sat drumming his dactyls on his writing table. Dammit! he inwardly cried.

His hand was large and square and heavily tanned. The voice crying in him was the voice of guilt. His four weeks in Italy had turned into nearer three months. He had returned to the pension a week ago. Now, he was just in the late poems of Hölderlin and therefore had most of the nineteenth century before him—plus next semester's class preparation. He was determined to spend an industrious summer. Well, maybe Manas wouldn't call. Meredith's fingers slowed and stopped over a line before him: *Sie lächeln, die schwarzen Hexen.* The menace of Manas gradually faded as Meredith asked himself should he translate it, 'How the dark fates laughed'? or, more rhythmically, 'The swarthy witches are laughing'? And he missed the point that the swarthy witches might be laughing at him for hoping to escape Nicolas Manas.

But Nicolas, too, was being interrupted, that morning.

Not by the 11:00 sun which had spread a warmth around his spot of grass in the English Gardens and sent him off to sleep, but by a blond girl in a sweater and skirt who stood a few yards off and tenderly regarded him. Should she wake him? She didn't have the heart. Her heart, her maternal feeling, in fact her . . . her being was too busy expressing itself, as quietly thrilled by this sight of her Nicolas curled asleep under a blanket, in a park like a scene from Poussin. She was just not able to break the spell. (Would she have been able to had she known that the blanket belonged to a young ballet dancer Nicolas had found his first night in one of Walter's marked bars? Nicolas: "Look, Nicolas doesn't go to bed with boys —no sex, see? So if all these beers was to get me in bed, man, you just spent a lot of money." Ballet dancer: Protests, tears, and "take what you want, Nicolas, I am a dancer, you are a poet, it is all beautiful." To this meek conjugation Nicolas had replied, "O.K. I can use this blanket. And when you get off this job tonight, well, you can gimme something to eat." And, as a matter of fact, Nicolas had slept in the park only part of one night, when he discovered that Munich's early mornings even in summer are laden with dew. He had always known how to find a bed, and on his own terms. He used the blanket for late morning naps when hosts of the night had gone off to jobs and proved reluctant to leave him in their small rooms with their few possessions. Mary Jane Lerner knew none of this.) Her Nicolas lay curled in the sun like a faun, black hair falling over his eyes. She was telling herself that this might just be her reward at the end of a long meaningful search for truth. This was surely a reunion in art, it was all that poetry promised.

That long night with Nicolas and marijuana in Venice had opened her eyes. His advice, his voice saying his poems, the fact that he had not so much as touched her—on the contrary, he had put his head back and she had stroked *his* hair—this was all new. Her eyes had opened, she had caught a glimpse of a new faith.

The next day he was gone.

Mary Jane might not be the most intelligent woman, but she was one of the most determined. Even so, it took her several days to force Walter to tell her Nicolas's whereabouts. Packing a small suitcase, informing her husband, whom she found in Harry's Bar, that she was taking a train to Germany to get away for a while, patting his arm, refusing a drink, getting on the train—all this had only taken her two hours. She had arrived this morning and come straight to the English Gardens. "Dear girl," Walter had finally said, "he writes me that he is sleeping in the English Gardens." "How like him!" Mary Jane had smilingly said. "His address," Walter added, "is that great foundling home, the American Express. And I will greatly appreciate it if you will not tell your husband. . . ." For the last half hour Mary Jane had crisscrossed half the length of the Gardens and, at last, come upon her knight. His presence there, asleep in the grass, confirmed all that Mary Jane believed it was in his power to teach her: freedom from the tedium of needs such as hotels, the meaning of nature, how to live, simply, with the angels.

She set down her suitcase. Should she wake him? No. Smiling, she sat down on the suitcase and waited and watched.

The sun grew hotter as it approached the midday. Nicolas was dreaming he had his head pressed against the dashboard of a speeding car. He began sweating. In his dream he cried, "Slow

down, for Chrissake!" He half woke and rolled over with his face
in the cooler grass. His nose was tickled. He sneezed. He blew his
nose expertly between his fingers. He spit. He half sat up and
scratched at the hair on his forehead and then, more vigorously,
between his legs. He belched, he stretched.

Mary Jane got up, quietly, and walked away.

Twenty minutes later she was at the desk of the Gräfin's pension,
her tears dried, signing a hotel form and asking for a bath.

Mary Jane belonged to a world acquainted with small attractive
hotels and pensions in all the major and minor cities. She had
retreated to this world. The Gräfin, who was charmed by her, told
her, "Your sister who was here two years ago has quite *dark* hair.
Families are *very* interesting. Nevertheless, there is no bath. But a
young American has a bath next to his room and I shall ask him if
you might use it this once. And then we shall see. . . ." (The
Gräfin was partial to the word 'shall'.)

Meredith was irritated when the Gräfin knocked at his door and
told him, "She is a great beauty! Shall we allow her not to have a
bath? Actually, she is a sad beauty, I believe. You shall see her at
dinner." Rather erotically he listened to the bath water running;
when it stopped he began busily typing, sitting up in a virtuous
way. Before dinner, he shaved for the second time that day. A thing
he did not like doing, generally. Singing into the mirror and his
interested eyes, he was pleased to note, when he stripped for his
own bath, that he still had the best part of his Italian sun tan. He
flexed his muscles for several minutes, got into the tub, and then
grew self-conscious of splashing as he washed.

In the small gallery used as the guests' dining room, Meredith
sat down at his place and, as always, began teasing the young waitress. He was asking had it been she who left the love note in his
sheets (she also served as maid) when he saw the Gräfin followed
by a stately blond girl approaching his table. It would be literary
license calculated to glamorize life to say that he, oh, dropped his
napkin, so startled was he by Mary Jane's beauty. Yet he did drop
his badinage with the ordinary country girl as much in deference
to the Gräfin as acknowledgment that here, indeed, was something
special. Mary Jane had made very little effort. Above a dark green
skirt she wore a pale green cashmere sweater with, as he soon

perceived, no brassière beneath. Her white blond hair was clean and brushed long straight down to her shoulders. Perhaps her eyes were larger and more of a summer blue for all they had seen and wept that day. She had touched her face, truly a noble and pure face, only with a lip salve which made her lips glisten but no redder than usual. The result was grace and modesty. As she was rather tired this evening, her simple "Thank you for the use of your bath"—when she sat down opposite him—spoken in a low voice, came across with coolnesses of intelligence and control. Meredith began falling in love.

Soup: "Only this morning"; veal cutlets: "Oh, I couldn't possibly eat all this!"; wine: "Then you were typing poems this afternoon?"; fruit compote: "If you think I would understand it"; a smile.

"What a beautiful room. Like . . . *as if* it were built of books."

Having opened the windows onto the terrace, lit the fire, translated the motto, Meredith grinned and took down a little triplet of books bound together in old calfskin. Opening these he brought out a schnapps bottle and small gold thimble-sized glasses hidden inside it. "I think the maids tipple in the afternoon."

"Those sweet girls? Oh . . . you're joking. It tastes a little like poppyseed. What's its name? *Steinhäger* . . ." She whispered *Steinhäger* to herself, several times, memorizing it. "Would you first read the poem aloud to me and then let me read it to myself?" Meredith's voice was always deep, with rough bass notes in it; in reading, on platforms, even in the large auditorium of the Y.M.H.A., Poetry Center nights, his voice was intimate, thoughtful, and a trifle shy. His new poem, a love poem, told of a young husband leading his wife upstairs to the bedroom when the lights in the house have failed. The husband points the steps out with his flashlight:

> *Its white stare filling her pale eyes*
> *To the blind brim with appetite,*
> *Bleaching her hands that grazed my thighs*
> *And sent us from the table in surprise*
> *To let the dishes soak all night,*

(Mary Jane asked herself if Meredith was blushing at this line, or was it the fire?) But he read on. In the bedroom before the husband and wife find their way to the bed, the lights go on:

> *In dull domestic radiance*
> *I watch her staring face, still blind,*
> *Start wincing in obedience*
> *To dirty waters, counters, pots and pans,*
> *Waiting below stairs, in her mind.*

Mary Jane took the page from him and began reading it, moving her lips with the words. "Oh, it's that myth, about Orpheus and . . . What *is* her name? I can never pronounce it." She repeated "Eurydice" several times, watching his lips, and then read the poem again. She raised her face and nodded, "It's sweet, and very sad." They discussed the way people never tell each other the things on their minds. They finished the small bottle of Steinhäger. She confessed she was unhappy, he asked was it her husband? She began to explain, "There was this poet, in Italy . . ." He interrupted, "Please don't judge all poets." They smiled.

At her door, two or three hours later, Mary Jane whispered, "Everyone is asleep." Kissing her he whispered, several times, "Eurydice." The third time rather urgently. But with her hand softly on his cheek for a last moment, she closed the door and he went back down the hall and into his bed excited, expectant, and finally faintly grinning with the feel of her hand against his mouth.

The next morning, promptly, when the American Express opened its glass doors, Nicolas appeared and demanded his mail. He was suspicious of the place because someone along the way had said, "Get your mail there but don't let them change your money." This kind of advice appealed to Nicolas and he followed it so faithfully he was hardly able to be civil to the girl behind the mail desk. He had a suspicion that they held mail back until they had an opportunity to check it with Authorities (nameless). He always examined it in front of the clerk, blocking others who were waiting, smiling in a knowing way as he studied the sealed flaps. "Uh huh!" he would murmur, if there was any trace of smudge along the gummed edges.

As he'd figured, there was a letter from his publisher in New York—his rise in publicity had secured him a large hard-binding-type publishing house. The check enclosed was about a tenth of what he'd expected. (Had it been exactly what he had expected it would have been half what he expected when it arrived.) This check was so small he thought of tearing it up and mailing back the pieces. Insult to injury were a mass of featherlight proof pages he was asked to correct and return (with postage money from the check, no doubt, the bastards!). "Jesus!" he said aloud. But as no one waiting behind him asked what the matter was, he stepped to one side, seized an American Express pen and change of address form, scrawled on the back, "You got editors, *you* read these, N.M." By reaching over the counter to the clerk's table he got an American Express envelope, addressed it to his luckless publisher, stuffed in the proof sheets, and, as an afterthought, added, "You call that money?"

Other letters were from other Beatniks and there was one from Walter Norman: "I've written Wilder. Look him up. Now, that blond muse left here to follow you. And I've been spending hours of my valuable time dodging her six foot husband who does not seem to believe I know nothing about it. Yes, look up Wilder. Why should he get off free? Or is there justice in that argument? No, I cannot send any money. As it is you left me begging crumbs. What do you think I am, the Doge?" Nicolas smiled to see how tough Norman could be, by mail. He composed: "Dogs and doges in Venice/Sniff around together," put it on a post card (he always carried several, a habit he'd picked up from Walter) to mail off to his former host. He then turned his attention to his other letters, garnering bits of news from them (which for all their claims of innocence were surprisingly worldly): "You ought to find yourself in Athens around September. W . . . will be there and he's told L . . . that he thinks our stuff has something. And he's got the gold," and: "Heard A . . .'s going to be in Venice in August. A connection, man," and: "We talked R . . . into an edition. Send some stuff. You getting any poems out of Germany?" Registering all this, Nicolas made a quick inventory. Yes, he could get out three poems, two he had in his head, one on paper. This, for kicks, had been conceived as a result of a German typewriter he had found in an apartment, two nights before. It was entitled, "Sputnik II passes Munich," and it began, *"The quick brown fox jumped över the möön,*" and ended, "*Öld gaschambers are nöw making Völkswagens.*" Its quick and foxy conception that night had much impressed the typewriter's owner and been good for a subsequent breakfast and two dinners, where he was widely introduced as America's most famous young poet.

Even so, and especially this morning, Nicolas was ready to kiss central Europe good-bye. Having used the myth book so often, he couldn't have helped glancing at some of its content and it had already occurred to him that a few poems, mailed from, say, some Greek village, would have an extra kick. Greek stuff was always hot. But the plans forming in his head always ran up against a wall of gold. With the twenty dollars left from Walter's checks, and this morning's check, minus postage—the Bastards!—he had about forty or so. Frowning, he looked up to study the crowd—you never knew. . . .

Mary Jane, just then, walked in. He watched her go to the cashier's window and cash two checks (he'd have to warn her). He tried remembering her last name (damn Norman!). Perhaps she'd come over to the mail desk. Slightly turning, he leaned with his back close to the mail girl's window. His wish was granted, and he heard her say her name. He waited. She left, not noticing him; he followed.

He had not approached her at the desk because there were other Americans around, one of them might be a spy of her husband's. Patiently he followed along two blocks, boarded the same streetcar back to Schwabing. He paused while she found a table at a café and then made a casual approach, passing, as he did, another table where some recently made fans hailed him, "Hey, Manas, you after something?" It was a sunny late morning and Mary Jane was opening her Paris *Herald,* asking for coffee, exposing her fair head to lightly swirl in the currents of air. She looked up.

"Hello, Nicolas, I saw you in the American Express."

For a moment he was stymied. He pondered swiftly and then remarked, "I followed you. How come you here?"

Mary Jane was too quick, she out-candored him, "*I* followed *you,* but changed my mind, yesterday."

By now he was sitting down, had ordered a beer to give himself

time. She turned back to her paper. Anyway she might stand him a
beer. He began gathering his wits.

"It was like a dream, that night, huh?"

She replied, "Yes."

"I been thinkin' about you."

She smiled, "I thought about you, too—for nearly a week."

"Listen, thoughts cross each other. I believe that. It's a great
feelin'. . . ."

"Is it?"

"Look, I don't get you. . . ."

"You're right, there."

Although none of this made any sense to him, he instantly perceived a prize flapping away on dollar signs. Assuming his little-boy
face he looked up at her from under several locks of hair. "You
going to be Nicolas's angel?"

Mary Jane was swayed. This assault had come quickly, and he
did look ragged in that blue shirt and those pants, his eyes . . .
She forced herself to think of her *new* poet. Yet only twenty
seconds passed before she said, "No," once again. And as she said
it she waved to the waitress.

Not listening to the No's, Nicolas had only heard the pause,
seen the wave as a call for help, and he moved in, instantly:

"Lemme buy that coffee for you. Nicolas wants to give you
something, see?"

It was a good stroke, it would have been felt by others; however,
buying and giving were the creativeness of Mary Jane's life. They
recalled the barterings in her marriage to a man almost as rich as
herself. Had Nicolas asked her to buy him his beer, he might have
laid a fresh claim. Instead she answered, "No, you save your money,
Nicolas," in a kind voice. And to the waitress, who had responded
quickly to her call, as did doormen, taxis, salespeople (even telephones performed for Mary Jane to extricate her from situations;
she was generous with tipping), "*Danke*," she said, picked up
purse and paper, patted Nicolas's hand, and left.

He watched her easily bringing a taxi to a halt, getting in, and
disappearing up Leopoldstrasse. Although his thoughts were black,
Nicolas registered nothing on his dark face which he turned toward
the friends at the other table. They hailed him again and he took

his beer over to them. A half hour later he left, a plan in mind, having added to his luster by writing something at the table telling them it was a poem inspired by the blonde. "I'll give it to her tonight." "The poem?" an acned student from Minnesota asked. Once again, Nicolas belabored them for only having sex on their minds, under cover of which he left, before they realized he had not paid for his beers.

Meredith had awakened about 10 A.M. As he was prowling around in his pre-coffee gloom, looking for clothes, feeling his face, he saw a slip of paper under his door:

"It's morning and I've gone to telegraph the outer world. Will I see you at lunch? Eurydice."

"Hm-m-mm," he muttered. Remembering, then, he brightened, smiling out at the sunny gardens. Two hours later, the maid brought yet another note:

"I'm outside at the door. Got a letter from Norman in Venice. Can I come in? Nicolas Manas."

"Damn!" cried Meredith to himself. Irritably, he followed the maid away from his work to receive his fellow poet. As they went out through the old house to the front he tried to recall any lines of Manas's he might know. His memory was excellent. Failing that, he tried to remember the names of any of the poems. Failing that, he was reduced to remembering his own quatrain and, inaccurately, the title of a pamphlet of Manas's.

For each, the appearance of the other was a surprise.

Thinking he was going to meet an Older Poet, Nicolas had put on a clean open-neck white shirt and washed and shaved. Meredith's frank face and tall, athletic body came as a shock. As the image of Robert Frost receded, he asked himself, "Why'd I use up a white shirt?" He began arranging his psyche to produce a youthfulness younger than his host's. Meredith saw, in the soft light in front of the Gräfin's desk, someone very young. Caravaggio came to mind and, thinking of Walter, Meredith understood the amusement Manas must provide him. There was something, Teen-age Tempter? Puberty's Spokesman? something, of impertinent youth about this Manas. And when he heard Nicolas's tough voice asking the Gräfin, sarcastically, "Guess you lemme go in, now?" he was more amused, himself, than shocked.

The Gräfin shrugged, raised an eyebrow, returned to her ledgers.
It was Meredith she was undecided about. She was fairly certain
his relationship to Mary Jane might turn into something she could
not tolerate in her house, if it hadn't already started. She could not
bring herself to mention it. She was relying on a new coldness on
her part to act as a warning.

Making their way back to Meredith's quarters, each was preparing himself: Nicolas, looking around, saying "Gosh!" every few
steps, was creating a boyishness; Meredith, being made to feel
expansive by this, was preparing an open mind.

They entered the large ex-library. Nicolas's cry, "Hey, man, this
is *great!*" did much to warm Meredith. Monkeylike, Nicolas danced
around the room stroking the bindings of the books, as if they
were so many bananas. He went back to open and close the door
and marvel at how it disappeared and became shelves. "Check
that, man!" he cried. Meredith stood by the windows, smiling.
"There are all kinds of gadgets. Look, these bars on the window,
they open out, like a shutter, see? And look . . ." he pointed to the
fireplace with its motto. "What's it say, man?" When he had translated it, Nicolas told him:

"Yeh, man. Now that's the truth! We all gotta burn, burn bright!
Like, you know, like real poets . . . right?" The accompanying
looks, while strangely flirtatious, were flattering and respectful. At
last they settled down, rather formally. One of them was less at a
loss how to begin than the other. Nicolas, after a brief pause in
which he studied Meredith's face with grave attention, said, "You
know? We gonna be *friends*. I like you. I like how you look."

Meredith felt this was a straightforward speech, although it embarrassed him, somewhat. "Well, thank you," he replied.

"No, I *mean* it, friends! We all poets, right? We gotta love each
other 'cause there's nothin' but cold outside, right? What they
know, they know how it is to burn? Like it says there on the fire.
No, they do not." The final jump from the basic English of Louis
Armstrong to the crispness of T. S. Eliot was of a virtuosity not
lost on Meredith. It bemused him, further defenses fell. He found
himself more and more pleased that Manas had come. This was
not work, of course, but it was as lively a substitute for it as he
had found in a long time. Nicolas continued: "Now if this was, say,

Greece, in the Golden Times, we'd a embraced. How's it go? The kiss of brotherhood. Right?" His dark, keen eyes looked for a sign, for with several homosexual poets this sentiment had had a marked effect. But seeing only an open nodding face he hastened on, "We's all soldiers in the army of Poetry, right?"

Meredith cleared his throat and clenched his fists a few times, releasing temporary embarrassments and showing, he hoped, a fraternal frame of mind. Suddenly, he was inspired to ask, "How would you like a bottle of beer. I think I'll send for some. How about that?" (He wanted to say "right?" but as yet he couldn't bring it out in his own tone of voice.)

"Great, man. No food around here, huh? I mean Nicolas didn't eat much today. . . ." At once, Meredith became guilty and compassionate. Nicolas saying "today" suggested hours of being abroad in the world, while he himself had slovenly slept. Next, he thought, "My God! He's not eating regularly!" He leapt to his feet, grabbed the telephone and asked the Gräfin, "Please, would you send a few bottles of beer and are there, is there some cheese and cold meat, something for sandwiches? Thank you." His lunch appointment had slipped his mind.

"Say, that's great, man," Nicolas said, laying his hand on Meredith's arm as he passed. "How about it, when all that gets here, will you read me a poem? And then I'll say one of mine. You do that for Nicolas?"

"Why, sure . . . certainly. That's a fine idea, Manas." Meredith's first uneasiness occurred, now, when he found himself deploring what he thought was a pompous note in his own voice, and the wish for a more engaging manner, something more involved with their experience. Putting one leg aslant across the other, he leaned back. This left him at an odd angle, the Gräfin's library chairs were spacious, so to divert attention from himself he pointed toward Nicolas's pants pocket:

"Is that a book, there?"

Nicolas grinned, delighted. "Hey! How *about* that? You just like me! Nicolas always say, 'What's that book?' These just some myths . . ." and he held out the book and riffled its pages.

Meredith looked, noticed the title, saw many scribblings on the margins. "Are you working on myths?" he asked, pleased that he had an opening to introduce his new Orpheus poem, and to discover that Manas did do research work.

"Look, I dream of going to Greece. That's Nicolas's dream, Meredith . . . Uh, that O.K. I call you by your first name? Nobody calls me like Nick . . . but if you wanna, fine! That'd be *our* name. But usually not."

"Fine, Nicolas."

"O.K. Great. Now it's like Greece was right in the middle of my dreams. Theseus! There's a myth, man. This Theseus is a bullfighter, see. I'm thinkin' of a play, a play about love, and this play'll be all about this bullfight with Theseus and how you get hung on poetry and how it's really *love*. Get it? You and me we fight out a poem and it's like everybody's lookin' at us, but who's gettin' hurt? I wanna feelin' of blood and this Theseus and this big bull and it'll have a line like: *Crete, there's a lot of sun there/And they yell 'Theseus, get in there!'/And . . .*" (At this point, the red-faced maid carried in the tray of food and beer bottles.) Nicolas looked, briefly, went on, "*And there's no hotdogs, no mustard/Nobody's selling anything. Just the big sound of Greeks!* . . . You get it?"

Meredith was fascinated. This kind of involvement, the immediacy Manas conveyed, made him at once grateful and a little envious. More than that, Manas calling on him now seemed to include him as a part of the vast action of poetry. For the moment, he could do no more than get to his feet and bustle around putting sandwiches together and snapping back the porcelain stoppers on the beer bottles. "You know, Nicolas," he said, as he worked, "it's a wonderful idea . . . Greece . . . I . . ."

"I'll just drink outa the bottle," Nicolas interjected.

"Oh, yes. Good idea."

Meredith went back to his sandwich-making. As there was a silence beside him, he imagined perhaps there was awkwardness because Manas was hungry. He tried bridging this by saying, "Your poems, Nicolas, uh . . . 'Flybait'? I . . ."

"'Jailbait', Meredith," Manas corrected him, through a large mouthful of cheese and ham, "Poems Out of Confinement—that's the way they described."

The following silence was extremely painful to Meredith until, looking up, he realized his guest was occupied eating, a bland look on his face. So he contented himself not explaining his mistake and merely sipped from his own bottle.

"Let's hear that poem you got up your sleeve, Meredith, and I'll tell you about my new book's coming out, *Hello Doom*. How's that for a title?"

Meredith sat and thought. Whenever his literary opinion was asked, he gave his answer hard thought, he always searched for an honest reaction. Finally he said, "Don't you think there's perhaps a little too much of the Françoise Sagan in it? I mean, you know, *Bonjour* . . ."

"Say, Franz . . . He's a German poet, right? I don't want anything Kraut about this."

"Well, no. Actually, you see it's a young girl, a French girl, she's written all these weird popular novels, and I just thought, perhaps . . ."

Tipping up his bottle, Nicolas had a worried look; swallowing, he said, angrily, "That title wasn't my idea at *all*. If that bastard's goin' to get me classified . . . Well, I'll fix him. You watch. Now read me your poem. What's it about?"

"As a matter of fact, Greek myth. The Orpheus-Eurydice myth, you know." Meredith found the poem and began reading it in his earnest voice. Nicolas chewed and swallowed and stared at him. He felt pretty sure he'd put himself across. On what grounds, he couldn't say, yet, but now he was relaxed and quite a bit more complacent about the hours ahead. The point was not to be too friendly. He started forming some words of reaction to the poem.

It was finished. He could tell because Meredith looked up at him. Nicolas nodded, "Say, I liked that sexy part in there. Now, you oughta . . . Wait a minute. Where's the can?"

"The . . . ? Oh, it's right out here." Meredith took Manas to the hall and pointed up to the end at the toilet door marked OO. He waited. And he waited, not realizing that Manas was several bottles of beer ahead. At last, he heard Manas calling, "Hey! Hey, man! Where are we!" Laughing, Meredith went out into the hall and said, "In here."

Through her door came their voices.

Mary Jane stopped writing in her journal. She raised her eye-

brows, thoughtfully. Could he have followed her, *here?* Weariness
and impatience, for a second or so, overcame her. Then her natural
resolve flooded back. Putting down her small gold pen, she took off
the plain summer dress she wore and looked around for something more interesting. Next, she brushed her hair and sat down to
work on her lips.

Meredith was rather depressed. They had not discussed his
poem, on the contrary, Manas had launched into an analysis of
Walter Norman, as man and poet, with considerable condescen-
sion. As a result Meredith was telling himself his poem was, indeed,
slight, not worked enough, not worth discussion. He was always
willing to believe the worst about his own work. And then he
noticed the bookshelves of the door moving in. A soft voice asked,
"Do I get any lunch?" And Mary Jane appeared.

The warm rose of her dress, the red of her lips, and her hair
introduced a whole new element of light. He looked at her with
renewed pleasure, as if reminded of the merits of a book he had
put down unfinished.

Nicolas's first thought was, "Geez' *She's* following *me!*" His
first look was clearly suspicious. Then it became apparent she and
Meredith knew each other. With that, his mind fell to work. Meanwhile, he had pushed to his feet, in imitation of Meredith, and
stood half smiling, half smirking at her.

"Yes," she was saying, "we do know each other. In fact, we
saw each other just this morning, getting our mail. What was in
your mail, Nicolas?"

Now, Nicolas knew very little about small talk—unless personal
questions, various forms of threat, innuendo, and streams of the
subconscious constituted the New Small Talk—as a result, Mary
Jane's question seemed to him almost insultingly pointless and he
answered, stiffly, "I got these proofs from my publisher and some
letters."

"Well, well," Meredith exclaimed, pulling up a chair for Mary
Jane, "maybe you would let me read some poems from the proof
sheets?"

More interested in watching Meredith's attentions to Mary Jane
than his own answer, Nicolas replied, "I sent 'em back, as was."

Meredith was amazed. He had always worked hard on his own

proofs, making minute changes, reluctant to let them go. "You *did?*"

"Look, those jokers don't pay *me* nothin'. So Nicolas don't do their work!"

"Well, I guess . . ."

"That's certainly *one* way of looking at it," Mary Jane put in. "Now how about lunch, Meredith?"

Such tricks were not new to Nicolas. He'd figure out why, later, Mary Jane wanted to be rid of him. The best thing now to do would be to put Meredith under obligation to him by leaving and making it clear he did not feel wanted. Even as he thought, he acted.

"Well, I guess Nicolas better be goin'?" he announced to Meredith, in slightly hurt tones.

"We could maybe all meet, tonight," Meredith hastened to suggest, peering at Mary Jane who went right on smiling. "I know a place, it's perhaps a little odd, called *Die Dritte*—it's a bar, with music."

"Yeh, I know the place. O.K." Nicolas looked at Mary Jane, "You comin', too?"

"If Meredith likes it, I'll go," she said, looking at Meredith.

And, "Swell," *he* said, as if everything were solved, "we'll get there at, oh, nine? How's that?"

"Great," Nicolas stood his ground a moment longer, a sullen moment further muddying the air and allowing responsibility its lead. Meredith started hesitantly toward the door when Nicolas was blessed with one of his improvisations.

With a wink, he shook his head at Meredith. "Look, that Frau at the door bugs me. Nicolas'll just take off through here." He went to the window, slipped the hasp, opened the bars and scooted over the sill, dropping lightly to the terrace. "See you later," he called to Meredith, then sauntered off across the lawns to the distant gate. There was a pathetic, jaunty look to the retreating figure, and a quiet in the room he had just left.

"He knows his way around," Mary Jane finally said.

"A friend of mine in Venice seems to have sent him to me."

"A *friend?*" she asked. But she quickly smiled and said, "What will it be today? More potato salad?" It took her a fraction of a second longer than she would have guessed to win him back, musing there, looking away over the sunlit lawns. In the end, she prevailed. Over the lunch table he had returned to her in force. In fact, it was Mary Jane who remembered their appointment at nine. "Oh," he sighed. "Well, it's across town. You needn't change, you are what we all will try to impress."

They were late.

Nicolas was discovered sitting with a group of five friends at a table for two, back by the small stand where an all German combo was playing *Sweet Georgia Brown* for the seventh time. One of the people Meredith knew, a young journalist. He was surprised, for it was a talented young journalist. He waved. Nicolas got right up and came over to the door.

"Hey buddy! Say, you come on back and meet . . ."

Mary Jane said, "It looks crowded back there to me, and loud. Let's sit right over here and Nicolas, you bring one or two of your friends over here." She smiled up at Meredith as she said this and explained, "We'd all be squatting back there on our haunches."

Nicolas studied her. "O.K." he said.

Smiling, in all innocence, Meredith suggested, "Bring Christian over." Then, immediately, he had to turn and help Mary Jane in behind a small table.

Nicolas did return with Meredith's friend, Christian, and another of his table, and a fresh tactic. He took a chair next to Mary Jane. All affability, he urged her, "Let Nicolas get you a beer."

"We've ordered, Nicolas, there'll be time." She had out a cigarette and turned to Meredith who lit it.

The Germans were dazzled by Mary Jane. "Does she speak German?" asked Christian, in German.

"*Ja,*" said Mary Jane, who had a German grandfather, from Munich, as a matter of fact. "*Aber der Manas, hier, spricht kein Wort.*" And she waved a hand at Nicolas. "We will speak English then, for our Nicolas," Christian said. He believed Mary Jane was Nicolas's possession, and he hoped to win favor with her. Nicolas, of course, had so persuaded him.

"Gee," Nicolas murmured, "you speak this stuff, huh?" He gazed at her with admiring eyes. "She is full of surprises," he announced. Mary Jane merely smiled and blew smoke up in the air.

Soon, Meredith and the other two were talking about the new Berlin ultimatum and Nicolas turned, confidentially, to Mary Jane:

"You hate Nicolas, right?"

"No."

"Why the freeze?"

"I'm occupied, that's all."

"Yeh, I'll bet!" Nicolas laughed, imagining she would join him.

"You're a crude one, Nicolas," she told him.

His voice was suddenly low and fierce, "Look, don't cross Nicolas up."

"You'll do that for yourself." And, thinking it was too easy a contest, Mary Jane made the mistake of turning away from him to listen to the others.

Nicolas waited until there was a pause, after an order for another round of beers, and he laid his hand on Mary Jane's arm, saying, as if unaware anyone could hear, "Let's not fight, huh? We all oughta love each other, right?" This was the first time it had dawned on Meredith there had been a fight. He looked at Mary Jane. She lost her head, a moment, shook off Nicolas's hand, and said, "Oh, do stop it!"

"O.K., O.K. . . ." he replied, grinning at Meredith, shrugging, as if to say, "These women . . ." Meredith's bewilderment deepened. And the others, as they always do, began talking again. Nicolas pursued his course.

"You wanna dance with Nicolas? We dance fine, right? Come on!"

He leapt up and did a few steps, holding out his hands, smiling.

All those eyes on her were too much for Mary Jane. She wavered, she laughed, falsely, shook her head; reaching for Meredith's hand she tried to re-establish her identity. He cried, "Come on, Nicolas, you give us a dance!" Which Nicolas, at last in his element, did.

It was a dance mainly of rotating hips, crotch out, accompanied by cries to the ceiling, "Gimme mewsik! Mew-ew-ew-*zik!*" The Germans loved it. In spite of himself, Meredith laughed, half embarrassed, half delighted. And at the end—it had been *Georgia Brown*, again—Nicolas fell back in his chair. They all went on applauding. He mopped his brow, black hair fell forward. At this point his modesty appeared, as it did when he knew indisputably all attention was his. He drank off his beer and cried, "Gimme time, hey, gimme time!" He had captured them all. Clapping her hands, smiling, Mary Jane stared at him; all the while realizing that she was indeed up against something she had better turn her mind to. "Next time you dance, too, O.K.?" Nicolas asked, in the easiest way rubbing his head against her shoulder and looking up to smile, then extending his smile all around.

"Oh, no, Nicolas, I could never do that!" she said, while asking herself, "There must be something I *can* do, now what is it?"

Nicolas began talking across her to Meredith, explaining how you had to get *with* it, with music, with everything. "You gotta know what *now* is!" he cried, excited by his own words. Mary Jane could see that Meredith was taking it all in—she had herself, once. Watching Nicolas manage to make an exclusive thing of experience, a unique, patented item, she reacted as if she were the magician's assistant eager to see the effect on the audience. But when she saw that this effect, on Meredith, was to minimize him she resented it, first as a fellow human being, next because she was womanly and, in Meredith, she wanted a man who would know who he *was*. It was as if, in considering the purchase of him, she did not want the goods tampered with.

The evening went right on being Nicolas's as glasses came, round after round. Eventually, her opportunity came. Meredith rose and excused himself, in a manner that proved how cowed he was. Nicolas's grin and remark, "Don't worry, man, we'll wait," seemed to imply that a Real Life Force Type would never bother with formalities if he had to go to the toilet. And so Meredith was more sent away than excused. Mary Jane was moved to action.

Ignoring the two others, she turned to Nicolas. They, seeming to expect this would happen as soon as Meredith left, did not listen.

"Look, Nicolas. Why don't you go back to Venice?"

Confident he had won, Nicolas settled back in his seat.

"Gold, baby. No gold."

"How much, Nicolas?"

"Two . . ." he looked at her, "three hundred."

"Two," she replied.

As a hundred and fifty would have done it, Nicolas shrugged.

"O.K. Two."

"I'll write them in the women's room," she told him, matter of factly, as if she did this every day. "And when will you leave?"

"Don't you worry, baby, I've *had* this place."

"Just remember, I can always claim these checks were stolen, if you don't. . . ."

Meredith reappeared, coming across the floor, self-consciously, as if they were all watching him. Nicolas had just time to hiss, "Dollars, that is!" and Mary Jane to give him one small contemptuous stare, saying, "God!"

She left the table as Meredith came to sit down. So few women came to this bar that she had the women's room to herself. Traveler's checks signed, a quick inspection in the mirror, a decision to leave, right away, with Meredith, took five minutes. She came back to the table, passing the checks to Nicolas smoothly, as she took her place. Refusing the next round of drinks, she suggested to Meredith that she would like to go home. He was surprised. She said, firmly, "Yes, I think I'd like to get back."

"All right! Let me finish this beer." He was attempting to preserve some independence in front of his friends.

But Mary Jane's habit was that once a bargain had been completed, the price paid, she wanted things her way. She saw money as a clarifier. She never had stores send purchases, for example, she always carried them. "Of course," she told Meredith, "I can go alone."

"No, no. Come on," he said, gulping his beer.

"You goin'?" Nicolas asked, showing surprise. Actually, he was anxious to have a look at the checks, just to make sure, and he was on his feet clearing the way even as he asked.

Meredith, always courteous, and in this case determined to make his exit his own, stepped behind Mary Jane, who only nodded and went off to the door. His farewells took a minute too long. Her impatience, shortening in a logarithmic curve, gave out. She was on the street and, with her usual good luck, getting into a taxi when he rushed out to find her.

"Hey!" was all that he managed before the black Mercedes moved away. He trotted a few steps, stopped, frowned, and stood there, irresolute.

Inside, the Germans speculated. They imagined that Mary Jane and Nicolas had made a later appointment. They told themselves that Meredith would come back in, alone. Almost instantly, they were proved correct.

Sitting down, deliberately indifferent, Meredith only said, "She took off."

"Man, that's a strange one," Nicolas informed him, looking up from something in his hands.

Now Nicolas expanded. He ordered more beers, Meredith was still there to pay. To insure this, he moved over into Mary Jane's chair to speak directly into Meredith's face, saying, "You know, Meredith, I read that little poem of yours about my kind of poetry. No, look, Nicolas's not mad. I gotta say this, we gotta stick *together*, man. This is a lonely life. . . ." Almost anytime, Nicolas could move himself to tears thinking of how lonely and misunderstood he was. The truth being, of course, that he passed scarcely an hour of any day out of company. He would have told you, the shine of water on his cheeks, that none of *that mattered*. "You sit there, like at a table, and the black wall closes in, right, man? You feel that, man?" Meredith nodded, distractedly. He wanted to go, he was nervous about Mary Jane; but this stroke about his Beatnik quatrain half paralyzed his urge and he sat on. He talked to his friend Christian. Then, turning, he was aware that Nicolas had left the table. He rose, paid the bill, said good-byes, and went off to the door. And he had just time to wave across the room to Nicolas before he went out. "See you around, man!" Nicolas called.

"Let me in."

"Tomorrow."

"Just for a few minutes."

"Please, tomorrow."

"I'll keep knocking."

"Well . . . Really, Meredith. I was asleep."

"Did you think *I* would sleep?"

The next twenty minutes were rather hard on Meredith. Mary Jane had begun her campaign. He was told she respected people who worked, realized their gifts, and depended on no one. Their parting was cool, but not final. He shut her door and started, rather dejectedly, for his own. "I'll let him think awhile before I go in," Mary Jane told herself.

When the door of the bar had closed on Meredith, Nicolas realized he had missed an opportunity. He still wanted company, he had not been lying to Mary Jane when he told her he had *had* the company of Munich bars. Besides, there was the question of where to sleep. Nicolas convinced himself he had felt only a tentative rejection in Meredith's departure. An eternal optimism gripped him on days when things went well. This was certainly one of them. He believed in wringing such days dry. Seize the moment! he might have said (and he would be saying when he read and approved of Emerson). He stood there ignoring several people and reasoning that, yes, for her treatment of him he had been paid back by Mary Jane, but for this poem about Beatniks Meredith still owed him something. Next, he was outside the door of the bar and inside a crowded Volkswagen about to leave those parts and willing enough to have him along. He fell into the back seat and cried, "Let me off up there around Pfy-fey-fee-lish, how-the-hell-you-say-it Platz." That got a laugh. He got another laugh when he lay back on three sets of knees and said, "Keep your hands off Nicolas's *lunch!*" (One of them who had had a scholarship out in Wisconsin translated for the others.)

Twelve minutes later he was unlatching the bars at Meredith's window. Then he was in the dark room.

There was a vast silence in and around the Gräfin's pension, the past-midnight silence of a house of the genteel poor. Some silences, such as this one, reduce even burglars to a nervous fumbling state. Hardened types, old-timers, have complained that the worst feature of the trade is the darkness and silence—there is no way to train for it. Nicolas whispered, "Hey, man, hey, Meredith!" and nothing but the dark responded. He tried again, the same ominous silence replied. He panicked. He felt out for things. He touched a chair. He found the pleated paper lampshade but he failed to remember that European lamps have the switch on the cord. And then his hands, as once before, groped along the narrow coldnesses of books —this time he cursed them. He came to a corner, more books. The smooth forearm of a leather chair brushed his thigh. And more books. Tears came into his eyes. He stepped into the fireplace, struck his head against its motto. He tried to remember. He stumbled against the bed and fell onto its silk comforter and lay there panting and listening. He wanted to get out, but the night had so darkened he could not see the windows. Yet, he was about to try again when he heard a door close, somewhere not far away, and steps come softly down the hall. He remained on the bed, his knees drawn up. There was a sound of air as the thick door opened, a click as it closed. A voice said, "Damn!" There was a snap and then a flood of light. And then he was focusing on Meredith who had already taken off his tie.

"What the hell!" This sounded like a shout, but was actually only in Meredith's normal deep voice.

They stared a second or so at each other.

Nicolas: "I . . . uh. Look, I figured . . ."

"You figured *what?*"

"Look, you got this room. Let Nicolas . . . It's dark out there. I . . ."

"Yeah, yeah. I'm in no mood for jokes. You better get out, Manas."

"Who's jokin'?" Nicolas had at last got hold of himself. In fast, near belligerent tones, he began stating his case: "You gonna let me stay here, tonight. This big place, all these books . . . Nicolas stay, read by the fire. We *poets*, man, and . . ."

As Meredith showed no signs of indecision, he hesitated. Realizing he had better try tougher tactics, he pivoted around and took a stand between the bed and the rear wall of books. There, with amazing speed, he got out of his clothes, throwing them, shirt, khakis, socks, shorts, toward Meredith as if he were making offerings. Then, naked, he got back on the bed and squatted facing Meredith.

Who, this while, had merely gaped at him. But now his jaw snapped shut and he took a step forward. Only Nicolas saw the door opening behind Meredith's back and Mary Jane come into the room.

"Oh," she gasped, staring at them, her anger lost in her horror. "I just came . . ." she faltered in childlike accents, "to borrow one of your . . ." With desperate fingers she plucked from the nearest shelf *Romantic Reykjavik*, and made her escape before either of them could speak. Returning to her room she collected herself enough to decide she must go back to Venice, as soon as possible. Feeling chaste as well as virtuous, she told herself that true adventures, after all, were those of the mind.

Meanwhile, Meredith had started for the door, stopped, turned, and, as he strode across the room, resolutely, was yelling, "Out! Out!" He reached for Nicolas, perhaps to take him by the ears.

"Hey, hey, easy! Hey!" Nicolas fell back on an elbow, his other arm held out defensively. By this he was grasped and brought to his feet so fast he tottered there like one of those weighted toys. Next, shoulders gripped, he was hustled to the window and thrust through onto the terrace, without even realizing how much he had helped by bending his knees. Outside, he faced the lighted library window and, piece by piece, had his clothes flung at him. Meredith leaned out and in a lowered voice declared, "And don't come creeping around here again, creep." The bars were shut, the windows, too. Through these, Meredith could be seen pacing around with his hands to his head.

Standing out there, a shiver took Nicolas, and then rage, and then—revenge! He gathered wind, cupped his mouth, shouted: "Kraut-lover! Phoney! No good verse-maker!"

He went on a little longer, improvising, until a light—controlled in the Gräfin's quarters—lit up the whole front of the house, the terrace, Nicolas, and part of the lawn beyond. In it, Nicolas posed, defiantly, confronting three elderly country ladies, an ex-Wehrmacht general, a family of four Swiss, the patroness, and five serving girls.

At last, he faced about and marched across the lawn into the shadows. The light, as if hospitably, faintly showed the way until he reached the gate. Having seen him there it clicked off and the scene was black. Meredith, at his desk, clutched his bowed head muttering to himself, "And tomorrow . . . ?" Mary Jane stopped listening and went on with her packing, intent on taking the first train out for Venice. All the others—but for the Gräfin—opened their bedroom doors, held their robes around them and peered at their neighbors up and down the hallways.

On the road, pausing only to get back into his clothes, pat his pockets to see if passport or money had been lost in the melee,

Nicolas set off for an all night newsstand where he left his traveling
sack and his blanket. His spirits were remarkably unlowered. Soon
he was under a chestnut tree in the English Gardens adjusting
himself to the hollows around the roots. And he was asleep some
time before the storm, descending from Alpine passes and valleys
around the Tegernsee, had reached the city's southern suburbs.
Shortly after, however, the thunder became Wagnerian, the lightning so operatic whole measures of an aria could have been sung
from darkness to darkness.

The rain came down for about an hour, perhaps, without waking
Nicolas. Only when his legs were drenched through blanket and
pants did he sit up and stare around. He huddled there horrified,
a solitary audience to this theater in the English Gardens. Trunks
of trees appeared, vertical whitenesses, like a speeded-up movie,
and left their imprint stuttering in his eyes. Curr-rr-*rash!* Bam! A
panorama of trees and bushes in a long pale fright. Intense blackness. It was as terrifying as it was plotless.

"Gee-zuzz!" Nicolas whispered. It was as nearly a prayer as he
had made in years. When he could move he was whimpering. In
a series of jerks he made a sack of the blanket to hold his belong-
ings. Time and again he jarred back against the chestnut, startled
by a particularly vivid onslaught. Clenching his teeth against their
chatter, he made a dash for the nearest path and while he ran down
it toward the distant street light he was protesting, "*O.K.! O.K.!*"

The rain tried to choke him as he ran. His course was a dotted
one of doorways. He burst into the Schwabing station where a
cleaning woman watched him drip on her wet floors and, generously, offered him a large dirty cloth to mop his head. "*Schlechtes
Wetter,*" she said. If not the words, he understood the gratuitous-
ness of the remark and mumbled, "*Ja, ja.*" He decided on the main
station and got there, extravagantly, by taxi. The driver, incensed
at his meager tip, complained about the wet seat left behind,
wasted on Nicolas who only slammed the door.

There is almost a spiritual air to railroad stations at four thirty
in the mornings. He wandering through it, idly, stood for a while
in front of a toilet mirror. At length, he sank down on a bench in
the third-class waiting room. He had the bemused air of a child
who has been thoroughly punished. For the first time in a life of

such public places at such an hour he was unaware of speculative
eyes turned upon him. He did not see a policeman looking his way
and talking to a janitor: "He is not an American. He is Greek. I
have been watching him for some time." Then, under their stare,
Nicolas gave a start. His hand reached into his breast pocket where
he had a package of cigarettes in which he had put Mary Jane's
checks. He was saying, "No . . . no . . . don't let 'em be . . ."
Slowly he pulled them out—they were dry. He breathed.

He need not have had that particular anxiety. Life, toward little
plots, is extremely permissive. All such small efforts are allowed.
Limited demands you are granted. Life says, "All right, now what?"
and sits back and watches.

Even his passport had not run. He relaxed against the bench.
Seeing his nervous search, the policeman nodded, wisely. But with
a burst of vehemence, the janitor said, "Those good-for-nothings!"
and in disgust went back to his work.

At nine that morning, the Gräfin was at her desk making out
Herr Wilder's bill. "There shall be no more of that," had been her
words to Meredith, a half hour before, "I shall make out your bill."
The others in the gallery dining room were waiting uselessly for
him to appear. Outside, everywhere, the sun was radiant, picking
out each detail with glistening edges. Regular walkers strode
through the English Gardens and marveled at such freshness.

When it opened, Nicolas sent a telegram at the Post-Telegraf
to Walter Norman, ARRIVE TONIGHT BY TRAIN ON MY WAY TO
GREECE MEET ME NICOLAS, thereby using all his last marks.

At nine five, the Venedig Express departed for the South. He
was on it long before it left. He did not see Mary Jane boarding
First Class. Nor could either of them know the kind of scene her
husband would make upon their joint arrival, that evening, in
Venice.

It would be interesting to relate, but people tell so many ver-
sions it is impossible to get at the truth.

JOHN GRAVES was born in Texas in 1920, received his B.A. from Rice Institute in 1942 and an M.A. from Columbia University in 1948. He has published one work of nonfiction, *Goodbye to a River*, and his shorter pieces have appeared in *The New Yorker*, *The Atlantic Monthly*, *Holiday*, *Esquire*, and other magazines.

THE AZTEC DOG

from *The Colorado Quarterly*

When, on sandal-shuffling feet, the young Indian maid had taken away the last plates, the two of them sat at the table smoking. The boy was reading a book, as he had been doing throughout the meal. The old man's bored forefinger made squares and triangles of crumbs of tobacco. The dining room was wide, floored and wainscoted with patterned green tiles, its three windows mullion-paned, but it had no ceiling and the roof that showed dimly above rough-milled rafters was of corrugated steel. Of furniture it held only the heavy table and the unmatched chairs in which they sat. In a corner, where the old man had tossed it before dinner, lay a quirt.

He had a gray mustache, cold dark eyes, and the face of a falcon, and wore a gray short riding-jacket and a white shirt buttoned at the throat without a tie. He said distantly, "Would you want a game of checkers?"

The boy raised book-focused blue eyes. It was poetry, the old man knew. He had glanced through the book where it lay on a chair that afternoon and had seen that it was poetry, in English. Not even good poetry, as far as he considered himself qualified to judge. . . .

The boy said in formula, "No. No, thanks."

Copyright 1961 by the University of Colorado, Boulder, Colorado.

He had been living at the hacienda for six weeks and had learned nearly all of his Spanish, which was good enough, in that time. It was one of the reasons given for his being there, to learn Spanish. When his father came again he would perhaps notice its excellence, not that the old man, whose name was Fernando Iturriaga, cared greatly.

Nor did he care about the checkers; the invitation was a nightly convention. At the beginning of the six weeks while feeling each other's temper they had played every evening. Later less, and later still not at all. But he went through the ritual of the invitation each night because irony and formality made living with the boy possible. He would have enjoyed carrying the formality to the point of coffee and cigarettes in the salón de estar, but that was not feasible because the salón, like the rest of the house except the dining room and two bedrooms and a kitchen, was without even a steel roof above it. Raw edges of mortared masonry left white marks on your clothing if you walked much about the unfinished parts of the house, though they had been unfinished for eighteen years. The porch lacked railings, and outside the back door gaped a staired, never-covered cellar-entrance into which a hog had once fallen to break three of its four legs. Much pork, that had been.

Rats danced sometimes in the moonlight on the tiles of the salón de estar. Fernando Iturriaga had seen them. It had seemed well.

The boy coughed and lit another cigarette. The old man went to the window and swung it open and looked out in the late dusk at his flower garden beneath old aguacates. Pallid small roses speckled the gloom and he smelled them. From a hole in the great wall beyond the garden, water he could not see trickled audibly. He was reassured by the roses and the sound of the water running from a wall his people had built two hundred years before and by the knowledge that among the roots of the aguacates violets bloomed as they had since his mother's time.

For a wife his father had gone to Spain—to Asturias—and she had brought the gardening with her to the moist valley where the hacienda spread, big in those days. His father's family had been hard, harsh, rawhide people, precipitate in pleasure and in work, and it was only now, after nearly seventy years of living, that Fernando Iturriaga could feel a little of his mother in himself.

When the boy came back with the blue-glass liter bottle of aguardiente it was his turn to be ironic. He set it on the table and asked Fernando Iturriaga if he wanted a drink.

As always, the old man refused. He drank, sometimes too much, but not with the boy. He valued the formality too highly.

The boy's father planned, or said he planned, to make the hacienda into a guest ranch. Fernando Iturriaga believed by now that the boy, who was there because he had slapped a professor, or had fecundated a girl, or something of that sort, was the only guest that particular guest ranch was ever likely to have.

Not that he wanted more. . . .

Watching the boy pour yellowish liquor into a glass, he said, "You rode into the upper valley today?"

"Yes."

The boy took a piece of bread and soaked it in the liquor. Fernando Iturriaga heard a quick tapping of claws on the tiles.

"You shouldn't," he said. "I've told you, with the elections coming on. You went into the cantina?"

"I do every day," the boy said. "Vidal! Look, Vidal!"

"You shouldn't," the old man repeated, risking a loss of formality in the irritation that cooled his belly when he thought of the boy speaking with the peasants of the upper valley in a brushwood bar, about Fernando Iturriaga.

The boy said indifferently, "Oh, it's all right. I get along with them."

The dog barked, dancing on quick white feet. It was tiny, brindle above and white below, with fragile legs and shadings of black about its muzzle and eyes. Before the American boy had come, the dog had never entered the house, though Fernando Iturriaga had played with it on the veranda in the afternoon, quietly, and had dropped bits of tortilla and meat to it out of his dining-room window when it begged from the garden. It was two years old and he had named it, whimsically, Vidal, because in his country's capital there was a street called that where the French mistress of a friend of his had once lived. It was of the ancient breed of alert Mexican mongrels from which the Aztecs had bred their even tinier bald dogs, and was symptomatic of a gentleness that had troubled him now for five or six years.

He had never seen gentleness as desirable, except in women. Insufficiently gentle, his own wife had left him eighteen years before, taking his sons, when the house was half rebuilt and the money had run out and she had found out about his relations with the cook they had had then.

He conceded now that there had been enough for her to be ungentle about. But he had several grandchildren whom he had never seen.

"Stand up," the boy said.

Fernando Iturriaga watched as the dog skipped on two legs before the boy. It snatched the piece of liquor-wetted bread from the air when he dropped it, gulping without chewing.

"Salud," the boy said sipping from his glass and grinning. "Salud, Vidal."

The old man said stubbornly, "They're troublesome people. Sooner or later you'll meet one of them drunk."

"One?" the boy said and laughed, glancing at him. "The half of them always are. They let me shoot a pistol at a cactus today."

"Sons of whores!" Fernando Iturriaga said forcibly through clamped teeth.

And wished that he had not, since it only meant that the boy had once more broken through the formality. Iturriaga sat for a moment swallowing anger like spittle, then went to his room to change his slippers back to half-boots and to shave. When he passed through the dining room twenty minutes later the dog was drunk. It had no capacity for the liquor. Neither had the boy, who crouched laughing on the floor, teasing it. It ran in short circles about him, yapping and dashing to tear at the flickering hands with its teeth.

Fernando Iturriaga thought that it was much like the rats' dance in the drawing room.

In the moonwashed court before the house a fresh horse stood saddled, as it did every night whether or not he wanted to use it. From the great wall's shadow two Indians' cigarettes pulsed; they murmured inarticulate courtesies and he grunted back in the same spirit. Leading the horse through the gate, he mounted in the road by the river. It shied, bouncing under him, a gray he had not ridden for several days. As he reined it into darkness under the cotton-woods lined along the little river, he was conscious of the valley's wide concavity to either side, more conscious than he had usually been when the valley had belonged to him. He had been there only occasionally during most of that time.

At its mouth, below the town toward which he rode, the earth fell away two thousand feet to malarial jungle, where the river ran turbidly wide to the sea. On clear days, from the flat top of a granary at the hacienda, the old man had often seen the shimmer of sun on salt water a hundred kilometers to the east.

Inland, the valley rose and flattened into a grassy bowl beneath the high peaks. His family's cattle had grazed there for seven generations, but now it was checkered into irrigated holdings of Indian agrarians. In the days of the change he had killed one of them. That had cost him a good part of the money he had had left, and they had nearly killed him later, skipping a bullet off his ribs as he passed a canebrake, six months before his wife had left him.

In the mornings the miserable dog had hangovers. Like a Christian, with thirst and groaning, and when you rolled back the thin black lids, the balls of the eyes were laced with blood.

He thought the gringos had begun to spawn rare ones, finally. Maybe they always had, but before, except for their nervous accessible women in the capital and the resorts, they had sent usually the meaty big ones like the boy's father, who knew cattle or oil or cotton or some other one thing completely and whom Fernando Iturriaga had always disliked a little because they profited from change and he did not.

But without obsession. Without what he thought of as the national obsession. He rode along on the pleasantly tense gray gelding toward the town where he would clatter dominoes and sip habanero with a drugstore owner and a grain dealer and a fat incompetent doctor who—though, with less reason then he, they shared his political bitterness—were not really friends of his. The kind of people he had chosen for friends lived in France, or the capital, or New York. Or were dead. He had not chosen well; he recognized that. Even the survivors had comfortably forgotten him when he had left that world.

But he had lived for five years in Paris and had known how to eat and drink and had bayed after actresses and gringas and such quarry, as a man of his background had been expected to do, and had spoken good English and French.

The gringo boy and his father did not know about all that, not even about the English, which he had never spoken with them. They thought of him as decayed indigenous gentry left over from feudalism.

That kind of feudalism had not existed since Iturbide, or before, but the old man granted that he was, at least, sufficiently decayed.

Riding, he thought without obsession about the gringo boy, and the dog, and gringos, and actresses with generals in long touring cars riding out to bull ranches, and how there ought to be green peace in the valley when, finally, you wanted peace.

Drink made the boy dizzy. He did not especially like it; it was a thing to rasp the old man's feelings with, like speaking of the cantina in the upper valley.

His name was John Anders and he was at the ranch because he had driven a pink unmuffled sports car into a culvert-rail near Amarillo, on his way to Hollywood with money from a considerable check forged in his father's name.

He had not known why Hollywood. An unpleasant hitchhiker with a ducktail haircut, sitting beside him, had died in the crash, but the boy had waked up on his back among prickly pears with a state patrolman bending cold-eyed over him and nothing at all broken in his slight body.

"No," he said to the dog sternly. "You've had enough."

He put down the book. It was Dylan Thomas; the boy's mother had had two nervous short stories published when young and all his life, in lieu of comprehension, had besieged him with literature. Some taste for it had stuck. He was nineteen, with one expulsion from college behind him and another school to try in the autumn, four months ahead now, and for two or three years poetry and kindred queerness had been serving him for armor in prep schools and around country-club swimming pools, where he did not fit well. Queernesses and a willingness to fight. . . .

His mother had wept emptily in her dove-gray bedroom and he had watched her, not for the first time or the fiftieth, and afterward had listened to his father's bellowing querulity in the same mood and had ridden with him on the peremptory trip down into Mexico, not listening all the way. He had learned to do that before he had been twelve.

When he got up from the table he found that the raw aguardiente had him in the legs, if not in the head. He lurched; the quickly counterpoising sole of his half-boot screeched in unswept grit on the tile. He stood, resisting the sudden idea of going out to see the Indian maid in her room beyond the laundry court.

Foggy guilt swirled in him when he thought of the maid, and he cursed aloud.

Turning, he walked through a hall to the old man's room and snapped on its light. It was monastic under the bare bulb's glare—a blue floor, a dresser of scarred oak, a table, a bed made of scroll-bent rods of tarnished brass, and a little wall Virgin. The boy stood resisting it. The old man's dignity was there like a smell, but did not explain itself. On the dresser stood a silver-framed photograph, cloud-haired, of an actress he somehow recognized to be Jean Harlow. It was a publicity picture of a special vintage, but was affectionately inscribed and signed. It did not fit with anything else that was there. He stared at it.

It stared back.

Him, the old bastard, he thought—but principally with puzzlement. . . .

In the beginning he and the maid had talked at night in the laundry court outside her door. She was shy, and alone a good bit, and giggled at his ragged confident Spanish, correcting him. Her people had worked there always and she would not talk to the boy about Don Fernando. She was not unhappy. She had a young man in the upper valley who possessed some education and would one day, maybe soon, be a power in the ejido there. But she saw him only on Sundays; Don Fernando did not encourage the upper-valley people at the hacienda.

"You have no life at all," the boy had said to her roughly, three nights before. He felt his own sophistication to be relative wisdom, and was enraged that ignorance and immobility could so brace the heavy contentment she expressed. "None of you," he said. "The ejido. Maybe they'll let him weigh sacks of grain."

"Maybe," the girl said, placid in the pallidity that came through the open door of her room. "Maybe so, señorito," she said. "But he won't end in the cantina, waving a machete with shouts. And there is no hurry. . . ."

Feeling wise still, and miserable, the boy said, "There's always hurry."

"Not in the valley," the girl said quietly.

She was young, with the Indian shyness and a round, brown, velvet face. Abruptly he put his hand on her cheek. She sucked in breath sharply through her teeth and ran inside, closing the door behind her.

That had been all, but it had shamed him; he had not wanted to be alone with her since.

He made a big embarrassed X-mark with his finger on the glass that shielded inexplicable Jean Harlow against the eatings of time, and left the room, the little dog's claws clicking along behind him.

He would apologize. . . .

You rode the bay horse (your father having paid for it, sight unseen, when Don Fernando had said someone was offering it for sale) hard up the valley by the river, under the big poplars, and then left the river before you reached the cantina, not wanting to go there first. Rising, the horse's flanks straining against your calves in labored effort of ascent, you passed oxcarts and laden strings of timid people in a roadlet that ran between terraces of irrigated grain and fiber, green. The world there smelled of green, and leather, and dung, and of charcoal and toasted maize in the huts between the fields, and on the higher mountains mists lay. The boy had not in his life known a freshness like that of the green upper valley as your horse mounted its side toward the mists.

Except that long before you were near the real mists you came to an almost vertical belt of cactus and stone and gray-green clawed plants, and trails were there that led to villages in the sierra. Clanking, clicking, shout-harried burro trains came along them. One trail ran simply parallel to the river, far below now. Taking that trail, you stopped somewhere along it and dismounted and sat on a rock, the cold feel of the mists above and behind you on your neck, the horse tearing irritably at clumps of inedibility among the stones, the quilt-patched green of the valley troughed below you, smoke tufted, split by the roving line of the river's trees.

Sometimes he would sit there for hours smoking Elegantes, coughing-strong. Once he yelled aloud in ferocious exultation of aloneness, "By God!"

The upper valley was, too, the brushwood cantina on the way home, and the taste of tepid black beer with loud peasants crowding toward his oddness. They liked him. He liked them, or thought he did, and was a little afraid of them—it was the main reason he went there. He would not talk to them about the old man, toward whom they felt the frank reflex hatred of crows for a crippled owl. They asked him about the States United and the flogging of wet-backs, and told him with pride that they were Reds. Once, when a stumbling-drunk Red with a drawn machete had cursed the boy and had gone outside to ride the bay horse away, one of the others had maced him from the saddle with a shovel and had courteously tied the horse again to its post.

"It is that at times one drinks," the courteous Red said.

"It is so," John Anders said with the solemnity of that dialect, and they laughed to one another to hear their intonation in his mouth, and slapped his shoulder.

And sometimes he ran the bay horse all the way back to the hacienda, the long-pounding lope downhill, and walked him cool in the courtyard there, and rubbed him slick with a cob.

The fact was, he liked living in the valley. It was a recent admission, and had had no effect on his prickling-war with the old man, who perplexed him. He had been at war with many adults, but had managed to touch most of them more painfully than he could touch Fernando Iturriaga.

Maybe, he thought, it was because the others had given a damn. . . .

He paused in the open door, winking against night's dark assault, and saw a yellow line beneath the maid's door. When he started down the unrailed steps, the aguardiente took him to the right. His foot pawed vacancy. Blackness jerked him cartwheeling down into the unroofed cellar-pit; he landed among shards of bottleglass, right-side-up and sitting, his right leg twisted back under behind him.

At first he knew only a shallowness of force-emptied lungs and fought to get his breath. Then a knowledge of the leg ascended through him like nausea. In sick shock, he knew that he was about to faint, but the little dog's whine cut into his ken and it was jumping at his face, licking. He took it in his hands and held it, speaking to it as it squirmed and licked and as the sickness went down, and waited while the dull but sharpening pain rose.

His hand was bleeding. The Indian girl was standing above him at the edge of the hole, uttering a mooing sound. He supposed he had made noise.

"Look for help," he told her.

She went away, still mooing. Without shifting, the boy held the dog and met the leg-pain full face and decided that it would probably be bearable. . . . She came back with the gardener, Elifonso. Elifonso gritted down the steep steps of the pit and loomed over the boy, smelling of peppers.

"If this is bad, señorito!" he said. "If this is very bad!"

"Don't touch me yet," the boy said.

But Elifonso grabbed him by the armpits and yanked upward, and the boy yelled and struck at him, and when Elifonso let go the hurt was twice what it had yet been. The boy's hand touched a stick; he flailed out with it and Elifonso went back up the steps. The boy shouted upper-valley words at them, and they murmured between themselves in the darkness, above him. He quieted, ashamed but still angry. After a time he asked the girl to bring the bottle of aguardiente from the dining room; when she gave it to him he drank five gulps of it, cold and oily, without stopping. It warmed him and pushed the pain down for a while, and he drank more. Then he vomited and for a long, long time sat coldly full of pain while the quiet Indian voices murmured on above him.

Finally a flashlight glared down into his face, reawakening dull rage. Fernando Iturriaga held it.

After a moment he said quietly to the boy, "You are a disaster."

John Anders said, "You aren't going to touch me."

"Go for the doctor Rodríguez," the old man told Elifonso.

Walking around the pit and down its steps, he knelt beside the boy and played the flashlight on the leg.

"How handsome," he said.

"Don't touch me," the boy said, and raised his stick.

Fernando Iturriaga took it from his hand and dropped it among the broken glass.

"Boy, I will touch you," he said. "I will hurt you, too. Shut up. You, Luz, come. . . ."

They were careful, but the pain was a twisting shaft up inside him, though it seemed that when the responsibility was no longer yours maybe the pain was not, either. The maid mooed all the way. When they had him on the bed in his room, waiting for the doctor, the leg as straight as they had dared put it with the big splinter sticking through the flesh above the knee, the old man said matter-of-factly: "It will have hurt like ten demons."

The boy rolled his head negatively.

"Don't lie," the old man said. "I know hurts. It will have hurt."

He considered, hard eyes candid. "Fat Rodríguez will hurt you more when he comes," he said. "He drank a lot this evening."

Weakened by the bed's comfort against his back, the boy began to cry. He cried because he hurt, and because the doctor would hurt him again, and because the old man clearly did not give a damn about him, and because he was a thousand miles from even a home that he despised—having, therefore, no home—and because the green foreign valley had turned on him and bitten him and was foreign now altogether, and hateful. He laid his forearm across his eyes and sobbed.

Astonishingly, the old man was patting his shoulder.

"Child, child," he said. "It will pass."

The boy stopped sobbing, and after a time uncovered his eyes. The formal hawk's face was smiling gently at him.

"I suppose it will," he said.

"Yes."

"All right," the boy said.

He was listening.

"At least a telegram," the boy's meaty father said earnestly, down-wiping damp hands against the front of gabardine trousers.

"Don Fernando, a letter that sat in the club in Mexico City for three weeks was . . ."

Fernando Iturriaga dropped his shoulders, flashed the cupped palms of his hands briefly upward, and turned away, unapologetic. He felt some pity for the big man, but he felt a little bit nationally obsessed, too. He considered that a telegram would likely have cooled in that club for three weeks also, awaiting the big man's arrival, and even had he known how to telephone him he doubted that he would have tried to do so. The bone had been set.

Crookedly, yes, healing with a bend like a pruned tree fork. Fat Rodríguez, gold spectacled, standing nervous now against the white-washed wall while the slim young doctor from the capital felt with long fingers the boy's humped femur—Rodríguez had thought of a thick fee but had not earned it. But Rodríguez had been all that there was; even the boy had understood that.

The slim capitaleño did not glance toward Rodríguez as he spoke to the boy's father.

"It will need rebreaking," he said. "There is also infection. A question of various months . . ."

"The hell it will," the boy on the bed said in English.

"Close your mouth," his father said. "For Christ's sake, you make any more trouble now and I'll . . ."

"I'm not going to let them bust it over again," the boy said unemotionally. "I watched them with Phil Evridge at school and he still limps."

The big man's voice shrilled. Rodríguez, his nervousness requir-ing expression, said to the slim doctor, "It is that sometimes, despite what one can do . . ."

The slim doctor turned on him for an instant two liquid slits, said, "Sí, señor!" and looked away, closing thin lips in punctuation.

Fat Rodríguez shuffled.

Fernando Iturriaga grinned and turned to go outside. My na-tionals, he thought. But the slim contemptuous capitaleño was of his nationals, too. Did he mean, then, those of his nationals who would end in a place like this valley?

Maybe.

On the gallery he dropped into a big hard chair of aguacate wood, and the little dog's nose shocked cold against his dangling hand. He caressed the bulb of its head and not looking felt its warm eyelids with his thumb.

Changing, he. . . . Gentling. A week after the boy's fall, three agrarians from the upper valley had come to the hacienda. With some pleasure he had gone out to tell them to go away again. But in their stubbled faces before he spoke, and in their politeness, he saw an actual concern for the boy. He had not expected that. Quietly, he led them himself to the boy's room, and afterward spoke to them about that year's crops. . . .

You are effeminated, he told himself.

Prepared for the big-meaty-gringo anger, he was a little disappointed when the father came out, alone, with cold control on his face.

He said, "Don Fernando, it was not well done."

"No."

"I don't mean that fat fool!"

His voice trilled at the end and Fernando Iturriaga glanced up hopefully, but the control was still there. The blue capable eyes glittered down at him like tile chips.

"There will not be a guest ranch."

"No," the old man said, and sighed courteously. Even in childhood, the line of the mountains where he was now looking had seemed to have the shape of a woman lying on her side. In childhood he had ridden there, on the high rocky slopes under the clouds, and the gringo boy had told him of doing the same.

Gently he pinched the small dog's ear.

"What a very great shame," he said in exact British English.

"By God!" Anders said, and stood above him for a moment longer, and then went out to the long brown-and-cream car to bring back a blanket.

The old man watched as all of them, the maid and the gardener and the doctor and even hopeful Rodríguez, bore armloads of books and clothes to load them into the luggage compartment. At last the capitaleño and Elifonso brought the blanketed boy between them through the door. They paused with him beside the chair.

"Well," the boy said. "Many thanks."

"Nothing, son," Fernando Iturriaga said. "May they make you a good oilman."

Crooked amusement split the boy's face, and he said a word from the upper valley that made the gardener laugh. They carried him to the car, and the old man watched still while the father strode past him unspeaking and managed to direct them into ramming the boy's head into a doorpost and the back of the front seat. At the end, the maid Luz ran out with the whittled crutches she had bought for the boy in the village, which he had refused to try.

By then, however, the car was moving; the maid stopped behind it holding the crutches and began foolishly to weep. Fernando Iturriaga saw the flash of the boy's face toward him from the rear seat. In the narrow gateway of the wall a stone tilted the big car's rear, and he felt a reprehensible surge of national pleasure as its finned fender gritted against the arch.

Fee-less, fat Rodríguez stood in the courtyard with the maid, his hands clenching and unclenching at his sides. Then he walked with head down and wagging to his old Ford, and drove away in it.

"Well, then," Fernando Iturriaga said aloud and for some reason in French.

He stared across the sunlit, slab-paved court at a section of wall where, mixed among the pocks of revolutionary bullets which in 1911 had killed his brother and a cousin and the peons who had stuck by them, were newer gray marks where he and the boy's father had held pistol practice some months before, speaking of the grandeurs of guest-ranching as they shot. It gave him satisfaction to think about how easily he had beaten the big American; then it disturbed him to recognize the satisfaction.

You are becoming nationally obsessed, he told himself.

He felt quite alone. Diffidently, the Indian girl came and asked if he would want his midday meal. He said that certainly he would. Hearing his calm tone as permissive, she said, "They left money. The big one said it was for room and food."

"Shut up," he said.

"Caray!" she protested.

"Shut up. What was he doing there in the laundry court, beside your house?"

She went back in. He was half certain she was his daughter, the child of the cook that had cost him his wife and sons. The cook had died quietly and quickly one winter, after the way of Indians, and the child had grown up there. He would give her something when she married her prim young man from the ejido. Not much. There was unhappily little to give.

The old man walked to his room, looked about it for a moment, and in leaving lightly, affectionately flicked the picture of Jean Harlow with his forefingernail. He had not known her; the picture had been some sort of joke from a friend, its point lost now. Or maybe he had bet and won it.

He went around to the shaded garden between his breakfast window and the wall. At its gate he examined the small perfect roses with pleasure, and he moved into the green gloom of the great aguacates slowly, so that hens in the path edged aside with only ritual cackling. He would tell Elifonso that the violets needed water; the outlet in the wall when he looked at it was closed with a whittled plug. Diverted river water, cool and vocal, ran in all the circumference of the peripheral wall. Two hundred years before, when his people had raised it—first, his father had said, the wall first of all for protection—the old Moorish water-love had made them build conduits inside it that ran into the houses, the gardens, the washwomen's court, the stables. . . . As a child he had leaned against the wall and listened while the water spoke its words.

Now he went to it again and put his ear against it and heard the water. In the pigpens these days there was only a drip from hairy green slime; he had meant for years to have it cleaned. A man lived in the town who could do that, somehow, with hook-ended wires.

Beside him there was a sound. It was the dog, squatting, one foot held delicately before it in the air as though in supplication. Its bright dark eyes were on his face.

"Vidal," the old man said.

The dog yipped at its name.

Fernando Iturriaga said, "You miss him, poor Vidal."

The dog whined and pumped the air with its foot and sat up as it had been taught. Commandingly it barked. The old man leaned down and picked it up, stroking its head as he glanced about himself. Against one of the aguacates leaned a section of rusted pipe. It had a familiar look. Holding the dog gently in the crook of his arm he walked to the tree and picked up the pipe, half a meter long, heavy, plugged with dirt. They had used it one year, he recalled now, as a stake for strung sweet peas.

He hefted it, and then in one deft motion, with Indian grace, he swung the little dog downward, holding its hind legs together in his left hand, and even as it yelped in surprise hit it a swift uncruel blow on its skull.

At the base of the tree he laid the dog and the pipe down beside each other, beyond the violets his mother had brought from Asturias, and rubbed the palms of his hands horseman-wise against his hips.

Now, he thought. Now maybe we will have peace here.

THOMAS E. ADAMS, 24, was born and grew up in Trenton, New Jersey. He graduated from La Salle College in Philadelphia in 1958 with a B.A. in English. From 1958 to 1960 he studied creative writing under Andrew Lytle at the University of Florida. He is currently serving a two-year tour of duty as a lieutenant in the U. S. Army. This is his first published story.

SLED

from *The Sewanee Review*

All the adventure of the night and snow lay before him: if only he could get out of the house.

"You can't go out," his mother said, "until you learn how to act like a gentleman. Now apologize to your sister."

He stared across the table at his sister.

"Go on," his mother said.

His sister was watching her plate. He could detect the trace of a smile at the corners of her mouth.

"I won't! She's laughing at me!" He saw the smile grow more pronounced. "Besides, she *is* a liar!"

His sister did not even bother to look up, and he felt from looking at her that he had said exactly what she had wanted him to say. He grew irritated at his stupidity.

"That settles it," his mother said calmly, without turning from the stove. "No outs for you."

He stared at his hands, his mind in a panic. He could feel the smile on his sister's face. His hand fumbled with the fork on his plate. "No," he said meekly, prodding a piece of meat with the fork. "I'll apologize."

His sister looked up at him innocently.

Copyright © 1961 The University of the South.

"Well?" said his mother. "Go on."

He took a deep breath. "I'm . . ." He met his sister's gaze. "I'm sorry!" But it came out too loudly, he knew.

"He is not," his sister said.

He clenched his teeth and pinched his legs with his fingers. "I am too," he said. It sounded good, he knew; and it was half over. He had control now, and he relaxed a bit and even said further: "I'm sorry I called you a liar."

"That's better," his mother said. "You two should love each other. Not always be fighting."

He paused strategically for a long moment.

"Can I go out now?"

"Yes," his mother said.

He rose from the table, glaring at his sister with a broad grin, calling her a liar with his eyes.

His hand plucked his jacket from the couch and swirled it around his back. The buttons refused to fit through the holes, so he let them go in despair. He sat down just long enough to pull on his shiny black rubbers. Finally he put on his gloves. Then with four proud strides he arrived at the door and reached for the knob.

"Put your hat on," his mother said without looking at him.

His face, toward the door, screwed and tightened with disgust. "Aw Ma."

"Put it on."

"Aw Ma, it's not that cold out."

"Put it on."

"Honest Ma, it's not that cold out."

"Are you going to put your hat on, or are you going to stay and help with the dishes?"

He sighed. "All right," he said. "I'll put it on."

The door to the kitchen closed on his back and he was alone in the cold gloom of the shed. Pale light streamed through the frosted window and fell against the wall where the sled stood. The dark cold room was silent, and he was free. He moved into the shaft of light and stopped when from the kitchen he heard the muffled murmur of his mother's voice, as if she were far away. He listened. The murmuring hushed and he was alone again.

The sled. It was leaning against the wall, its varnished wood glistening in the moonlight. He moved closer to it and he saw his shadow block the light, and he heard the cold cracking of the loose linoleum beneath his feet.

He picked it up. He felt the smooth wood slippery in his gloved hands. The thin steel runners shone blue in the light, as he moved one finger along the polished surface to erase any dust. He shifted the sled in his hands and stood getting the feel of its weight the way he had seen his brother hold a rifle. He gripped the sled tightly, aware of the strength in his arms; and he felt proud to be strong and alone and far away with the sled in the dark cold silent room.

The sled was small and light. But strong. And when he ran with it, he ran very quickly, quicker than anyone, because it was very light and small and not bulky like other sleds. And when he ran with it, he carried it as if it were a part of him, as if he carried nothing in his arms. He set the rear end on the floor and let the sled lean against him, his hands on the steering bar. He pushed down on the bar and the thin runners curved gracefully because they were made of shiny blue flexible steel; and with them he could turn sharply in the snow, sharper than anyone. It was the best sled. It was his.

He felt a slight chill in the cold room, and in the moonlight he saw his breath in vapor rising like cigarette smoke before his eyes. His body shivered with excitement as he moved hurriedly but noiselessly to the door. He flung it open; and the snow blue and sparkling, and the shadows deep and mysterious, and the air silent and cold: all awaited him.

"Joey!" From the kitchen came his mother's voice. He turned toward the kitchen door and refused to answer.

"Joseph!"

"What!" His tone was arrogant, and a chill of fear rushed through his mind.

There was a long awful silence.

"Don't you forget to be home by seven o'clock." She hadn't noticed, and his fear was gone.

"All right!" He answered, ashamed of his fear. He stepped across the threshold and closed the door. Then he removed the hat and dropped it in the snow beside the porch.

He plodded down the alley, thrilling in the cold white silence—

the snow was thick. The gate creaked as he pushed it open, holding and guiding the sled through the portal. The street was white, and shiny were the icy tracks of automobiles in the lamplight above. While between him and the light the black branches of trees ticked softly in the slight wind. In the gutters stood enormous heaps of snow, pale and dark in the shadows, stretching away from him like a string of mountains. He moved out of the shadows, between two piles of snow, and into the center of the street; where he stood for a moment gazing down the white road that gradually grew darker until it melted into the gloom at the far end.

Then he started to trot slowly down the street. Slowly, slowly gaining speed without losing balance. Faster he went now, watching the snow glide beneath his shiny black rubbers. Faster and faster, but stiffly, don't slip. Don't fall, don't fall: now! And his body plunged downward, and the sled whacked in the quiet and the white close to his eyes was flying beneath him as he felt the thrill of gliding alone along a shadowy street, with only the ski-sound of the sled in the packed snow. Then before his eyes the moving snow gradually slowed. And stopped. And he heard only the low sound of the wind and his breath.

Up again and start the trot. He moved to the beating sound of his feet along the ground. His breath came heavily and quickly, and matched the rhythm of his pumping legs, straining to carry the weight of his body without the balance of his arms. He reached a wild dangerous breakneck speed, and his leg muscles swelled and ached from the tension, and the fear of falling too early filled his mind; and down he let his body go. The white road rushed to meet him; he was off again, guiding the sled obliquely across the street toward a huge pile of snow near a driveway.

Squinting his eyes into the biting wind, he calculated when he would turn to avoid crashing. The pile, framed against the darkness of the sky, glistened white and shiny. It loomed larger and larger before him. He steered the sled sharply, bending the bar; and the snow flew as the sled churned sideways, and he heard suddenly a cold metallic snap. He and the sled went tumbling over in the hard wet snow. He rolled with it and the steering bar jarred his forehead. Then the dark sky and snow stopped turning, and all he felt was the cold air stinging the bump on his forehead.

The runner had snapped; the sled was broken. He stared at the shiny smooth runner and touched the jagged edge with his fingers. He sat in the middle of the driveway, the sled cradled in his lap, running his fingers up and down the thin runner until he came to the jagged edge where it had broken.

With his fingers he took the two broken edges and fitted them back into place. They stuck together with only a thin crooked line to indicate the split. But it was like putting a broken cup together. He stared at it, and wished it would be all right and felt like crying.

He got up and walked slowly back down the street to his house. He sat down between the back bumper of a parked car and a pile of snow. Cradling the sled across his legs, he put the two edges together again and stared at them. He felt a thickness in his throat, and he swallowed hard to remove it, but it did not go away.

He leaned back, resting his head against the snowpile. Through his wet eyelids he saw the lamplight shimmering brightly against the sky. He closed his eyes and saw again the shiny graceful curve of the runner. But it was broken now. He had bent it too far; too far. With his hand he rubbed his neck, then his eyes, then his neck again. And he felt the snow coming wet through his pants. As he shifted to a new position, he heard the creaking of a gate. He turned toward the sound.

His sister was walking away from his house. He watched her move slowly across the street and into the grocery store. Through the plate-glass window he saw her talking with the storekeeper. He stared down at the runner. With his gloves off, he ran his fingers along the cold smooth surface and felt the thin breakline. He got up, brushed the snow off the seat of his pants, and walked to the gate to wait for his sister.

He saw her take a package from the man and come out of the store. She walked carefully on the smooth white, her figure dark in its own shadow as she passed beneath the streetlight, the package in her arm. When she reached the curb on his side, he rested his arms on the nose of the sled and exhaled a deep breath nervously. He pretended to be staring in the opposite direction.

When he heard her feet crunching softly in the snow, he turned: "Hi," he said.

"Hi," she said, and she paused for a moment. "Good sledding?"

"Uhuh," he said. "Just right. Snow's packed nice and hard. Hardly any slush at all." He paused. "I'm just resting a bit now."

She nodded. "I just went for some milk."

His fingers moved slowly down the runner and touched the joined edges.

"Well . . ." she said, about to leave.

His fingers trembled slightly, and he felt his heart begin to beat rapidly: "Do you want to take a flop?" In the still night air he heard with surprise the calm sound of his voice.

Her face came suddenly alive. "Can I? I mean, will you let me? Really?"

"Sure," he said. "Go ahead," and he handed her the sled very carefully. She gave him the package.

He put the bag under his arm and watched her move out of the shadows of the trees and into the light. She started to trot slowly, awkwardly, bearing the sled. She passed directly beneath the light and then she slipped and slowed to regain her balance. The sled looked large and heavy in her arms, and seeing her awkwardness, he realized she would be hurt badly in the fall. She was moving away again, out of the reach of the streetlight, and into the gray haze farther down the road.

He moved to the curb, holding the bag tightly under his arm, hearing his heart pounding in his ears. He wanted to stop her, and he opened his mouth as if to call to her; but no sound came. It was too late: her dark figure was already starting the fall, putting the sled beneath her. Whack! And her head dipped with the front end jutting the ground, and the back of the sled and her legs rose like a seesaw and down they came with another muffled sound. The street was quiet, except for a low whimper that filled his ears.

He saw her figure rise slowly and move toward him. He walked out to meet her beneath the light. She held the sled loosely in one hand, the broken runner dangling, reflecting light as she moved.

She sobbed and looking up he saw bright tears falling down her cheeks, and a thin line of blood trickling down her chin. In the

corner of her mouth near the red swelling on her lip, a little bubble
of spit shone with the blood in the light.

He felt that he should say something but he did not speak.

"I'm . . . I'm sorry," she said and the bubble broke. "I'm sorry
I . . . your sled." She looked down at the sled. "It'll never be the
same."

"It'll be all right," he said. He felt that he ought to do something
but he did not move. "I can get it soldered. Don't worry about it."
But he saw from her expression that she thought he was only trying
to make her feel better.

"No," she said, shaking her head emphatically. "No it won't!
It'll always have that weak spot now." She began to cry very
hard. "I'm sorry."

He made an awkward gesture of forgiveness with his hand.
"Don't cry," he said.

She kept crying.

"It wasn't your fault," he said.

"Yes it was," she said. "Oh, yes it was."

"No!" he said. "No it wasn't!" But she didn't seem to hear him,
and he felt his words were useless. He sighed wearily with defeat,
not knowing what to say next. He saw her glance up at him as if
to see whether he were still watching her, then she quickly lowered
her gaze and said with despair and anguish: "Oh . . . girls are so
stupid!"

There was no sound. She was no longer crying. She was looking
at the ground: waiting. His ears heard nothing; they felt only the
cold silent air.

"No they aren't," he said halfheartedly. And he heard her breathing again. He felt he had been forced to say that. In her shining
eyes he saw an expression he did not understand. He wished she
would go in the house. But seeing the tears on her cheeks and the
blood on her chin, he immediately regretted the thought.

She wiped her chin with her sleeve, and he winced, feeling
rough cloth on an open cut. "Don't do that," his hand moved to
his back pocket, "use my handkerchief."

She waited.

The pocket was empty. "I haven't got one," he said.

Staring directly at him, she patted gingerly the swollen part of her lip with the tips of her fingers.

He moved closer to her. "Let me see," he said. With his hands he grasped her head and tilted it so that the light fell directly on the cut.

"It's not too bad," she said calmly. And as she said it she looked straight into his eyes, and he felt she was perfectly at ease; while standing that close to her, he felt clumsy and out of place.

In his hands her head was small and fragile, and her hair was soft and warm; he felt the rapid pulsing of the vein in her temple: his ears grew hot with shame.

"Maybe I better go inside and wash it off?" she asked.

With his finger he wiped the blood from her chin. "Yes," he said, feeling relieved. "You go inside and wash it off." He took the sled and gave her the package.

He stared at the ground as they walked to the gate in silence. When they reached the curb he became aware that she was watching him.

"You've got a nasty bump on your forehead," she said.

"Yes," he said. "I fell."

"Let me put some snow on it," she said, reaching to the ground.

He caught her wrist and held it gently. "No," he said.

He saw her about to object: "It's all right. You go inside and take care of your lip." He said it softly but with his grip and his eyes he told her more firmly.

"All right," she said after a moment, and he released his hold. "But don't forget to put your hat on."

He stared at her.

"I mean, *before* you go back in the house."

They both smiled.

"Thanks for reminding me," he said, and he dropped the sled in the snow and hurried to hold the gate open for her.

She hesitated, then smiled proudly as he beckoned her into the alley.

He watched her walk away from him down the dark alley in the gray snow. Her small figure swayed awkwardly as she stepped carefully in the deep snow, so as not to get her feet too wet. Her head was bowed and her shoulders hunched and he humbly felt her weakness. And he felt her cold. And he felt the snow running cold down her boots around her ankles. And though she wasn't crying now, he could still hear her low sobbing, and he saw her shining eyes and the tears falling and she trying to stop them and they falling even faster. And he wished he had never gone sledding. He wished that he had never even come out of the house tonight.

The back door closed. He turned and moved about nervously kicking at the ground. At the edge of the curb he dug his hands deep into the cold wet snow. He came up with a handful and absently began shaping and smoothing it. He stopped abruptly and dropped it at his feet.

He did not hear it fall. He was looking up at the dark sky but he did not see it. He put his cold hands in his back pockets but he did not feel them. He was wishing that he were some time a long time away from now and somewhere a long way away from here.

In the corner of his eye something suddenly dimmed. Across the street in the grocery store the light was out: it was seven o'clock.

MIRIAM McKENZIE was born in 1923 in Wilmington, Delaware. She received a B.A. in English from the University of Delaware and then did graduate work in Psychology, receiving a PH.D. from New York University. She lives in New York City with her husband, a theater director. This is her first published story.

DÉJÀ VU

from *New World Writing*

She stood at the hedge, only her head visible, looking more than ever like a wood creature—startled, vulnerable, remote. Her face was lit by a strange excitement, and there was the suggestion of a smile, but she said very innocently, so still-ly, "Poor Miranda, I believe her mother is dead."

Coffee cup still at her lips, Lucy looked hard at the beautiful child, so like her own that she could read, with care, her mysterious face. Lethargic, as only the obese or insane can be, burdened by her own flesh and slow-oozing blood, Lucy used her eyes alone for the world, and like the blind man's heightened sense of touch, her sight had grown keen with exercise.

Her hand, frozen now on the cup handle, for well she knew that innocent smile, she said, in a cold, tight voice, "Martha, where is your mother?" and the child laughed, in mad, hoarse glee, and answered: "On the kitchen floor." She bounded off, just a head skimming the hedges, with plaits in suspension, as Lucy lurched out of the chaise, cup dropped more than placed on the grass, the opened book sliding noiselessly from her lap.

For a moment she just stood, a short, heavy girl-woman, backed against her chaise, looking about pleadingly, bewilderedly, as if

Copyright © 1961 by J. B. Lippincott Company.

jolted from sleep by a bad dream, and needing to place herself. Sudden movement, sudden feeling, were antipathetic to her nature, and she stood, faint and thick, inert, wounded, disoriented. The May warmth, spring warmth, and air heavy with the scent of damp earth, early flowers, in which she had, only a moment before, been reveling, was transformed into the feel and smell of a sickroom, and she was the patient, abandoned too soon in her convalescence, weak-kneed, frightened, and fragile.

She looked toward the house, even started for it, dazedly, but remembered it was Laura's day off; there was no one else, child or adult, and she ran, in a strange slow-motion, as if through another's will, into her driveway, barefooted, shapeless feet hardened to the large stones that covered it. The drive, overhung by new leaves, covered by dappled light, was like a tunnel seen in sleep, and Lucy, who never ran, felt the surprise of the dreamer, watching herself in an unexpected action. She was in flight, but she knew not from what, where to, and she looked, running so awkwardly, her pony-tail still uncombed, in a soiled white shirt of her husband's, tails out, and a blue denim skirt, like the fat little girl she must once have been, running home to a mother who couldn't comfort her.

Though she still dressed like that child, in ruffled calico, Liberty Bell buttons, and corduroy jumpers, she no longer recognized her in her mirrors, taken in by the woman who puffed on her pink powder, drew on the red mouth. Smoking three packs of cigarettes a day, always with a cup of coffee at her elbow, she never recognized that little girl, in her quilted skirt, her denim skirt.

But the slow, clumsy running did what no mirror could, and she sank into a walk, biting her thumb hard, as she remembered her mother, slim in black linen, her tanned arm, jangling in its golden bangles, extended, while she tucked a crisp bill into Lucy's counselor's breast pocket. She remembered how the counselors had gathered about her whenever she came, a court to her beauty and wit, so pleased, in their new adult status, to be included in her little jokes, her quick flippancies. For days after, they would speak of her as if she were their mother and not hers, and as if they shared some wonderful secret with her from which she, Lucy, was excluded.

It took her two minutes to reach the end of her short drive, and emerging from its shade, she crossed the strip of road, bright with sun, that separated the houses, with no awareness of having done so. It was only after she had taken a few steps into the other drive-way, still a hundred feet to the house, that she remembered her errand, and she stopped, completely, not moving a muscle, only panting, shallowly, rapidly. She looked at nothing and felt unseen, and stood there, like a large animal, obstinate in its terror, trying to blend in with its surroundings, to take on the shape and color of a rock. Her body was rigid in its withdrawal, her eyes strained with not seeing.

A side of the house was visible from this point, and when she looked (how long later?) and saw that the shades were drawn, she sagged in stunning relief; with the cunning of the practiced self-deceptive, she concluded that Isabel was taking her midmorning nap, and Martha had, after all, only been playing one of her sick little tricks. That child was really a monster, something that had crawled out from under a rock. Isabel had confided that there were days when she couldn't look at her small, hidden face, and Jack would have to take her off somewhere, anywhere, until she re-gained her composure, always, for this child, a steel-like control. She said she didn't trust herself at those moments, so enraged was she by the very sight of her, and Lucy was swept by an impulse to hunt her out and slap her, an instant's fury that disappeared as she dawdled in the drive, painfully catching her breath. She had an uneasy sense of something being out of place, of the dream continuing, and she lingered, breathing heavily, pinching off the black-green leaves from the hedge detachedly with her left hand.

Perhaps it was the sun on her hand, a strong, past-noon sun, or the kind of hush, not of the morning, or the children's voices, from a distance, muffled but shrill, that shattered her feeble illusion; it was past noon, and she knew that Isabel, efficient housewife, would long ago have been up and at her scheduled tasks. Lolling in her own garden, she hadn't thought of the time, knowing a neighbor, probably Isabel, would feed her children if they didn't turn up.

The shades were drawn to the same point, room to room, and Lucy remembered, nauseous now with fear, the time she had gone to Olive Lane's house, one childhood morning, to ask her to draw more paper dolls, and she couldn't touch the bell because of the

ugly gray crape that concealed it. For months after, she was torn
between her need for Olive's dolls, so like Olive herself—bow-
mouthed, rouged, spit-curled—and her terror of that house in
which Olive's grandfather, brown with age, the monkey-man, had
died.

She moved forward, involuntarily, almost stealthily, as if she
must be on guard; she had a sudden image of an oversized funeral
wreath, gaudy flowers stiffly wired, and she looked to the ground,
afraid a snake might slither across her path. Now she concentrated
on the path, absorbedly, formulating the precise color and shape
of its fine gravel, almost counting her steps. She liked the feel of
her feet sinking in the gravel, and she stopped a minute to dig her
big toe in more deeply.

A crescendo of shrieks, like birds frightened from a cover, sent
her scurrying instinctively, head still bent, into the rustic playhouse
that sat just back from the turn in the drive. She had to duck a
little at the door, but once inside she could stand, and she leaned
against the log wall, trembling, feeling the beat of her heart in her
back.

The room was as trim as one of Isabel's, and though she had always been intrigued by the real windows that pushed out, the
child-size rocker, the doll bed, the stove, the tea set, she saw nothing, only welcomed the concealment. Standing so, just inside the
door, against the wall, she had the posture of a child in hiding,
hiding inadequately, and just as sure that a furious mother would
storm through the door and discover her. She felt very warm,
clammy with fear, and there was that pain, and yet thrill, in her
throat. She read *Rock-a-bye, baby*, painted in gold script across the
top of the black, lacquered rocker, and she watched a spider make
its way slowly, somnambulistically, across the opposite sill.

Their voices were coming from the kitchen, just paces away, a
rising and falling, the essence of extreme excitement, phrased by
very brief, very breath-holding silences, and she began to mumble,
as if telling a rosary, making extravagant promises to God and the
possibly deceased, if only she were spared this one time more. She
made little spitting sounds with her lips, reviving a long-forgotten
defense against the Devil, and her mumbling and spitting mingled

with the buzzing of a bee, out of sight, lost somewhere in the rafters.

It was David's shout, "You kick her, Mandy" (she had heard no words before, could only take in the rumble), that wrenched her from her hiding place, walking rapidly, pitched forward, the mother, herself, ready to pounce. His voice drew her as red magnetizes the bull, with the first response always that of rage, and though she felt her fear just behind it, she was up the back steps and at the screen door with a burst of energy that left her, pulsatingly, palpitatingly, as she looked, transfixed, at the tableau within.

Four children, shocked, laughing, anguished, were pinching, kicking, touching, and recoiling from, the dead young woman, face purple and swollen, who lay on the floor. They formed a circle that undulated as one child would suddenly dart forward, daring contact with the dead, the others, nerved, following, and then one by one, pulling sharply back, stricken. Each became the leader, unchallenged—they brought an order to death they had never brought to play—only quickly to relinquish his position to the next brave one. Goliath lay slain, but could one be sure?

The afternoon sunlight, mote-filled, fell on them from the two windows like giant spotlights, carefully angled, and in their brightly colored summer dresses and jerseys, they looked like dwarfed Breughel peasants, dancing in their drunkenness. The gleaming white stove and sink and refrigerator, the snap beans in a colander on the drainboard, the electric clock, with its second hand sweeping around, served as ground to the figures, oblivious, impervious ground. —The herd impelled to stampede, a crowd moved to destroy, their pace accelerated; they shrieked and squealed and circled and spun—a merry-go-round of small demons, out of control.

She collapsed against the door, and the dull thud was followed by an immediate hush. For moments, minutes, the four of them were fixed, just where they were, staring at Lucy, an all-seeing monster, two-dimensional and immense, flattened up against the screen. And with glazed, mad eyes, Lucy stared at this pack that had once been young children. The hum of the clock, a large, evil eye, could be heard, but no human sound penetrated this timeless silence.

David spoke first, hushedly: "Isabel's dead, Mom," but Lucy didn't move, didn't hear. He was more shrill, the good boy reporting: "Look, Mom, Isabel's dead." Jennie, just four, the tag-along, began to cry, and ran to the door, but Lucy was unmovable, lifeless. Martha and Miranda hung back, almost bashfully, as if out of modesty—it was so much their show—, David with them, prepared for flight, never taking his eyes from Lucy. Unable to get out, Jennie began to scream, and to pound on her mother, scratching her small fists on the screen that separated them, and though none of the others moved, they, like animals, gave small signs of rising panic, and it was these that brought Lucy slowly, confusedly, into consciousness. Faint, on the verge of retching, she saw the four children, two hers, two Isabel's, and Isabel, neighbor and best friend, dead, in a checked gingham apron, mustard and white.

Slack-mouthed, leaning against the door as if deflated, a larger than life-size Boppo, the clown balloon, aslant and dying on its cardboard feet, a mute in deep pain, she looked at David, and he stood, also dumb, his face already concealing, though subtly crossed, a sensitive surface, by a swift succession of emotions. He waited for her sign, Fagin's waif watching his master, and finally, with a hand she couldn't raise, she just visibly, so vaguely, pointed to the back of him, and he, who could obey no order directly, especially hers, ran into the hall, glad to begin the long atonement.

Though only six, he could be relied upon to make the call to the hospital, just as he could have led one to any road in the community at two, told the time accurately at three, and read the newspaper, adult word for adult word, at four; so bleakly lost within, so mother-lost, he could not risk losing touch without. The incongruity of this undersized boy, who looked like a sad Buster Brown, with his round, dark eyes, and thatch of blond hair, trudging home from the library with his books of facts, amused the townspeople, who called him a "character," and liked to engage him in conversation just to hear his serious, little old-head remarks. The children were still tolerant—he was so gentle in his pedantry —but they thought he "talked like a book."

The three girls were all at the door, Jennie hysterical, and the other two, stiffly silent, looking patiently at Lucy, already orphans, knowing their place. Miranda, the younger, round and sturdy, secure as the second child in her mother's love, sensed her new status through Martha, who had been rehearsing this role daily, all of her seven years. Here, in this moment of final triumph, her magnificent face was, as always, inscrutable, and her bearing as tautly erect, but her *raison d'être* was gone, and Lucy saw, even with the screen between them, a new hollowness in those eyes.

Her throat too tight for more than a cracked whisper, she told them to come out, stepping back weavingly so they could open the door. Jennie grasped her leg, almost tumbling her from the steps, and the two sisters walked into the back garden, Martha stooping to pick up a broken toy barrow, Miranda just behind, watching her in silence. Lucy looked back at her friend, always so freshly lovely (honey-blond hair in a high bun; soft, fragrant cotton dresses), now mottled and grotesque, twisted and rigid, and with an involuntary shrug of revulsion, turned away, breaking into a loud hiccough as she stifled a sob, bile filling her mouth. Jennie looked up in alarm, through blurred, tear-filled eyes, and then took up her crying, nuzzling her head deeper into her mother's soft, thick thigh.

She stood a moment longer, struggling with the thought that she should go into the kitchen to see if Isabel were truly dead (Was she dead? Is that death's face?), and then sat down heavily on the top step, her back to the door, trying to shut out what was behind her with all of her body and thought. She pulled Jennie onto her lap, and looked out into the garden with blank, sick eyes, and she sat limply huddled, holding the child in her arms as if she were trying to pull into herself her own escaping entrails, a gesture of self-preservation. She only thought of David, waiting for him to come take up the lead, like a child staving off panic in the dark with one sing-song phrase, and she began to rock back and forth, loosely, rhythmically.

Somewhere in her dark web of feelings for David, there was the dependence upon an older brother, hated, envied, and needed, so that mother and son were often brother and sister, taunting, imploring, destroying, supporting. Sometimes she was the big sister, fat and aggressive, shriveling his budding masculinity with a quick, murderous hand on the back of his neck, and sometimes he was the older, triumphant and mocking in answering her needs. The transitions were swift, but each knew his part, recognized his cue.

(With horror and fascination, she had watched Isabel in the same terrible game of destruction with her first-born, and the irony of the perpetual *déjà vu* did not completely escape her: her neighbor mirror-imaged her own evil. Closest friends after a time, they played scrabble in the afternoons, locked in one another's homes, their own children shut without.)

The afternoon sun, which dominated this open patch, seemed to hold them like lizards in its grasp, and the only sounds, except for Jennie's chantlike wails, mechanical, fading, were small and very clear: Lucy's hiccoughs, quieter now, and that of the one good barrow-wheel that Martha was spinning with close attention. Lucy was growing listless, sitting there in the warm sun, hypnotized by her one thought; she was not so afraid sitting there in the warm sun, huddled over—she was never so afraid once she sat or sprawled or curled up.

But the sound of David, running through the kitchen, and the slam of the screen door, exploded the silence, shredded Lucy's cocoon. She turned toward him, but pushing off from her shoulder, he jumped the two steps to the ground, and stood before her, panting, pale, and tense. His lips were quivering, he was close to tears, and mother and son, anxiously scrutinizing each other's faces, were for the first time, deadlocked by panic, complete equals. Each grew more terrified by what he saw in the other's face, and had it not been for Miranda's casual "What are we going to do, Lucy?" they might both have broken into a terrible weeping, two babes in the woods.

Lucy began to bustle, avoiding David's eyes, lifting Jennie, almost asleep, from her lap, and smoothing out her skirt, as she arose, with nervous hands. She announced they were all going to take a walk, and suggested they hurry if they wanted to play on the swings and to get some ice cream. She sometimes slipped into the voice, even the stride, of the senior camp counselor, the quickly assumed voice and demeanor of this moment. She knew that David heard the forced good cheer, the nursery school and "hup-two" rhythms, that he, clearest of all, like the dog that hears the pitch beyond human range, also heard the breathless fear just behind

them, and understood that she was determined to get away before
the ambulance turned into the drive.

Like the faithful collie, he helped collect, and urge on, the children, pulling away at the head of what looked like a crack-the-whip
chain, everyone having reached for everyone else's hand. Miranda
was next to David, laughing each time he swung her arm hard, or
complained, like a querulous old man, of her pokiness, and Martha
was in the middle holding Jennie with her other hand, gently
hurrying her along—they practically ran the length of the drive,
each knowing some need for haste—talking in her pretend-mother
voice, the voice she used for Betsy, her doll and alter ego. Jennie
was pleased (she loved attention, and only by chance was not
wearing her tutu, her favorite play dress), but wary, never before
having been Martha's "baby." She held her mother's hand firmly,
while permitting Martha to direct her around a puddle, to murmur,
"Jennie-sweetie," and "darling baby."

Lucy came last, and looked as though she were unbalancing,
pulling back, this fragile line of children, spread ahead, S-shaped,
on the steep hill that ran between the houses. She pushed forward,
determinedly—in her mind transporting herself over the turnings
and by-ways to the village green, her goal, her haven—struggling
up that road she rarely walked, her attention so directed ahead
that she ignored her bursting lungs, her audible puffing. The children were growing noisier now that there was a distance between
them and the dead, but Lucy said not a word, raptly following their
zigzag course.

They were on level ground again, on the road that led past the
outdoor Shakespeare theater and the community hall, Tudor setting for the weekly square dances and the meetings of the "guilds."
(This was a suburb with a purpose, more cooperative and art-
conscious than most, with its woodedness enhancing its narcissism,
provincialism.) She hadn't been by here since the Valentine party,
and she remembered Isabel, regally beautiful as the Queen of
Hearts, sitting next to her, making her terse, acid comments, as she
looked on with a jaundiced eye. (My God, Isabel was dead! My
God! My God! With whom would she ever talk or laugh again?)
She moaned, a low sound of fright, but the sound was swallowed
up in the light babbling of the children.

The road was deserted, the hour falling short of meeting time, school dismissal, and Lucy, wanting no delay, no encounter, was remotely grateful for their solitary course. They were scattered across the road, and, followed by two of the many dogs that paraded about, patrolled, the town, all day long, they looked like a band of ragamuffins, disheveled and rootless. A bread truck turned out of a drive behind them, and Lucy, absent-mindedly, called everyone into the ditch. She scarcely looked up as it passed, but the children shouted, "Hell-o, Don."

They circled with the road, making only a small noise in the large afternoon silence. The cars on the highway, a half mile away, could be heard distinctly; there was even the hum of a distant vacuum cleaner. Lucy felt the weight of her usual afternoon melancholy, intensified by the shadow of a terrible thought lurking around its edges, and her face was alive in its new anguish. Later, trying to remember the walk to the green, she could only catch that sadness (like a dread spreading through her body), and a few images: the bread truck, and wild mushrooms, looking obscene, clumped along the roots of an old tree. When had she lost those ten minutes? How many years ago?

There was the green, a patched oblong, with its bald spots of earth, the base of the vacuum into which they had been drawn, irresistibly, sinking, sinking—empty, deserted. The baseball diamond with its markers, the swings in a row, the jungle-gym, like an ancient ruin, looked to Lucy like cemetery plots, and sickened by their stamp of death, their loneliness, she quickly turned away from them, following the children into Murphy's "general store" just opposite.

The cowbells on the door jingled loudly, and the children ran to the ice cream case, throwing open its little black doors, reaching in for popsicles. Murphy was rarely in the front of the store and everyone helped himself, going behind the old-fashioned walnut counter, or into the turn-of-the-century candy case, with its sliding doors and curved glass front. The candy was displayed in small glass dishes (Murphy had all the penny varieties) on dirty shelf paper, and the shelves lining the sides of the room were less than half full, with a few brightly wrapped loaves of bread, cans of soup and beans, bars of soap. There was a grappler hanging to a side, though there was nothing on the top shelves except for a peeling Coca-Cola sign, and a large metal samovar (Murphy had visited Russia in the twenties). One of Murphy's cats was asleep on the counter, and Lucy, seating herself on the one stool, off in a gloomy corner, felt for the first time as if she had wandered into a child's play-store.

She noted the children's choices (Jennie, to infuriate, was copying David again), and thought, with shame, of the double-dip cone she would wait for Murphy to get for her. She looked hungrily, furtively, at the rack of ten-cent cakes and pies, and began to tremble with the push of her compulsion, the anxiety it always gave her in public. She felt a terrible guilt as she thought of Isabel, dead, not yet gently lifted from the kitchen floor, and she wanted all the cake and candy and ice cream in Murphy's store.

Murphy came through the door at the rear, a short man, in his Western shirt, Levi's, and sandals, with his customary look of slight surprise and empty geniality. He never made conversation unless one insisted on it; Murphy only seemed to come into his own on square-dance night, when he flew about and promenaded-home like a man half his age, always partnering his ugly, suspicious Scottish wife. He gave Lucy her cone, covered with chocolate sprinkles, and wrote the sale on a slip of paper, since Lucy had no money with her; they exchanged no more than the few words necessary for the transaction. The children were teasing Murphy's cat, an orange one, and trooped out after Lucy, comparing how much each had left as they crossed to the swings.

Miranda and Martha were already swinging, and David was taking his last bite, only half on his swing, when the siren splintered the afternoon quiet, growing immediately louder, more loudly immediate, and Jennie, who had just handed her popsicle to Lucy, en route to the low swings, started to cry again, as if she had never stopped. David jumped down, and ran to stand by Lucy, looking wildly at the two sisters, bent toward them, a frantic, angry terrier. He shouted, "Your mother is dead, don't you know your mother is dead?", repeating and repeating, with more fury and agitation, as Martha and Miranda, never looking down, continued to swing, pumping harder, flying higher. Lucy licked at her dripping cone, quickly, expertly, her eyes fixed on her task.

MAUREEN HOWARD was born in 1930 in Bridgeport, Connecticut. After graduating from Smith College, she worked for several years in publishing and advertising in New York City. Since her marriage, Mrs. Howard has lived in Rome and London, and now lives in New Brunswick, New Jersey, where her husband teaches literature at Rutgers. She has previously published several short stories, reviews, and a novel, *Not a Word About Nightingales*.

BRIDGEPORT BUS

from *The Hudson Review*

FIRST I WILL WRITE:

When I go home, I walk through all the dim two-family-house streets where the colors are brown and grey with what they call cream trim. On the route I take—eight thirty in the morning, five at night—there are four houses which are repainted in pastels, pink and pale green, with aluminum around the doors; the windows and their front stoops are faced with quarter-inch fake stone. When my nerves are raw from the meaningless day at work I see nothing more than four ugly houses, their vulgar shapes, their sameness, defined by the light colors and bright metal. On better days I think these houses have beauty, reflect some hope shared by the Italians who own them: I suppose their blank painted faces would look fine in the Mediterranean sun or in a summer town on the Long Island shore.

I turn to walk up the hill where I live—here the dark houses are equally bad, though they are presumed to be better, with an extra bedroom in each flat and the upstairs flat bulged out over

By permission from The Hudson Review, Vol. XIII, No. 4, Winter 1960–61. Copyright 1961 by The Hudson Review, Inc.

the downstairs porch. When I look up the hill there are dirty window eyes and huge indolent growths on each idiot brow, a row of monster heads to greet me. I turn back and see the city stretched out dead at my feet. I think about New York or San Francisco or Paris, the scene in which young Gide (it's the first entry in his journals) looks down on beautiful and mist-grey Paris across the imaginary writing desk of an artist. I started that book but something happened, my brother's children, my mother's gall bladder, something happened so I never finished. The actor says, "You see all that down there," (panorama of city at night) "all that," he says to Rita Hayworth, "will be yours." When I look down I see my city on the banks of the exhausted Naugatuck. There is a line of rust along the shore that smells of rubber—the gardens, if I may be allowed, of factories, and then the hills with all the streets of brown houses coming up towards me and towards my street of superior brown houses.

When I go home my mother and I play a cannibal game; we eat each other over the years, tender morsel by morsel, until there is nothing left but dry bone and wig. She is winning—needless to say has had so much more experience—she meets me in the front room, hiding behind the evening paper, a fat self-indulgent body, her starved mind hungry for me. I am on guard when I first come from work—what means has she devised during the day for devouring me? I stand under the dark-stained arch, an anxious thrill rising in me, and just wait, watching but not seeing the elephant chairs and my bloated old mother behind her paper. This room, stuffed with darkness, day or night, any season, is a monochrome of immobility; heavy chairs, lame tables, parchment shades and curtains of ecru lace, all colorless as time—all under a layer of antediluvian silt. Arrangement in grey and black, portrait of my mother profiled, soft and bulky in her sagging chair: a big Irish-woman full of life with eyes ready to cry. For contrast, her white hair crimped in a prim and Protestant roll, seen against the walls (a deeper tone) papered in potato skins. A coat of yellow varnish, the years of our aboriginal love, over the entire picture. I have not long to wait, contemplating the classic scene of home, for she speaks up right away.

"Ag?" she says, not looking at me, and I don't answer, but I entertain myself with the notion that one day it will be someone else come in the front door, a rapist or a mad killer and she'll be caught there reading the obituaries or the society page or looking up her TV programs for the night. "Ag, I bought snowsuits today for the children downtown."

"In April? That's fine."

"On sale, Ag. Sometimes I don't think you use your head. There's been sales advertised downtown all week. I bought them big for next year." She smiles at me, puffy and red in the face, self-satisfied, imitating all the well-to-do Irish.

"I don't read that paper. How much?" I ask.

"Well, that's it—only twenty dollars," mother says.

"Sixty dollars?"

"Yes, for *three* children. I guess I can multiply as well as you Mary Agnes." Then she's had enough and pushes herself out of the chair to waddle off and get supper.

"Sixty dollars," I say after her, "and what's wrong with the ones you bought last year, not on sale. Can't they pass the clothes on? Can't Catherine wear Patrick's snowsuit? I didn't know a goddamn girl's coat buttoned from right to left when I was their age."

"I don't like to hear you talk that way, Mary Agnes." And then she will say, hurt to wrench my heart—and it works every time— my heart *is* wrenched looking at her raw face, tears swelling. Her blood pressure is up. "Your father, rest his soul, was poor. It's a sad thing, Ag, when you've no more feeling left for your brother and his family way up there in Buffalo. It doesn't matter about me, but it's sad."

We never get more violent than that. I am cursed with gentility and can hardly do better than an occasional name of the Lord in vain, but after each argument I like to look at myself in my own room or in the blue glass mirror in the dining room. There I can see what part of me she has picked at—her favorite soft flesh around the eyes or my shamefully concave chest. I am gaunt, you might guess it, five-foot eleven, one hundred and eighteen pounds. But why do I start with such heightened drama when there are the usual tidbits: my mail is opened, my bureau drawers rearranged, Clorox put in the machine with a new dress, or: "Ag?" (Once again it is only me, not the sex maniac I dream of, and she goes on at me behind the paper.) "Christine Doyle called about the Sodality Tea and she said wouldn't you pour. Isn't that nice?"

"And you said yes?"

"Yes, isn't that nice." Then she is wise enough to hurry right on and read me something out of the paper: "Well poor Tom Heffernan died, that's a blessing. They say his body was full of it."

You will think now that I am stupid and incompetent, but you would be surprised how I can gnaw at my mother just by reading for hours, or not speaking, or muttering "Christ" in the direction of the television set as I pass through the front room. And, my choicest bone of contention, I take night courses every year instead of making myself one bit attractive to the gelded, balding boys that my mother is able to find in limitless supply. "Tess Mueller is coming over with that nice son who works in the bank," she announces from behind her paper. I get a quick flash of Fred Mueller, a harmless pudding-beast caged at the People's Trust, counting out my money and saying, "Cold enough for you?" or "Long time no see."

"That's a shame," I tell my mother, "because I'm going to the library in New Haven tonight."

"The library, the *library*—" shrieks of coronary outrage.

"The University, mother. Hundreds of men."

But she is gasping now and slaps her beloved *Evening American* against the brown velour chair. "That's what I'm to tell Tess when she brings that nice boy, that you've gone to the *library?*"

"Oh, you'd be surprised—hundreds of men . . ." But never use even the simplest sarcasm on children because they don't get it, and I wonder if I should illustrate my point for mother: maybe a story about a nun, a Sister of Mercy, working on Cardinal Newman in the stack; she meets up with an emeritus professor, a medievalist who has just been writing a piece on the clerical orgies at Cluny. Scene: the Sterling Memorial Library in the $9860.2n$'s. Time: four o'clock in the week of Septuagesima. It is a moment of transition and the lights have not yet been turned on. . . .

Mother smooths out the newspaper, folds it, tucks it under her arm with finality: she is finished, through with me. "Ag," she says, "you are thirty-five years old."

This is her master stroke. What I should have written to begin with is that I am Mary Agnes Keely, a thirty-five-year-old virgin. All narrative should begin with essentials, instead of the oblique device—picture of a city, a house—that flirts with the truth in a maidenly way. I am called Ag, named Mary after guess who and Agnes after the child martyr. She defended her virginity before it had even a literary value, so I have never had much sympathy with her. At the age of thirteen can you honestly say there is a choice—I mean between a lion and a dirty, nasty man. I can not believe in a world which honors that prissy little girl, and dishonors me as no more than one of a million social misfits, and lets me be fed daily to my ravenous old mother. "Ag," she will say, her mouth watering, "you are thirty-five years old."

As I write this I am calm for the first time in years, sitting at my dressing table where I can look at myself often, and I admire the freshness that has come to my cheeks this evening and what seems to be a new firm quality to my throat. I have laid out a thick pad of yellow theme paper and with a smooth, satisfying ball point pen I have begun to write. I can hear my mother at the telephone out in the kitchen. She is whining, aggrieved, to the long distance operator and is asking again, the fifth time in the hour, if the girl will dial her son in Buffalo. My brother and his family don't seem to be at home; that's the straw, she tells my Aunt Mae in a lengthy call, that broke the camel's back in her already broken heart. She has told her sad story to Aunt Mae and to her younger sister Aunt Lil. From what I can overhear, Aunt Lil will be over after supper, done up in her ranch mink stole, to talk to me and try to straighten things out, though nothing is tangled as far as I'm concerned—things are straighter than they have ever been, and I intend to set the whole scene down on my pleasant yellow pad.

It is spring now, but nine weeks ago tonight it was winter, the beginning of February. I came in from the wet gloom of the brown streets to the shriveled gloom of our house—there was mother with the *Evening American*, but she didn't ask who it was standing under the arch, so immediately I knew there was to be an announcement on a grand scale.

"Is it still raining, Ag?" she asked, sweetness itself.

"Yes," I said.

Then she put down the paper so I could see that she had been to the Edna-Lou Beauty Shop. Her hair had a fresh rinse of purple and was kinked in to the head. She was wearing her best stylish-stout wine crepe with a surplice top, and her new Enna Jettick shoes. "Well, wouldn't you just know," my mother said with false petulance, "wouldn't you just know it would rain tonight." She waited, preening out her fat bosom, but I wouldn't ask, so she heaved out of the chair. "Dinner is almost on the table. We have to eat early tonight, Ag, because of the novena."

"The novena!" I said. Her backside looked broader than ever as she hustled out to the kitchen. Ever since I was a girl, for over twenty years that would be, I had to drag my mother to that novena in the winter, tugging her up the church steps like an impossible rolled mattress and stuffing her into a pew. Then the Rosary, the Aspirations, the Benediction, the Prayer for Peace . . . the whole thing started just before the war and was addressed to Our Lady of Fatima who, as I recall, appeared to some prepubescent Portuguese and said the world was coming to an end—as though that were news. So off to the novena and afterwards from St. Augustine's to Friedman's Dairy with the Scanlan sisters, Aunt Mae, and a toothy schoolteacher named Louise Conroy, there to reap the reward: heavenly hot fudge sundaes, topped with whipped cream, and a symposium on every hysterectomy in town. Unfortunately, when the novena was four-ninths or five-ninths over it coincided with Lent, so that my mother and her friends would stand in the back of the church and debate about going to Friedman's, but they always went, denying themselves nuts and whipped cream to commemorate the forty days and forty nights in the desert. Nine weeks ago tonight the novena began.

"I've put your dinner out," my mother called and I walked slowly out to the kitchen. She had already settled herself behind a dish of glutinous brown stew.

"I have my course tonight, mother." *En route* I had switched from the Spenser-Milton seminar which was to be given on Friday evenings to Modern French Poetry.

"You have what?" Poor mother, she saw I was serious.

I sat down opposite her, just as loose and easy, and said, "My French course. It comes on Thursdays."

"God knows," she started her harangue right away, "you were

brought up a good Catholic girl that you should choose a lot of dirty French books over your religion. And thank the good Lord," (with a tremolo) "your father is not here to see you an ingrate to your mother . . . a woman the age of you, Mary Agnes, thirty-five years old . . ." and on and on with a sad scum forming on her stew. She looked hateful with all the veins jumping in her face, yet I almost cried, out of a perverse love for her ravings. I was consumed, ready to say yes I would go with her and try to stop the end of the world, but she said, "I will pray for you, Mary Agnes," with her lips all pursed up. That was new, as though she were sucking the marrow out of my bones, and for eight weeks I have heard it—how she is praying for me, for a woman who would let her old mother go down the slippery hills and up the church steps alone at night.

It must have been her praying for me that started me on the pastel houses. I had to have something to come back with after all. Three or four times a week when I came in from work, I told my mother about the Italian houses, the houses that are painted pink and pale green. I would mention how gay they look on a rainy day or remark what a lovely aluminum curlycued C the Capizzolis had put on their front door, or how I admired the Riccios' empty urn, a cemetery urn painted red, standing in front of their peachy pink house. And all the while I had no knowledge, I will swear to it, that I was provoking her more than usual. Yes, I was nibbling! And there were the expected retorts about foreigners: "They weren't stupid. They knew how to improve their property." But when I told her I liked the Italian houses it was only partially true. I had come to love them. I left the house early to hurry down my street and around the corner to the first one, the Marcuccis', who had left corrugated metal awnings up all winter long waiting for sun, and then on to the Riccios' splendid red urn that promised to have flowers and to the Capizzolis' with all the twisted aluminum and the pressed stone that had no geological limitations. A few grey blocks on, near my office, was the last house—I don't know the people—a three-family aqua wonder with glass bricks set around each window to modernize it and the front yard cemented up except for a small patch of dirt the shape of an irrigation pan. There some hardy ivy grew all winter, green.

It was an oasis that I rushed to, and one day I walked into the cement yard and picked an ivy leaf. The urn, the awnings, the ivy remembered another season, though I suppose it was the future that I really admired in them, because I had none.

One night I said to my mother, "That's how I get to work and back, from one bright house to the next. I think lots of people go on that way, from one bowling night to the next, or even from meal to meal."

I thought she hadn't heard—she hardly ever did when I explained things—but later by the blue light of the television set she said, "You used to be a good, plain girl, Ag. I can't see what's changed you."

I bought a red silk dress at this time and let my hair grow. At the office they all said how snappy Miss Ag was looking—there I command respect for seventeen years as a cheerful drudge. I am secretary to the president of the Standard Zipper Company. Everyone knows the type, a pinch-faced lady, supports an old mother, can locate every paper clip and advise her boss not to merge with Reddi-Zip, Inc. It makes the salesmen laugh to say I know all the ups and downs. It is pathetic . . . I think of a million flies all over America, zip, zip, zip down the trolley—miners, truck drivers, farmers, junior executives, Hollywood stars—never an embarrassing moment, due to the efficiency and diligence of Mary Agnes Keely. I think of the harassed women catching their flesh . . . you must never hurry it, I know that . . . and the tossing babies kept warm for the night and the suitcases and tents and silver bags, everything is closing and opening like breath going in and out, while I am sealed—as though our 72-inch model were stitched into me from the toes up and the zipper stuck forever on a broken track under my hawk-Irish nose. It's pathetic, but funny.

I mentioned the dress, the novena naturally, and I shall want to write about my course. My brother went to college, but after my father died my mother took the money that was meant for me and bought our wen-browed dark house so that we would always have a roof over our empty heads. I started filing at Standard Zipper and taking courses at night, and I discovered that being a homely gawk, I was smart. Well, I was smarter than anyone at the Teachers College and as smart as the Saturday morning crowd at Columbia.

I have a world now, about the size of a circle of light thrown by a desk lamp, that is mine and safe from my mother and the zipper company and my brother's children. It is the one space in which I am free of self-pity and I hold it sacred like some impossible belief in guardian angels, because when I am outside of the circle of light I can see that it is dim and small. Someone is always saying how fine it is and what a mark of maturity to be able to think, to read; but I'm sure it is cowardice for most people. I mean that we should want to stand in an amphitheater with spotlights on us, like F. D. R. in a black cape, and say something significant: "At last, my friends, we know the world can come to an end."

Well, my small circle of light, the reading lamp, had been shining with special brightness since the beginning of February because of my course in the modern French poets—they spoke to me. That happens now and again, even when you become a sophisticated reader with all kinds of critical impedimenta: you read something that is so direct, so pertinent to exactly where you are—the way you feel and your precise frame of mind. That is the rapport I had—I still do have—with Nerval, with Baudelaire, with Rimbaud. Not only what they say in brilliant, disparate images but with their diseased, eccentric lives. I feel pain where I have never been touched, dissipation in my early-to-bed soul. (Have I written an Illumination?)

(My mother has got through to my brother in Buffalo. She has only to hear his voice to cry, so what must it be tonight, an ancient keening racially remembered that cannot stop. I wonder if she will ask me to talk to him, way up there in Buffalo. "Hello," I will say, "how are you? How are the kids? Yes," I will say, "everything is fine here. The weather is fine. I am going away." She is wailing. She will not ask me to speak to him on the phone, but no matter where I may go I will get the bill . . . I always pay. If I were to leave my room and see my mother leaning heavily on the refrigerator, daubing at her wet eyes and nose with a disintegrated Kleenex, weeping and weeping to the child she loves, my brother . . . then I could not go. I would offer myself to her, the last sweet bite, a soupçon airy and delicious to restore her, humanity fudge. Warriors did that—not as long ago as we like to think—ate the heart of the enemy . . . I will stay in my room.)

Now let me tell you what has happened. I have told you about the red dress, the novena, the pastel houses and the French poets. Tonight I came home, a Thursday, and turned up the hill to my house. The scene was wrong: the weather had been fine all day, from the window of the zipper factory, and the sun still glowed, low and late on my dirty brown street, but there was a flash of electric blue—intense Immigrant Blue. Then I ran up the hill to my house, because it was *my* house with that cheap blue all over the front and half way down the side, and I ran up the steps, my feet sticking to the gluey wet paint. Inside there she was with the newspaper held up higher than usual, waiting for me. "Ag," she said, "is that you?"

"You know it's me," I shouted. "You know that." I tore the *Evening American* from her face. The smile she had prepared to greet me with was plastered on her speechless mouth. "You have gone out of your mind," I said evenly, "*out of your mind.*"

"Now, Mary Agnes, the painters came today . . ."

"The house is blue."

". . . the painters came today, Mary Agnes, and I had it in mind for a while with the house so run down, and I wanted to do something for you, something to please you, Ag."

"The house is blue."

"Well that's it." Her voice rose an octave—her face was flushed. "You've been talking up those houses the Italians own for weeks now, every day it seems you're at me about the colors and the decoration." Now she got up and began to gather the torn newspaper, stooping as best she could with the blood rushing to her head and those veins jumping faster than I have ever seen. "You've been plaguing me with those colored houses, but there is no pleasing you, Mary Agnes."

"In the first place we are not Italians," I said.

"Well you don't have to tell me," she screamed, "you're the big mixer, aren't you, with all your talk about those wops. . . . It wasn't me wanted the house blue."

"We are not Italians," I said again—and in a whisper: "We are withered brown people. Can't you see that? Can't you see one rotten thing?"

"No, I don't like the way you speak to your mother—out of dirty French books I've seen in your room. I bless the day your father died, not to see you like this, a heretic and a spiteful woman."

I grabbed her fat arm when she turned from me and held her. "Now tell me," I said, "how much does it cost to paint a house?"

But she only started to cry, so that I had to answer. "It's my bank account, isn't it?—spread all over the front of this house."

"You'd go off and leave your mother to die, Mary Agnes." Then I saw the working of her voracious mind. Her words grated through the sobs: "You've no more feeling than stone; you'd go off to Europe with the money, and let me walk up to church in the winter and go off in the summer and leave me alone, all alone when I chose that color for you."

Then I began to cry and threw myself into an elephant chair. "For me. For me. That is the color for your Holy Mary. Must the whole street know, the whole city that I am a virgin and thirty-five." I pounded the bulky chair thinking it was my mother's body. She must have felt I was wild—staring up at her with my ravaged face. I was suddenly smiling and sure. "All this," I said pleasantly looking around the front room, "has no importance." My mother thought I meant only our house. "Now I am going to play Bridgeport Bus, once and for all I am going to play Bridgeport Bus and I will go away." (It is a wonderful game, Bridgeport Bus: you line up the dining room chairs in two aisles and you collect fares and joggle along through the Naugatuck valley talking to all the passengers and then get off at Bridgeport.) Mother went out weeping into the kitchen, but I stayed there hugging the large bosom back of the chair.

Aunt Lil has come and gone. She stuck her head into my room and seeing that I was calm, writing on my yellow pad, she went to comfort my mother, saying, I imagine, that it was one of our arguments like any other. Then I could hear mother, loud and choking to Aunt Lil that she would not finish her novena tonight. She is too ill from the exertion and all the shouting. Oh, M. Rimbaud

—"This can only be the end of the world, kept going." It is obvious that I will not finish my course . . . no matter.

I intend to travel light, only the red silk dress, some books, my cosmetics, though my face has a surprising fullness and the skin on my neck seems tight, like the skin of an out-of-season, hothouse fruit. I am like that, maturing too late, therefore I may be more valuable . . . that is one of the questions to be asked, still unplucked. My girlish head luxuriates in absurd decisions: I will take the Bridgeport Bus and joggle to the railroad station and then choose between Boston and New York. I may take my rhinestone earrings or I may leave them behind. Shall I call a taxi to take me to the bus depot or shall I walk so that I can see for the last time my obscure, night-dark city with its hills rising—unlit funeral pyres, grey and brown, rising from the beach of industrial rubble . . . and the river used up, ashamed like a deserted woman. "So long!" I will say, "You have loved me like a mother. I take nothing from you but the bare necessities; one suitcase, the beginning of this story. So long, sweet Mother, good night, good night."

The wise boy Rimbaud writes: "The hour of flight will be the hour of death for me." Let me establish that I *know* this as concretely as I comprehend a world of zippers. So having cleared myself of some naïveté, I have only to put on my coat and go— through the living room where my mother is soothed at last by her television, watching lives much more professional than ours. "Let's not say good-bye, only *Adieu, bon appétit.* . . ."

REYNOLDS PRICE was born in 1933 in Macon, North Carolina. He graduated from Duke University, after which he attended Oxford University as a Rhodes Scholar. In 1958 he returned to teach English Literature at Duke. His story "One Sunday in Late July" received third prize in *Prize Stories 1961* and his first novel, *A Long and Happy Life*, will be published by Atheneum early in 1962. Mr. Price is now in England, completing a volume of stories and beginning a second novel.

THE WARRIOR PRINCESS OZIMBA

from *The Virginia Quarterly Review*

She was the oldest thing any of us knew anything about, and she had never been near a tennis court, but somewhere around the Fourth of July every year, one of us (it was my father for a long time but for the past two years, just me) rode out to her place and took her a pair of blue tennis shoes. (Blue because that was her favorite color before she went blind and because even now, opening the box and not seeing them, she always asks, "Is they blue?") We did it on the Fourth because that was the day she had picked out fifty years ago for her birthday, not knowing what day she had been born and figuring that the Fourth was right noisy anyhow and one more little celebration wouldn't hurt if it pacified my father, who was a boy then and who wanted to give her presents. And it was always tennis shoes because they were the only kind she would put on and because with her little bit of shuffling around in the sun, she managed to wear out a pair every year. So now that I was doing it, the time would come, and Vesta, who was her daughter and had taken her mother's place and who didn't

Copyright 1961 by The Virginia Quarterly Review, The University of Virginia.

have much faith in my memory, would look up at me from string-
ing beans or waxing the floor and say, "Mr. Ed, Mama's feets
going to be flat on the ground by next week," and then I would
drive out, and it would be her birthday.

My mother goes out very seldom now, so late in the afternoon
of the Fourth, I took the shoes and climbed in the broiling car
alone and headed down the Embro road where she lived with
Vesta and Vesta's husband, where she had lived ever since she
took up with Uncle Ben Harrison in the Year One and started
having those children that had more or less vanished. (My grandfather asked her once just when was it she and Ben got married.
She smiled and said, "Mr. Buddy, *you* know we ain't married. We
just made arrangements.")

All the way out there the shoulders of the dirt road were full of
Negroes dressed up in a lot of light-colored clothes that were getting dustier by the minute, walking nowhere (except maybe to
some big baptizing up the creek) slow and happy with a lot of
laughing and with children bunched along every now and then,
yelling and prancing and important-looking as puppies on the
verge of being grown and running away. I waved at several of the
struggling knots as I passed just so I could look in the mirror and
see the children all stop their scuffling and string out in a line
with great wide eyes and all those teeth and watch my car till it
was gone, wondering who in the world that waving white man
was, flying on by them to the creek.

There was still the creek to cross that I and a little Negro
named Walter had dammed up a thousand times for wading pur-
poses. It would follow along on the left, and there would be that
solid mile of cool shade and sand and honeysuckle and the two
chimneys that had belonged to Lord-knows-what rising from the
far end of it and the sawdust pile that had swallowed Harp Hub-
bard at age eleven so afterwards we couldn't play there except in
secret and always had to bathe before going home, and then on
the right it would be her place.

About all you could say for her place was it would keep out
a gentle rain, balancing on its own low knoll on four rock legs so
delicate it seemed she could move once, sitting now tall in her
chair on one end of the porch, and send the whole thing—house,

dog, flowers, herself, all—turning quietly down past the nodding
chickens and the one mulberry tree to the road, if she hadn't been
lighter than a fall leaf and nearly as dry. I got out of the car without
even waking her dog and started towards her.

She sat there the way she had sat every day for eight years
(every day since that evening after supper when she stepped to the
living room door and called my father out and asked him, "Mr.
Will, ain't it about time I'm taking me a rest?"), facing whoever
might pass and the trees and beyond and gradually not seeing any
of them, her hands laid palm up on her knees, her back and her
head held straight as any boy and in that black hat nobody ever
saw her without but which got changed—by night—every year or
so, a little deaf and with no sight at all and her teeth gone and her
lips caved in forever, leaving her nothing but those saddles of bone
under her eyes and her age which nobody knew (at times you
could make her remember when General Lee took up my grandmother, who was a baby, and kissed her) and her name which my
great grandfather had been called on to give her and which came
from a book he was reading at the time—Warrior Princess Ozimba.

I climbed the steps till I stood directly in front of her, level
with her shut eyes and blocking the late sun, which had made her
this year the same as every year the color of bright old pennies
that made us all pretend she was an Indian when we were children
and spy on her from behind doors and think she knew things she
wasn't telling. I wasn't sure she was awake until she said, "Good
evening to you," and I said, "Good evening, Aunt Zimby. How
are you getting on?"

"Mighty well for an old woman," she said, "with all this good-
feeling sunshine."

"Yes, it *is* good weather," I said. "We'll be calling for a little
rain soon though."

"Maybe you all will," she said, "but it's the sun and not the
rain that helps my misery. And if you just step out of my light,
please sir, I can take the last of it." So I sat down on the top
step by her feet that were in what was left of last year's shoes,
and the sun spread back over her face, and whatever it was my
great grandfather thought the Warrior Princess Ozimba looked
like, it must have been something like that.

When she spoke again it seemed to confirm she knew somebody was with her. "I been setting here wondering is my mulberries ripe yet?"

I looked down at her knobby little tree and said, "No, not yet."

"My white folks that I works for, they littlest boy named Will, and he do love the mulberries. One day his mama was going off somewhere, and she say to him, 'Will, don't you eat n'er one of them mulberries.' So he say, 'No ma'am' like he swearing in court. Well, I give him his dinner, and he go streaking off down the back of the lot. That afternoon I setting on the kitchen steps, resting my feets, and Mr. Will he come up towards me through the yard, no bigger than a mosquito, and ask me, 'Aunt Zimby, what you studying about?' I say to him I just wondering if them mulberries back yonder is fit to eat yet. And he don't do nothing but stand there and turn up that face of his, round as a dollar watch and just as solemn but with the mulberry juice ringing round his mouth bright as any wreath, and he say, 'I expect they is.'"

I thought she was going to laugh—I did, softly—but suddenly she was still as before, and then a smile broke out on her mouth as if it had taken that long for the story to work from her lips into her mind, and when the smile was dying off, she jerked her hand that was almost a great brown bird's wing paddling the air once across her eyes. It was the first time she had moved, and coming quick as it did, it made me think for a minute she had opened her eyes with her hand and would be turning now to see who I was. But the one move was all, and she was back in her age like sleep so deep and still I couldn't have sworn she was breathing even, if there hadn't been the last of the sun on her face and the color streaming under the skin.

I sat for awhile, not thinking of anything except that it was cooling off and that I would count to a hundred and leave if she hadn't moved or spoken. I counted and it seemed she wasn't coming back from wherever she was, not today, so I set the shoe box by the side of her chair and got up to go. Vesta would see them when she came at dark to lead her mother in. I was all the way down the steps, going slow hoping the dog wouldn't bark, when she spoke, "You don't know my Mr. Will, does you?"

I walked back so she could hear me and said no, I didn't believe

I did. There was no use confusing her now and starting her to remembering my father and maybe crying. Nobody had told her when he died.

She felt for the tin can beside her chair and turned away from me and spat her snuff into it. (She had said before that if she was going sinning on to her grave after dips of snuff, it was her own business, but she wasn't going asking nobody else to watch her doing it.) Those few slow moves as gentle and breakable as some long-necked waterfowl brought her to life again, and when she had set her can down, I thought I ought to say something so I got back onto how nice the weather was.

But she held her eyes shut, knowing maybe that if she had opened them and hadn't been blind anyhow, she would have seen I wasn't who she had expected all year long. "Yes sir, this here's the weather you all wants for your dances, ain't it?"

I said, "Yes, it would be ideal for that."

"Well, is you been dancing much lately, Mr. Will?"

She seemed to think she was talking to me so I said no, there wasn't much of that going on these days.

"You a great one for the dancing, ain't you, Mr. Will?" All I did was laugh loud enough for her to hear me, but she wiped her mouth with a small yellow rag, and I could see that—not meaning to, not meaning to at all—I had startled her.

She began with a short laugh of her own and drummed out a noiseless tune on the arm of the chair and nodded her head and said, "You *is* a case, Mr. Will."

I asked her what did she mean because I couldn't leave now.

"I was just thinking about that evening you went off to some dance with one of your missy-girls, you in your white trousers looking like snow was on the way. And late that night I was out there on you all's back porch, and it come up a rain, and directly you come strolling up with not a thing on but your underwear and your feets in them white shoes you was putting down like stove lids, and there was your white trousers laid pretty as you please over your arm to keep from getting them muddy. Does you remember that, Mr. Will?"

I said there were right many things I didn't remember these days.

"The same with me," she said, "except every once in a while. . . ." A line of black children passed up the road. They everyone of them looked towards us and then towards the older tall yellow girl who led the line and who had been silently deputized to wave and say, "How you this evening, Miss Zimby?"—not looking for an answer surely, not even looking to be heard, just in respect like when you speak to the sea. ". . . What put me to thinking about Mr. Will is it's time for me some new shoes."

And there I was with the shoes in my hands that I couldn't give her now and wondering what I could do, and while I was wondering she raised her own long foot and stamped the floor three times, and there was considerable noise, as surprising as if that same bird she kept reminding me of had beat the air with its foot and made it thunder. Before I could guess why she had done it, Vesta came to the front door and said, "Lord, Mr. Ed, I didn't know you was out here. Me and Lonnie was in yonder lying down, and I just figured it was Mama going on to herself." Then she said louder to Aunt Zimby, "What you call me for, Mama?"

It took her a little while to remember. "Vesta, when have Mr. Will been here? It ain't been long is it?"

Vesta looked at me for an answer but I was no help. "No Mama, it ain't been so long."

"He ain't sick or nothing is he? Because it's getting time for me some new shoes."

"It won't be long, Mama. Mr. Will ain't never forgot you yet."

And that seemed to settle it for her. The little tune she had been thumping out slowed down and stopped, and next her head began to nod, all as quick as if she had worked the whole day out in the cotton and come home and fixed everybody's supper and seen them to bed and pressed a shirt for Uncle Ben, who drove a taxi occasionally, and then fallen dead to sleep in the sounding dark with the others breathing all round her.

Vesta and I stayed still by her until we could hear breathing, but when it began, small and slow, I handed Vesta the shoes. She knew and smiled and nodded, and I told her to go on in and let her mother sleep. I stood there those last few minutes, looking through sudden amazed tears at all that age and remembering my dead father.

Evening was coming on but the heat was everywhere still. I took the steps slowly down, and as I expected the old dog came up, and I waited while he decided what to do about me. Over the sounds of his smelling there came a crowd of high rushing nameless notes and her voice among them, low and quiet and firm on the air, "You can see them little birds can't you, Mr. Will? I used to take a joy watching them little fellows playing before they went to sleep."

I knew it would be wrong to answer now, but I looked without a word to where her open eyes rested across the road to the darkening field and the two chimneys, and yes, they were there, going off against the evening like out of pistols, hard dark bullets that arched dark on the sky and curled and showered to the sturdy trees beneath.

THOMAS WHITBREAD was born in 1931 in Bronxville, New York. He attended Amherst College (B.A. 1952) and Harvard Graduate School of Arts and Sciences (A.M. 1953, PH.D. 1959). At present he is a member of the English department at the University of Texas. Mr. Whitbread has published poems in *Harper's, The New Yorker, The Atlantic Monthly,* and other magazines. This is his first published story.

THE REMEMBERER

from *The Paris Review*

"Have you met the man who's lost his memory yet?" said a tall stranger, breathing at me. He wore brown tweeds. His hand held his mahogany-colored highball unsteadily. His presence was offensive.

"No," I said, turning aside.

"You must see him!" said the stranger. "You must see the guest of honor!" He swung his free hand toward my arm. Forestalling its grip, I nodded assent and followed him.

I hadn't wanted to attend the party. I was sick of 5:30–7:30 cocktail parties that began at 6:15 and extended, for some of the few interesting people, till either 9:45 or 3 A.M., depending on who ate when, where, with whom, and who got to a liquor store for replenishments before 11:00 closing. I had definitely decided not to go. I sat sipping a highball in my room, congratulating myself on saying no for once to the alcoholics—I refer to an activity, like fireworks or acrobatics, not to people—of Cambridge in May. But my sips gradually became swallows, I reflected that this was my last spring in academic lotos-land, and at 6:01, spurred by the bells of St. Paul's campanile, I began dressing.

Paris Review, Inc.

Now I was following an unknown fool toward a destination known only as some promised, glorified amnesiac. My host had casually told me, had evidently also told my bourboned guide, that an unusual and wise person, to whom he would like to introduce me, would be there—there in a disguise of reticence. This sage had requested that no special notice be paid him until the crowd had thinned, until he was ready for it. I suspected that my guide had forgotten or chosen to disregard this request, or hadn't been told of it; or, less likely, that the great amnesiac himself, in a kingly whim, had commanded my presence.

The crowd had thinned slightly, though the noise level gave contradictory evidence. Even so, our quest was hazardous, including one spilled martini and Gale (née Gail) Henderson, one of those well-thatched Radcliffe girls with metaphysically different costumes for each party, party, party, a soft-bottomed well into which men must fall. "My Jimmy," Gale breathed, her downy red cheek surprisingly close to mine—I had an instant's sharp glimpse of the delicate purple lines under her moist witch hazel eyes, the stiffened lacquer on her black lashes, and knew that tonight she was playing one of Hoffmann's girls, possibly all three—as we passed out of that room into a corridor. Our host was saying good-bye to some guests. As we passed him, he turned and saw my glass. "Jim! You need another drink! Let me—"

"Thanks, Paul, I'll get it myself. We're looking for your guest of honor."

"He isn't here yet." A study of his watch. "He should arrive around 8:30."

A glance at my watch: 7:40. "OK. I'm looking forward." I escaped my guide, reached the kitchen, and poured myself a fourth scotch-and-soda. Off the kitchen was a third-story back-stairs sun-porch. Not wanting to retrace my recent steps, I moved toward it. Five or six people, one of whom I vaguely knew from a February weekend party of red wine and guitars in a snowed-in Rhode Island lodge, were talking. The one I vaguely knew—I couldn't think of her name—screamed "Ah! Here's Jim! He knows op-er-a!" and froze me smiling in the doorway. "Oh! you know opera?" said a large, sweet, plain, open girl, scurrying up to me. "Do you know *Il mio tesoro?*"

"Yes," I said.

"Oh! Do sing it! Sing us *Il mio tesoro!*" She cast excited looks at the others, none of whom looked excited.

I stepped onto the porch, engaged in preliminary badinage, allowed myself to be further teased, then sang the aria, pitched lower than written, since I'm a baritone. I was in unusually good voice, for me: no sense of tightness, no quick wearing out. Applause followed. I was so happy that after little conversational pause I sang another aria. *De miei bollenti spiriti,* with even greater resonance, ease, and verve. More applause, though my audience had become three or four. Then I sang several more arias, not caringly noticing the departure of almost all audience and applause, until no one was left but the sweet, open girl. My voice felt tired, and I decided to go inside. "Thank you for listening, my dear."

"Oh! Won't you sing some more?"

"No. Alas!" I pointed significantly at my neck.

"Oh! I understand! Thank you, oh thank you!"

Most of my audience had moved no further than the kitchen. One member of it, a stubby, swarthy fire-plug, returned to the porch after I left it. He was the husband of the girl I had deserted. Or so I gathered from their rings and the way, with no preliminaries, they solidly kissed. I excused myself past the others, read one of the poems by guests which Paul had scotch-taped here and there on the walls, thought ill of it, and returned to the main room. Thinking "best defense, good offense," I approached the first person I saw, extended my hand, and said "Jim Turtledove," pronouncing "dove" very much like "taub."

"Hugh FitzHugh," said the person, shaking my hand vigorously. His face was mottled, bristled, and bespectacled, his torso portly, his palm wet. "Jim, let me introduce you to my friend, Timothy Steele," he said.

"Hello," I said. "My last name's really Thomas."

"Are you a poet?" Timothy said.

"Yes."

"So am I. FitzHugh here mostly writes prose—or so he says."

"I have tried my hand at poems—in free verse, you understand —but I feel happier in the less rigorous medium," FitzHugh said.

"Have you submitted any poems to magazines?" Timothy said, looking at me.

"Yes," I said.

"Have you sold any?"

"Yes."

"Where?"

I told him.

"I want nothing more than to sell a poem to *The New Yorker*," Timothy said. "But they anticipate every move I make! I was just finishing a poem on the decline of Boston, getting it ready to send in, when what did they do but publish that one by Starbuck! You've seen it?"

"Yes. I like it."

"So do I. But why couldn't I have written one first! It happens every time. I get a good subject, think about it, brood over it, get to the point where I can start to write a poem, put down some lines, revise, tear up, start over, get a whole poem, revise, revise, brood some more, polish and revise, and then, when I have the thing almost in submissable shape, what do they do but—" He broke off, exasperated.

"Yes. I don't blame you for being upset. That's happened to me. Once—"

"Sorry to interrupt," said Paul, interrupting. He turned to me. "The guest of honor has arrived and would like to meet you."

"Fine, Paul. But I'm talking with Timothy"—I nodded capaciously in Timothy's direction—"and I don't—"

"Oh. Well. Bring Timothy along."

So Timothy and I followed Paul toward what must be the true throne, leaving Hugh FitzHugh, who had already left us, his gin-and-tonic being empty, behind.

We walked through the main room. Gale Henderson was off in a corner seducing someone, or pretending to do so; anyway, they were occupied, playing in her sandbox. No one cried or whispered "Jim" to me. With no incidents, our procession reached a second bedroom. The only person in the room, so far as I could see, was Harry Samson.

"Hello, Harry!" I said. I had met Harry at several parties during the winter and had liked him. Name a topic, subject, theme: Harry would say what he thought straight out, then give, in dendritic detail, seventy-eight corollaries, qualifications, other sides.

But instead of returning my greeting, Harry looked at Paul brightly, expectantly, as if ready to be introduced to new acquaintances. "This is Harry Samson," Paul said. "Jim Thomas, Timothy Steele."

"Delighted to meet you," Harry said, smiling at me, then at Timothy. I shook his hand mechanically, Timothy did so naturally. Then I came to: *this* was, after all, the guest of honor! the man who had lost his memory! Had Harry—a blow on the skull, a trauma, an inner dislocation—become amnesiac?

"How did you lose your memory?" I asked.

Harry looked at Paul.

"I told Jim that you had," Paul said.

Harry looked at me. His eyes shone. "That isn't the right question," he said.

"What is?" I said.

"That's for him to know and you to find out," Paul said, smiling like a satyr.

Timothy cleared his throat. "Why did you lose your memory?" he asked.

Harry looked, his eyes burning, at Timothy. "Ah! that is the right question! And I'll tell you why. Because there was nothing I could do."

"What do you mean?" I said. Harry kept looking at Timothy.

"I knew there was nothing I could do—nothing at all—to prevent the destruction of the earth. I knew I could never stop some sub-genius imbecile from starting, by a finger pressed on a button, perhaps, or more likely an order telephoned to an ICBM range, a conflict ending with the end of mankind. I knew I had no influence, no position, no voice; I couldn't be elected if I ran for senator, I have no chance of telling my senator what to do and wouldn't know what to tell him if I did, I'd be overwhelmed if I were senator; I saw no way of swaying the course of events. So, I thought, what shall I do? Suicide? No: better to wait for genocide. Discovery of a balm named *pax*? I haven't the talents. So, I decided to lose my memory."

"You gave up hope?" I said.

"No. I gave up fear that each day might be my last."

A silence. In it I examined Harry: a stocky associate professor of history, who played the violin. The fingers of his right hand tapered delicately, like limp steel. His left hand was a claw. I swallowed the residue of my drink.

"Harry, you've met me before," I said, looking at him.

He stared at me, at Paul, at Timothy, back at me. "I beg—"

"No. Harry, you have met me before," I said.

He chuckled briefly. "No. You are mistaken, Jim, I fear. I have never met you before. Because I have lost my memory."

"How do you remember, then, that my name is Jim?" I said.

"Come off it, Jim," Paul whispered.

Timothy looked interested and shrewd.

"Don't you see?" Harry said, eyes of beads. "I *can't* remember having met you before, *because* I have lost my memory. But I only lose my memory once a day. I'd say I'm like Cinderella if I lost it at midnight. But I don't. I lose my memory at 3:30 A.M., every day, while sleeping."

"You don't dream? You're never awake?"

"Never at 3:30 A.M."

"You never recall anything from your childhood? Despite yourself?"

"Never. *Because* I have lost my memory."

"You're trying to play a fantastic role. Poets do this every day. But you're not a poet. And if you don't watch out, you'll stop being a person."

"I doubt that. I have already become more of a person than I ever was. I am the man who has lost his memory."

Could Timothy have been the interlocutor in that last exchange? I tried to imagine him trying to press Harry back into the ordinary molds of intercourse. But I couldn't. There Timothy was, having been aboveboard, cynical and silent. I had said the obvious.

"Excuse me," I said, waving my glass at Paul's chin. "Another drink."

It pleases me to think I can do certain mechanical things imaginatively. One of them is driving a car in New York City. I enjoy trying to collapse Kenneth Burke's terms, to make the jagged, arhythmic pace of city traffic approach the condition of lullaby. An acquaintance of a friend of mine has studied the traffic lights on Queens Boulevard in both directions so fully that in non-rush hour situations he can travel the 3.2-mile stretch of it he habitually uses without coming to a full stop, going nine mph here, twenty-six mph there, three mph during the amoral suspension of red's reluctantly yielding to green at some tricky intersection. This is his chief claim to fame. Not wishing so limiting an excellence, I haven't yet gone so far. But I have my devices. Approaching a red light from a distance, usually just after shooting through an amoral suspension, I brake, downshift, dawdle, and, corner of my eye fixed on the light governing the cross street, time my acceleration into an open lane past stopped dummies (who, if Imperials, Cadillacs, or even Fords, soon zoom past me, unless I and some news-truck—a double-parked car helps on three-lane drives, while nothing will do on most of the newfangled one-way avenues except, of course, utter congestion) at the precise moment when red joins green on it. Using Park Avenue to get north or south, I know I have seven or eight blocks in ordinary traffic, ten to twelve in the middle of the night, between red lights; I have fun choosing the appropriate moment to turn off. Sixty-seventh? Sixty-ninth? Seventy-first? (On Fourth Avenue, Brooklyn, I once made fifteen blocks in a stretch. Brooklyn's arteries relax more than Manhattan's.) The one-way avenues, with staggered lights attuned to a steady twenty-four mph, are less exciting. The only game I play with them is Entering the Intersection as the Green Turns Red— the exact reverse of the sport motormen of A trains enjoy between 125th and 59th. I am aware of the use of that old tunnel, sometimes blocked off, in the middle of Fourth-Park below Grand Central, and of the rectangular Alpine route round Grand Central itself. I have theories as to the relative merits of the West Side Highway, the East River (pardon me! Franklin Delano Roosevelt) Drive, or one and another of those one-way avenues for getting from Bay Ridge to Twenty-third and Sixth, or, indeed, to the mid-Bronx, at various times of day. And, being a poet, I love working my way back to sanity from the intersection of West Fourth and West Eleventh.

I reached Manhattan this time in the late morning, and could have spent the whole afternoon driving here and there, outwitting or being nonwitted by lights. In my new VW, with its positive thirst for downshiftings, its four forward speeds, its delighted roars and whines, the fun would have been immense. But my mildly puritanical upbringing—I attended a Congregational Sunday School, summers only, and remember innocently embarrassing the teacher, a gentle, open-faced breeder of cocker spaniels, by asking the meaning of "circumcision" in *The Acts of the Apostles*—asserted itself. I left the Henry Hudson Parkway, tortuously ascended Washington Heights, parked my car near where I might stay, and entered the Independent subway.

Where next? I thought of telephoning an old friend at his midtown office, but decided against it. Better to be anonymous awhile. Or what's a city for? Or some such rot. The idea of going to the 125th Street station of the New York Central–New Haven presented itself. It would be fun to watch trains. Once, when I was thirteen, I visited my aunt and did just that. She was astounded and hilarious when I told her about it: astounded that I would think doing such a thing worth my while; hilarious because, thinking, as I did then of most signs, that the sign "SHOW YOUR TICKETS: NO PERSON ALLOWED TO GO TO PLATFORM WITHOUT TRANSPORTATION" meant what it said, I bought a ticket from 125th Street to Morrisania for I think it was eleven cents. The ancient guardian of the staircase nodded suspiciously at me, in appropriate response to my tremors, as I showed him my ticket; I watched many trains; then I crept guiltily down, not looking at the guardian, and out to the street. I still have that ticket, being one of the tribe that likes to keep things—including, especially, memories.

But 125th Street station wouldn't do. For one thing, here I was, token intaken, physically, emotionally, psychosomatically ready to rocket south. For another, there wouldn't be many trains at 125th Street at midday: not many, anyway, in contrast with the racketing thunders of 5:40 P.M. I thought, for no reason, of No One, New Hampshire—or possibly Noone, though I prefer to think otherwise—a stop on a little-used branch line of the Boston and Maine, visible from route 202 south of Peterborough. Was I no one? I preferred to think so. As I began pretending to think so, an AA train arrived and took me in. I switched at 145th Street to an A train, front car, and from 125th to 59th stood with renewed pleasure, one hand on blue metal, face against wire-webbed glass, body swaying, a child to my right and down, as the anonymous motorman, chain-bolted in his cab, came steadily, without slackening speed, to a red light, went, without slackening speed, through the light just after it turned green, and approached, without increasing speed, steadily, steadily onward, the next red light.

At Forty-second Street I got off, emerged, and scanned movie marquees. The Apollo, where I twice saw *Rigoletto* with Tito Gobbi, had a double-feature made of teen-agers, guns, sex. The Astor had Barry Fitzgerald being Irish, either with or without the assistance of Bing Crosby. The Palace had some earth-shaking extravaganza, featuring one or another Hollywood sinuosity as a Mississippi, Nile, or Sea of Galilee slut, very good at heart, ready to be readily translated, near the end, by the reformed handsome clear-cut daring con-man, into romantic heavenly bliss. The Waverly was probably playing a vintage Guinness and *Great Expectations*, but it was way off in left or right field, certainly not in Times Square. I entered the BMT subway.

My plans until then had been unclear. But with that move they crystallized. I would take a West End or Sea Beach—no matter which, no special preference for elevated clattering or tunnelly rumbling—to Coney Island. This I did. (A Sea Beach if you *must* know.) When I arrived, did I buy a hot dog and orange at Nathan's? promenade the boardwalk? ride the parachute-jump? ogle other onlookers? No. I climbed to the walk over all the tracks, found a good point of vantage, and watched trains come in and out. Sea Beaches and West Ends, from the west. Brighton Beaches and D trains, from the east. I stared, as if I planned to remember them, at the numbers of the various cars, although I already knew from past observings that Sea Beaches were in 6000s, West Ends and Brighton Beaches in 2000s, D trains between 100 and 1600 or so. The City of New York moves in unmysterious ways in numbering its subway cars. It avoids duplication. For example: some of the postwar, fluorescently lit cars on the IND line, with numerals in orange-red instead of white, took up their numbers where the old, riveted, incandescent (some by ACF, some by Pullman Standard, some by Pressed Steel) cars left off. But they soon approached 2000. So the powers caused them to jump clear over the BMT's 2000s and to start, as most postwar IND cars do, with a 3. I have seen the car 3000 and the car 3333. What the IRT has been doing in the meantime with its 4000s and 5000s is outside the scope of this discourse.

Trains coming into and out of Coney Island made a maze for me for a couple of hours. Then, thirsty, I descended to the street, had three or four quick beers, and, remembering a past excellence, got into a D train and hurtled north. At Boro Hall I changed to a GG, frequent stopper, up to Queens Plaza. I was just in time. On the top shelf of that frenetic intersection I saw the sun, big red passionless bomb, drop on Manhattan with no force at all. I saw the sun set. When all of it was gone, I entered a BMT train bound for Times Square and sat down. A few people, not many, were standing; the rush was still mainly away from offices, though partly toward restaurants and theaters. I thought of walking up to the front and watching the lights change, but rejected that idea; I was tired of seeing, and the front of the train was five or six cars ahead. Then I looked at the people seated across from me and saw Harry Samson.

Harry was reading the New York *Post* and was partly hidden by swaying standees, but he was unmistakably Harry. What was he doing here? on this train? It took me a minute to remember that this was summer, not spring, New York, not Cambridge, and Harry probably had relatives or maybe a house of his own in Kew Gardens or Forest Hills. I stared at him, thinking, for some time, until, putting his *Post* away decisively, he looked straight in my direction.

I smiled what I felt to be greetings and pleased recognition.

His eyes were utterly expressionless.

And yet we stared at each other, my smile fading, for more than a minute until his eyes detached themselves, like the suckers of clams from sand, to seek a happier habitat. He looked hungry. He never reopened his *Post*. His eyes focused, so far as I was able to tell between standees, either nowhere at all or inward, into his brain, the rest of our trip separately together. I thought for a moment of going over and introducing myself. But it would be, at best, like that evening in Cambridge: he would look surprised, say he was happy to meet me, ask me who I was? what I did? why I was there? Or worse: who could ask such questions on a subway train? And some standee would take my seat, leaving me lurching in uneasy, pockmarked talk with the amnesiac Samson. So I sat still. And I thought, as the train racketed along, of how Harry began life anew at 3:30 that morning.

When the train reached Fifty-ninth Street, I got up to leave. Harry Samson had not yet left. Then I felt a sudden resistance to my exit, a tugging against my left arm, a strange refusal to let me leave. I redoubled my efforts toward the platform. The resistance grew in response. In desperation, fearing that Samson had at this last minute grabbed my arm, I turned around. I found instead a large Negro lady, trembling with rage and indignation, on the verge of the outcry which decades of subjugation had taught her (through her mother) would be unseemly. My left arm had inadvertently come between her purse and herself. She had been a standee; I had been glancing at Samson. I excused myself, freed my arm, and, just before the doors closed, lunged through them to the comparative air of the platform. I looked back through the window at Samson, who was looking out toward me, unseeingly. What was he doing? Would he go on to Times Square and then get out? Or was he riding this train back and forth, back and forth between Queens and Manhattan, not knowing what he was doing, unknowingly, not knowing what he was undoing?

I climbed up to street air, turned southwest, and walked. This involved skirting a few buildings at right angles. I thought of phoning Gale Henderson, who would almost certainly be in New York, but decided dinner must come first. I ate it at some halfheartedly pretentious place, by no means a cafeteria, certainly less than a restaurant—a jaded place-to-go or to-have-gone, with a complete spaghetti-and-meat-balls dinner for $1.65—between Fifty-ninth and Times Square. Then I thought again of phoning Gale —but decided instead to think of The Time, the great first time. . . .

"Hello?" she said.

"Hello," I said.

"And who is this?" she said.

"This is Jim Thomas," I said. "Cambridge."

"Oh?" she said.

"Can you come to dinner with me tonight?" I said.

We had a wonderful dinner, with talk, jokes, cheap wine, and not much to look forward to. When we left the restaurant Gale exclaimed over the sunset, the sunset that still let itself be seen, lingered down West Fifty-second. "Yes," I said, gathering her in. "Fine sunset." She exclaimed some more as we walked toward my old car.

That car was '49 Chevrolet, not new VW. But when she got in, it was chariot toward our goal. I didn't know this at first. I have always been too cerebral. As we meandered down Manhattan, I thought we might simply be going back to her apartment. But I soon sensed she didn't want that. So, in reaction, I took us over Manhattan Bridge.

"Where are we going?" she said.

"To Brooklyn," I said. "Smell the coffee."

We smelt the coffee. Then we penetrated Brooklyn. Up Fulton, to the Grand Army Plaza; then down the side of Prospect Park, by zigzags to the sides of the cemetery wherein my grandparents lay buried, whereby teen-agers smooched; then onto Fourth Avenue, and her hand entered my hair. We drove along, many blocks, I not trying to outwit the lights, and her hand kept moving in my hair. I thought where would be the best place. I turned here, there, her hand in my hair, through Bay Ridge, until finally we came to rest somewhere, on an avenue in view of the bay above Fort Hamilton, below the Sixty-ninth Street Ferry. I parked. I began to move my hand in her hair. Then she drew me to her, and I moved to her willingly, mouth to her mouth, body to her body. We kissed a long time. I very much liked her taste. We kept up excited kissing, and stroking each other, and feeling (I speak for myself) detachedly engaged, until something snapped, some barrier broke, and I felt that both of us felt that nothing stood in the way of ourselves, and we clasped, embraced, involved ourselves in new intimacy. We stayed in this feeling for what seemed a long time. Then I heard a voice somewhere outside.

"What?" I said, stupidly sticking my head out my window.

"Would you please move your car?" said a stranger, smiling intimately. I started the car, moved it backwards four feet, and the stranger drove his car into his garage.

Then we resumed kissing, confronting, being passionate. Our intimacy, though, seemed less. Then it was over, and we drove back toward Manhattan, along the elevated highway, into the Brooklyn-Battery Tunnel, up through Manhattan's oldest veins.

"I love you," I said, letting her off.

"I love you," she said. "See you again!"

She let herself into her building without looking behind.

I drove off into the later night, wondering, Who am I? . . .

But I hadn't decided, now, to phone Gale Henderson again. Why not? What else? Anything else?

I had walked, while remembering, into Times Square. I entered a Whelan's, bought an El Producto Bouquet, lit it, and puffed. On Forty-second near Sixth I passed a cut-rate bookstore where I once bought *H. E. Bates* by Edward Garnett, *The Enchanted Grindstone* by a poet-professor named Robinson, a third title I can't remember, and, *pièce de résistance*, *The Unstrung Harp* by Edward Gorey, at nineteen cents each. *The Unstrung Harp* so struck and tickled the lyres of my friends in Cambridge that when I next weekended in New York I bore with me commissions to buy six more copies of that dark, wry work. My mission was easily accomplished: a large stack remained to be remaindered. O fate of authors? destiny uneschewed! Fount of self-pity! I cut short my lament, reasserted my transient anonymity to myself, rejected the notion of seeing if any copies of *The Unstrung Harp* lingered now, in 1959, four years later, in that bookstore, and turned down Sixth. Fortieth Street between Sixth and Fifth is very quiet at night. I walked over to Broadway for a view of the Met.

I had seen many operas here, in this solid, doomed, grimy brick-and-mortar tetrazoid. And my most vivid memory, as I stood watching the Elgin clock move from 9:16 to 9:17, 9:18, 9:19, was of what seemed to me a magnificent performance of *Götterdämmerung*. It was and is the only performance of that monument I have seen. I was sitting in the last row of the Family Circle with a friend, so I naturally valued big voices that carried. The biggest, most carrying voice that evening was Deszo Ernster's. Astrid Varnay could be heard most of the time, and managed her faithful steed Gräne: the horse, a trouper, neither leapt into the pit nor nuzzled a tuba in search of oats. Hans Hötter, one of my favorite artists, sang and acted impeccably the unrewarding role of Gunther, which required him to play dead, spread out on the cold, cold stage, for almost half an hour. But Ernster as Hagen, keeping his lonely watch with immense, guttural, analytical statements about his role, summoning his tribe with tremendously loud and barbaric "Hoi-ho!"s in which his whole frame visibly rose and fell, shook and vibrated—Ernster, Hungarian *basso profundo*, with the longest time and space between the peaks of his sound waves of any singer I have heard, stole, for me, the show. I reveled in his every utterance.

Less than two minutes from *Ring*'s end, when the Rhine overflowed in every direction, Valhalla crumbled in fire and quake, and the orchestra cataclysmatically played fifteen or twenty motifs in kaleidoscopic sequence, some of them simultaneously, all quadruple fortissimo, a couple in front of us got up, blocking our view of the stage. I was annoyed. My friend was furious. "Yes! Go!" he spat at their backs. "Get out!" He dismissed them with one hand, a taut, angry claw, as spontaneous and incisive as the gesture with which Wotan, saying "Geh!", contemptuously kills Hunding at the end of Act II, *Die Walküre*. His face was red, his protuberant brown eyes glare ice. "Get out! Get down to the street before the rest of us! Get home five minutes sooner! Don't give a damn about the music! Why did you come here at all?!" The offenders, without turning around, scurried sideways over three or four others, then away down the aisle. We saw the last minute of the end without obstruction.

After yelling "Bravo!" a few minutes and clapping our hands crimson—not sore, since we played enough tennis and squash to keep our palms in condition—we walked down the many stairs to the street. Then we decided to go to the stage door, on Fortieth near Seventh. It was windy and cold. Twenty-five or thirty people stood there, jumping from foot to foot, some wondering aloud when Varnay would come out. Most had autograph books. We had stood there about fifteen minutes when a large, late-middle-aged man, wrapped in a heavy fur coat, emerged from the sacred portal. I have never seen a more tired face. The lines of age were inlined with fatigue and some strips of unremoved grease paint. An ample woman detached herself from the group and moved familiarly toward him. "Come, my dear," he said to her, patting her black-gloved hand. He was unmistakably Deszo Ernster. No one asked him for his autograph. He had sung the longest, most taxing role in the opera, and had sung it well. He and his wife got into a taxicab and drove off. Ten minutes later Varnay appeared, gave autographs, drove off. Then my friend and I walked away, but didn't repeat our performance of the night after the first opera I attended: *La Traviata*, December 31, 1948. Albanese, Peerce, Warren. Afterward, Times Square. Warm gin-and-ginger-ale from my friend's hip-flask. Mob movements here and there in the screaming crowd. Midnight! the descending electric bomb! the New Year! Victory! Fresh starts! An end to traumas! And then the ride back to my friend's New Jersey home on a Public Service bus: we entertained our fellow passengers, or some of them, perhaps, with an almost complete rendition of *The Mikado*, first to last, taking all parts. God, we were drunk.

I left the slumbering Met and its moving clock, which now said 9:29, and entered a nearby tavern. I sat on a stool near the street side of the oval bar and ordered draft beer. While I sat there, slowly drinking beer after beer, various people came in: two or three probable bums; one or two slick ones, panderers or co-proprietors; one definite propietor, to whom the arrogant bartender was all deference; a boy, in need and fear of company; a lone soldier, totally lone, ice-tight; three unaccompanied women, perhaps whores, though one was carried off by a man, strickenly debonair, who called her "my wife"; and many pressmen, compositors, newspapermen. The last group formed the steady core of the place, gave it its tone. They came in, were served by the arrogant bartender with *PM*, or *Philadelphia*, or *Carstairs*, or *Four Roses*, to their accustomed two or three shot limits, usually with beer chasers; they chaffed each other and their patron, told jokes, and left. Home to their wives? and, for most of them, families? via

detours? Who knows? God knows I didn't know, though I guessed.
Meanwhile the TV kept going constantly, showing during the last
hours of my sitting there a World War II movie I had once seen in
a theater, with romantic subplot, deaths of people beyond game-
limits, grenades tossed into kerosened stage properties, the hero
court-martialed, judged innocent, happy end. I couldn't feel cynical. People had died—Americans at Guadalcanal, Japanese at Nag-
asaki—and many Americans, Japanese, British, Germans, French,
Australians, Chinese, Canadians, Poles, Italians, Russians, Czechs,
Bulgarians, Turks, Egyptians—the sides soon merge, in any narrative of nationalities—North Koreans, South Koreans—in too many
wars and conflicts for me to feel cynical. I only felt sad and depressed, looking at Mitchum and Ryan, or their World War II
Hollywood counterparts, moving on their bellies against the
enemy. Maybe, I thought, I remember too much. Then I finished
my last beer, moved to the telephone booth, dialed the number
of a couple I know on the upper East Side, woke the better half,
got permission to stay the night, and went there by foot and bus.
I couldn't stand going underground at that point. She had left
the door unlocked, the couch-bed made. I could think about my
VW in the morning.

JOHN UPDIKE was born in Shillington, Pennsylvania, in 1932. He attended the Shillington public schools, Harvard College, and the Ruskin School of Drawing and Fine Art, in Oxford, England. From 1955 to 1957, he was a member of the staff of *The New Yorker*, to which he has contributed short stories, humorous essays, light verse and poems. He has published two novels, *The Poorhouse Fair* and *Rabbit, Run*, a collection of short stories, *The Same Door*, and a collection of poems, *The Carpentered Hen*.

THE DOCTOR'S WIFE

from *The New Yorker*

"Sharks?" The tip of the doctor's wife's freckled nose seemed to sharpen in the sparkling air. Her eyes, momentarily rendered colorless by thought, took up the green of the Caribbean; the plane of the water intersected her throat. "Yes, we have some. Big dark fellows, too."

Ralph, hanging beside her, squatting on buoyance, straightened up, splashing, and tried to survey the beryl depths around him. His sudden movements rendered even the immediate water opaque. The doctor's wife's surprisingly young laughter rang out.

"You Americans," she said, "so nervy," and with complacence pushed a little deeper into the sea, floating backward while the water gently bubbled around her mouth. She had a small face, gone freckled and rosy in this climate; her stringy auburn hair had been dulled by daily sea-bathing. "They rarely come in this far," she said, tilting her face upward and speaking to the sky. "Only in the turtle-killing season, when the blood draws them in. We're fortunate. Our beaches go out shallowly. Over in St. Martin, now, the offshore water is deep, and they must be careful."

Copyright © 1961 by The New Yorker Magazine, Inc.

She turned and, with the casual paddling stroke of a plump woman who floats easily, swam smiling toward him. "A shame," she said, her voice strained by the effort of curving her throat to keep her lips free, "Vic Johnson is gone. He was a dear soul. The old Anglican vicar." She pronounced "vicar" rather harshly, perhaps humorously. She stood up beside Ralph and pointed to the horizon. "Now *he*," she said, "used to swim far out into the bay, he and his great black dog Hooker. Vic would swim straight out, until he couldn't move a muscle, and then he would float, and grab Hooker's tail, and the dog would pull him in. Honestly, it was a sight, this fat old English gentleman, his white hair streaming, coming in on the tail of a dog. He never gave a thought to sharks. Oh, he'd swim *way* out, until he was just a dot."

They were waist-deep in the sea, and at a motion from Ralph they walked toward shore together. The calm warm water leaped from their strides. She was small beside him, and her voice piped at his shoulder. "I'm sorry he's gone," she said. "He was a lovely old gentleman. He had been here forty years. He loved the island."

"I can see why he would," Ralph said. He turned his head to review the crescent of landscape around the beach, as if through his fresh eyes the doctor's wife could renew—what obscurely seemed to him to need renewing—her sense of the island's beauty. The white beach was empty. The natives used it only as a path. Their homes were set behind the ragged hedge of sea grape that rimmed the sand. Bits of tarpaper, pink-painted cement, corrugated roofing reddened by rust, wooden walls weathered to silver and patched by flattened kerosene tins, shacks on stilts, and unfinished cinder-block shells peeped above the dull, low foliage. There were few flowers. This was January. But the clusters of coconuts nested under the shuffling branches of the palms, and the high, small, soft clouds, like the quick clouds of spring in his own climate, suggested that here the season of bloom and the season of harvest were parallel and perpetual: germination and fruition ceaselessly intertwined. There were no mountains in the view. The island was low; when they came in on the airplane, it seemed a two-dimensional twin, or sketch, of St. Martin, which thrust from the sea like a set of Vermont mountaintops. There, the beaches were steep and dangerous; here, they were safe. There,

Dutchmen and Frenchmen built bustling hotels and restaurants to entice American dollars; here, strangers rarely came. Here, even the place names were bestowed without enterprise or effort. East End, West End, The Road, The Forest—thus the island was geographically divided. The uninhabited ridge of scrub and coral rubble that formed one side of the bay was named High Hill. The village was called The Bay. The orange cliffs on the other side of the bay were called The Cliffs. During these short winter days the sun set on a diagonal above them and, between six and seven o'clock, touched the sea at the fingertips of the most distant arm of land. Yet after the sun had drowned, light, itself lazy, lingered among the huts and the oleander bushes. Now it was late afternoon; the tiny tropical sun, not yet swollen to red, patiently poured white brilliance down through the hushed air. The air was as soft, as kind, as the water; there was no hostility in either. The two elements, as Ralph came out of one into the other, seemed tints of a single enveloping benevolence.

"Oh, yes, but not merely that," the doctor's wife said. "He loved the people. He built them three churches and, oh, did all manner of good works. We're talking of Reverend Johnson," she explained to Eve, who had remained on the beach with the children. "The Anglican padre. He retired last year and went back to England. Sussex, I think."

"He loved the people?" Eve asked. She had heard. Voices carried well in the air, disturbed, during the day, by only the whispering beat of the surf and infrequent voices calling in English made musical by an unintelligible lilt.

The doctor's wife dropped down on the sand. "These are my children," she intoned gruffly. She chased the abrupt parody away with her sharp laughter. "Oh, yes, he loved them. He gave his life to them." The youthful excitement of her voice and the innocent clarity of her eyes went queerly with her body, which was middle-aged. Her plump legs had gone lumpy and sodden, and her small face was finely wrinkled, each wrinkle accented by a line of white where the pinched skin had evaded the sun. "He didn't have any children of his own," she thought to add. "Just this dreadful dog Hooker. Such a funny old man. You might have liked him. I'm sure you never see his kind in America."

"I know we would have liked him," Eve said. "Hannah often mentions Reverend Johnson." Hannah was their cook, a woman of over thirty yet as shy and subtle as a girl. Her skin was always shining as if in embarrassment, but she had a jaunty way of crooning hymns to herself in the kitchen. The children, at first timid of her color, adored her, and listened with eyes rounded by delight when she held up a two-tone forefinger and told them to be good. Goodness had never before been presented to them seriously. Ralph and Eve had not expected a servant. They had picked the most obscure island they could find. But Hannah came with the house; the owner, a svelte widow who had children in Florida, Peru, and Antigua, assumed they would need her. As it turned out, they did. They could never have unravelled alone all the riddles of this novel world. Eve could never have managed the shopping, which was carried on by gossip—invisible voices as liquid as the wind, telling who had just slaughtered a pig, and whose fishing boat had come in with a catch. The village was full of stores; almost every shack at least sold—for disturbingly discrepant prices—American cigarettes smuggled from St. Martin. But even the business hours of the most official store, a cement corridor of shelves attached to the customs office, had proved a mystery the Americans were unable to crack. They always found barred the large green door bearing in wobbly chalk script the ancient announcement, "Attention Members! Attention Friends! This Store will be CLOSED Thursday afternoon."

"Oh, Hannah. She's a good girl," the doctor's wife said, and rolled over on her stomach. The corrugated backs of her thighs were frosted with sand like wet sugar.

"She *is*, you know," Eve said. "She's lovely. I think they're all lovely. They've all been lovely to us." Such insistence was unlike his wife. Ralph wondered what was between the two women, who had just met a day ago. "I can see why Reverend Johnson loved the people," Eve added in a deliberate, though cautiously soft, voice. "The people" were all around them; their huts came down to the edge of the sand, and, windows shuttered, the patched walls seemed to be listening raptly.

The doctor's wife rolled over again and returned to a sitting position. What was making her so restless?

"Yes," she said, and an especially heavy curl of surf foamed up the white slope and soaked in just short of their feet. The sand was porous; innumerable punctures dotted it, the breathing holes of crabs. The doctor's wife's eyes fixed on the horizon and became, from the side, colorless lenses. Her nose in profile turned acute. "They're simple souls," she said.

The doctor's wife was a queen here. She was the only fully white woman resident on the island. When the rare British official and the rare, fantastically minor member of royalty came to grace this most remote and docile scrap of empire with a visit, she was the hostess. When she roared along the dirt roads in her spattered English Ford—its muffler had long ago rotted away—the older natives touched their foreheads ironically and the children flapped their arms in her wake of dust. When she and the doctor condescended to call upon the American family staying three weeks in The Bay, Hannah had trembled with pride and broken a cup in the kitchen. The doctor was a slight, rapid-voiced man with a witty air of failure. His fingertips were dyed deep yellow by smuggled cigarettes. He preferred Camels, but Chesterfields were all that were coming through now. He had never seen a filtered cigarette. He and his wife had been ten years in the tropics—B.G., Trinidad, Barbados, now this. He had some vague scheme of getting to America and making a fortune and retiring to a Yorkshire village. He was off for the day to St. Martin.

"In America, now," the doctor's wife said, vehemently brushing sand from her knees, "are the coloreds well cared for?"

"How do you mean?" Eve asked.

"Are they well off?"

"Not really," Ralph said, because he sensed that it would be better if he, rather than Eve, answered. "In some parts better than others. In the South, of course, they're openly discriminated against; in the North they by and large have to live in the city slums but at least they have full legal rights."

"Oh dear," the doctor's wife said. "It is a problem, isn't it?"

Eve's face flashed up from studying a shell. "Whose problem?" she asked. She was a graduate of one of those female colleges where only a member of a racial minority or a cripple can be

elected class president. News from South Africa made her voice
thrash, and she was for anyone—Castro, Ben-Gurion, Martin Lu-
ther King—who in her mind represented an oppressed race. That
such automatic sympathy was itself condescending had not occurred to her. Of English blood, enriched by remote and aristo-
cratic injections of French and Russian, she denied the less favored
even the compliment of fearing them.

The doctor's wife returned her gaze to the horizon, and Ralph
wondered if they had been rude. In the woman's pointed profile
there was a certain perhaps deliberately noble thrust. But, the
hostess, she relented and tried to make the conversation go again.
She turned her head, shading her eyes with a quick hand and exposing her neat white teeth in a tense smile. "The schools," she
said. "Can they go to your schools?"

"Of course," Ralph said swiftly, at the same time realizing that
for her there was no "of course" to it. She knew nothing about
his country. He felt firmer, having gauged her ignorance, and having moved to the hard ground of information. "Nobody denies
them schools. In the South the schools are segregated. But in the
North, and the West, and so on, there's no problem." He hunched
his shoulders, feeling at his back Eve's disapproval of his saying
"problem."

"But"—the doctor's wife's freckles gathered under her eyes as
she squinted into the focus of the issue—"would *your* children
go to school with them?"

"Sure. Good heavens. Why not?" He was relieved to clear this
up, to lock this door. He hoped the doctor's wife would now turn
away and talk of something else.

She sighed. "Of course, you in America have lived with the
problem so long. In England, now, they're just waking up; the
blacks are *pouring* into London."

A wave, pushed by one behind it, slid so far up the slant of sand
their feet were delicately shocked and soaked. For a few seconds
their ankles glittered in rippling sleeves of retreating water. Eve
said slowly, "You talk as if they had asked to be made slaves and
brought here."

"Mommy, look! Mommy, look!" Kate's voice, mingling with
Larry's babyish yips of excitement, came from far down the beach.

Their little silhouettes were jiggling around something dark at their feet, and out of the sea grape an old woman in a kerchief and a young sailor with a naked chest had emerged to watch them, amused to see what amused these strange children. Eve rose, casting down, for Ralph to see, a startled and indignant look at the doctor's wife's body, as if it were an offensive piece of rubbish washed up on the pure sands of her mind.

As Eve walked away, the doctor's wife said, "Doesn't she take a tan beautifully?"

"Yes, she always does. She's part French." With his wife out of earshot, Ralph relaxed into the sand. Mediating between the two women had demanded an exhausting equilibrium. He resigned himself to listening; he knew the doctor's wife's tongue would be loosened. The presence of another white queen inhibited her, diluted her authority.

"Do you want to hear a frightening story?"

"Sure." He acquiesced uneasily. The attention of the houses behind them seemed to grow more intense. He felt that he and his family were liked in the village; the doctor's wife, driving down from the center of the island to enjoy their beach, assumed an incriminating alliance which he did not wish to exist. For when the sun went down, she would go home, leaving them alone in the village with the night and its noises.

"When Vic Johnson left," she said, lowering her voice and sinking back on her elbow, to bring her face closer to his, "they had a party to greet the new parson, a very nice young colored boy from St. Kitts. *Very* nice, I must say, and they say very intelligent, though I haven't heard him preach. Well, the Warden—you haven't met him, and I daresay you won't, a big smooth Jamaican, takes himself oh *ever* so seriously—the Warden makes this little speech. He of course mentions Vic, forty years and so on, but right at the end he says that he knows we will not miss Reverend Johnson, because the new vicar is such a fine young man, comes to us with such an excellent record of study, and the rest of it, and furthermore, *furthermore*, what makes us especially happy and proud, he is one of us. Imagine! One of us! Of course, the young parson was embarrassed to death. It made me so mad I would have jumped up and left if the doctor hadn't held my hand. *One of us!* Vic had given his life to these people."

Her voice had become shrill; Ralph spoke in the hope of restraining it. "It seems unnecessary; but natural," he said.

"I don't see anything natural about it. *Un*natural, in my book. Unnatural, childish ingratitude. You just don't know how unnatural these people are. If you could see one-tenth of the antics, and then the selfishness, the doctor puts up with. At two in the morning, 'Doctor, Doctor, come save my child,' and then a week later, when he tries to collect his poor little dollar or two, they don't *remember*. They don't remember at all. And if he insists— 'The white people are stealing our money.' Oh. I hate them. God forgive me, I've come to hate them. They're *not* natural. They're not fully human." Seeing his hand begin a protesting movement, she added, "And for that matter, do you know what they say about you and your wife?" It was as if a shadow cruising through her words now made its lunge.

"No. Do they say something?"

"This is just to show how malicious they are. They say your wife has a touch of the brush." It took Ralph a moment to expand "brush" into "tarbrush." He laughed; what else?

The doctor's wife laughed, too; but under the blond eyebrows her blue eyes, the pupils pinpricks in the sun, were fixed on his face. She expected his face to crack and the truth to escape. "You see how dark she is," she explained. "How tan." He watched her tongue tick as she suspensefully pronounced the last two words. Girlish curiosity gave a taut surface to her mature malice.

Blood rushed through his body; the wound was confused; his anger entangled him with his attacker. He was supplying an absurd assault with teeth out of himself. "She just naturally gets that brown."

"And you see," the doctor's wife went on, still not unpinning her eyes from his face, "that's why they say you came here. No tourists come here, least of all with children. They say your wife's being part Negro has kept you out of the hotels on the better islands."

He felt certain that this ingenious argument was wholly her own. "We came here because it was cheap," he said.

"Of *course*," she said, "of *course*," and giggled, sensing that she had exposed herself to his defense. "But they can't believe that. They believe, you see, that all Americans are *rich*." Which was just what, Ralph knew, she and the doctor believed.

He stood up, wet sand collapsing from his legs. In an effort to rein his excitement, he threw several unrelated laughs, as if out of a renewed realization of absurdity, outward into the air. He looked down at the woman and said, "Well, that explains why they seem to like her better than me."

The doctor's wife, having strained her neck to squint up at him, collapsed the rest of the way. She pillowed her head with one arm and threw the other over her eyes. Without her eyes her lips seemed vague and numb. "Oh, no," she said. "They hate her for getting away with it."

His laughter this time was totally vacant; it humiliated him. "I think I'll go in again," he said. "Before the sun fades."

"It won't fade," was the faint answer.

From the safety of the water he watched his dark wife herd two pale, burned children up the beach. The distance between her and the doctor's wife's inert body diminished; he had an urge to shout a warning, then smiled, picturing the laughter that would greet this story when they were home, at a cocktail party, secure among their own. Abruptly he felt guilty in relation to his wife. He had betrayed her. His seriousness had been unworthy of her. She would have wanted him to say yes, her grandfather picked cotton in Alabama, in America these things are taken for granted, we have no problem. But he saw, like a movement glimpsed in a liquid volume, that the comedy of this response depended upon, could only live within, a vast and unconscious pride of race. That since this medium was poisoned all its creatures must be evil. That he and the doctor's wife were immersed together; he hated her blue eyes because they were pinned to his face, hated the taste of her because —could it be?—she was dying. His guilt could not be mapped. Its intricacy was as dense as a simple mass. He moved backward in the ocean, touching the ribbed bottom with his toes, until the water wrapped around his throat. Something—seaweed or the pulse of a current—touched his calf. He thrashed, and peered down, but saw nothing. He was afraid of the sharks, and he was afraid of the doctor's wife, so he hung there between them, bleeding shame, while the water forgave him.

MAGAZINES CONSULTED

ACCENT — University Station, Urbana, Illinois

THE ANTIOCH REVIEW — 212 Xenia Avenue, Yellow Springs, Ohio

THE ARIZONA QUARTERLY — University of Arizona, Tucson, Arizona

ARTESIAN — 2223 S. Main Road, Ann Arbor, Michigan

THE ATLANTIC MONTHLY — 8 Arlington Street, Boston 16, Massachusetts

AUDIENCE — 140 Mt. Auburn Street, Cambridge 38, Massachusetts

AUDIT — Box 92, Hayes Hall, University of Buffalo, Buffalo 14, New York

BETWEEN WORLDS — Inter American University, San Germán, Puerto Rico, U.S.A.

BIG TABLE — 1316 North Dearborn Street, Chicago 10, Illinois

CARLETON MISCELLANY — Carleton College, Northfield, Minnesota

THE CAROLINA QUARTERLY — Box 1117, Chapel Hill, North Carolina

CHICAGO REVIEW — University of Chicago, Chicago 37, Illinois

THE COLORADO QUARTERLY — Hellums 118, University of Colorado, Boulder, Colorado

COMMENTARY — 165 East 56 Street, New York 22, New York

CONTACT — Box 755, Sausalito, California

CONTEMPORARY FICTION — Box 1323, Milwaukee 2, Wisconsin

COSMOPOLITAN — 57 Street and Eighth Avenue, New York 19, New York

CROCODILE REVIEW – 230 East 80 Street, New York 21, New York

THE DIAL – 461 Park Avenue South, New York 16, New York

ENCOUNTER – 25 Haymarket, London, S.W.1, England

EPOCH – 159 Goldwin Smith Hall, Cornell University, Ithaca, New York

ESQUIRE – 488 Madison Avenue, New York 22, New York

EVERGREEN REVIEW – 64 University Place, New York 3, New York

FIRST PERSON – Box 273, Boston, Massachusetts

FOUR QUARTERS – La Salle College, Philadelphia 41, Pennsylvania

GQ (GENTLEMEN'S QUARTERLY) – 488 Madison Avenue, New York 22, New York

THE GEORGIA REVIEW – University of Georgia, Athens, Georgia

HARPER'S BAZAAR – 572 Madison Avenue, New York 22, New York

HARPER'S MAGAZINE – 49 East 33 Street, New York 16, New York

THE HUDSON REVIEW – 65 East 55 Street, New York 22, New York

THE KENYON REVIEW – Kenyon College, Gambier, Ohio

LADIES' HOME JOURNAL – Independence Square, Philadelphia 5, Pennsylvania

THE LITERARY REVIEW – Fairleigh Dickinson University, Teaneck, New Jersey

MADEMOISELLE – 575 Madison Avenue, New York 22, New York

MAINSTREAM – 832 Broadway, New York 3, New York

THE MASSACHUSETTS REVIEW – University of Massachusetts, Amherst, Massachusetts

MIDSTREAM – 515 Park Avenue, New York 22, New York

MINNESOTA REVIEW – Box 4068, University Station, Minneapolis, Minnesota

MUTINY – Box 278, Northport, New York

NEW MEXICO QUARTERLY – University of New Mexico Press, Marron Hall, Albuquerque, New Mexico

NEW WORLD WRITING – c/o J. B. Lippincott Company, 521 Fifth Avenue, New York 17, New York

THE NEW YORKER – 25 West 43 Street, New York 36, New York

NIMROD – University of Tulsa, Tulsa, Oklahoma

THE NOBLE SAVAGE – Meridian Books, 119 West 57 Street, New York 19, New York

NORTHWEST REVIEW – Erb Memorial Student Union, University of Oregon, Eugene, Oregon

THE PARIS REVIEW – 45–39 171 Place, Flushing 58, New York

PARTISAN REVIEW – 22 East 17 Street, New York 3, New York

PERSPECTIVE – Washington University Post Office, St. Louis 5, Missouri

PLAYBOY – 232 East Ohio Street, Chicago 11, Illinois

PRAIRIE SCHOONER – Nebraska Hall, University of Nebraska, 901 North 17 Street, Lincoln 8, Nebraska

QUARTERLY REVIEW OF LITERATURE – Box 287, Bard College, Annandale-on-Hudson, New York

THE REPORTER – 660 Madison Avenue, New York 21, New York

SAN FRANCISCO REVIEW – Box 671, San Francisco, California

THE SATURDAY EVENING POST – Independence Square, Philadelphia 5, Pennsylvania

SEQUOIA – Box 2167, Stanford University, Stanford, California

THE SEWANEE REVIEW – University of the South, Sewanee, Tennessee

SOUTHWEST REVIEW – Southern Methodist University Press, Dallas 22, Texas

STORY – 135 Central Park West, New York 23, New York

TEXAS QUARTERLY – Box 7527, University of Texas, Austin 12, Texas

THE TRANSATLANTIC REVIEW – 821 Second Avenue, New York 17, New York

THE UNIVERSITY OF KANSAS CITY REVIEW – University of Kansas City, 51st and Rockhill Road, Kansas City, Missouri

VENTURE – Box 228, Old Chelsea Station, New York 11, New York

THE VIRGINIA QUARTERLY REVIEW – University of Virginia, 1 West Range, Charlottesville, Virginia

VOGUE – 420 Lexington Avenue, New York 17, New York

WOMAN'S DAY – 67 West 44 Street, New York 36, New York

THE YALE REVIEW – 28 Hillhouse Avenue, New Haven, Connecticut